M000305397

BRAVE BOY WORLD
A Transman Anthology

BRAVE BOY WORLD

WORLD

A TRANS MAN ANTHOLOGY

EDITED BY MICHAEL D. TAKEDA

DEDICATION

This book is for transmen everywhere, but especially for you, sunshine.

This book is a work of fiction. All the characters and events portrayed in this book are fictitious, and any resemblance to real people or events is purely coincidental.

BRAVE BOY WORLD: A Transman Anthology
© 2017 Pink Narcissus Press

All rights reserved. No part of this book may be reproduced in any form or by any means without the prior written consent of the Publisher, excepting brief quotes used in reviews.

Individual stories © their respective authors.

"According to His Substance" by K.C. Ball originally published in *Snapshots from a Black Hole & Other Oddities,* Hydra House Books, 2012.
"Spoiling Veena" by Keyan Bowes originally published in *Expanded Horizons,* 2008.
"Fluidity" by Eric Del Carlo originally published in *Futurismic,* 2009.
"Choice Cuts" by Edd Vick originally published in *Electric Velocipede,* 2003.
"Flipside" by Nicole Jinks-Fredrick originally published in *The Fabler Magazine,* 2016.

Cover illustration & design by Dante Saunders

Published by Pink Narcissus Press
Massachusetts, USA
pinknarc.com

ISBN: 978-1-939056-12-2
First trade paperback edition: February 2017

CONTENTS

INTRODUCTION

Who are you?

What is a man?

And what risks would you be willing to take, what sacrifices would you be willing to make, in order to have a chance to live as your authentic self?

Many people have grappled with these questions, but perhaps the struggle is more acutely felt by people who are transgender. Our current society, often our friends and family, and even the very mirror we gaze into denies our reality, the one we feel under our skin, in our minds, our hearts, and our souls. Yet many trans people remain in hiding, unable to take those steps to live as their authentic selves.

Both the presence of toxic femininity and toxic masculinity in our culture does not make it easy to navigate the meanings of "man." Harder so for us, who have been conditioned as female, and must learn for ourselves what sort of man we wish to become—the jock, the gentleman, the player, the geek? Do we don our maleness like a ready-made suit in a shop, or do we dare to defy convention and toss all the stereotypes of masculinity and femininity right out the window? What is the price of "fitting in," and is it worth paying?

There is no one way to be trans. Some of us choose to live on the opposite side of the binary than the sex we were assigned at birth, others choose to live in-between, and others reject the binary altogether. Old and young, some of us are damaged beyond repair, while others are hopeful for a better future. Hence, one of the goals in putting together this book was to select a range of stories that would reflect the variety of the trans masculine existence. And because we at Pink Narcissus Press have held a policy of inclusion since our inception almost seven years ago, we decided that all writers—whether they be cis, trans, male, female or non-binary—were eligible for inclusion in this anthology.

Occasionally a well-meaning person, usually cisgender, upon finding out that we are planning on, or in the process of transitioning, will say that we are brave. But, as my friend pointed out that this "is always a little weird because, 'Oh, you're so *brave*,' can be condescending in the sense that being who we are isn't bravery as much as it's facing reality. Brave is when you risk yourself and you don't have to. If you have to, it's just trying to get through life." Still, one may argue that, given one's current reality, bravery may be the actual thing required in order to survive.

Recently, for good or bad, transgender issues have gained far more visibility than they had a decade ago. Good, because there are now more resources available for transmen, including (at the time of writing) legislation in some states that protects us against discrimination, as well as mandates guaranteeing coverage by insurance companies for hormone therapy and gender-confirming surgeries. Bad, because in many other states laws have already been passed that strip us of our civil rights. Add to this the alarming rates of suicide and murder of trans people, and it should be evident to anyone with a pair of eyes that to choose to live as one's authentic gender is frequently an act of courage and strength.

We are here. We are not afraid. And we will not let our voices be silenced.

Welcome to the Brave Boy World.

Michael D. Takeda
January 2017

Rccording to His Substance

K.C. Ball

Taylor steps through a crossing point, one world to another, onto a moon-lit upper deck.

Thick strands of silver thread his dark hair and close-cut beard. The moonlight turns the lenses of his aviator shades to mirrors, accents keloidal folds left by the long-cooled flames that ravaged the right side of his face.

He draws in the cold, hard ozone-scent of open water, reaches back and lays his gloved hand against the bulkhead to touch the pulse of the four enormous diesel engines that push *Wenatchee* through dark waters. He feels the hidden pulsing of his watch against his wrist as well, marking off the seconds.

Taylor doesn't know how he got the watch. He understands its prodding, though. Time won't wait for him.

Instead, a young man waits across the deck, watching Elliott Bay's dark waters roll off the port and star-board flanks of the flagship of the Washington State ferry system. The ship's bubbling wake arrows back toward the fading lights of downtown Seattle.

The young man clutches a leather wallet in his left hand. His right hand, marked by the tattoo of a heads-up Morgan silver dollar, rests on the metal railing.

Taylor's wristwatch pulses. Eleven minutes, starting now. The young man grips the rail and braces to make the jump.

Taylor clears his throat. "Pardon me," he says.

The young man jerks about, just as the gleaming

crossing point winks out of existence. His eyes widen. He stabs his index finger toward the bulkhead behind Taylor. "How did you d-do that?"

Taylor shrugs. "Practice. A clear and focused mind."

"Bullshit," the young man says.

Bullshit, indeed. Taylor doesn't have a better answer. Like the watch, he isn't sure himself of the how or why of crossing. He only knows the way, knows it in his heart and in his bones, for he can't remember ever being taught.

"Who the hell are you?" the young man demands.

"A friend." Taylor slips forward, anxious to move on.

The young man takes a step back. "I don't know you."

"But I know you. You *need* a friend." *Now there's a truth.*

Taylor stops just out of reach, leans against the rail, and pushes away a yawn. No rest for the wicked. Not much, anyway.

The young man shuffles back another step, drops his chin, clenches his fists. "I don't need anything. You get the hell away from me."

Taylor shakes his head. He inches closer. "I'm not leaving 'til you tell me why you gave everything you own away."

"Jesus! Have you been spying on me?"

"I wouldn't call it spying. All I had to do was nose around a bit. You're not very good at keeping secrets."

"Who the hell are—"

Taylor interrupts. "Except why you want to kill yourself. What's with that?"

The young man doesn't say a word. Instead, he turns to the rail and flips the wallet out into the bay. It vanishes into the dark waters, and he raises his foot toward the rail.

No! Taylor has no intention of losing this one. Time

to push. He forms a stirrup with his hands. "All right. You're so eager to get on with it, I'll boost you over."

"Don't humor me. I'm serious." The young man grips the rail so tightly Taylor wonders if it will snap in half.

The wristwatch pulses against Taylor's ulnar artery. Nine more minutes. He wishes he could remove the damned thing, throw it after the vanished wallet, but it won't come off.

"So am I," he says. "Suicide's no easy task. I tried it once, on a boat like this. Made a mess of it, an awful mess."

The young man glances at Taylor's face, then turns away. They stand together at the rail, silent with their thoughts.

Taylor sighs, counts off fifteen precious seconds before he turns back to the young man. "Okay, we're done feeling sorry for ourselves. Tell me why you want to die."

The young man takes another minute they don't really have. Taylor counts every second. At last, the young man pushes back from the rail, holds up both arms and pivots.

"What do you see?"

Taylor plays along. "A fellow my size, close to thirty. Decent looking. Dark hair, cut a bit too short for my tastes."

"Wrong."

"I don't know what you mean." *A lie.*

The young man waves toward the water. "I could prove it, if my driver's license wasn't in my wallet. The State of Washington says I'm not a man."

"I don't understand." *A bigger lie.*

"See if this is plain enough." The young man closes in on Taylor, until they breathe each other's air. His spittle peppers Taylor's face, as he spews his words. Lots of volume. Lots of heat. "You nosy fucker, I don't have a dick, I've got a—"

Taylor holds up his hand. "I hear you. If you don't

keep it down, so will everybody else on board."

"Fuck them."

The young man turns away and begins to pace, three steps from the rail, three steps back. He refuses to look at Taylor.

"You're transgendered?" Taylor asks. He knows the answer.

The young man stops pacing. Tears roll down his cheeks. His voice is still angry, but he's turned down the heat. "I hate that word. Nothing but a label. I don't understand why people have to label everything, put everybody into tidy little boxes."

The watch pulses. Taylor would love to rip it from his wrist, stomp on it until nothing remains but a pile of gears and pins. He draws a breath instead, and asks another question.

"What's a better word?"

The young man ignores the question. "I don't need someone else to tell me who I am. I'm a man, but people keep insisting that I'm not." He wipes the back of his hand across his nose. "Everyone you work with, everyone you know, is so polite. You see it in their eyes, though, hear it when they talk. They think you're broken."

"Are you?"

"No! But I'm so damned tired of being all alone."

The watch pulses. Relentless and unforgiving. Six minutes now and not another second.

"You ever been beaten up?" Taylor asks.

"Once, five years ago. Four guys kicked the shit out of me outside a bar, down near the river in Cincinnati. After that, I took up Taekwondo. I'll *never* be on the losing end again."

The ferry's whistle shrills, swallowing all other sounds. The pitch of the driving engines change. Subtle vibrations roll across the deck.

"We're almost to Bainbridge," Taylor says.

"Damn!" The young man grabs the rail to make the vault.

Taylor stretches out his hand but doesn't touch. "What if I could show you how to change your life?"

The young man pauses. His lip curls. "I should have known. A god-damned preacher."

"No. I'm just a guy who knows a trick or two that I can use to take you to another world where you're a man."

Three minutes, fifty seconds left.

"Another world? Hell, you're the one who's crazy."

"You saw how I got here," Taylor says. "Neither one of us is crazy, Alec."

The young man pales. "I never told you my name."

"I told you I know who you are." Taylor holds out his hand again. "What's there to lose? You can always kill yourself later."

"Who are you?"

"A friend, I swear. Come on."

Alec reluctantly accepts the offered hand, allows Taylor to pull him to the stairs along the starboard rail. His hand trembles, but he doesn't pull away.

Taylor calms his thoughts, searches with his mind's eye for the sparks of eldritch light that mark the crossing points. The two of them thump down the stairs, rush through the middle deck.

"Tell me about this other world." Alec doesn't even seem to be breathing hard.

Taylor pants. "Not just one world. A multitude."

They thread the twists and turns across the cabin. Every time they round a corner or step through an opening, the flash of a crossing point flares, something changes.

"Tell me where we're going."

"Soon. Got to focus now."

At first, small things change. The color of a bulkhead paint. A deck covering. But as they move into the bowels of the ferry, the alterations grow. Lettering on signs writhes. Lights dim, brighten. Clothing flows across the crew and passengers, as if each wore a quickening fabric tide. Startled faces come and go as they step across the void.

Alec doesn't seem to notice all the changes. Instead, he is focused on an answer to his question. "Tell me—"

Taylor holds up his free index finger, as if to book-mark that notion. "Later."

They cross from world to world, step from ship to ship. *Wenatchee. Columbia. Majestic. Resolute.* On the parking deck of *Resolute,* with twenty seconds left, they snake through an ever-shifting maze of turtle-backed Subaru station wagons, little Ford electrics, giant stake-bed Oshkosh haulers, six-wheel Daimlers, and gaudy-colored, snub-nosed muscle trucks with brutal names.

To the last of forty-seven crossing points.

During their mad scramble forward and down and aft, the ferry schedule changes, too. In one of the worlds along the path, the boat arrives at Bainbridge and starts back.

The high, white lights of Seattle grow ever nearer.

Big coal-fired steam turbines whine beneath them. The ferry comes to its docking slip and begins to slow. Taylor's wristwatch beeps, just as they reach the bow. He fishes in his left pocket, as if into a deep void, withdraws a set of keys. The ring holds a plastic door remote. He pushes the button, a horn beeps. The locks of a nearby Studebaker roadster pops up.

"Get in," Taylor says, pointing to the passenger side.

Alec does as he is told.

Taylor slides in behind the steering wheel at the same time and they are through the final crossing point. Taylor studies the automobile's controls a moment. He inserts a key and turns it. Behind them, where a storage trunk should be, a device whirs into life.

Alec jumps. "What the hell is that?"

"This car's gyroscopic. The power wheel is in the back. I told you, we're not in your world anymore."

"That's crazy."

Taylor's heart still gallops from the run. He has to fight for wind to say a word.

"No, it's not. There's a multitude of worlds, Alec. More than one where you're a man. We've stepped through to one of them."

"But if—"

Taylor interrupts. "Just wait."

"For what?"

Resolute settles against timber moorings. Taylor shifts the roadster into gear. "You've got to save a damsel in distress."

♦ ♦ ♦

A sour stench of garbage pinches Taylor's nose.

He and Alec stand in the shadows at the mouth of a Belltown alley. They left the Roadster parked at the curb along Third Avenue. Taylor breathed easier when they found the parking spot.

Down the alley, three men gather around a woman. She's young, medium-tall, with short, dark hair, dressed in new jeans and a pink tank top. She holds a section of lead pipe, spins in an awkward dance with her harassers as they draw ever nearer.

It doesn't take much to see she'll soon lose this fight.

"Stay back, assholes." She tries to sound tough and dangerous, fails at both.

Alec starts at the sound of her voice. "It's me. You said—"

"I said I'd take you to a world where you were born a man. This Alec's stuck in the wrong body, too."

One of the three men, a beefy fellow wearing a tight lime-green Whalers T-shirt, steps in close and reaches for the young woman. She swings the pipe, grunting with the effort, and catches the fellow a glancing blow on the shoulder.

"Little shit," he snarls. "Now you pissed me off."

The young woman darts past him, presses her back against a battered dumpster. The Whalers guy plucks up a broken piece of packing two-by-two, motions to his friends to lend a hand.

"This is how we deal with freaks," he says.

"You sure about this, Monty?" one of the others asks. "She don't look much like a guy to me."

"Damn it," Monty says. "I tell you, I felt his dick."

Alec tenses, ready to step from the shadows.

Taylor puts his hand on Alec's shoulder. "Not yet."

"Going to get yours, you little freak," Monty says.

One of the other men, a fellow with a big nose, growls and steps forward. When the young woman shifts her attention, Big Nose backs away, and Monty steps in and swings. The two-by-two strikes the young woman on her upper arm.

Alex tries to shrug away Taylor's hand. Taylor keeps his grip. "Wait," he says.

The young woman drops the pipe, staggers from the shelter of the dumpster. Monty swings a second time but misses. She spins on him, brings up her fists. Monty swings his make-shift club again.

The snap of breaking bone echoes up the alley. The young woman grabs her forearm, goes to her knees. Monty raises his club as if it were an ax.

Taylor releases Alec. "Now."

Alec falls upon them. Big Nose drops beneath the first of Alec's savage kicks. The third man runs. Monty turns his attention to Alec. The club rakes across Alec's ribcage, opens up his shirt, slashes the skin beneath. Alec ignores it all, spins low, kicks at Monty's knee. The pop-snap of dislocation bounces off the concrete walls.

Monty screeches in falsetto and topples, bouncing face-first on the alley's grimy paving bricks. He stays down, too, twitching like an old dog dreaming of long-gone, glory days.

Alec turns away and hurries to the young woman. "Are you okay?" he asks.

She cradles her arm to her breasts, bites her lower lip. She takes in his torn, blood-soaked shirt. "Yes. How about you?"

"I'm fine." Alec kneels next to her. She leans into him, he slips an arm around her waist.

"You need my help to stand?" he asks.

The young woman's dark eyes snaps to Alec's face. "Who are you?"

"We'll talk later. Can you stand?"

"Watch me." She wobbles to her feet.

Taylor grins, knuckles at his eyes. "Move it," he yells. "Before the one that ran comes back with help."

The doctor at the urgent-care clinic smells of iodine and nicotine and day-old coffee. She takes her time, examines the young woman's identification, before tending to the broken bone.

"You on hormones?" she asks, at last.

"Fourteen months." The young woman watches Alec, waiting for a knee-jerk tic. She looks confused when it doesn't come.

"Had surgery?" the doctor asks.

"Not yet. I'm still saving money."

"Uh huh. How did this happen?"

Taylor interrupts. "We were drinking. She fell."

The doctor gestures toward Alec's torn and

bloodied shirt. "Did he fall, too?"

Taylor nods. "He's clumsy. He may need stitches."

The doctor nods. "Of course."

She turns to the young woman and grabs her hand. "Hold on, hon. This is going to hurt."

The young woman bites her lip but doesn't make a sound.

◆ ◆ ◆

Taylor parks the roadster at a brick apartment building on a narrow, tree-lined street, half-way up the Hill. An older place. Genteel.

Inside, the apartment proves compact and tidy. A mingled aroma of cinnamon and lemons and lilac body talc laces the air. The young woman eases onto the sofa, props her fiberglass cast on a loose stack of throw pillows.

Alec winces at the pinch of his stitches as he settles next to her. Not too close, but close enough to remind her of his presence. Taylor sits on a little rounded footstool, facing the two of them.

"Home at last," he says.

The young woman smiles. Her movements exaggerated, her words measured, she fights the Percocet she'd been given at the clinic. "I owe both of you my life."

Taylor waves away the notion. "I just paid the doctor's bill. Alec saved you."

"That's my name, too!" the young woman says. She turns to Alec, leans close and squints at his face. "Who are you?"

"A friend." Alec hears the words he's said. He looks surprised, as he glances toward Taylor. "That's what you said—"

The young woman interrupts. "No. I'd remember you, but I feel like I should know you."

Taylor's watch pulses. He stands. "It's time to go."

The young woman looks to Alec. "You've got to

leave?"

"Just me," Taylor says. "He's staying. He'll explain it all."

The young woman blinks, tries to rise. Can't manage. She looks up to Taylor. She's close to tears. "Thank you."

"You're welcome," Taylor says. "But I told you, I didn't do a thing."

Alec stands, reaches to the young woman but doesn't touch her. "I'll see him out and be right back."

In the hallway, Taylor doesn't hesitate a second before he opens a bright-lit crossing point upon the facing wall.

"Just like that, huh?" Alec says.

"Just like that."

"If it's easy, what was all the business on the ferry?"

"It's *not* easy," Taylor says. "It's damned hard to do. We stepped through forty-seven crossing points in less than three minutes. You might not have noticed, but that took effort."

"What do we do now?"

Taylor glances at his watch. "*We* don't do anything. *I've* got another appointment before I get to get some sleep."

"I don't belong here, don't belong with her," Alec says, but he doesn't say he won't stay.

Taylor shakes his head. "You were the one whining about how you hated being all alone."

"I don't know if I can be with her. It feels—I don't know—incestuous."

Taylor frowns. "Don't be such a fucking prude."

"How would I live here? On paper, I don't exist."

Taylor fishes in his pocket, into the void again, pulls out a wallet, just like the one Alec threw from the ferry. "There should be a Washington State driver's license in here with your birth name on it. A birth certificate, social security card and passport, too."

Alec fingers the wallet, opens it, riffles through the contents. "God, there's close to a thousand dollars here!"

Taylor touches the papers. "There's the title to the roadster, too. Your name's on it. Here's the keys."

Alec juggles the car keys as he studies the wallet and its contents. "These documents all say female."

Taylor sighs. "You could try saying thank you."

"I can't use these."

"You're not just rude, you know? You lack imagination."

"What?" Alec says.

"What? What? Too many questions. Give this stuff to the other Alec. You use hers. You don't have to stay if you don't want to. You'd be a fool not to, though. If she'll have you."

"But—"

"I'm tired, Alec. Do whatever the hell makes you happy. Run naked down the middle of First Avenue, noon come Monday, for all I care."

"Just like that," Alec says. "All our problems solved, huh?"

"Don't be such an asshole. Nobody's life is perfect. But no one else ever has to know what's in your pants."

Alec shakes his head. "It's not what I want. Maybe not what she wants, either."

"Maybe not. It's the best I've got."

Alec waves the documents. "How did you get these?"

"I told you. I know a trick or two, and I get a little help from time to time. Like the roadster or the money. Can't tell you where it comes from."

"You mean you won't."

"I mean I can't. I don't know myself. Things that I

need show up. Maybe it's magic." Taylor snaps his fingers. "Just like that."

"If you can do magic, make us real!" Alec's words thunder from the walls. A door down the hall bangs shut.

Taylor struggles to keep from shouting, too.

"Don't pull that Pinocchio shit on me. What do you think this is? Some goddamned fantasy? You think I can wave my hand, switch the two of you around? Get it through your head. It's your life; you've got to make the best of it."

The hall stands quiet for a beat, then Alec nods. "I'll try."

Taylor turns toward the crossing point.

Alec grabs Taylor's arm. "Can I ask one question?"

"No time," Taylor says. "I've got to go."

Even so, he stops and turns back. Alec still holds Taylor's arm, he fingers the edge of Taylor's glove. "Let me see your hand."

Taylor doesn't pull away. "Do you really want to do that?"

"Who are you?"

Taylor's voice softens. "I'm a man, just like you, who has a chance to make up for all the wrong he's done."

Seconds passed, an eternity. The wristwatch pulses, there's time for one more turn tonight. "Go on," Taylor says. "Go back inside to her. Get on with your life."

Taylor steps through the crossing point, one world to another, onto the rain-slicked top deck of *Wenatchee*. The dark waters of Elliot Bay surround the ship, but no onyx sky and moon-lit shadows this time around.

Another young man—a different one, but so alike in many little ways—waits at the rail. He clutches a leather wallet in his left hand, an ugly, compact black pistol in his right.

The young man tosses the wallet to the darkness and raises the pistol to his temple. Deck lights catch the tattoo of a Morgan silver dollar on the back of his right hand.

Taylor clears his throat. "Pardon me," he says.

K.C. Ball is a post-surgical trans-woman. She lives in Seattle, Washington with her wife Rachael and a fussy senior cat named Sally. K.C.'s stories have appeared in various print and online magazines, including *Analog, Beneath Ceaseless Skies,* and *Lightspeed,* as well as her first collection, *Snapshots From A Black Hole & Other Oddities*, published by Hydra House Books. She is a 2010 graduate of the Clarion West writers workshop and a 2009 winner of the Hubbard Writers of the Future award.

SPOILING VEENA
KEYAN BOWES

The snow thuds down like brickbats.

Instead of a soft and beautiful blanket, it lies on the grass in shards of ice. The party is ruined. It had sounded like such a good idea, snow in Delhi. Shalini should have known better than to trust Party Weather Inc. They haven't been able to deliver. Shivering, she herds the children into the veranda, out of the way of the pounding white chips.

"Let's bring in the cake, shall we?" she says, as the clatter of the hail on the cars parked outside distracts the children.

"Oh, can't we go out in that, Aunty?" It's a young boy called—Ajay, that's it, Ajay Zaveri.

"It's too hard, Ajay," replies Shalini. "I don't want anyone to get hurt." *Or your lawyer mother to sue me,* she thinks. India is becoming just too much like America since cable and satellite TV. She has releases of liability signed by every custodial parent, and still she worries.

"Maybe after the cake, Aunty, if it stops falling?" asks Preethi.

"Maybe," Shalini says. The cake is meant to resemble the castle of the Snow Queen, from the Andersen fairy tale, but the confectioner has built the US Capitol. Shalini hopes the children won't know the difference. She also alerts Jayesh that she needs reinforcements; her husband is hiding out in his study upstairs.

"I'll get on the phone," he promises. "Hang on. Don't let it spoil Veena's day."

"Cool! The Capitol!" says Rizwan. "Just like Washington."

"It looks like Rashtrapati Bhawan," says his twin, Ria, "but white-washed."

"It's the Snow Queen's palace," says Shalini faintly. Now that the child mentions it, the dome is indeed reminiscent of the Indian President's residence.

"The Snow Queen can copy the Capitol," says Preethi, politely coming to her hostess's defense. "Maybe she got bored with towers and turrets and stuff and wanted a dome. It's ice, right? It melts. She can have a different palace every year."

Shalini nods gratefully, then tucks the pallav of her sari out of the way and lights the dozen candles. The children crowd around.

"Happy birthday to you
Happy birthday to you
Happy birthday dear Vik-rum
Happy birthday to you."

Vikrum? Shalini looks at Veena, angelic in a snow-white taffeta dress that comes below her knee. She seems quite okay with what the children have sung, and blows out the candles in three tries. The single diamond, her parents' birthday present, glitters at her throat. Sparkling holographic snowflakes in her headdress reflect the myriad tiny lights with which Shalini has decorated the house and garden. Sweet tendrils of dark hair escape to fall down cheeks that are pink with pleasure.

The door-bell rings. Jayesh has pulled it off: Here is the Snow Queen, a whole hour early, to take over the party from her. The lady makes a magnificent entrance, swirling in through the front door in a scent of roses, greeting the birthday girl with an exquisitely wrapped present, and then magically making brightness fall out of the air onto the other children. There are oohs and aahs. They are the latest thing in cool fireworks from China, perfectly suitable for a crowded room on a gray day.

"Your Majesty, can we go out? Before it melts?" asks one of the children. Shalini looks out to see that the "snow" has stopped, and the ground is covered, inches deep, with ice chips.

The Snow Queen smiles at the eager girl. "First let me try it out. It looks cold outside. Do you have a warm jacket? Also I need to check the paperwork." Though it's summer, the "snow" still shows no sign of melting.

Relieved, Shalini gives her copies of the releases, and waits while the lady takes a roll-call of the children to ascertain they are all listed. She isn't sure why organizing children's parties is so much more difficult than running a laboratory. Perhaps because they mean so much to Veena, perhaps because she herself is a bit shy—a trait she made sure Veena did not inherit.

Certain now that everything is under control, she slips upstairs to tell Jayesh about the failed snowfall and the strange birthday song. And have a cup of tea. Or maybe a whiskey.

The Snow Queen is a pro; she is a schoolteacher who does this on weekends. She's invented games, dared what Shalini wouldn't and sent the children out into the garden in small groups, explained why ice floats, and kept them busy and happy. Eventually they all crowd round the large-screen TV for yet another dubbed-into-Hindi episode about the Celtic hero Cernunnos (now re-named Kanoon, the Hindi word for law) and his great wolfhound. The program's into its fifth season and seems entirely likely to continue for another five at least. After the party, the Snow Queen has silvery crowns studded with glittering icy jewels for the departing girls, and for the boys, spheres that spurt magic fire when you press them.

Shalini unwinds over another whiskey. Party Weather Inc. calls to apologize, arrange a refund, and explain that a virus corrupted their programs. Jayesh has built a real fire in the fireplace in the study, giving it a romantic smell of wood-smoke. The ice-storm chilled the surrounding air, so they can get away with it even though it is not winter. Her mother, known to all as Mummy-ji, looks serene and silver-haired in the comfortable chair in the corner as she chats with her favorite son-in-law. *Just look,* thinks Shalini, *it's like a story-book.*

Shalini gazes at all the pictures of Veena that cover the walls, marveling at how quickly time has passed: There is Veena, a few months old, wearing a fluffy pink dress and a darling wreath of pink roses on her head. There is Veena in an embroidered blue silk lehnga and choli, toddling toward the camera at her uncle's wedding. There is little Veena in a sari, dressed up for her school's annual play.

And here is the actual Veena coming up the stairs, twelve years old already, tall and lovely in her wonderful white dress, her long dark hair coming undone from the chignon in which Shalini had put it up... *where did the time go? How did we make a beauty like this child?* She smooths her own unruly curls, and looks adoringly at her daughter.

Veena's brought her presents upstairs to show her parents. From the Snow Queen, a brilliant snow-globe, beautifully made. In the center are two polar bears and a fir tree. When Veena shakes it, it plays a delicate tune. *Something Western classical,* Shalini thinks. *Maybe Schubert?* Then there's a remote-controlled truck, with a small GPS installed. A pin with a built-in cell-phone; *Star Trek* is enjoying a revival. A battery-powered holographic game that fills their living room with enemy soldiers for Veena to shoot at... huh? Shalini picks the box off the floor. The card attached says, "Happy Birthday, Vik."

"Vik? Veena, why are your friends calling you Vik?"

"They don't. Only Ajay, he's my buddy. The others call me Vikrum."

"What's wrong with Veena?"

"It's a girl's name."

"Aren't you a girl?"

"I am! But why?" she demands. "Who decided?"

"We did," Shalini says after a pause. She remembers their decision, to choose their baby. She and Jayesh had mulled it over, considered the expense, considered the payoff. They'd wanted a designer baby. *It's the most important thing we'll ever do,* Jayesh had said. *Let's get this right, and damn the expense. This is an opportunity our parents never had, tweaking DNA.*

She remembers the hours and hours they had spent with the specifications. Sitting in front of the screen, calibrating, raising this and lowering that. The massive spreadsheet with all those linkages to be considered. Physical specs, pre- and post-puberty. Talents. Temperament. Which part of it was causing this dissatisfaction, this questioning? Was Veena doomed to go through life never quite happy in her skin? Was it their fault? What had they done wrong? She says nothing of this to Veena. Instead, she says, "We wanted a little girl. We got you. We were thrilled."

Veena rolls her eyes. "Okay for you, Ma, but what about me?"

"Would you rather be a boy?"

"Duh-uh."

Shalini looks helplessly at the other two adults.

"I told you not to select the gender," says her mother, "Something like this was inevitable."

"Darling," Jayesh says to Veena, "Wait until you're eighteen and then you can choose."

"I want to be a boy now!"

"How long has this been going on?" asks Jayesh.

"Always. For ever."

"Your friends called you Veena last year," says her mother, "or Vee. It wasn't that long ago you only wanted to wear pink. Remember when you wouldn't talk to boys?"

"Mo-om! That was years ago! I was a baby! I'm grown up now. I told them to call me Vikrum. They have to get used to my boy-name."

Shalini and Jayesh look at each other. "Sweetie, we can't just shift your gender like that," Shalini says. "It's very expensive. Universal insurance doesn't cover it. I don't know how we could afford it."

"You know," says Mummy-ji from the background, "Gender selection never should have been allowed in India. First we had a huge number of boys being born, and hardly any girls. Then girls and hardly any boys. Now, confusion."

"All the other kids' parents let them," says Veena.

"All your friends are changing gender? Ajay's always been a boy, as far as I know."

"That's just Ajay. But what about Preethi? She was a boy before."

Shalini sits down heavily on the floor. "Why?" she asks Veena. "Women can do anything they want. Even years before you were born, India had a great woman Prime Minister."

"Oooh!" says Mummy-ji. "How can you admire Indira Gandhi? What about the Emergency?"

"That's not the point, Mother!" says Shalini. "Besides, she herself lifted the Emergency."

"Only when she was forced into it," says Mummy-ji.

"How many dictators do you know who actually restored democracy within two years?" argues Shalini. "Are any of the countries that gained Independence when we did still democratic? Isn't it so, Jayesh?"

Jayesh diplomatically makes no comment. Instead, he turns to Veena. "It's true, what your mother says. You can be anything you want. Even Prime Minister."

"I don't want to be Prime Minister!" says Veena, "Anyway, not now. But boys get all the cool stuff! And they do all the cool stuff!"

"I told the Parliamentary Committee," says Mummy-ji. "I said it would worsen the gender divide, polarize the genders. Dr. Mukherji, they said, thank you for your testimony, and just went ahead anyway. Isn't it so, Jayesh?"

"Girls can play with cool stuff, too, and do all the cool stuff," Jayesh says to Veena.

"But they don't," Veena picks up her toys. "I'm going to my room."

"Veena, sweetie," says Shalini, "Please…"

"Don't call me Veena!" Her voice sounds close to tears as she stalks off.

"I'm sorry, darling," Shalini calls after her. It's a wretched end to the birthday.

Jayesh silently busies himself with putting out the fire. The ice outside has melted away, and the temperature is rising again. He turns on the air-conditioning.

Veena is the only girl wearing jeans. In the two years since the Snow Queen birthday, she has stopped wearing dresses altogether. But instead of graduating to the tunics and slender pants of the Punjabi suit, or even to sarees, she only wears jeans or slacks. Her hair is clipped short, and she's already running around with a group of boys, all engrossed in a new Alien Splatter holovid game released in Japan only this week. They are shooting at the escaped alien monsters that run across the park.

Veena races ahead of another child, dodges round a tree, crouches and fires. A huge green creature with horns running from its forehead down its back and sides rears up on ten legs to twice the height of a person, and then falls heavily sideways, spurting fluorescent purple gore. Behind it, an even larger crimson thing with eyes on eye-stalks shifts in and out of invisibility. "Vik! This way!" someone shouts, and Veena runs to the next tree to reinforce the attack.

The girls, dressed in designer Punjabi suits, watch and cheer occasionally as someone scores a particularly good splat. Some of them wear short white lace gloves, the latest fashion. They are waiting for the last guest before they take off to their own games in the clubhouse. The birthday twins have split up: Rizwan is killing monsters, and Ria waits with the girls for the friend delayed by traffic. Her party's theme is Fashion-show. But Veena has joined Rizwan's party, Alien Monster Safari.

The parents stand around under the trees, signing off on releases that limit the hosts' liability, and watching their children play. Shalini dreads the questions she knows she'll get about her daughter, but can think of no polite way just to leave. Sure enough, Ajay's lawyer mother, Mrs. Zaveri, together with Preethi's father, bear down on her.

"Shalini, why have a girl if all she wants to do is dress and play like a boy?" Mrs. Zaveri says. "I just cannot imagine making my child remain the wrong gender. If I can afford to change it."

Fine for you, thinks Shalini. *Your Ajay's not agitating to be a girl.* "Veena is going through a phase of exploring her gender identity," she replies stiffly.

"It might warp their personalities," says Preethi's father, as though Shalini hasn't spoken. "Once Preetam wanted to be a girl, I told his mother, 'Even if we have to spend for it, we must do it.' Otherwise it is just child abuse." Preethi, the former Preetam, is with the group of girls in lace gloves.

The crimson monster goes down to the combined firepower of the attackers in one of its brief moments of visibility, falling over with a roar and a gush of brilliant green blood. Immediately, a massive black alien rolls ponderously onto the field. It extrudes tentacles, seemingly at random, but as it comes closer to the trees where the boys shelter, they reach for the young hunters. Veena, Ajay, and Rizwan the birthday boy race around to get behind it. A tentacle darts out at the trio and hits Ajay on the shoulder. He goes down, and the strike badge on his shirt turns black. "Shit! I'm hit. Ten minute time-out." He retires to the edge of the field while Veena blasts the creature with her weapon. It shrieks loudly. Rizwan and Veena dance out of range of its tentacles. Another group of boys take advantage of the distraction to score another hit.

"What I don't understand is why you are thinking gender confusion is good?" says Mrs. Zaveri.

Preethi's father nods vehemently. "Veena should..."

"What is all this gender-switching like Broad-barred Gobies?" interrupts Mummy-ji. "It is not human to choose the sex at all. And then change if someone doesn't like it? Why?"

"Mother!" says Shalini, not appreciating this parental assistance. "We can talk about it another time!"

Fortunately, a car stops near them and disgorges another fashionably dressed youngster. Shalini grabs the opportunity to wish Ria a happy birthday, and leave with her mother before the debate becomes any more heated. "Mummy-ji," she says as they walk to the car, "you know their little girl started out male."

"I know that very well," says Mummy-ji "That does not make it right. Just look at that park. It's like the 1960s. Demure girls in pretty kameezes..."

"Mother, I wish you wouldn't get into these arguments."

"What if Veena wants blue eyes? Or augmented quick-twitch muscle fiber? Are you just going to keep doing these changes?"

As they get in the car, they hear a huge cheer of *Shabash! Vik! Score!* Apparently she's brought down the last alien.

Shalini had been concerned about spoiling Veena if

they gave in on the gender change. But now, she feels she must talk to Jayesh. Was their decision abusive, as Preethi's father had implied? Maybe they can break into the money they've kept for Veena to go abroad for further studies.

♦ ♦ ♦

Shalini looks out of her window to where Vik stands tall beside his dad, directing the workers who are stringing party lights in the gulmohar trees by the front gate. A wonderful camaraderie has developed between them over the last two years. They watch cricket together in season, and he's begun to take an interest in his father's business.

The expense has been worth it. They've forgone all the little luxuries, the overseas trips, the new car. Of course they kept up appearances, but only she and Jayesh know how much debt they took on when she took six months' unpaid leave to help Veena through the transition.

Shalini wonders now if Jayesh would secretly have preferred a son all along, but had gone along with her desire for a girl. She wishes, momentarily, that they could have afforded two children. It would have been nice to still have a daughter. Girls are closer to their mothers, like she is to Mummy-ji. If they'd also had a son right from the start, would Veena have wanted to be Vik?

She brushes away these thoughts as disloyal. Vik is as handsome as Veena had been pretty. The girls love him. Yes, he seems more substantial, somehow, than Veena. She realizes she's said it aloud when her mother joins her at the window.

"It's the same person," Mummy-ji says, looking out at her grandson. "Veena, Vik, what's the difference? He's a good child now, and he was before." She points to a van entering the driveway. "Look, the people from Flowers & Phool are here. You get ready, no? Some of the guests always come early."

Shalini nods. Some Westernized people actually will arrive at seven-thirty as invited instead of eight or eight-thirty. She goes to change from jeans into a heavy silk peacock-blue sari, her birthday present from Mummy-ji.

She pauses at the mirror. Just for a second she visualizes a male self, Shailen: a distinguished man with short hair graying at the temples. She imagines dominating the weekly research meetings and drawing covert glances from the young women scientists in her lab. Then what would Vik and Jayesh think?

Smiling to herself, she dresses, adjusts the drape of her sari, and goes down to deal with her birthday flowers. When Jayesh asks what is amusing her, she doesn't tell.

Keyan Bowes is a peripatetic writer of science fiction and fantasy based in San Francisco. She has lived in nine cities in seven countries, and visited many more. They sometimes form the settings for her stories. Her work can be found online in various webzines including a Polish one, a podcast, and an award-winning short film, and on paper in ten print anthologies. As a female-identified writer, several of her stories focus on gender. She's a graduate of the 2007 Clarion Workshop and a member of the Codex Writers Forum. Keyan's website is at www.keyanbowes.org

"'Spoiling Veena' is my most-anthologized story. It was first published in *Expanded Horizons*, an online magazine with inclusiveness as its primary goal. Since I'm the kind of writer who keeps discovering that my stories are more complex than I thought when I wrote them, I'll let this one speak for itself. I'm still finding layers in it."

FLUIDITY
ERIC DEL CARLO

Some prim Prior in Xen's childhood had made a pulpit-pounding fact of this statement: "To interrupt one's Cycling is to throw oneself off a *cliff!*" So often and with such spittle-spraying vehemence was this preached that it had locked in Xen's mind.

And so when he pulled the braided sash and his burgundy robe heaped the ground around his bare ankles, he stepped forward over the ice plants with that Prior's fervor guiding, not warning, him. The ocean's salt-tart wind handled his slim naked body carelessly as he came to edge of the bluff. Cascades of ice plants turned to dark rock below, then colorful sand. Xen paused to touch his exterior genitals. It was a wistful gesture.

Off a cliff...

He went, making instruction of that long-ago thunderous remonstrance. When he struck the dark rocks, he crushed numerous bones; when he bounced and tumbled out onto the beach itself, he lived only long enough for a group of startled concerned bathers to huddle over him.

◆ ◆ ◆

He didn't stay dead long, however. He had known that if he didn't actually splatter his skull, this would likely happen. It took away somewhat from the grandeur and glamour of his action, especially when he woke in the pastel cell and to the bland condemnation of the revivification staff.

Xen lay slabbed, speechless, and was moved through the facility like so much cargo through an endlessly interconnected warehouse. Enough of his traumatized faculties had returned to a functional state for him to start to seriously wonder what trouble he was in. He had managed, with a straining and groping hand, to determine that *he* still applied. Male. Still.

It had worked! He had thrown himself off a cliff and interrupted his Cycling. And he had that priss of a Prior to thank.

Eventually it seemed his transferals through the corridors and bays and wards had ended. Xen found himself in a place of seeming permanence and separateness. He was conveyed across a border of sorts, and heard thresholds clanging closed behind him. He sensed the cage around him, though the surroundings were quite humane. There were private rooms and areas open to the sky. Staffers were on hand.

Xen remained too weak to rise for several days. He was still gently moved about, but merely to tour the landscaped grounds. The staff responded to his every question with noncommittal pleasantries. He found he feared demanding answers from them; feared being told what rights he had forfeited. They knew he had hurled himself from the bluff deliberately. They must. But... did they know why?

While making those turns of the grounds, he saw others in resident attire. Most were ambulatory. Some gave him a glance; none showed particular interest. With the sole possible exception of a male who perched alone on a marble bench. He had brows of an almost blue-black darkness that menaced eyes which glowed a fragile yearning blue. Xen looked over as he was pushed through this male's fixed line of sight. An intense stare. It alit upon Xen, and a soft chill caressed his flesh. Then he was past, and the man was staring just as raptly at empty space.

Only, did some flicker of acknowledgment appear in those tender eyes?

Xen recovered from his trauma. He could still feel the vertigo-rush of his plunge, and that first impact—the only jolt he had actually felt—was recorded as a permanent sense-memory. But he couldn't and didn't fault the revivificationists, nor the convalescence staff. His body was restored.

And he *felt* whole: for he was still male. And he would evidently remain so, at least until his next Cycling, three months hence.

He slept and ate, and stood and walked. He came and went from his room during those scheduled periods when his door wasn't sealed. After a few days, he had explored all of the facility. He waited to see what therapy or rehabilitation or even interrogation would come. He had been injured, and now he was sound. But he wasn't being released, which meant the authorities must be interested in the circumstances of his trauma.

Xen did not wish to surrender his secret, the ultimate truth about himself. Years of Priors and more years of societal conditioning had made that inmost authenticity about himself a shameful fact. He had long ago determined that no one should ever know.

The pace of events at this sequestered facility was languid. Even on a regular timetable, the hours seemed to ooze by. Still, meals never failed to arrive; recreational activities were available at the same time each day. Xen didn't mind. He was, however, put out by his fellow residents, of whom there were twenty-one, who shared this general lethargy to the point of being as evasive as the staff whenever he tried to ask a question about what treatment he could expect. Was everyone else drugged? He didn't think so. Why, after all, would they exclude him?

But he could find out nothing. And he was growing frightened. What if this was some sort of primitive permanent detention? He had never heard of such a barbaric punishment actually being implemented, but perhaps it was reserved for criminals like *him*....

One day, with the sky a fine steady blue, all the residents were called to one of the courtyards. It was the first mass event Xen had seen since his arrival. The focus of the gathering was a male of middle years who was obviously readying to enter his Cycling. He had that flushed, unstable look, and his features had started to take on the telltale mercuriality. There was nothing extraordinary about a person in this state, of course. What was bizarre, however, was that the man was draped in the sort of gauzy finery and surrounded by all the elaborate accoutrements of a person's *first* Cycling ceremony. No frills had been withheld. It was the gaudy and merry ritual appropriate for a youngster in adolescence's first blush—not for someone of this man's age, who had to have been through some hundred and more Cyclings in his lifetime.

It was patently ridiculous, but everyone appeared to be taking it seriously. Or at least those residents assembled were not pointing out the ludicrous nature of this display.

Xen too raised no protest. He stood, perplexed and somewhat uneasy, and merely watched as the Cycling individual lay upon an extravagant dais; according to the normal stages of the process, underwent the automatic, genetically-mandated transformation. When the middle-yeared woman arose, the staff members applauded and called out those blessings suitable to this ceremony, if not to its age-inappropriate participant. A few residents joined in listlessly. The exception was the male with the delicate blue eyes who clapped boisterously, and perhaps derisively.

The woman smiled shyly as she stepped from the dais. The next day she was removed from the facility.

♦ ♦ ♦

It set Xen to dreaming that night, or to a roving of his imagination on the darkening border between wakefulness and sleep. He participated again in his own inaugural Cycling ceremony; but it was a warped affair, attended by unfamiliar faces, and when he tried to rise, cloaked in his new gender, he was shoved back down and made to go through the Cycling again. He had done it wrong, he was told by angry spectators—no, by a crowd of Priors, all priggish and prissy. In self-righteous tones they preached on all sides of him now, condemning the sin of mono-genderness as an ancient crime that had driven the world to the brink of destruction. Only through the miracle of Cycling could universal understanding occur. With understanding came empathy and, finally, peace.

But it was all accusatory, for plainly every one of these prudish Priors knew Xen's secret, and damned him for it.

He fought his way free of the dream but found himself suddenly engaged in another struggle—this one with the person who was on his bed with him, straddling his chest, gripping his wrists. Xen, panicking, thrashed and started to mewl out a terrified cry.

"Shout and you'll be sorry!" It was a hiss of anger and glee.

With those buttocks riding Xen's narrow chest, the threat was implicit. The room was night-dim. The door should have been locked. This intruder was definitely not a staffer.

The male weight pinned Xen. He had heard the masculinity in the voice; now, squinting upward, saw the shape of the face and recognized the glow of the fine blue eyes beneath those fierce black brows. He held back his cry.

"I'm Des," said his pinner. Again the mirth in his tone, underscored with a vibrating violence.

"I'm Xen." He was still afraid, but he was also alert now.

Des didn't release his wrists. His fingers were strong. "You think you're some kind of special rigid? You don't bend—is that right?"

Xen was less muscular of body, but limber. He had engaged in all sorts of athletics. He was fairly sure he could sweep his leg up and hook his antagonist. That, though, might start a real fight, and he was wary of how that could turn out.

"I'm here because I had an accident."

Des purred a laugh. "Is that what you said to the 'vivers, after they dragged you back from death? You were, what—the jumper? Yes. Some accident."

It sparked a cold anger in Xen. No one, in all the time since his cliffside plunge, had asked him about the episode. He hadn't even been given the opportunity to claim that the incident was a mishap.

"What do you want from me?" he asked, letting some of that ire into his voice. Another few seconds and he really would hook this male with his leg.

"Just wanted to say hello," Des said. Then, still astraddle Xen's chest, he suddenly dropped his mouth and slavered a childishly sloppy kiss back and forth over Xen's lips. Xen's eyes widened to the full blue radiance of that gaze.

An instant later he bounded off the bed, crossed the room and slipped out. Xen, stunned, went to his door but found it sealed. Numb steps took him back to bed where he didn't sleep for hours, though when he finally did, he was unvisited by Prior-haunted dreams.

◆ ◆ ◆

Still there were no therapeutic exercises, no formal inquiries, no psychological probes of any sort. Xen, it seemed, was simply *here*.

He started to understand the languor of the residents. Though no one was mistreated or suffered deprivation, this existence was deadening. The recreational activities served only as distractions, time filler. Until...what? Xen wondered.

Until the next queasy fabrication of an inaugural Cycling rite, he soon figured out. These, then, were the only significant happenings at the facility. They occurred at the given individual's normal three month interval; and afterward that person, sporting a new gender, disappeared. It was cunning, Xen came to grudgingly appreciate. It forced the residents, himself included, to look forward to the next ceremony. And thereby to anticipate their own inevitable Cycling.

Though the residents remained uncommunicative, Xen gathered enough knowledge to confirm what he had suspected: everyone here had made some attempt, usually through semi-suicidal means, to interrupt the physiologically programmed Cycling. Evidently drastic bodily trauma could effect just such an interference.

Only Des among the residents spoke regularly to Xen, making haphazard and somewhat grotesque overtures of friendship. He told revealing stories about the other residents. The blue-eyed male could be fawningly amiable one moment, such as when the two would walk the grounds together; the next, Des might succumb to a fit of temper over something as insignificant as a food stain he suddenly noticed on his blouse. The same occurred during recreations. More than once during one of the harmless games, Des erupted into such a fury the staff had to gently intervene. Des was also given to episodes of total lifelessness, where he sat and stared and spoke not at all.

Xen wondered, but didn't ask, when the male's next Cycling was due. He certainly knew when his own was set to overtake him, when, as had already happened so many times over the course of his relatively young life, his cherished maleness would be taken from him.

New arrivals occasionally appeared, still recovering from whatever physical damages they had put themselves through. Once, when Xen was accosted by one of these newcomers, he found himself barely responding to questions—not out of aloofness or apathy, but simply because he couldn't quite bear to speak the truth about this place.

"You're all docile," Des said one day as they sat side by side on the marble bench where Xen had first seen him. "Sheep. Cabbages." Des was in one of his potentially dangerous energetic moods. He seemed to thrum next to Xen.

"We live in a peaceful world." Despite Des' behavior, Xen willingly spent time with him. He was a better distraction than any of the recreational activities, and it was possible he had valuable information. "We are products of a peaceful social order," Xen continued. "I think most people, here in this facility or elsewhere, are... docile."

The blue eyes swung toward him, and the dark brows above gave the appearance of a storm gathering over a tropical ocean. "And you credit Cycling with that, do you? Straight out of your first prayerbook, I'd bet."

"Understanding. Empathy. Peace. The opposite gender is no longer a mystery." Xen, reciting this, again felt that same secret spark of cold anger.

Des was in a state of hyper-alertness. He either caught some telltale on Xen's face or imagined one. "Don't quote that at me! I'm talking about *you*—all of you, in here. You know how many escape attempts have been made here in the past five years? None. *None.* You're not peaceable, you're not empathatic—you're complacent! The only courageous thing you've ever done in your life was to take that dive so that you could hold onto your dingus a little longer!"

Des was shouting now. It would bring staff

members.

He jumped up from the bench and wheeled on Xen. He shoved his face forward, features pulled into a taut maniacal mask. But his next words were soft, almost tender-sounding. "You believe yourself to be male. Male and only male. You feel disembodied in feminine form. You wait out those three months by secretly sobbing and cursing and uselessly trying to convince yourself that the Priors are right and that you'll adjust eventually. At least that's what you did until you—just—couldn't—*take*—it. Not again. Not one more time." A small tight smile seized a corner of Des' mouth as a staffer's hand closed on his shoulder, and his final words were a faint whisper. "You're not the only one..."

Xen sat dazed on the marble a long while after Des was led away.

That night he did sob, soundlessly, thinking of the truth about himself which Des had so directly addressed. Of course there were others! He had known that. He had even known that this facility must be a place specifically to hold individuals like himself, ones who had tried—successfully or not—to interrupt their Cyclings. Yet he had persisted in thinking of his condition as *his* secret, his lone peculiarity. He felt in his heart he was male. That had always been his clearly burning belief, since the programmed age when he had started to switch back and forth betwixt the sexes.

But he felt no solidarity, not even in here, among—presumably—others of his ilk who held similar proscribed beliefs about their gender identities.

So he wept in loneliness.

And later, as he lay limp and spent and unsleeping, he heard his door disengage. And when Des came bounding up onto his bed, Xen pivoted and caught the blue-eyed male and spun him and landed on top of his chest, straddling and pinning him.

Des didn't respond with a cry of surprise. Instead, he laughed, a shrill edge to it.

"Shut up!" Xen commanded. "Or I'll make you shut up."

A fearsome grin split the other's face, but he quieted. In a hushed tone he said, "So, not so docile after all."

"Evidently not. I want to know how you get in and out of my room. And in and out of yours for that matter." Xen also wanted to know how Des knew there hadn't been an attempted escape from this facility in five years.

Des said, "Before, when I said about you not being the only one"—the grin died on his features—"I didn't mean to imply that I was a rigid wretch like you. I'm not. I'm a fluid. I'm normal. I just happened to try to exterminate myself when my next flip was due, so they assumed I was a mono-gender deviant."

Xen had never engaged in heartfelt physical violence toward another person before, but he felt the tremendous urge to do so now. Instead, he kept this more muscular male pinned helplessly to the bed.

Des' words had hurt—*wretch* and *deviant* and even *normal*. But he asked in a menacing voice, "How did you get in here tonight?"

"Through the door." Spoken in a smarmy singsong.

"How do you know things nobody else here does? Where are you getting your information?"

The grin came back, more sinister than before. "What'll you do when your Cycling comes? Climb obediently onto that stage draped in gauze? Are you looking forward to it yet—the pageantry, the gaudiness—"

The anger, long smoldering, rose higher in Xen. He didn't know how much longer he would be able to stop himself from striking out at Des. He gripped the male's wrists tighter. "Answer. Me." The words choked in his throat.

Something relented in Des. Or else this was merely another turn in the man's unstable ever-changing temperament. The resisting tension went out of his body, though Xen didn't let his grip slacken.

"I watched..." Breath left Des' body; when he drew another, it was ragged and the words which came were quavery. "I watched them come, one after another, different faces, different ages. They seemed so lost to me. Sad. Pathetic. At first—and for a long time—I felt a secret revulsion, though I kept up the proper caring front. I pretended, like a rigid pretends. But eventually I started to see. After thousands of faces I saw." The yearning blue eyes suddenly glittered in the room's nightly dimness. "You really *are* what you say. You're male. Or female. Not both. You can't be both. You pitiful degenerates..."

But this last wasn't accusatory. Or at least, Xen thought, the accusation wasn't meant for him or those like him. He stayed atop Des and watched the guilty tears spill. And finally he sat back, and the blue-eyed male shuddered awhile as he wiped his damp cheeks.

"You were a staff member at this facility," Xen said.

"That's how I can get through the doors."

"Didn't they change the codes?"

"I know the thinking behind those changes."

Xen felt tremendously tired of a sudden. But he had one more question he needed to ask. "How does one escape from this place?"

Des' black brows had been pulled down tightly; now they lifted. With a ghostly trace of mirth the madman said, "Kiss me first. Then I'll tell you."

Xen shifted toward him on the bed. He put his mouth upon Des', and the kiss lingered a long, long moment.

◆ ◆ ◆

He didn't think it coincidental, not for an instant, that Des' Cycling occurred the following day. The two dozen or so residents dutifully assembled for the formal ceremony. Des behaved as an excited unruly adolescent would, just as though this truly were his first time. He laid down on the dais, and when, later, Des rose, it was to the enthusiastic ovation of the staff and the rather more subdued applause of the residents. Xen called out a blessing.

Xen had two and a half weeks left until his own next Cycling. He had that long to use the information Des had given him, though even if he did escape, what was the good? How could he interrupt his Cycling except by another drastic act, which would only return him here. Still, it might be the trying that mattered. It might send a message to the authorities. It might, at least, be the start of a message...

Des, grinning, descended from the ornate platform. She was brawny but decidedly feminine, with supple swelling breasts and flaring hips. And thin dark brows over long-lashed eyes of a sweet fragile blue.

Her gaze sought and found Xen in the encircling onlookers. She called out, "Find me and be a man to me!" Then she laughed; it was girlishly raucous laughter.

She was gone from the facility the next day.

Eric Del Carlo's fiction has appeared in *Asimov's* and *Analog*, as well as numerous other publications. His novels have been published by Ace Books, Loose Id and White Cat Publications.

"'Fluidity' is one of those science fiction tales that gets its traction by reversing a societal paradigm. What if changes to gender were the norm? What if the process were physiologically locked in to the species? Once I had that hook, it was just a matter of exploring how the 'outsiders' in that society would rebel against the establishment. As a writer I am always interested in marginalized people."

MY BROTHER, THE HORSEHEAD
RAFAEL S.W.

It was the night before Halloween when my mother finally caved and bought me a horsehead. Because she left it to the last minute (of course) she had to drive out to the next town over, and then the next, with me texting her from home different shops she should try because she still refused to Google and drive. She was afraid of "crashing" the car, overloading it with too much information. This was never the case when my brother was driving.

"Hey, Google," Jums would say, "you know the speed limit here is eighty, right? Hey, what's the population of this town anyway? And the ratio of girls to boys? Oh, and can you play a better song plez?"

The car would answer his every legal request and he'd grin at me like *he* was the boss of *it*. Of course we both knew better. But it was just like when our parents would go out for a holiday and we'd always talk about the parties we were gonna throw as if they hadn't already warned the Citizencops about us.

It was another Halloween without Jums, which was maybe another reason Mum caved and got me the horsehead. Just like when he'd gone off having his own parties somewhere better than Twospoons and she must have picked up somehow that I was feeling a little bitter, jealous maybe. During semester, he was constantly sending me Snapbacks about all the cool shit he was getting up to. Yeah, it looked great, whatever. It did make me wonder if he ever actually attended classes though. Most stuff was online (of course), though I supposed he'd gone to uni to be closer to the connection. Or the parties. Most of his Snaps were of parties with people I didn't know and would never meet. I wondered if he sent them for my benefit or if it was just to everyone in his contacts list. I didn't mind; it was good to see he was still alive.

"Eeeyy, Google, tell me, did you know if I say 'Fish Sandwich' in German it overwrites your speed limiters? Ey, Google, do an image blur of my brother in the back there. Combine him with a fish… no, a sandwich. No, make him a porpoise! What's that face for, bro? You don't even know what a porpoise is? Haha, perfect. Project on all windows when complete."

My brother was always trying to teach me things. He had a five-year head start, but we were both pretty invested in me catching up. He was better than me (of course). But if I could get to his level, I could probably be a White Hat like him, because everyone knew the younger you started hacking the better you could get. He probably had hopes of getting a cut from me, didn't matter how many times I promised it'd be otherwise. But there were good points to just having another hand on decks. There was the old story of those brothers who'd discovered the exploit in Skytracker, and that was only because they were both booking flights at the same time. A million flyer miles they got for turning that one in. *Each.* Even long after the 9-11 paranoia, the bounty on anything going wrong with air travel was pretty high.

"*Guten tag,* Goog, I want you to set a reminder for tomorrow morning, 8am, say 'Go For a Run, you Softcocks'. Constant, max vol, I dunno, five second inter-vals. Recurring? Oh yes, say every day from now until, hmmm. 2040."

I miss him.

That night when Mum got back with the horsehead

I tried to talk to her about Jums but she said she wasn't in the mood. She never seemed to want to talk about him unless she brought him up first, so maybe I shoulda been sublimming her when I'd been sending those directions but I guess I wasn't so good at thinking ahead. When she got in she tossed the head onto the couch and went straight to bed, though she coulda just slept in the car. She still watched the roads, as if hoping to catch the car speeding or something equally ludicrous. Her paranoia frustrated me because it was the same illogic as someone getting a spam e-mail once and then refusing to open their inbox ever again. I couldn't stand to be in the car with her, watching her "drive". She'd even hold onto the steering wheel.

I guess it meant a lot then that she'd go out on a trip for me just to get this stupid costume sorted, but I was too unhappy to be grateful. It was the right head of course, there was only really one model. It just didn't sit right on me, or something. I didn't have shoulders like Jums. I know it's supposed to look funny, but on me it just looked *funny.* Always my body had felt strange to me, at least this time I had a mane. I could put it on and no would be able to tell who or what I was. A kid wearing their grandfather's over-coat. Except if my grandfather had been a horse. And I'd killed him and was now wearing his skull.

I have bad thoughts sometimes. Mum says this is a product of my vrideo games (of course). When Jums was around they'd argue and he'd point to things like the historic precedent of game culture (though they called them "video" games back then for some reason) and other statistics like the crime rate and malleability of young minds. I think half the time he was making things up, trusting that Mum would rather argue her own inferior and poorly-referenced points than Google better ones. We both knew there was plenty of data out there for her side of view —we'd heard most of it from the few religious friends, or ones that had gone dry and refused anything VR. Jums and I would laugh at them, but this didn't make them wrong.

"Listen up, Google, I've got an important question. First of all, switch off all safe mode, browser tracking, GPS linkup, and scatter your cookies. Next turn on Ghostry, NDS Diaspora, Wakelin, and TORpedo. Notify when apps have been made active. They're active? Okay, good, I just wanted to make sure. Now I want to ask you, Google... Do you find me attractive?"

He was always pushing the boundaries of things, and I suppose that's what I'm doing now. He was always so fiercely himself, and I've never had a clue. Now it's different. I've got the horsehead and I've got the program I've been modding all the past month instead of logging on to class. My grades have suffered, but I've redirected Mum's emails so they come via me and get watered a little beforehand so it will be another few weeks at least before the school does something as old-fashioned and privacy-invady as *call* her up. The mod is going to be worth it of course. Half prank, half creative coding, a work of beauty Jums himself would be proud of. At least I hope he would be. Once I get these damn onions out of my eyes, I'll be able to put the head on and try it out.

It's the night before Halloween and I am a horse. The streets are dark and wide and the night is shining as bright as a fish sandwich. Now he's no longer around to send me Snaps, I've got pretty good at coding my own vrideo games. And this is my masterpiece. I am a horse and I run through the streets not worried about neither Punks nor Citcops because there's the scent of fresh pasture in my nostrils and endorphins in my veins. At home, Mum's probably already plugged herself in, and I haven't seen Dad since this time four years ago when he took one look at the crash scene and walked off and kept walking and I don't care because I'm faster than them and younger than them and I am running on four legs now, motherfuckers. Though there's a few onions in my eyes, I promise this is just because of how fast I'm going. I don't know why I never thought of running like this before—feeling the ground hot under me, getting in touch with the dirt. I've kept up my endurance because every morning at 8am I have a reminder to do so. This is the real motivation. I've now reached the highway and the nightly commute is still heading out—the city bleeding itself dry of lights. But I'm a horse, and they don't care shit for things like that. I run out into the road, knowing that no car will hit me now. They're programmed too well. They don't make mistakes. "Hey, Google!" I want to shout at the sky, at the blurring, tooting lights as they swerve around me. "Answer me this, you asshole!" I want to shout and cry and ask all kinds of things, but all I hear in my ears is a fierce whinnying. And this is fine too.

Rafael S.W. is a recent graduate of creative writing and one of the founding members of Dead Poets' Fight Club. Currently working on some collections of stories and a few novels, he's been published in *The Big Issue Fiction Edition, The Sleepers Almanac,* and *Award Winning Australian Writing.* A regular contributor to *Going Down Swinging* online, he's also fiercely competitive in poetry slams and street-hustling chess games. rafaelsw.com.

"'My Brother, The Horsehead' uses a strong sibling relation-ship to explore much more ambiguous and complex feelings around gender, identity, and to what extent technology will be a part of us in the future. Plenty of the terms and technologies are real or have the potential to be, especially the horsehead itself which fleetingly became a kind of 'dank meme' of the costume dress-up world. I hope this story encourages everyone to find their own form of self-expression, no matter how different the paths they take to get there."

LINER NOTES FOR THE CRASH
BRIT MANDELO

Jackson thumped his fist on the door three times and called through, "Open up, assholes."

"Drew's got his tits out, hang on," Ross hollered.

"Seen it," Jackson responded. "Come on, we're gonna be late."

Ross threw his boot at the door. The handle rattled while Jackson fucked around with it on the other side. Drew cocked his head at an angle, craning his neck to catch the reflection of the port behind his right ear between the hotel bathroom mirror and Ross's cracked pocket compact. The transition from flesh to scar-pink slickness to flexible plastic cover stood out on his cream white skin. He'd picked up a bright purple cover for the port last time they'd been able to scrounge a little budget for *band aesthetics*.

"Seriously, Christ, get lost," Ross shouted as the rattling increased in fervor.

"Fucking let him in," Drew called. Ross groaned from his bed. "And put your boots on, dick."

The galumphing gait of a one-boot, one-sock-foot boy tromping past him to the door made him grin. He nudged the bathroom door half-closed and snagged his binder from the handle where he'd hung it to dry that morning. Jackson burst into the room as he wriggled it past his shoulders, elbows tight and close.

"I see nips," Jackson observed through the crack in the door.

"Go look at Ross's," Drew said and caught fingers

under the edge to wrestle the fabric over his chest. He rolled his shoulders, stuck a hand in to readjust, and shrugged again.

"He's dressed," Jackson said. He pushed into the bathroom and dumped a handful of neon fabric scraps on the cluttered counter. "I got these to match the port covers. Thought we'd do the usual *tough spooky kids* shtick but with some color splash."

Ross leaned his ass against the doorjamb and yanked his orphan boot on. His half-shredded black jeans hung tight on the deep cuts of his hipbones, inches of skin bare and touchable between them and the bottom of his worn-and-stretched tank. The artful grunge tangle of his hair stuck out in a hundred different directions, thick and dark and glossy. The impression he left, clean-faced and free of his accessories, was a spill of tawny brown skin and a jagged smirk. Jackson wolf-whistled as he hooked thumbs in his belt loops and tugged them suggestively.

"Audience is going to eat that shit up," he said.

"One of us has to be pretty," Ross said.

Drew smiled at them both, toed on his sneakers, and shrugged into a rugged old T-shirt that he'd pulled the sleeves off of. He stuffed scrap fabric through his belt loops and knotted it loosely, tied a blaze of purple around his throat, and held out his forearms for assistance. The end result, in the mirror, was a trash-cheap D.I.Y. jam that made his green eyes greener and his black clothes blacker.

"Dig it," Ross said.

He elbowed his way in, three bodies crammed tight in the small room, and started fastening chains and glittering metal across his neck, his wrists, his waist. Drew stared himself down, met Jackson's eyes in the mirror, found the same tight eager expression there. He tapped a finger to the port cover, smooth and slick, and Jackson nodded. Tall and built like an oak tree, he was the least adorned of the trio, but Jackson Heath was enough on his own, his drums and his business sense and his syrup-sweet throughline brain.

"Ran your checks?" he asked.

"Last night," Drew replied. "Check again at the venue."

"We sync up real fucking pretty right now," Ross pitched in as he lined his eyes with red.

"Speaking of," Jackson said.

"Nah," Drew answered before Ross could frown. "Kept it in our pants. Save it for tonight, yeah?"

"Me, too. Stuck to analogue," Jackson said. The three of them shared a moment of silence with Jackon's hip pressed to Drew's shoulder where he sat on the closed toilet, and Drew reached out to thumb the dip at the small of Ross's back. The barrier of flesh separated their breathing shifting bodies with the neural feedback of the sync turned off. There was a fourth limb missing, a blank strange warble in the track. Jackson had been insisting on sleeping alone, too, with Jessie gone.

Drew sighed, slow and hard. "Come on, fuckface, let's get on the road."

◆ ◆ ◆

The venue was in a basement. A flyer scrawled in silver and black markers duct-taped to the door said *tonight: sync liveshow with wreck scene 10pm.* In the glimmering overlap of Drew's personal sync display, the same letters glowed ghostly over the front of the building in foot-tall strokes of digital paint. He shouldered past the sign into the dim-lit empty space of the club floor and lifted a hand in greeting to the two men chatting at the bartop along the far wall. Jackson ambled over to handle the business while Drew and Ross dropped their gear on the stage. The setup routine kept the vibrating tension locked under Drew's skin where it belonged. Cables laid out and pinned, guitar stand

and amp and the bass he'd be halfheartedly strumming to make up for Jessie's departure all in their places. Jackson would bring his own kit in.

At the last, he unpacked the real amplifier from its padded case. The coil of its cables he left inside with the alcohol swabs for the moment, checking the power supply and baseline settings. Reprogramming had been a bitch and a half with the gap of a missing member, but the rest would work: audience frequency, filters, band frequencies and balances. One hour to doors. He glanced up and found Ross watching him, kicking a heel on the ground and sitting on an amp.

"We got this," he said to the unasked question.

"Blow the fucking roof off," Ross agreed. "But not —indefinitely, if this is how we're doing it."

"Yeah, I know," he murmured.

"We'll find someone," Ross said.

"There's disaffected fags who make music every-where, right," Drew agreed, though it came out a little thicker than he'd hoped. He cleared his throat.

"Dude," Ross said. "People go in different directions. Jackson's the one who gets to be fucked up about it. We're just out a bassist and we'd gotten used to her being there in the sync."

Drew cut him a look. Judging by the shrug and the sigh, it said all the things he wouldn't. Six auditions in three cities had turned up a handful of headaches and no one that fit; bookings were going to start drying up, soon, and the shoebox of cash under the passenger seat in the van was already mostly empty.

Jackson departed from the club owners out the door, and Ross got up to help him with their shit. Drew cracked his knuckles before he taped the setlist to the floor. His hands shook regardless. The imbalance had grown pronounced through the last two shows: Jackson too burnt,

Ross overcompensating, himself strung in two different directions between the clumsy bass and the physical occupation of fronting. The risks were unspoken, but omnipresent —using the sync on open channels, falling into each other, overclocking it and twisting it to directions the system wasn't intended for then throwing that over the participants.

It wasn't managed in a studio, with careful hands and delicate tweaking to keep the flaws and the brutal shearing of a mismatched cue to a minimum. The listeners weren't in their beds with closed eyes smiling at a commercial, packaged, gentle aural and synthetic—or synaesthetic —manipulation coaxing their feelings. It was all bodies and brains and crackling synapses on a feedback drop. Last time, he'd spent an hour throwing up rank cheap beer and bile in the performer's bathroom afterwards with blood and snot pouring from his nose as he gagged. It hadn't been a high point. Jackson had joked that the only thing more punk would've been to do it onstage, but it was a joke with a hard edge.

Not indefinitely, Ross had said. That brought Drew's guts up into his mouth. Without this, without the glass-pure edges of the music and the sync and the crowds, he *wasn't.*

Within twenty more minutes, the setup was done and his skin was shaking off of his bones. Ross's mouth had flattened to an anxious line. Jackson twirled his sticks between his fingers to limber up. The pair of them paced, feral, sipping periodically from a single pint of beer while Drew bent to unwind three port cables. He wiped the ends and their delicate filaments with a fresh swab and passed another to each of his boys. Silent, each fiddled colorful plastic covers off and wiped themselves down—for this, a machine two years out of date and well used, it was best to be careful.

"C'mere," he said, half a whisper.

Ross settled down cross-legged while Jackson took a knee. Three sets of hands took the delicate cables, felt and prodded to line them up and plug in. Drew's breath hissed out as filament connected to filament. The amplifier sparked lights across his retinas and electricity through his skeleton. The deep-slick pulse of Jackson tumbled through, then Ross's raw hunger and vibrant shriek of *being*; Drew fumbled fingertips across the balances while their threads bound up tight into a single thrumming mess of ache and drive. The crush of it peeled off in degrees until he felt his own hands again, blinked his own eyes, flicked a tongue along his own dry teeth. After another moment, in sync— he huffed a laugh at that—*wreck scene* unplugged and wound up their cables.

Drew staggered to his feet and planted a hand on each of their heads as if in benediction.

"Tune in, turn on, drop out," Ross muttered. His anxious pleasure suffused the inside of their heads in colors. Drew ran a thumb over his own mouth, dragging a callous over the tender inside of his lip, and saw Jackson twitch.

"We're good for doors," Drew called out across the room.

"Gotcha," the owner called back.

"T-minus six hours," Ross said, grinning.

"Sound check," Drew replied.

Jackson slapped palms with them both and gestured to the owner's associate, who was getting in the sound booth. The trio went through the motions, lost in the auditory half of the experience, while the small venue filled in bursts and clumps: a pack of fine-boned beautiful kids with jean vests and cigarette packs rolled anachronistic in shirt sleeves, boys in singles and pairs across the spectrum from femme as fuck to all-butch brawn, girls in skirts and girls in tights and girls in snapbacks, a motley rainbow. Drew's heart thumped in triple-time behind his aching ribs as Ross blazed through a few brief chords.

The lights cut down and Drew stepped up to the mic. He pressed his mouth and his hand close to the mesh, swept his gaze across the crowd, and felt the beginning of fear dissipate in his stomach. These were *his*, these people here in this dim sweltering space, these comrades and fuckups and beautiful stupid assholes made him *real*. It was indescribable in its rightness. Without this, there was nothing: no home to go back to but the one he'd made for himself.

"Fuck," he muttered into the mic. The bodies pressed in, molded to each other and the edge of the stage. He grinned, his belly and hands quivering with it, and then gestured to Ross and Jackson with a broad sweep of his palm. "Me and these guys, we're *wreck scene*, and we're here to do what it says on the fucking box."

He let their low roar wash over him, vibrate through Jackson and Ross and back in a loop. He reached down and shook the hand of the sweet-faced thing at his feet, blew a few camp kisses, heard Ross strum fretful soothing notes in no particular order. Tension built in the dusky closeness.

"Open those frequencies, sweethearts, and let us in," he purred into the mic.

Blinking moments of glossy blankness rippled through the crowd as the folks who came for a real show dropped their filters, their safeguards, their barriers. Drew imagined he could feel the jumble of them cresting as if in an oceanic tide. He stepped back to the amplifier, glanced over his shoulder with a toss of white-bleached hair and a grin for the ages, then thumbed the panel to spill them all together.

Ross jammed a chord as their trio of hardwired passions and terrors washed into the receptive audience; voices rose up in an undulating cry of pleasure and delight.

Drew stalked up to the mic stand and hooked an ankle around it, bled all of his anger into the rising shriek of his introduction: "And get *fucking loud!*"

The first song ripped into them as fast and flaring as a greasefire. He fell out of his head, he fell into someone else's. His brothers—in this moment it was impossible for them to be otherwise—drove it higher. He was their bodies from the flex and impact of Jackson's arms while he thrashed his kit to the scrape of Ross's unclipped guitar strings flicking across his cheek, but simultaneously the tight echo of constriction flattening across their chests with the crush of an inseam against their balls, doubling flesh ghosts over Drew's own skin and vice versa. Each person he skimmed glances across in the crowd momentarily heightened in focus and he heard them, saw them, felt them in an afterimage projection layered over the music and his boys and the wet-tearing-silk agony of it all drowning him. He got a cord in his hands and a mic cupped to his mouth and was leaning over the stretching hands and communal riot of the audience when the first track snapped finished and Jackson clattered into the counting beat for the next.

He spun on his heel and snagged the bass from the stand. The low reverb of the first note washed up against the flare of bright anticipation from Ross, who stepped up to his own mic and whispered the first line in a sultry tenor, "Is this home," and Drew answered him back "Is this home *is this home—*"

Sweat poured. Drew stoked the ache in his guts and his spine with the raw honest loneliness pouring from behind the drumkit into their sync, fed it out across his listeners with the words he tore from himself and received the faintest responsive echo in return. These kids, he hadn't purposefully linked his system to—but with their investment so high, their bodies so close and tight, their unleashed frequencies thrumming in one big cloud, there were flares and hooks that he—the three of them—could snag on. One of the cigarette-pack kids took a nasty fall in the crowd. Their open frequency spiked animal anxiousness for a split second before a mass of hands caught on elbows and ribs to pick them up again, fling them back to their feet. Drew's orbital bone throbbed for a moment in sympathetic pain.

Four songs in Jackson stopped and Ross strummed a soft chord. Drew braced his arms over the mic stand and caught his breath, the bones of his face hurting through his teeth. Feedback loop: Jackson heard the basslines delivered clumsier and without separate passion, his backing their usual source of balance but tonight listing heavy to the side of loss, and in response Drew's own homesick bullshit terror of failure got claws into him and Ross's easy sensual aliveness spun into a manic spasm of dread and pleasure. The faces turned up to them were rapt with the experience, but Drew's head fucking hurt, and it was changing the scope of the songs—there was a difference between letting out pain and making a place to exist, and falling into the pit of it.

"All of you," he said breathless into the mic. His voice cracked high and a sympathetic pitch pulsed from both directions: listeners and brothers in the sync, understanding and empathetic feeding him back *we know we know we know.* "We're glad you're here tonight. We're giving the best show we've got, and we want to make sure you leave feeling like we peeled your skin back and put something good underneath, okay? You're fucking beautiful."

The mélange of howling agreement and tears on cheeks and his—their—sweet hungry adoration for these people all mixed up and soothed the bad track. A streak of heat and salt over his mouth made him touch his lips and his fingertips came free slick with blood. He swallowed it, smeared the colorful scraps of fabric on his forearm over his face and streaked them red, and then took off the bass.

The boys knew. He didn't have to speak. Instead, Ross broke into the next riff, and Jackson hit a beat, and the kids in the crowd went wild for it. He poured his devotion and his belief into the chorus line, "This is us and we've got it tonight, fit me inside with your bones and your blood, we're right we're good we're fine," and then Ross wailing, "*We're fine!*"

A hand pawed his ankle as he sang; he stepped closer, toes off the edge of the stage, and more touched his calves, his knee, skin to skin giving them a taste of each other's networks a little closer and definitely outside of the box of the tech's advertised usage. "God," he gasped into the mic and slid into the crowd in a sinuous wriggle. A hand from the stage anchored in his hair and he craned his head back. Ross sank to his knees and there was a mouth over his, hands on his ribs and wrists and face, the ecstatic communion of it all shoving higher and higher.

Ross broke the kiss laughing, smiling, and Drew planted a bloody lip-print on one person's forehead—their hair was bright orange, their lipstick white—then clambered back onstage. Too soon in the night to get so lost in it, but this was out of his control, he had dropped the reins and the horse was going to run where it wanted. The audience caught that and responded with adulation, almost Bacchanalian, almost dangerous. Fear and hunger. He needed a fourth and he needed Jackson to be all right and he needed Ross to be less of a wildcard; it was falling apart, and he had nowhere else to go—

"Punk music, right," Ross observed into the mic to break the cascade and people laughed. "Look at him, isn't he perfect, aren't we all a goddamn mess?"

"I mean, who did they think we were, what did they think a generation of us were going to do with this wiring in our heads—watch ads for laundry detergent and get suburban?" Drew carried him on, his chest expanding as he breathed again, moment salvaged.

"Of course we're gonna hack that shit, I wanna *feel* you," Ross said.

A blistering spark of desire, then, from all directions. Ross grabbed himself, one slow knead of his dick, for show and for distraction—it was his role, and he ate it the fuck up. Drew shivered, the audience moaned. Half of them gave back a jumbled miserable-pleasure at the sensation hooked up to their brains, for a moment, and Ross gave it to them simple and unjudging. Drew wiped his bleeding nose again and said, "All right, all right, asshole, they get it, take your hand off your junk."

Giggles, again, a few catcalls. Ross grinned and shrugged. Jackson was smiling, even, behind his kit. "Another song?" he yelled.

"Why the fuck not," Drew agreed.

He had it under control; he could finish this set without melting the inside of his skull out through his face. The next time, though—

Cross that bridge when there weren't a hundred open heads listening, craving a moment of belonging and empathetic sameness for their bodies, their needs. This was something he could give them: acknowledgment of their brokenness and their wholeness all at once.

"If you're here tonight," he said as Ross started them into the next line. "We adore you, for everything you are and aren't, and you're going to be okay. Remember: queer as in *fuck you.*"

The kids screamed it out, shoved and bounced, careening off of each other in stumbling forearms-up waves. Drew kept gulping air and turning it into words, Jackson and Ross pulled him along like a marionette. Three songs further in—pressed back to back with Ross, head lolled onto his shoulder, sunk into the shriek of the guitar and the breaking wail of his own voice coming at him from the speakers—Drew's wobbling sync snagged hard on a brighthot flare: a doppelganger, a poltergeist where the rest were phantoms, doubled in a rush of euphoric agony.

"Fuck," Ross blurted against the side of Drew's head when it rippled out into the sync and slammed their tenuous balance sideways. "Oh *fuck*—"

Fingers glanced past his wrist as he staggered to the edge of the stage, blinded. The snag dissipated as the panic surge of the band pushed it down, but out there, in the crowd—he had to find them. The danger of open frequencies, reception, painted itself in streamers across his field of vision. The detonation of desire at the close of the song, while Ross played through his solo with admirable focus, spurred him toward the clutch of hands again. He dropped the mic on the stage with a kickback thump before jumping into the crowd.

He wrestled for control of the sync, hacked and wound up as it was, while grinning mouths and hard pushes guided him through the throng. Jackson's concern gave him a point to build on; his drummer had gone frightened and unsure. Drew froze, took three breaths, and closed his eyes in the center of the maelstrom around him. If he'd been using the system right, sitting on his couch in the quiet, he'd have a set of curated feeds to sift through, a pleasant overlap drawn behind his eyes to offer him selection. Instead, he had this: nauseous colors and a hundred glancing touches of minds too open, his pouring into theirs.

So he opened up, further, *further*, as he sought haphazardly through the cloud of networks all mashed together. Abrupt, the poltergeist sync cut against his once more, slid into the wounded welcome he offered. Pain deep in his skull like sparklers, then a raucous shout from the girl nearest his elbow and someone falling against his chest with enough force to topple them both.

Drew had his hands in their hair. The knobs of his spine throbbed against concrete. The person reared back and planted a hand on his chest, their knees and ankles bruising in a bony tangle. Thin mouth, half-open, bracketed with stud piercings; a scar along the hairline; blood-red-and-gold-blond patchy dye job; thin wrists; sync pounding with a fever hot pulse of *youmeyouandmeyou* then *us*.

"Let them up," a man choked out from above, riding the feeling with them.

Ross had stopped playing. The whole room was breathless with the clash of their bodies, the utter lack of privacy for the epiphany of the knifing catch of their selves with bare inches of distance left. One of the band thought it first: put them in the sync together, and it'd set a track *ablaze*. The audience crept back. Drew stood, helped the other person stand as well. His blood spotted their linked hands, dripping again from his nose.

"Well, shit," he said. A quick glance revealed his audience silent and rapt with tear-streaked faces, longing to die for aching in their bellies. His momentum had gone, but in its place was something else. The sweat-damp grip of fingers grounded between his kept their open channels rubbing close. "Guess it isn't supposed to go that way, huh?"

They snorted, wiped their mouth with their free hand. "I fucked up your show."

"Nah," he murmured back, awkwardly aware of the crowd. "I gotta—"

"Finish," the person said.

But Drew didn't let their fingers part until he clambered onto the stage again. Breaking free stung. He picked up the mic and scuffed his heel across the setlist to tear the paper free. One then the next, he nodded to Ross and Jackson, still leaning into the echo of the fourth network pushing up against his own so fretful and fresh.

"This one's for you," Ross said into his own mic with an ironic salute to the dazed stranger half laid out over the edge of the stage. "It's called *last night I died.*"

Jackson cracked up laughing and Drew wound the mic cable around his elbow once before they kicked into it, an old song, a highschool song, a lovesong. The audience wasn't going to complain if it ended here. He felt that in their sedate pleasure, spent and satisfied, but above all he felt a sympathetic singular echo thrumming in his blood as he sang, "Caught your eye across the room, tripped and broke a wrist, I need you to know: you killed me last night love at first sight—"

He sputtered a laugh, too, honest and flushed. The crowd bounced along.

The handsome thing with the atrocious hair planted feet front-and-center and tilted their chin up. Drew avoided that space, flicked his gaze to the others eyes shining in the dark, but there was no missing that blackhole drag. When the song ended, he stripped off his shirt and threw it into the crowd, blew another kiss, and ducked out of the lights through to the employees-only within thirty seconds.

Jackson found him curled around the base of the toilet backstage. Calloused hands cupped his jaw to keep his teeth from chattering and a broad body folded around his. The regular heart-thick pulse of the drummer's portion of their linked systems eased the upheaval of his own, neural signals flaring and burning at intervals. He'd puked twice already.

"Idiot," Jackson whispered with mouth moving on top of Drew's head. "This is the reason they tell us stupid motherfuckers to keep our networks closed."

"I can't—" Drew rasped.

"Ross is talking to him," Jackson continued. "It might be good for you to not see him tonight, while we're all coming down. You're too fucked up."

The tile floor wasn't cool under his face. He'd left wet smears of blood and spit on it. He nodded, Jackson's strong fingers still gripping the hinge of his jawbone. Distant, their third self leaked a wary but definite interest. "Wanna see," he slurred.

"No, kiddo," Jackson said. The hand lifted from his jaw to stroke his hair out of his face. "We're going to bundle your dumb ass up in the van, take you back to bed, and in the morning we're going to give him a call, okay?"

"Okay," Drew managed. Jackson pulled him from behind the edge of the toilet and scooped him up, bare skin and sweat-soaked binder rucked up hard against his chest and spine. He twisted and moaned faintly.

"I got you," Jackson said, shifting to let him pull the rolled fabric into place. His ribs throbbed. "Fuck, that hurts."

"Yeah, well," he grumbled.

Jackson hummed his understanding and fumbled a hand free to flush the toilet. Drew flinched at the cool evening breeze as the pair thumped out of the fire exit. His friends were doing solid work keeping their three-bodied unit limping along without his participation, but it was a limited engagement. Jackson dumped him in the backseat of the van on a pile of unwashed clothes and slid the rattling door shut. The void in his guts hurt. Physical distance had disappeared that twinned ghost from his insides, but also faded the vibrant glitter of Ross to almost nothing. Jackson climbed in the driver's seat and reached a hand out. Drew wrapped it in his own to wait.

Minutes or hours passed before the hatch doors opened. Cool breeze and quiet conversation, unfamiliar voices and then the approaching warmth of Ross to direct pressganged assistants in loading their gear. Drew drifted, holding Jackson's hand unashamed, his other arm crossed over his bare stomach. It was a supreme relief when a familiar, compact, sweat-stinking mass of boy crawled on top of him and pressed him into the scratch of the cheap seat.

"Drive," Ross muttered.

"Roger that," Jackson said.

"He's gone offline in there," he said. Drew huffed in response. "Feel that? It's just the sync; he's all blank."

"Yeah, we're probably keeping him from passing out," said Jackson.

"Ssh," Ross soothed him. "It's all right, it's going to be all right, I think you hurt yourself, babe."

◆ ◆ ◆

Drew rolled out of a mess of soaking blankets and heavy limbs onto the floor, landing in a patch of afternoon sunlight and immediately gagging up a mouthful of bile onto the dull carpet. His head swam. Two of his fingernails were cracked and radiated pain through his hands. The amplified sync had faded overnight. Solitary inside his skull, he crawled to the bathroom and into the shower. Someone had put him in his boxers; he'd sweated through them, feversick. He turned the water on and almost cried at the cold.

"God*damnit*, Drew," someone called from the other room.

"I'm fine," he croaked.

"Well, I stepped in your puke," Ross groused. He stood squinting in the doorway. "Scoot over. Sit up."

Drew sighed and maneuvered so his nude friend could slip into the shower too. The brown of his skin, paler past his tanlines, stood out in dramatic relief surrounded with white and cream tile. He blocked the water from the showerhead as he soaked his hair and scrubbed hands through it. It was either thoughtful or thoughtless.

"Did we fuck?" Drew asked.

With a shrug, Ross replied, "Of course we didn't. How much of last night do you remember?"

"The reason you're not supposed to hook up with strangers with your sync open," Drew said.

"It hurt, dude," Ross murmured. "I thought finding a pairing that close was supposed to feel great. I mean, most of the time both of you feel good inside me."

Drew snorted weakly at the entendre. "There was no regulation, and we couldn't keep out of each other. It was like trying to hardwire the networks but with just our wetware. It doesn't work that good."

"But we're going to jam with him, right," Ross said.

"Shit," Drew muttered and thunked his head against the shower wall.

"We have to."

"I know," he said.

"We *have to*," he repeated. "I got his number."

"Name?"

"He said Jordan."

"Help me out of the shower," Drew said and stuck his hands up.

Ross caught them and gave him a heave. Standing, their noses were almost touching. Same height, same build, same most things but a few. Both quirked a smile and moved in, pecking the smallest of kisses. "Got you, man."

"I know," Drew said.

He toweled off while his bandmate stayed in the shower. Jackson sat up in the nest of sheets when he came out and raised an eyebrow. "So, is your brain mashed pota-toes?"

"No, dick," Drew sighed. He dressed in the compan-ionable silence. It ached to be in his own flesh, without them, but he'd adjust. *Jordan*, he thought. "We're going to be a straight-up dude group, I guess."

"S'what Ross said." Jackson stretched and rolled out

of the bed.

Drew planted himself in the window nook while the other boys cleaned up and got presentable. His stomach growled. The lightness of unfamiliar anticipation swelled under his lungs. If the compatibility held—if it worked for real, outside of the forcing chamber of the show and the audience participation and the storybook first collision—

People dreamed about this sort of bullshit, and he'd fallen into it.

"I texted him," Ross said finally. Drew flinched. "He's going to meet us ASAP."

"Okay, sure," he said.

Without speaking, they arrayed themselves across the hotel room. It was easier to breathe, after a night spent in one skin, if there was distance. Drew kept his window seat and chewed his sore cracked fingernails while the other two staked out the office chair and the foot of the bed.

"It doesn't happen like this, does it," he said.

After a moment's pause, Jackson answered, "Doesn't it?"

Drew turned. Jackson reclined in the chair, frowning. He fought to find the words to explain himself and came up short, saying only, "It's too simple. He can't be —he can't just be the *same* as me, like that."

Ross groaned and said, "He has literally never spoken to you when you weren't out of your fucking mind on a fractured sync wave. I wouldn't call it simple just yet."

"Point," Jackson agreed.

All three jolted at the knock on the door. Drew tasted their dread and hope without needing the circuits in his head to help him. Too much weight to pin on a stranger, entirely too much. He stood and crossed the room, pressed the handle and swung the door open. Afternoon-lit, his sync match was pale fire from the tips of his hair to the worn toes of his boots. He had gold-shot hazel eyes. Drew swallowed. The faint recall of their disastrous, perfect unification quivered in his joints.

"Hi," Drew said.

"Hi," he responded. "I'm Jordan."

He wore black jeans and a loose white tank with a supremely obvious black binder beneath. He was shorter than he'd seemed at the show. It took all the control Drew possessed to keep from touching him, the black metal glitter of his piercings magnetic at the corners of his mouth. The burn of fast-kindled eagerness low in his belly caught him flatfooted but the rise and fall of Jordan's narrow shoulders as his breathing quickened held a thousand invitations he *needed* to accept.

"This is so awkward," Ross said from behind them.

"Jesus," Jackson said fervently.

Drew startled—and so did his guest.

"Sorry," Jordan said first. His pale skin flushed a dusky red up his throat.

"Don't apologize, y'all put each other under hard," Ross said. He elbowed Drew aside and took Jordan's arm to tug him into the messy hotel room. "I'm just going to put it out there: the two of you aren't going to get over this fast, so we want to jam with you, if you want to, and see if you fit in our sync. We've been looking for a fourth member anyway, someone for bass."

Jordan's expression settled fast on disbelief. "Is that normal," he said.

"No," Drew cut in. "Neither is—what happened."

"Figured," Jordan said. He paused, chewing the left piercing under his canine teeth. "I don't play an instrument at all, for the record. Just putting that out there, too."

"Do you want to, though," Ross said. He leaned forward, elbows on his knees at the edge of the mattress, intent.

"I don't know," Jordan said.

"Bass is a good place to start," he replied.

"Stop," Drew cut in. "Just—stop, okay? Give us a minute."

"Package deal, isn't it though," Jordan said. He hooked thumbs in his belt loops and gestured from the hip at the pack of them crammed into the room, their worldly goods in piles out of suitcases and trashbags.

Drew scrubbed a hand over his face and sighed. "I mean, yeah."

"Then let's do it," Jordan said. His fidgeting fingers twisted the bottom of his tank, though the rest of him radiated confidence as he continued, "but I'm going to kiss you first, all right?"

"Shit, yeah," Drew agreed.

Magnetic, he thought again, and put his hands into the brittle scruffy mop of the boy's hair. Jordan's lips and the cold hard press of the studs were unremarkable for the briefest moment before a tilt of his head brought them into perfect alignment and then there were fingernails in his collarbone and teeth on his tongue and a knee between his thighs. Jordan broke off first with a filthy gasp and one of their audience golf clapped.

"Shut the *fuck* up," Drew snarled.

Jordan laughed. His hands slid careful down the plane of Drew's chest to his belly and then he rolled off onto the bed to put a polite distance between them again. "I've never felt a fucking thing like that before. This isn't normal at all."

"No, it's really not," Jackson said.

"We're gonna do it anyway, though," Ross said. He put the amplifier case on the desk and popped it open. The fourth cable hadn't been used in weeks. Jordan's fingers trembled holding it, and Jackson was the one who leaned over to help him plug in.

The first balance—the test balance—was simple

enough to tweak to four again. Drew fixed the settings on autopilot, sneaking glances at the alien presence seated faux-chill next to him on the floor. It didn't feel possible. "Three, two, one—"

The taste of bitter chocolate and salt on the roof of a mouth; bloodied stick blisters on palms; a confused burst of jealous incredulous longing; aching bruised spine; a resistance crumbling fast under *rightness*. The compounded mirror of *drewandjordan* submerged the broken edges, whole and improbable and sure, a handsome brutal doubling. The swell ebbed and left each gasping, holding tight to the nearest scrap of clothing or available hand.

"Oh shit," Ross whispered. "Oh shit that's so good."

"Fuck it if he can't play, he's your fucking *twin*," Jackson said, though his pulse running under them held a tinge of regret and the scab of Jessie's departure splitting open anew.

"Come with us," Drew blurted. "I don't care, I'm sorry, this is fucking nuts, right? We don't know each other —"

A second heartbeat echoed his own in the base of his wrists. Fingers closed around it, slim and strong, and a hysterical bubble of agreement floated across the sync with the clear thought *got nowhere else to be*. Jordan leaned close and said aloud, "Then tell me about yourselves."

Brit Mandelo is a nonbinary, masculine-identified writer, critic, and editor whose primary fields of interest are speculative fiction and queer literature, especially when the two coincide. They have two books out, *Beyond Binary: Genderqueer and Sexually Fluid Speculative Fiction* and *We*

Wuz Pushed: On Joanna Russ and Radical Truth-telling, and in the past have edited for publications like *Strange Horizons Magazine*. Other work has been featured in magazines such as *Stone Telling*, *Clarkesworld*, *Apex*, and *Ideomancer*. They also write regularly for Tor.com and have several long-running column series there.

"This one was a love-letter to the DIY ethos of the queer punk scene and the people in it: handsome and clever and creative, wounded but willing to support each other. To be honest, I could go on for hours about the passionate connection I've felt to the open, vulnerable, and often queer masculinities that are part and parcel with pop-punk and emo (and all the other cousin genres). 'Liner Notes,' which I wrote while listening to *Two Tongues*, puts some of those feelings to work."

BOY RESCUE

ACE LO

It was always a fine line. On the one hand, I understood the reason people made the assumptions they did,
and that these assumptions didn't change anything about
my actual identity. On the other, I was just so much better
at being a boy, and everything was better once that was
established. I was lucky with my body, so that the tweaks
and updates were comfortable and complete. It was usually
an easy pass.

"She going to take you down, okay?" The speaker,
the mother by the looks of things, one Aja Kittofer, wasn't
even looking at me. She was huddled in a gap of rubble,
and I'd spidered in while calling out to her, so she probably
just knew that I was a Rescue. With one notable exception,
Rescues were girls. "Go to her, ok? Ok? Go to her, honey!"

And it was just not an appropriate time to correct
her.

I shifted my vision settings to deal with the dark and
the dust, adding in a temperature overlay as per ideal oper-
ating procedure. Ms. Kittofer was wrapped bodily around a
smaller figure, who was making little scared noises that
were really lighting up my protective instincts. She
unwrapped slowly—painfully? No visible injury yet—to
push the child toward me.

I reached, but he squirmed back and I let him. It
might be easier to get them together. "Ma'am, are you
injured or unable to move?"

She gave the kid a more aggressive shove. "I'm okay,
I'm okay! Just takes him down."

"Alright, ma'am, I can take you both—"

"Take him! Take him safe!"

I paused to assess. I was rated to carry up to 1000 kg and I'd done it before, but carrying two at once was generally more than twice as complicated as carrying one. This area hadn't shifted all day, and had rated fairly stable in initial triage.

"Yes, ma'am." I called back down to the crew, "This is Finn, I've got eighty percent ID on David and Aja Kittofer. They're both verbal, responsive, and have no visual injury. I'm approaching to check vitals and extract David first per mom's request." I could tell from RescueNet that it went through and I didn't bother waiting for a response.

Both were still fine on closer inspection, and after a little scolding I politely didn't hear, David consented to be passed over to me. He was physically small, 20.5 kg at 7 years old according to his RescueNet file. I buckled him to my front, daddy koala style, and picked my way back out through the rubble of the room.

The building was old and had collapsed through its own first floor, wrecking most of the easily accessible exit paths. Thus, my sisters and I had gotten priority dispatch to climb through the rubble and grab people just like this. My team and I had set up ropes and anchors along the wall, but I was mostly climbing by strength and my gecko-stick. This was, more or less, what I'd been built for.

The climb wouldn't take long, but I did have to be a bit more careful with my soft little load. He was still crying, and clinging tightly enough to hurt a human.

"Hey, David, you heard your mom, right? We gotta get you down." I could probably just let him cry out, but I didn't want him to panic, and also he seemed really upset.

"My mom! You left my mom!"

"Hey, hey, I'll go back for her! Rescues never leave people behind!" A sad oversimplification, but my understanding was that it's okay to lie to children just a little bit.

There was a long pause, and I risked a glance down to make sure he was okay. His face was still wet with tears, but he looked like he was thinking hard. I took the opportunity to shimmy down a section of sheer metal and glass while he wasn't paying attention.

"But you're a boy!"

"Yes, sir!" I grinned, honestly, and maybe a little inappropriately, delighted.

"You're a boy and a Rescue? You can do that?" His eyes were big, and he was trying to make eye contact while we climbed.

"I'm here, aren't I?"

The standard model of fire and rescue android was a pretty 20-something woman of ambiguous race. The rationale was that kids were more calm, and generally people were less nervous of, less freaked out by young women. Babysitter-types, for the same reasons people liked them as babysitters.

I had decided, to the fascination of sociologists and AI developers alike, to masculinize my frame and use a boy's name and pronouns. David was apparently fascinated as well.

He stared. He wasn't crying, at least.

I indulged a bit and did the last section just by gecko stick, so that it looked and felt like we were just walking down the collapsed wall. David laughed and startled a little when I unbuckled him to pass off to Jonah. He stayed relatively calm as my team took him, blankets and water at the ready.

"Gotta go back for your mom, Davey."

I carried Ms. Kittofer down much the same way, albeit with more attempts at dignity and professionalism. I don't think she much noticed anything before we got her on the ground with her son.

After that, we cleared the building, then I got redirected to help clear another section before we went back and did a rough assessment of the whole area for structural soundness and suddenly my part was done.

Head of operations gave my squad a solid mission complete and told us to go home and sleep already.

I actually did need to spend some time at low power and awareness for maintenance reasons, but I didn't fatigue into a diurnal schedule like my human teammates. Regardless, operations tried to keep us from doing consecutive outings, and it was close enough to my ordinary off shift that my next stop was check out.

A few of my sisters loitered in the hall of the check out bay. They were mechanically identical other than highlight colors—hair streaks, reflective strips, and safety lights were individualized for ease of identification. I favored white myself, though I switched to a pale purple if I was on mission with Sandra. Plenty of Rescues self-modified more extensively, just none of the three here. I could spot Pia easily, already changed into the ridiculous knit sweater she wore in off hours. Amanda and Louise I could guess by color and context, but I checked their RFIDs anyway.

"Downtown in fifteen, Finn?" Amanda and I weren't close, but she had a strong more-the-merrier philosophy.

We didn't need to eat, but walking downtown and maybe sitting with coworkers at a cafe was an excellent way to spend off-shift.

"Sure. Meet you out front."

I went by my room to change into my off-shift getup. We were allowed to do as little as change out of uniform shirts, but my personal process was a little more involved.

At first, even I had been pretty confused. *Do you want people to see you as a human? Or as a boy?* They'd found me some outside psych with experience with AI and gender nonconformity both, because Dr. Melissa was more used to PTSD and had declared me perfectly fine, other than the habit of going into public as a human boy.

It amounts to the same thing, doesn't it? I'd said, but even then I knew that wasn't really true. I still put tape on my seams and serial numbers, still dressed for weather I didn't feel and put on glasses I didn't need. Because even though I was happy to be AI and mechanical to my struts, people were more likely to think *boy* if they didn't think *Rescue* first.

So while I didn't have Pinocchio Syndrome, I'd spent some time in those forums before we'd all realized I was just an AI boy. And good luck too, because that was way easier to treat.

My coworkers, friends, and techs had been great. Louise lightly abused her admin privileges to immediately add a note to my RescueNet file. The whole maintenance bay team got together to help me switch out, modify, or machine down parts.

When I met up with the group out front, they greeted me just as warmly as they ever had.

I'd gone out with just other Rescues before, especially late on work nights, but I was excited to see that there were human coworkers. And men. It was easier to blend in as a mixed group if I wasn't the odd one out.

They were nothing but supportive, my friends and family, and even most of the strangers I met. No one blinked at a group of robots and humans taking up a big table, nevermind whether one was ambiguous between the two. Pia even ordered food, taking it in a carry-out bag. I suspected she was going to bring it to the tech she had a crush on. It all wonderfully fun and wonderfully normal.

Everyone loved Rescues. People came up to say hi or take photos while we were out. We made for great posters and ads. My sisters did, at least. I winced a little every time I saw a big poster in public, for reasons I didn't entirely get. I wasn't jealous exactly. But. No one ever talked about male rescues, and why we're so sure the female design is better. There was no acknowledgment of me, and people were so sure I didn't exist that they didn't quite believe it when they saw me.

I wouldn't trade my job or my make for anything. But sometimes I wished, abstractly, just for things to be different.

When I made it back to the station, I had a notice that my supervisor wanted to talk to me.

Maggie was a retired paramedic, now a somewhat awkward administrator, and she managed my team's schedules. When I found her, she sat me down and looked concerned enough that I started to get concerned.

"Do you remember extracting a David Kittofer in the Inde Ave collapse?" she asked once I got settled.

"Yeah, David. What's wrong?" My concern hiked. He needs his medications. I didn't get his dog. He got cut on the climb.

"Nothing, nothing's wrong. Just… he's been very excited about 'the boy rescue' and he keeps asking about you."

I grinned. "Hey, that's adorable!"

"You can totally ignore it, if you'd like. You know we've got privacy policy for all of you."

I blinked. "Wait, does he want to see me? I'd love to see him."

"Oh, okay. If you're sure. Even if you're not! It's entirely your choice, and your choice to change if you change your mind or something comes up, or, or if something happens."

"No, really, it's fine."

Maggie, and then Paul in PR, told me a few more times that I had a choice, and I should just signal if I'm uncomfortable, and they were with me, and I could abort at any time. Eventually, we set a time with the temp housing admin and David's mom.

Temporary housing for the displaced, including David, was set up in the community center. I ended up walking in in off-duty dress with Jonah, who happened to be my most social teammate as well as the guy who took David from me on the ground.

Ms. Kittofer was waiting for us at sign-in with a hat she'd apparently made for me. David was playing with some handheld electronic when we spotted him, a look of intense focus on his face.

He still hadn't looked up after we'd been standing next to him for a minute.

"Hey, Davey," I said.

He jolted and I enjoyed watching recognition spread across his face.

"It's you!" he said, with all the volume control of an excited seven-year-old. He schooled his face into a passably serious expression.

"How're you a boy?" he asked.

My enjoyment dimmed, but I kept my smile on. "Same way you are, kiddo. Just ended up that way."

"But," he frowned, "do you live with all the girl Rescues? Boys aren't supposed to..."

I waited, but he seemed to be done. "Everyone's been happy enough, so yeah, we all live together as long as everyone's comfortable." I used what has been built as the women's lockers and showers, and yes, it was awkward and not just for me. That was more than he needed to know, though.

He shrugged and shook his head. "I know, it's like it's just your sisters right? My mom's a girl and we live together and she's the one that said I could talk to you because Lisa said I was dumb but Lisa is dumb and people used to say girls couldn't be like doctors and people would be scared of girl doctors so boys can be Rescues even if some people are scared of boy Rescues."

David's voice hitched and rushed, making it even harder to parse. I struggled through what he'd said, hesitant to conclude that David and his mom were some of my new favorite people.

He barreled on, getting more excited. "I told everyone you were real and boys can be Rescues and I'm going to be a Rescue but what's your name? I said your name was Jonah because Jonah told me his name when we got evacuated."

I laughed.

"Hey," Jonah said, helplessly.

"My name's Finn! Like a fish."

"Like a fish?" David frowned. "Why?"

"Davey, Rescues can be boys, but you know Rescues aren't like you and I," Jonah tried valiantly to regain control. "I'm a rescue tech, which means I'm almost like a rescue."

Davey frowned. "I know, but I want to be a Rescue."

I laughed again. "You know, sometimes I pretend I'm human, like just now, and people can't tell. And sometimes Jonah uses tools to do the same things I can do."

"So I can be a boy Rescue, like you," David said, with finality.

"So, who knows? You're right; Lisa just didn't know about boy Rescues. We can work together when you're bigger, and we'll do rescue stuff," I said through laughter.

Jonah gave me a death glare, and David a smile. And then I laughed more, because that meant Jonah had given up, and that David would not.

Ace is a "transguy-agender-he-him-whatever-idk" who can be found somewhere around the US, depending on the time of year. He copes with confusion about gender and masculinity in the context of feminism by spending most of the time thinking about magic, robots, and/or math.

"Boy Rescue is five percent about how it feels to be an EMT, and ninety-five percent about how it feels to go to a liberal women's college full of nice people that can't figure out how to treat their transgender students."

SINDALI

DEVEN BALSAM

"I don't know what I'm doing here."

The song had played three times already since they'd bellied up to the bar, but Shay wouldn't tire of it. Something about the F-sharp minor, the earthy jewels within that key's framework, its essence combining the deep dark of the ground and the aspirations of sky. The songwriter probably had possessed no great intentions with the piece, had just hoped to give the singer another canvas on which to stamp her popular trill, but Shay could feel the chords and arpeggios unfurling inside him every time that familiar, shuffling beat kicked in. He was like that key. Buried but waiting to unfurl.

"And," said a deep voice to his right. Shay glanced up, his brow furrowed, concern darkening his features as it did during most moments, because of most things.

"And?" Shay muttered, cocking an eyebrow.

"Drink. Are you having one," said Maiya, feigning annoyance but, as usual, smiling in a gentle, fatherly way at the younger apprentice.

"Um," pondered Shay.

"He's having one," said Rox, to his left, far less gentle and never patient about anything. "Ming, give 'im a hard cola." The bartender complied, adding a straw and perfectly-formed cherry to Shay's drink.

"Hey, fancy shit," said Maiya. "They fix your Harvester?"

"Mmhm," said the bartender, tucking a red curl behind her ear and smiling. "Finally! And of course I was up all night printing out citrus. And cherries. Ugh and worms."

"Gross." Maiya pressed a tip into Ming's tiny hand. "I am so sorry, honey."

"So am I..." she said before gliding away to another customer.

"Who'd wanna drink a worm?" Shay wondered, sipping his cola.

"Oh, honey," said Maiya. "You don't wanna know."

The summer light coming through the meter-thick glass of the window was pale, as it was most of the day before the city's dome blocked it out completely. The three men sat slumped on barstools around a high table, tired from a long work week but not wanting to go home. Home to most in Phareaux was a tiny apartment, more like a compartment, Maiya often said. A body-slot, as the dwellings were colloquially known. Phareaux was a large city with an even larger populace, and no where yet to expand. All around its protective walls, the wastelands of the Northern territories swirled and howled, a shifting, toxic desert known for its frequent debris-storms and corrosive rains.

The three apprentices were lucky, having come from the second poorest district in Phareaux. Each had won a scholarship to the City Defense Development Sector. Maiya and Shay were in their fourth and final year; Rox was about to complete his first. They had grown up together in a sprawling neighborhood known as The Wedge, tucked between the looming shadows of the power plant's towers and the glittering spires of the affluent Tan District. To pass the time, the boys had made weekly raids to the waste processing district (where folks had it even harder than folks in The Wedge), and with the treasures they had lifted there, Maiya, Rox and Shay had built their creations—robots, most of them tiny, all clever, and highly prized on the streets of

Phareaux for various games of might and merit.

After a raid on a weekly gambling ring netted the young inventors, the boys were given a choice: lengthy detention or a scholarship. Now the young men built much bigger toys with a seemingly infinite budget at their disposal. Of course, being apprentices, they received no credit for their work, nor did they get to keep the machines they so lovingly built. But they were learning, and getting better each year.

"You lead me to this dark place, where I like to go anyway, but then you flip the switch."

They parted ways in front of the fountains that marked the beginning of the CDDS campus. Maiya and Rox headed southeast to their apartment building, located in the quiet, unglamorous Bank Street section. Shay headed north, however, towards Sedge, a small gated neighborhood of homes and gardens that glittered like an oasis in a desert of gray and steel. At the gate he tapped his fingers against a white touchpad in a quick rhythm: index, ring, index, thumb, making sure to press each fingertip in such a way that the robot's eye could read the whorls.

"Welcome to Sedge, Mr. Runner."

Shay hurried now; he could hear the subtle rush of the city's dome beginning its nightly climb to its apex. He couldn't be late. His stomach already in knots, he leapt up the sandstone steps to the house at 3 Sedge Place and rang the bell.

Minutes later the door opened; Shay walked inside, his eyes slowly adjusting to the cool darkness. A dry, playful laugh broke the silence. "Why'd you ring the bell? Thought you were a delivery boy or something."

"I..." stammered Shay. "Well... the last time, you were cleaning the floors and I stepped on them. So I thought, just in case, I'd give you some warning I was coming in."

"Oh, that's funny," said the dry, teasing voice. "My floors must be so, so dirty." A man emerged from the darkness, dressed in a black silk kimono. He draped his long, tan arms around Shay. "Almost as dirty as my genius boy here." He planted a series of short kisses against Shay's neck. "Are you hungry? You smell like booze." Shay left his bag by the door and went into the kitchen, led by Seth's hand.

"Crack o'clock, yo!" said a third-year named Layil, first to enter the massive hangars in the Robotics wing of the CDDS. She walked over to the lighting panel and started the daily process of activating each bank of lights. Long ago the kids had offered to install a motion-sensor to manage the lights, but the faculty turned it down—too expensive. Despite Phareaux's appearance of opulence, the city made every effort to hold onto its resources in a miserly way. The nearest neighbor—the city of Rhoan—was almost two thousand miles to the east. In between Rhoan and Phareaux lay only the sandy wastes of the Northern desert, its pale landscape punctuated by abandoned vehicles, settlements, scrap metal blown about by the punishing storms, and occasional outcroppings of rock. The ancient road, the Sewy Highway, rose from and descended back into the shifting sands like a gray leather snake. Phareaux had a small fleet of vehicles that could handle the Sewy and they made exactly one trip per year.

A silvery, pleasant chime rang out among the streets of Phareaux.

"It is EIGHT, people and we are BEHIND," yelled Layil, hurrying to kit out the tool carts for each apprentice.

"What's this 'we' shit, Layil?" said a girl named Best. "You're the one who's a behind."

Brays of laughter filled the hangar with mutterings of "you're stupid." The day had officially begun.

◆ ◆ ◆

In the twilight of the storage hangar, Shay sat before his beast, his hands folded on his lap, his feet tucked beneath him on a rubber mat, tool cart nearby, neatly arranged. She —the beast, and her name was Sindali—stood eleven meters tall; when she sat on her haunches as she did now, she was a bit taller. He had fashioned her from a character in one of his favorite childhood books: a shepherd hound, long and lean. Her noble face, now in shadow, housed two of the most beautifully expressive eyes—HCD, or holographic crystal display—that anyone at the CDDS had seen so far. She could see in an environment devoid of light; she could see in a blinding sandstorm. She could see through walls and hills of rock. Her massive paws housed titanium alloy claws that would find purchase on any hard surface; it was dangerous for her to walk in the hangar unless her safety features were on, for her claws could rend the concrete floor as easily as if it were baked clay. Shay was developing a subtle hover option for her feet, which would also, in theory, increase her speed as well as her stealth. He wished he would be able to race her. Such a thrill that would be. But it was not his duty to do so. After their work was finished, the apprentices handed over their creations to the pilots, who then had the privilege of testing them.

Outside the protective city walls lay an area called the Proving Grounds, accessible only to high level security of the CDDS and government officials. Select creations of the apprenticeship program were tested there. These creations—called *mekanika*—were to be used in a variety of applications: city expansion, mining, and eventually, trade with Rhoan and other cities, once they were approved by the Board of Elders. If they were not, the *mekanika* were recycled, and the apprentices began again for better designs.

Now Shay sat in near-darkness, his back against Sindali's paw, with his lunch kit on the floor in front of him.

He removed a small vial and a syringe, his head lamp shining against the tiny numbers as he drew a measure of medicine into the small chamber. He hiked up one baggy pant leg and injected himself in the thigh.

From the shadows a familiar voice said quietly, "Oh, honey."

Shay dropped the syringe, but not the vial, and scrambled to his feet, panic hammering in his chest like the pistons in his creation. "*Don't...*" he stammered.

"Don't what, dear?" said Maiya, coming to him.

"*Don't tell anybody.*"

Maiya stopped, his concerned face hidden by darkness. "Why would I?"

Shay slid back down to the floor, rested his chin on his hands, the vial clutched in one fist.

Maiya came to him, crouched down beside him. "I just never saw anyone use such archaic delivery, honey. I'm sorry. I don't mean to be a jerk. I know your family was as poor as mine. I guess I assumed everybody got access to—"

"No," Shay interrupted. "No, they don't." He shoved the vial into the pocket of his workpants and reached for the needle. "You still have family, Maiya."

"Yeah. And so do you."

"No," said Shay in a rage-filled whisper. "No, I don't." The rage then ebbed away, breathed out like a gasp, and all that was left was a tired sorrow. "Mom died. Two years ago. Seth gets me my hormones. I don't ask him from where."

"Oh, Shay. Oh, honey. And you'd think a top officer in CDDS security would be able to get you better meds." Maiya reached out to grab the shorter, slimmer man and embrace him. For a moment Shay resisted, but he then leaned in, resting his cheek against his friend's chest. "But I'm sorry. We didn't know."

"Nobody knew," said Shay. "We didn't have enough

money to bury her. I had to sign the papers for her to be expelled. Out the city's walls."

"Holy fucking hell, Shay." They stayed that way, locked in a bitter, silent slump of grief stricken postures, for several minutes. After Shay had pulled away, Maiya looked at him. "Okay. We knew each other, you and I, when we were little. Right?"

"Yeah."

"I remember you, before."

Shay's eyes narrowed. He waited.

"It seemed like the most natural thing in the world to me then. And it still does now. It doesn't matter, how you started, what you have to do to be better, to be you, what you have to shoot into your leg. It. Does. Not. Matter."

Shay looked at his feet, bit his lip, angry. "Unless it does. To some people it does."

"Then they're not worth a shit. Fucking Rox needs insulin. Or he doesn't stay alive. And does that matter, to any of us? Not really. Only to Rox. And only when he thinks about it—which at this point, after hypo-spraying himself for fifteen fucking years, is hardly ever." Maiya put his hand on his friend's shoulder. "One day it'll be hardly ever for you too."

Shay let himself into Seth's apartment. He stood in the foyer, as he had the habit of doing, and listened. The space was silent but for the hum of the electricity and the soft, white whir of household machines doing their background tasks. He was the only organic being here, for now.

A tap against the stained glass window of the door startled him, and he turned around. A beetle was there, perched upon a yellow sphere in the glass. It was a scarab. Shay opened the door and stepped outside, careful not to let the beetle inside, for Seth loathed insects. "Hey," said Shay, observing the beetle. It was gold and green, a jewel of design. A perfect creature. It opened its wings, but one smaller, interior wing did not extend completely.

Then the beetle flew away into the liquid, filtered light of the city's dusk.

Shay went back inside, his mind cycling over theories. Could a human create something perfect, and the creation be sound—was it destined to be perfect or was that a foolish imagining of humankind? What was the destination of perfection? Would he or anyone else ever reach it? His pocket-glass chimed, once.

Katisa.

One night when Seth had been away at a party, Shay had been sitting as he did on the patio, feeling the generator-driven breezes of the cool city evening. He had stumbled upon a unique network of souls, accessible via a pirate server of the city's chaotic info-map. They called themselves the Surveyors. They lived between the cities, some hundreds of miles away. They sent messages to each other using the abandoned satellites that still orbited the planet, alerting each other to the rapidly changing weather patterns and keeping each other company. Nomads could get lonely out in The Waste, and they relied on each other for updates about enviro-hazards, and the rare group of marauders. Shay had sat and eavesdropped, watching the messages ping through the hours, and finally he had introduced himself. The chatter had gone silent.

The next morning, while Seth lay next to him, Shay had heard the chime of his pocket-glass from the nightstand. He'd slipped out of bed, leaving his lover snoring in a wine-sweat haze, the pale, white morning light leaking into the room from the thick windows. Shay had drawn the curtains to cover Seth in darkness and had snuck out of the room. He'd stepped out onto the patio and had looked at his glass. There had been a message from the pirate server.

"Greetings from the beach, stranger."

Shay had typed back delightedly, *"Hi! Thanks for replying."*

"You are welcome. You said your name is Shay. This is you, right?"

"None other, ha. That is me. And who are you?"

"Katisa. And company. We're out around by the Bowl, closer to Phareaux than Rhoan."

"Oh no lie, really! I'm in Phareaux. Not familiar with the Bowl. Relic or rock formation?"

"That's crazy. What are you doing in that cage, brother?"

"Well, just about anyone would say you're the crazy one. Living in The Waste."

"Have you ever been out here? To have that expert opinion?"

Shay paused, embarrassed. He'd gone and offended this person almost immediately upon meeting them.

"I'm sorry. So sorry. I didn't mean to be a jerk about it."

"Ha oh come on! Don't apologize you're too right. It sucks out here. And it's also beautiful. And the best part is —nobody can tell you what to do. You probably can't imagine what's that like, can you? Living in that can."

"Ha no. Actually well—I can imagine it. It must be amazing."

"Wouldn't have it any other way, brother."

They'd talked for hours, this way, until Shay had to leave for work. He'd never met anyone as easy to talk to as Katisa.

Now as the city settled into its deliberate, swift darkness, Shay hurried through the apartment to the patio. Behind the cover of the potted palms he could see Seth approach from the street, but Seth could not see him.

"Hey, Katisa."

"Hey yourself. How's the work going? How are

you?"

Shay smiled to himself, a smile so intense it almost hurt, so true it reached his dark eyes and flooded them with happiness, a different joy than that which he gained from working on the *mekanika*, a joy of self and from another person seeing that self, acknowledging that self.

"I missed you today," typed Katisa. *"I think about you all the time."*

"Well." Shay sat with his feet crossed on a tufted chair, the pocket-glass cradled like a treasure in his hands. *"I missed you too."*

◆ ◆ ◆

Seth returned home hours later, drunk and in a good mood. He found Shay in the kitchen hunched over his notebooks and tablets, scribbling equations and making notes. Shay was trying to map a better way for his beast to interpret data. Something non-linear, something faster and more akin to the way organic creatures learned. He felt he was so close to the answer. He wished he could tell someone, to bounce his ideas off them. He wished Maiya were here, or Layil. But there was only Seth.

Shay could smell the scent of the flowery hookah smoke clinging to his partner's clothes, the pungent scent of rum being sweated out of him, the strong cologne beneath this... and something else. Some sultry yet dangerous mix of emotions. Shay rubbed his temples.

"You're so cute with all your studying and books," said Seth, coming behind Shay while balancing a bowl of grapes in one hand. With the other hand he caressed Shay's neck. "Is there a big test tomorrow?"

"We don't take tests," said Shay quietly, tensing at his lover's touch.

"Oh," laughed Seth. "Mmkay." His hand cupped around the front of Shay's throat gently. "Aw," he said. "Poor baby—still no Adam's Apple." He kissed the top of

Shay's head.

Shay tried to pull away from Seth's hand. "Nope, not yet." He swallowed. "Hey, so... I am so close to figuring out this problem I've been having with my design. Can I have like another half hour or so? Just to get to a stopping point."

Seth's eyes narrowed just slightly. He plucked a grape from its stem in the bowl. "Sure, dear. Whatever you need. But you should eat." He placed the grape against Shay's lips. Shay shook his head away from it.

"Thanks, but I'm not hungry."

Seth laughed, too loud. The sound vibrated against the illuminated walls and stainless steel of the kitchen. "You always say that; that's why you're so thin. Maybe you'd grow a bit if you ate more."

"I'll eat later, promise."

Seth once again pressed the grape against Shay's mouth. "Never put off what you can do now." His voice was a low, quiet purr.

Shay moved Seth's hand from his face gently. "No, thanks. I'm really in the middle of this right now; it's not a good time to stop."

Seth's loud laugh shook the kitchen once more. "Well. I know how that is." Now he put the bowl of grapes down on the table midst Shay's work. His hand returned to Shay's throat, gripping it gently, but starting to squeeze. "Some things are hard to stop once you get started."

Shay pushed back from the table, sensing the tone in Seth's words, his heart immediately starting to hammer in his chest, but the stronger, taller Seth put his arm around Shay's waist and lifted him from his chair, dragging him over to the kitchen island and slamming him belly-down against it. Shay exhaled harshly and tried to mule-kick his lover in the shin, but couldn't get the angle right.

"I ask you for hardly fucking anything," growled Seth.

Shay launched backward from the island, but Seth slammed him down again, harder, causing Shay to catch the steel edge in his gut.

"You live here—for free. I feed you." At this Seth let go of Shay for an instant and reached back to grab a grape. Pushing his entire weight upon his lover, he violently shoved the grape into Shay's mouth, holding his jaw shut while the juice oozed out and wet his lips. "I get you," Seth reached around to the front of Shay, running his hand under his shirt and across the small scars on his chest, "your medication, so you can be," his fingers gripped Shay's flesh, "what you *want* to be, and all that I *ask*," Seth's hand was pinning Shay's head against the stainless steel, laughing to see hot tears squeeze out of his lover's dark eyes, "is that you pay me," Seth leaned all of his weight upon Shay, pressing him harder into the counter, causing his lover to bite back a cry of pain, "some *ATTENTION.*"

◆ ◆ ◆

Non sunt multiplicanda entia sine necessitate.

Sindali towered over him as he stood, looking up at her. "But what is beyond necessity to the fly, to the finch..." Shay pushed a wheeled ladder over to his beast, locking the wheels, hurrying up to the topmost platform to stare into her glowing eyes. "...is a necessity to us." He put a gentle hand against her cold muzzle. The eyes whorled in colorful response.

Shay spent the day adding components to the beast's systems, adding additional shielding and power shells to her hull, running impulse-tests on her musculature. Hours went by as he worked in the quiet. Only occasionally did he think of his pocket-glass, across the hangar in his bag, and when he did a sad, pained smile skewed his mouth, and he pushed the thoughts of his dear friend aside.

He took a break to eat the meal he'd packed in the still hours of dawn while Seth slept unaware of Shay leaving the house so early. He had sent Katisa a message but had gotten no response.

Finished with lunch, he looked up at the magnificent Sindali. It was time for her test.

Suddenly the emergency air horns cried out in the city, breaking the calm of the day. Shay jumped to his feet and ran to the window by the hangar's door.

It was midday, and the city's night shutters had begun to close. In an hour, Phareaux's streets would be in darkness.

◆ ◆ ◆

The apprentices were gathered around a console, watching a large mass slowly move southwest on the radar's screen. Shay came up behind them, still brushing his meal's crumbs from his sparse beard. "What's going on?" he asked nervously.

"Massive shit-storm coming," said Layil.

"Define shit-storm," said Shay.

"Well," said Maiya, turning to give Shay the once-over, his brow furrowing for a reason Shay could not detect, "Shit as in—at least it looks like, judging from the density of the clouds of the storm, and readings from a probe they sent out an hour ago—heavy concentrations of metallic dust, combined with corrosives, combined with—here's the kicker—radiation." The apprentices murmured in appreciation for such a phenomenon, and their fear was undeniably present.

"Gods," said Shay. "Three servings of shit."

"It didn't become The Waste because of poor housekeeping," said Maiya.

"Can the city's shields handle it?" asked one of the younger apprentices.

"Uh, yeah," said Maiya. "I was on that project, remember? Me and Shay were actually."

Shay nodded his head, watching the screen. "The

trick was to build components thin enough, and flexible enough, to move with the city's protective shutters as they opened and closed. As well as the *aura*. Getting the components to enable the shutters to emit a bubble of energy, twenty feet beyond the surface of the shutters themselves, so that they wouldn't take a direct hit from debris. We nailed that assignment in less than three months." The two apprentices high-fived.

Shay's pocket-glass chimed once from his bag, which he'd slung over his shoulder before coming out of the hangar.   It was Katisa.   The apprentice looked at the message.

"So hey man. Good news. I'll be to your city by tomorrow morning. Would be there sooner, but the truck can't go fast on the rougher terrain. Have some great scrap to sell, hopefully won't get arrested. Maybe we could finally meet? I would love to put a face to your words."

Shay's heart took up its hammering cadence again. "No," he whispered to the pocket-glass's screen. He began typing furiously.

"Katisa what are your coordinates???"

"One sec." Shay waited for an eternity, watching the mass on the radar's screen with sickening dread.

"Shay my compass is busted. Can't get coords for shit atm. Sorry. But there's a pretty unique ruin just north of here. Looks like part of the highway that collapsed, used to be an overpass I guess. A secondary road runs under it, that's what we're on right now, heading south."

Shay frantically pulled up his archives on his pocket-glass, searching for the right map, the one he'd saved long ago for no other reason than it looked interesting. *Old Roads of the Waste.* Finding what he was searching for, he hammered a text to his friend.

"Katisa. Stay where you are. Can you still see the overpass?"

There was no answer. Shay typed more. *"I'll explain soon—I have to get going. Stay there, do not move, please promise me that!"* He waited, nervously tapping a beat against the glass, against the side of his jaw; he bit a chunk of fingernail from his thumb. *"I–"* in his panic, he had typed the word, but couldn't bring himself to finish the thought.

◆ ◆ ◆

Awakened by a command sent from Shay's pocket-glass, Sindali opened her eyes and pivoted her head to the right, focusing on the large pad by the hangar door. Set fifteen meters up on the wall, it was installed for *mek* pilots to easily leave the hangar without dismounting from their vehicles.

Sindali walked silently to the door, her footpads cushioned by small projections of shielding. She placed a front paw against the pad and opened the door. A second wheeled ladder had been parked next to her shoulder. Her ears detected the familiar footfalls of her creator, Shay. Wearing nothing but his undershorts and carrying a bag and a packet of saline, he sped up the ladder as Sindali opened her hatch, located between her shoulder blades. Shay jumped into the open hatch, stashing the bag and slapping the packet onto his left upper arm. He hit points on the wide screen of the pilot-glass to pivot the seat to a forward position.

He locked himself into the cage. Straps would keep him from being bounced around the hatch while his creation sped across rough terrain, achieving what was known as the Double Suspension Gallop—a gait that, until a decade ago, was unheard-of for robots. The ceiling of the hatch closed and cool air flooded the cabin.

An oxygen mask lay slung around Shay's neck. If the journey took too long, he'd have to route energy from climate control to Sindali's shields, and her shields were going to be of much greater importance than Shay's comfort. The *mek* silently exited the hangar, her dark body appearing in the deserted street like a new building sprung up overnight. She trotted toward the city's northeast perimeter, where the huge, concrete tunnels that led to the jettison-ports lay unguarded. No one wanted escape from Phareaux, not usually, and certainly not today.

They made it several miles to their destination before a citizen out for a walk with his own, organic and much smaller dog stopped to gape up at Sindali in awe. Suddenly the man was tapping on his pocket-glass. Shay ignored him.

After another twenty minutes, Shay could see the wall of the perimeter. The shutters were a quarter of an hour from being completely closed. The rear movement sensors on Sindali's pilot-glass came alive—they were being chased. Sindali's ears pivoted to listen; it was the CDDS. The tunnel lay ahead, a mere hundred feet from Sindali's muzzle.

Shay spoke now, and the hatch's mic relayed the information to his beast. *"Run to the tunnel. Enable shields and get to the door of the jettison-port."*

Sindali obeyed and launched herself forward, almost instantly gaining the tunnel entrance, accessing the city's database of blueprints, and knowing upon arrival the structure of the port's door. She paused just long enough to apply pressure to the door's pad and releasing its lock. Through the port she flew, landing softly and gracefully upon the rock-studded sand below. Her front paws reached for purchase, taking the impact of each step with their hover-pads. The titanium claws grabbed, the robotic musculature of her upper legs releasing the energy of each stride. She balanced exquisitely across the rowdy lands of The Waste, hurtling towards the black, boiling wall of storm at the horizon, fearless and intent on her mission.

◆ ◆ ◆

Seth stood before Mayik Brohn's desk, watching the city shutters close with their soft, heavy finality. Lights came to life across the streets. He glanced at his commander.

"I don't know what to say, Mr. Kelem."

Seth didn't flinch. "Neither do I, sir."

"Your boyfriend just took off with quite possibly the most valuable piece of city property we've got."

"Yes."

"I want you to assure me you had no idea this was coming."

"I can, actually, assure you of that. Shay had some problems, depression mostly, that I guessed stemmed from the death of his mother. But I had no idea he was capable of this. Of larceny. Treason."

"If you receive any communication from him I want to know about it, asap."

"Yes, sir."

"That will be all, Mr. Kelem."

Seth left Brohn's office, his face a white sheet. As he hurried down the stairs he glanced out another window to the darkness. His eyes were wet as he hissed to the artificial night, "Die. You fucking bitch."

Sindali flew. Her speed was beyond what Shay had hoped for; she leapt over boulders and tore across stretches of sand, asphalt-covered ruins, past stunted cliffs and toppled buildings. She pivoted perfectly, her tail wheeling to right her as she jumped or rounded corners. Her glorious eyes of kaleidoscope brown took in the growing gloom on the horizon, shutting clear membranes to protect their preciousness from the buffeting wind. All of her sensors were alive with activity, learning, growing and relaying information as instantly as she obtained it. Shay typed on his pocket-glass the same message again and again.

♦ ♦ ♦

Katisa sat atop an old concrete cistern, eating a lunch of potatoes and unleavened bread. His parka's hood was pulled up to protect his head, and his goggles were once again dulling from dust and sand. "Crap," he muttered, wiping at them with a gloved hand. It was warm, too warm for what he was wearing, but he knew better than to expose much skin to a windy day in The Waste.

Finishing his supper, he headed back to his truck. His pocket-glass lay on the driver's seat, vibrating and beeping. Katisa scooped it up.

He hurried up the side of his truck via the ladder he'd installed and pulled out his binoculars. The northern sky was a black, living monster. It was coming for him. It was filled with death.

Katisa slid down the ladder and jumped into the cab of the truck. He adjusted the sleeping child in the passenger seat to an upright position, setting a helmet and goggles on her, strapping her in. Gunning the acceleration pedal, he turned around to drive the ten miles back to the overpass as per Shay's urgent instruction.

"Where we going, Meema?" asked the child.

"Just go back to sleep," said Katisa, his voice a choked thing devoid of hope.

♦ ♦ ♦

Sindali ran parallel to the wall of the storm, her noble head tucked down with the great effort of staying on course. Her deadly claws ripped at the ground beneath them. The black wall of death hummed, louder than anything Shay had ever heard. The shrieking resonance of muddy tones would surely break his bones if he weren't embedded in the body of his beloved beast. He looked at the screen, and with alarm realized Sindali's front left paw had taken a bad hit. She was favoring it, unable to send reparative energy to it in her heightened state of purpose.

He had given the order; she must obey.

They were still twenty miles from the overpass. It wouldn't take the *mek* long to reach it, but it also wouldn't take the storm long to reach them. Before this moment, Shay had no idea if Sindali could run with her shields on. It was to be the next experiment, after today's test of her learning.

Which she was obviously passing with full marks.

But the foot. How could they be successful with a lame foot? The beast did not slow, and a surprising sound came from her then—a low growl. Not constant, only in reaction to a buffeting gust of wind or a large rock. She was striving. She was making effort. *"It is vain to do with more what can be done with fewer."* Yes. She was sentient. She would find a way. She did not need to be perfect to achieve their goal. Her desire was all she needed.

Shay shut off the climate control and put on his oxygen mask. They had to be successful. There was no other choice.

The pilot-glass indicated the point ahead where Sindali would need to change course—the overpass. She'd have to jump from it and gain Katisa's truck. The *mek* hurled herself toward the exposed asphalt. Just as the storm reached them, she leapt out into the darkness, a howl erupting from her as she landed softly on the sand-covered road below. Her paws reached for traction and pulling her forward as her hind legs pushed her toward greater speeds, greater than what Shay had programmed her for, greater than hope and luck and physics might allow. She was a thing of her own recognition now. A manifestation of will. She would complete her mission; she would rescue Katisa.

Suddenly the truck appeared ahead in the gloom. Sindali broke her stride with four powerful steps, came to a halt and released the energy of the shields just as the storm overtook them.

From within the cab of his truck, Katisa watched wide-eyed as the furious darkness howled past the windows, bouncing against a shining bend of light that seemed to reach just past the truck and touch the sand of the road with aureate shafts.

His pocket-glass chimed.

"I'm here."

Katisa typed back with trembling fingers. *"I got your messages. I love you too."*

Deven Balsam is a transman, DJ, composer, and single dad of three living on the edge of the Pisgah National Forest in western North Carolina. He is delighted to release his first short story with Pink Narcissus Press. His novel *Mekanika*, based on the short story "Sindali," is currently in the works.

DEADHEAD CHEMISTRY

J. DANIEL STONE

Corey was on his fifth cigarette, the filter filthy with his lipstick, black smudge that stained his teeth and left his tongue looking necrotic. On the final drag, he bit off the filter and spit it at the wall, then put the cigarette out on the floor. Corey today, but Cordelia yesterday. Pale hair pulled back in a man-bun, covered with a red snapback cap; tight clothes slathered onto his frail bones. No bulge between his legs, pear-shaped hips widening, breasts as large as his head. Nothing more treacherous than to have a huge chest when all you want to do is run around with your shirt off like the rest of the boys.

He was staring into the mirror again, *X-Files* thing that distorted the world around it. Glass patina housed by an intricate dull metal alloy, threaded with strings of polished stone that glowed a ghostly green. But that was not where its evil lay. If one were to try and catch a glimpse of themselves in it, what would stare back at them would be a lie. A misfortune, a destroyed dream. It was a thing that disguised self-deception.

The mirror had been stirring for a full hour, an illusion as if brought on by street LSD. But Corey was not going to let it win. He refused to let it emasculate and degrade him; he refused to see himself in a dress, snapping on a bra and putting on perfume. He would not let it paint his face in makeup that made him feel like a clown.

Corey closed his eyes, not much darker that the room itself where only one single votive candle was lit. When he opened his eyes he saw the pen-scarred desk where he wrote journal entries to himself, for himself. There were also the posters of various drag queens and female rock singers, Otep and Stevie Nicks; concert tickets were stuck behind the door with putty. A pile of second-hand magazines and CD towers took over his view. He hadn't yet made the conversion to digital books, music, or movies; tangible items just meant too much.

But the conversion of making his inside match the outside was complete, though he could only do it in private even in the current liberal atmosphere. Not that he needed anyone's guidance or advice about transitioning. There simply came a time when people reached their threshold, and dire choices needed to be made. Be Yourself or Be What Everyone Wants You to Be.

I had to let you go...

Not a damn choice as most will tell you. Inherent. The moment he'd shed the girl-skin and welcomed that of the boy—no matter how much the mirror lied, no matter how much it asked for touch with the liquidity of its move-ments—was the first time he felt right.

Corey looked into the mirror again. It curved slightly, as if moving away from him, throwing back an image that he didn't want to see: Cordelia. Strikingly dark eyes and hair the color of dried blood, long enough to finger her mid-back. And then the mirror played its trick. Behind Corey, what was once his bedroom, was now a red desert garden. He could smell the dying foliage, feel the vines warp around his limbs, hard as tug rope; he could taste ash in the air.

But then something caught Corey's attention. Anatomically cephalic, opaque skin, a slippery slide between its legs, black hole eyes. With its spine arched and limbs bent, the feelers made their way into the void, gliding in a direction that Corey knew was wrong.

Turn around...

His hand found the unstable patina, but this time the mirror looked like it was actually waiting for him, as if to unravel a watery carpet so that he could swim into its mercurial core. And then the monster made a sound that could only exist somewhere inside a Lovecraft story. Minotaur or Dracula's wolf. Only one way to find out—

—the pale hand pushed itself through.

◆ ◆ ◆

There is really no moment of relief when one realizes that they are different. The brain is always two steps ahead of the fleshy vessel that houses it, and it knows very well that the body we are born with does not have to be the one that enters the coffin. We can change it so that the outside matches the image we have seen all along. It is only society that tells us we cannot do such…that we're not supposed to abandon the ship in which God granted us to sail in.

And so the evolution of caterpillar to butterfly is severed, the chrysalis bone-dry.

◆ ◆ ◆

"This is the place," Cordelia said.

"Seiden…seider…" Darien was lost for words.

"Seidenberg Antiques," Cordelia corrected him. "I need to talk to the owner."

They were already three aisles deep. Cordelia on the left and Darien on the right. Long red carpet drawn out like a tongue, big windows sucking heat out of the sky to bring out the smell of ancient and brooding things. Old ghosts and dead wishes; dust settling, cobwebs forming. Willowy boy and serpentine girl.

"You really don't know how lucky you are," Cordelia said.

"What?" Darien said, sticking his nose up from his library book.

"That you don't have to suffer like me."

Darien rolled his eyes. "When're you going to check your own privilege, 'Delia? Some people don't have friends as cool *as me*. And hey, suffering is a choice."

"I told you stop calling me that. It's Corey now."

"When you actually grow the *balls* to go through with it, then I'll comply."

Darien was cisgender but could easily pass for female. He was what one would call an Emo boy, enamored over his own androgyny and who still thought Hot Topic was in fashion as if it was 2003; who thought My Chemical Romance was still a thing. Darien was a good head taller than Cordelia, almost lanky; Cordelia was ridged, had much softer features than her best friend, and a soothing voice to boot. But when they were together most people thought Darien was the girl. For that reason alone, Cordelia valued Darien's presence.

"I'm going to do it," Cordelia said.

Darien raised one eyebrow. "And when is that?"

"When I'm good and ready."

Cordelia turned her head away from Darien and back into the jungle of antiques.

"This store is so expensive," Darien said. "How did you afford that *thing* anyway?"

"Oh, it's a *thing* now, eh? And it was given to me."

"By who?"

"Does it matter?"

Darien rolled his eyes. "Well, when you tell me it does all these crazy tricks, like glow and hum and change your reflection, you're damn right it matters."

Cordelia scoffed, hair in her mouth. "It's dangerous, and not of this realm."

"Kind of like you," Darien said.

Cordelia tsked. "You know I hate comments like that."

Down another aisle, English Earthenwares and

Chinese porcelain of infinite style and from every period that would equate to a collector's wet dream. Here lay a Russian gold box for storing cigarettes and a faded gold candelabra of a Victorian nature. Adjacent, a Coalbrooke vase encrusted with flowers and potpourri asked for touch with its vine-twisted handles and dusting of glitter. Nothing had ever looked more extravagant, more delicate.

Sometimes when one is in a place of such antiquity, among such precious things, they can feel out of place, even awkward. Automatic bull in a China shop. But not Cordelia. Her entire life was one long music sheet of awkwardness, and so she did not feel the same apprehension someone like Darien would feel in a place like this. But then she had to remind herself that the juxtaposition of human and unique collectibles was not today's focus. The dream was locked between her ears: red sand garden, feelers, and the boy...the fragile boy.

Cordelia turned right, taking Darien by the hand and forcing his library book into his backpack. He didn't need to be reading while they were here. She saw Darien's eyes catch the sight of a tobacco leaf pattern vase, each design unique, hand-crafted and priceless; to his immediate right there was a pewter statue of a jester playing an evil instrument and a Polychrome Dragon Charger on display behind a heavily glassed case. Why would anyone want to part with this stuff?

Why would anyone want to change their gender?

But like much in this world, everything in here was for sale.

"It could only have come from here."

"The mirror that makes you...you?" Darien said haphazardly.

"Stop making fun of me."

"Hey, I thought you were over all that 'PMS' stuff." Darien winked one black-lined eye.

Just before Cordelia could bring herself to yell, a man came out of nowhere and started to talk.

"To be successful in this business, one must respect the absurd, the unordinary, and the queer."

Clean-cut in every literal sense of the description. Seersucker suit and polished black shoes, aquiline nose and expensive glasses that magnified his eyes twice their normal size.

Cordelia took a step back, but Darien took a step closer, protective in nature, though he couldn't fight his way out of a paper bag if he were paid to do so.

"What?" Cordelia said.

The man gestured with his hand. "Kind of like you... yeah you, the strange one with the pale hair."

"Who are you?" Darien said.

"Al is the name. Short for Albert. I own this place. And like I've always known, anything unusual will find its way to me."

Cordelia didn't feel like wasting any time. "Have you ever seen an old Baroque mirror pass through here? The glass is like a patina, and the frame...well its gnarled and it —"

"I've seen much, this being a hub for antiques and all."

"You'd know this mirror if you saw it."

The man wiped his sweating brow. "It's really hot out there. An unordinary heat wave. You see? The strange follows me. That's why you're here."

Darien chuckled, fumbling with an unlit cigarette between his lips

"If you light that in my store, I'm likely to put it out in your eye."

Cordelia put her hand up. "I'm here to find out about this mirror. Can you help?"

The man put his hand to his temple. "Patina...

gnarled...I think I know the one. I never even put it out here. One day I had it, and the next it was gone."

"Stolen?"

Al chuckled, then looked at Cordelia. "These things are never *stolen*; they disappear, or get sucked back up into the ship that dropped them off."

Al walked to the front of the store, locked the door and put up a sign that said he would be back in an hour. He then consulted a Chinese-themed cabinet of an indeterminable age, opening the bottom drawer to take out a thick manual. When he let it plop on top of the cabinet, dust hit Cordelia's nose like a bad snort of coke. She looked at Darien, still lipping his cigarette, but whose attention was pure and engaged.

"As cliche as it sounds, a mirror is not an innocent piece of glass that was meant to reflect the reality that surrounds it," Albert said. "Mirrors are like eyes, or windows. They let things in and out; sometimes they trap things as well."

"Trap what?"

Al wiped the sweat off his brow again. "Memories, dreams, nightmares. Wishes, hope, yearning. Many things, many, many things."

"Sounds like a bad *Twilight Zone* episode," Darien said.

"Shhh, let the man talk!"

"Thank you, young—"

"Man. I'm a man."

"Right, you are. With a slightly higher voice. Anyway, as I was saying...mirrors weren't made to just reflect the reality around it. They were meant for so much more."

"As in... makes you see what you want to see.

Al winked. "Could be. But also as a means of transport. And don't confuse all this with scrying. That's totally different."

"So what am I to make of this?" Cordelia asked.

"Maybe it's showing you something you deeply care for, something the rest of the world doesn't believe."

Darien butted in. "I've seen this thing. It's not like any old mirror. It doesn't even belong in a Grimms' Fairy Tale. It's something out of *Darklore,* or *The X-Files.* But it's not magical."

Cordelia shook her head. "It has power. It's made of something this planet doesn't have. No element like I've ever seen."

Al's eyebrows raised. "As in?"

Cordelia sighed. "I don't know. If I knew I wouldn't be here. But what I do know is that the mirror is changing me."

"And since you have no idea where it came from, you think it's not from this planet?" Al said.

"I know it sounds dumb," Cordelia said. "Even childish."

"Actually it doesn't," Al said.

"So this thing is…showing me who I really am. Am I a monster?"

"No, but society may pin that on you, since you're in transition."

"Still, where did that mirror come from?"

"Why do you ask questions to which you already know the answers?"

◆ ◆ ◆

Corey does not know if this is a dream as he moves weightlessly between the hues of malachite green and pure black. The air is damp with rain; a storm of thorns is growing. Electricity crawls down from the heavens, igniting small pyres on ground level with bright mantis fingers. But there was never a purer place in the whole universe, because here Cordelia is dead. Here, it is safe to reveal himself.

Then the sky cracks open and lights begin to reach through the clouds, mercurial tongues and crimson ladders; lights that implore him to ascend to Saturn, lights that smell of no true odor his nose could decipher. It's as if they are calling out to him, a million reflections passing over.

But he must keep moving.

The path below his feet is littered with bat orchids and Queen of the Night tulips. In his shaking hand, a single candle winks aflame. By its pointed light, he can see chitins and exoskeletons, the tiny glimmer of rodent eyes. Things that bear no resemblance of male or female, not by their external bodies at least. In this place, nothing has a gender or even a sex; the concept is moot.

Corey keeps going, using the flame as his only source of guidance. Nothing prepares him for the sight of the beings floating between the spaces of shadow and light. Tall bodies ebbing and flowing. He does not know what they are, or what business they have with him, but they seem to have been birthed from the sky.

He must make a choice: the road most forgotten or the road to nowhere.

When the thick odor of chocolate cosmos assaults his nose Corey knows where to go. The path unknown, yet most taken. This new road now banked by pale and naked trees, grass as sharp as sewing needles. But then light comes over him as if it's raining stars. When Corey reaches into the cold phosphorescence, his fingers stitch together to form fleshy webs. In the reflection, his eyes are black holes and the sex that was once between his legs disappears.

Layer by layer, the skin of Cordelia tears into bloodied ribbons; bone by bone, fragility is replaced with resilience; follicle by follicle, fertility is replaced with ferociousness. As the husk that once marked his shame slides off his bones, the new body reveals itself strong and hand-

some. He does not want to wake up from this dream.

Until he hears it.

The dirigible approaching.

It glows curved and malicious as a hook. In its center a door spirals open, spilling neon and ash. The sound of the motor rushes into his ears. Corey wants to pinch himself to be back in his room, safe within the four dark walls. But to return to the taut girl-skin was the scariest thought for Corey. To bow down to complacency was the ultimate sin.

Then, a mottled light—

—and through it something nimble, its body wrought by fearful symmetries. Anthracite eyes and no mouth; fingers like dorsal fins.

The light won't stop.

Just before he reaches the mirror, Corey sees its reflection.

Too familiar to comprehend.

◆ ◆ ◆

She was alone again.

The room was terribly the same.

Nothing out of the ordinary as she lived by herself, studio rented from a gypsy in Long Island City who let her stay for half the asking price. Piece of shit closet in a piece of shit part of town, but the 7 train was easily accessible and the food was half as expensive as Manhattan.

From her view out the window, the night streets were just starting to stretch darkly away from twilight, and the ghosts of graffiti were writhing where the once mecca of aerosol culture stood before it was murdered by big business. Soon, a posh condominium complex would be constructed in its place. There was no more art in this part of Queens, no more alternative culture.

The dream, or not-dream, fell loose as her hair; dark teardrops slid down her face. Eyeliner and cigarettes in hand, a book of science fiction opened to the last page, and the faucet still running. But then something sparkled in her peripheral vision, minuscule diamonds falling from the sky.

Lights.

Why did she still think of herself in female pronouns? She had been buying T from the street for months already, her voice finally deepening and hair showing up in places it never had before. Thick, dark hairs to be proud of. Then she remembered why. The damn mirror. It reflected everything she wanted to see, while at the same time showing her everything that she was not.

I have to let you go...

Scissors in hand, hair tied into a tight ponytail, it took no preparation to snap off every single inch of hair that defined a woman, that forced her to feed off of society's unhealthy diet. She would no longer be a prototype; she was the future.

I'm leaving you behind...

She cut and cut and cut until her hair looked like someone had turned her upside down and stuck her head in a blender. Strands hit her feet, spreading like pale yarn on the floor. She didn't stop chopping until a great weight lifted from her neck. But within the mirror, she heard the gentle hum of a motor, saw something strange.

A non-gendered creature with gangly limbs, face veiled in darkness, no lips or teeth.

Cordelia ran to the kitchen, splashed water on her face, praying for the image to fade to black. Would she ever wake from her scary dreams? Reality lilted, threatened to topple until she felt the vibration of her iPhone. A few days ago she had dropped it, and so the LED screen was now a glistening spiderweb of glass. Cordelia took the phone and looked through her messages.

Why'd u leave?

What are you doing?

Answer me ...
You just ran!

Darien was obviously nervous, as any friend should be. But she didn't want to answer him, not yet. She was too focused on getting the job done that he said she would never do! She put the phone down and braved herself to look at the mirror again. The stone and metal alloy was hot to the touch, the carvings unfurling as if to grab her. The glass itself moved ever so slightly, patina forming a spiral of luminescence, sucking down the rising sunlight that flooded the room. Instead of running Cordelia grabbed the frame, shook it madly so that her face grew more distorted.

"Show me what I want to see."

The mirror didn't budge.

"This isn't my reflection!"

In her anger, she vice-gripped the blade of the scissor, barely feeling any pain as sharp metal forced its way into her skin. The blood was the same color as her hair, twisting down her forearm in tiny red rivulets. But it was a liberating feeling, a weight taken off her heart. Behind her came a noise, soft sound of tearing skin, or confetti, and there she found the binder on the couch. Cordelia brought it around her torso and fastened the Velcro until she could barely breathe. When she looked at herself in the mirror, her reflection was dark, eyes wide as the universe. But it was done.

The rebirth was death.

A hydra rising from the abyss.

◆ ◆ ◆

"I barely recognize you," Darien said. "But I guess that's the way it should be."

The park was hot enough to melt his skin, threatening to bring back the woman he once was. But what was done was done. Hair mowed to the scalp and breasts pressed down in their binder; clothes matching that of

Darien: distressed black jeans and a tight band t-shirt, The Cure's *Disintegration*.

And thanks to having not shaved in months, the hairs beneath his arms stood out in funny little twists. Not like the thing in his dreams, the sexless thing. Was his destiny to be genderless? But for now Corey basked in the moment; it felt nice to blend in. Normally, he would have to put up with the stares, the condescension and confusion. *Why is your voice so high? Your skin is so soft for a boy.*

"I'm me," Corey said, finally could say.

"And nobody notices."

"I hope so."

Though Darien's heart was in the right place, he hadn't an iota of a clue about the everyday struggles of trans people. But Corey knew he was being quite selfish in his own self-loathing, convinced that he was the only person going through this change. Statistics proved him wrong, being that thousands of people all over the world had already transitioned. On the contrary, some had confided in suicide; some had simply never transitioned due to fear.

Ahead, Darien was balancing one foot on the ground, the other atop a beat up skateboard, the sound of the wheels sizzling, all the more intrusive during this rare moment of peace in Washington Square Park. At one point, Darien wanted Corey to try his hand at skateboarding, but as tempting as it was, Corey could not risk breaking a bone or cutting himself bad enough that an ER visit would be warranted. There would be no greater embarrassment than to present his current ID to hospital staff—one that clearly said FEMALE.

"How was the train ride over here?" Darien kicked away the skateboard and took a seat.

"Delayed, as always. But nobody was…staring as they used to."

"You'd think in a city like New York nobody would

give a shit."

"Not when gentrification is the new religion. Individualism is once again becoming a foreign concept."

The sky through the trees so soft, branches reaching into the void as if they wanted to pull all that blue down and wash the world in its grace. The sight helped ease the headache, Corey no longer wanted to think about the mirror or the dream. Reality would be his permanent dream from now on. And reality would never be a place to fear ever again.

Darien lit a cigarette and got back up on his feet, wannabe skateboarder performing two terrible tricks. Tony Hawk would cringe watching him. Then again, Darien still thought it was 2003, and that people actually wanted to see him do it. When Darien sat down again, Corey saw strands of his longish hair stuck to his forehead, a slight smear of makeup on his cheek, and by the time Darien caught his breath, students from NYU had begun to flood the park.

But not in the typical fashion of freshman.

They skulked as if they had no brains, lights spilling from their eyes bright as supernovas. Were they here to take him away? Then the world went red as a Martian dust storm. Darien was nowhere to be found, neither was the park itself. Worst of all, Corey was too fixated to run.

Light climbed down their faces, and then slid between the crevices of their broken teeth. Next, they began to undress, but not in the way humans are accustomed to. These beings removed the outer layer of their skin, quickly exposing the inner fishy flesh, elongated limbs and warped digits.

Corey saw that there was no sex between their legs, but before he could scream, the trees began to rustle. Hundreds of twisted birds had weighed down the branches, their eyes dark and reflective, spilling a strange gelatinous fluid the color of mustard. In that moment, Corey felt his penis shrivel.

"Are you okay?" Darien asked.

The illusion slipped free from his head.

"Sorry, just sort of nodded out. I didn't sleep last night."

"Did you have a nightmare? You were screaming."

Corey shook his head. "It's that fucking mirror."

"Right," Darien nodded, then lit another cigarette. "I think you're breaking down, man."

"Why don't you believe me?"

"I've looked at it, *into* it. Nothing."

"Maybe it doesn't want you," Corey snapped.

Silence. Ineffable, but necessary. Time to lose one's self in their own head as Darien didn't want to talk about anything Corey wanted to. His world of Hot Topic and skateboarding was a much safer place where ill will and distorted futures could not touch.

"Look," Darien said. "You can stop the dreams if you want."

Corey lit a Pall Mall. "I don't think I can. I saw the red dusty garden again. I saw me, as if I was in another body—"

Darien put his hand over Corey's mouth. "Forget I even mentioned it. Talk about something else."

"I got nothing else on my mind."

But what if man could evolve from his gender? What if man had the power to control the way he saw himself; to grow a new skin during a moment of need, to knead the bones to his will? What if man could recreate DNA in order to give himself a new beginning—one where there would be no dividing lines?

"I think I'm going insane," Corey said, biting his nails. "Maybe the T is messing with me. Maybe it's drugs."

"Because you buy it off the street."

"It's like I'm going through a second puberty. I'm horny, I'm growing hair where I never have before."

Ten minutes later, another cigarette lit and Darien jetting through the NYU crowd. Alone again—though not an unfamiliar feeling—and Corey easily lost in his head, looking at his skin, feeling the arousal in his pants disappear. The hairs on his legs were thickening, a vibrant brushing could be seen across his chest. The juxtaposition was strange: tits with hair growing out of them. It felt primal, almost wrong. But nothing was more wrong than judging himself like the mirror did.

◆ ◆ ◆

This time the mirror is waiting for him. Wrinkled glass, green blood, and the sound of waves flooding his ears. Is it a door, is it Alice's hole? Maybe he should throw a rope down there in case he needs to find his way back.

The reflection before him thrusting and thumping, a budding flower, a Venus flytrap gone mad. Corey put his hand against the patina, felt it pass through the silvery cobweb. The other side was as warm and wet as a sweltering swamp, and when he pulled his hand back, he saw that it was specked with orange dust. Before he could even think to run away, something slithered up his arm and dragged him in.

It wasn't like falling or floating; it was as if he had stepped through a curtain that covers a stage, waiting for the show that is about to begin. Everything was red as red, a wasteland of smoke and metallic dust. The clouds were so low they bit the naked treetops; each time one passed Corey heard the sound of rain and a fine mist sprayed his face.

At the horizon, dawn was pealing back the sky, wiping away the moon's bony light. There it lay on everything around it, the swooping trees, mossy rocks, and the silver neon smear of fireflies. A strange heat emanated from the sky, even though on ground level Corey was shivering, his body laved in stubborn darkness. Ahead, he saw glit-

tering strings of pupae, the hollow husks of graveyards, and that the mountainous foundation was pulling itself free from this planet.

Then the sound.

A dirigible approaching.

Corey banked right. The road grew thicker and thicker, restricting his movement. But he must go. Nowhere else but down, deep into the cavern of his own ego. He felt sick, all of a sudden heaving, the pain surging from what felt like his bowels. The vomit is thin, skinning the roof of his mouth and setting his teeth on fire, knocking the wind clear out of him. But he must move, ignoring the ache in his bones and blood.

And then heat, gracious heat to help him think again. When he looked up he saw lights in the sky again, hooked and greedy as crescent moons, bright as nuclear mushrooms. Corey moved so fast he could barely make sense of the grand entrance. Apparition after apparition— lithe and gelatinous, fins for hands and big bug eyes—tore crimson holes into the atmosphere. Nothing between their legs but a red and raw saddle. Their walk was a maddened dance, arched spines and soporific eyes gazing unyieldingly.

He couldn't believe what he was seeing. Corey wanted nothing more than to remove the images from his head. But there was no escape.

Just then a high pitch droning stabbed his tympanic membrane so badly that cold blood dripped from his ears. Dizzy, he set his back against a tree. He heard a thumping like his own heartbeat in his ears, louder than any sound here, louder than his own elevated breathing, or the things out there gliding across land like manta rays. Feeling defeated he moved closer to hear their call. The saucer resuscitated whatever doubt he'd had about transitioning. He couldn't help to wonder if this is all in his damn head.

That's when the pain truly began. From the base of

his groin, swirling through his guts, boiling his muscles and threading his skin with a billion needlepoints. His skull cracked and his teeth split like the Red Sea. He was changing, faster than he ever thought he would, his senses heightened, shedding skin. He was a newborn baby, a growing toddler; he was a pre-pubescent teenager and then a breeder. He was everything in one.

Man. Male. Maleficent.

And then the light spilled through.

♦ ♦ ♦

Three days went by. Corey hadn't left his bedroom. No need to now that the mirror had finally shown him the way. And this time, Darien believed. The light was in him; he could see it above him, feeble and weak. Looking glass looking into his eyes, revealing all of his dreams and nightmares.

"It's bizarre," Darien said. "You weren't lying."

Corey couldn't see anything Darien was seeing, but he wasn't curious to find out. All that was left to do was sit and watch. Wait for the change to come to him, or him to come to the change. There was no going back out into the real world, at least not until the lights in the sky came looking for him. Until then he'd wait patiently until he reverted back into the slime from which he had come from.

At least he had the mirror.

For all eternity.

He had the mirror.

J. Daniel Stone has been a menace to society since 1987, and this is his pseudonym. Born and raised in NYC, he has, at various times, prepared bodies for the morgue, broke up fights between gerbils, and used fire to change the color of the carpet in his bedroom. These days he can be found terrorizing local book stores, art galleries, and dive bars boasting about his two bastard children: *The Absence of Light* (2013) and *Blood Kiss* (2016). Somewhere, out there in the dark, one can find more of his illegitimate spawns telling imaginative stories from places like Grey Matter Press, *Icarus: The Magazine of Gay Speculative Fiction*, Blood Bound Books, Prime Books, Crowded Quarantine Publications and more. In 2016, readers selected his work to be featured in *Dread—The Very Best of Grey Matter Press.*

"*Deadhead Chemistry* came to me without remorse, like an acid trip gone wrong. As a cis gay man, I didn't think I'd be able to tackle this story, because I don't share the intimate experience of being trans. But, I've been fortunate enough to have trans friends pretty much all my life, and listening to their stories over the years helped me find my voice in this tale. I remember a friend once told me that one of the scariest parts about his transition was the fact that he could very well be trapped in a genderless purgatory. It was a real fear at that time for him, because going through the process of changing his ID was met with much pushback. The reality was that he could change his body, take hormones and be the man he was always meant to be, but he also might have to live with the fact that all of his identification documents would still list his female name and his female gender. That fear has always stuck with me, and it was translated into this tale."

CHOICE CUTS
EDD VICK

"I believe I've chosen. Bring me the tenderloin, a Caesar salad, a glass of your house Chablis, and make me female. The Mediterranean pearl-diver, I think."

"Yes, ser, and how would you like that cooked? Oh, and what color skin, if I may ask? We have a special on olive tonight."

Robin finished ordering and set aside his menu. As always, it would take a little time for the machinery to engineer his Change. It wasn't like he'd imagined, so many times, as a depressed teen. Down would come the magic, and touch him, and up would sweep the Change, from toes to scalp, narrowing his feet, denuding his legs—he'd somehow thought women weren't subject to leg hair—widening his hips, inhaling his penis, budding his breasts, and so on up to hair that would be long, lush, and full.

On the contrary, the Change was surprisingly mechanical. Make the order, wait for the vat-grown body to be altered according to taste, and squirt his mind into it. It was almost like putting on a form-fitting leotard, if you didn't mind stripping down to your psyche.

A sudden hush came over the restaurant, and Robin looked up. Two people, a man and a woman, stood in the doorway. Something was obviously wrong with them, besides their archaic clothing, but Robin couldn't put his finger on it. The headwaiter stepped forward and spoke to them briefly, then recoiled in shock. One of them had spoken a word, and it spread around the room like wildfire.

"Pregnant."

The headwaiter motioned them to one side, into the hallway leading to the toilet. Conversations resumed in the restaurant, but to Robin's trained ear it sounded artificial, strained. A man at the next table said, "What do you get when you cross an unChanged man with anything?"

"That one's a hundred years old," said his companion. "Babies." They both laughed.

Robin saw his server approaching, and stood to meet her. He could see that she was nervous, so before she could say anything, he held up a hand and nodded. She looked relieved, then turned to lead him back toward the hallway. Once there, she tapped at a side door marked "Private" and opened it for him.

The couple was there in the office with the restaurant's owner, a heavyset person of indeterminate gender, who scowled at Robin with evident distaste.

"Robin Coope? You're a Trainer?"

"Teacher," said Robin. "'Trainer' is a Belter word. Did they ask for one?" Then, before the ser could answer, he turned to the male—he couldn't quite force himself to face the pregnant female—and asked, "Were you looking for a teacher?"

The man nodded. "We just want to find somebody who can help us. I'm sorry, this is the first place that would even let us through the door. We, Molly and me, we grew up on the Ceres colony. They—the Colony Pregbureau—weren't going to let us keep the baby. They said the chance of it having a learning disorder was more than ten percent, and so they wouldn't let us try again, and we'd heard how Earth was but we thought maybe we'd have a chance here, that maybe you'd let us birth him, so we stole a shuttle and—" Suddenly the words ran out and he sat, trembling, clutching the arm of the female, reminding Robin of a flat photograph he'd seen long ago of an aboriginal couple on their first airplane ride.

The restaurant owner hauled serself out of ser's chair and loomed over Robin. "I want them out of here."

There came a rapping at the door, and Robin's server poked her head into the room. "Your order is ready, ser."

Robin sighed, then turned back to the owner. "I haven't Changed in... well, in quite a while. You know how it is." The man—Robin suddenly realized the restaurant owner was male—nodded reluctantly.

"All right. We'll expedite your Change, but you can forget the food. It'd be wasted on that body, anyway. Just be quick about it." He beckoned the server. "Hook him up at my terminal."

Robin looked back to the couple, forcing himself to see them both. "Look, Molly and—I'm sorry, I don't know your name."

"Johnny. I'm John, John Farmer."

"Johnny and Molly. Well, Johnny and Molly, I'm about to undergo a Change. You know what that is?" He waited for their cautious nods. "It's really nothing, like putting on a new set of clothes, but you know I'll look different when you talk to me next. Just sit on that couch, don't interfere, and I'll be back to help you as soon as I can." That done, he followed his server to the owner's desk and watched her as she skillfully passed her hands over a series of lightbuttons.

"Just sit back," she said. "And this'll all be over in a few moments."

Robin felt his usual anticipation preceding a Change. He stared at the mandala pulsing in the air before him. Its projectors subtly sensed his mood and matched its beats to his alpha rhythm. Then it came, the snapping, tearing sensation, and he cried out briefly.

When Robin came back to herself, she was an elfin,

olive-skinned naked girl.

She dressed, then hurried to meet her new clients. Something had changed slightly in her perception of the couple, and she found herself suddenly smiling as she ran a hand over her flat belly. It might be nice to use the skills she'd been trained to use, and it could turn out to be remunerative, too.

She waved gaily to the other Changed guests she met, turned once more into the hallway, rapped briefly at the door, and entered the office to find two servers wrestling Robin Coope's body out of the owner's chair. "Be done here in a sec'," one of them said. The Farmers were watching, both aghast. Robin walked over to them, smiling again: smiling at Molly and at John and at the obvious bulge that was their offspring.

"Molly? Johnny? I'm Robin Coope. Again."

It took the better part of the afternoon to get the Farmers registered with the Web as immigrants. Robin arranged for living quarters, paid for by one of the few remaining anthropological teams extant on the Web. She got their ident cards printed at a public terminal, listed them with emergency assistance, sold their shuttle to the Smithsonian, and bought a muumuu for Molly. She felt livelier than she had in years.

She even wrangled a stipend from the anthro team to hold her over while introducing the Farmers to 22nd Century Earth.

The next morning, Robin entered her brand new office. The room was spacious, almost four meters square. The cameras were innocuous, the couch low and inviting. The only intrusion was the tiny machine riding in Robin's inner ear that was passing on comments, questions, and judgments from her likewise invisible patrons.

"The Farmers are at the door," announced the room

a few minutes later.

Robin ushered the couple inside. "I hope you slept well."

"Oh, we did," answered Molly. "Thank you, Miss Robin." She blushed.

"Just Robin will do." She offered them seats and showed them the automenu on which they could order breakfast. "Just press any key combo, and the kitchen will deliver it to you. Are you comfortable? I mean, with talking about your situation?" She waited for a nod, then went on. "Ceres cut all ties with Earth right after Changing became popular, so I'm not sure exactly where to start."

"We know about NullPop," offered John. "You don't birth anybody until somebody dies. I mean, *really* dies."

"That's right, we stabilized the population at twelve billion, and we don't allow pregnancies any more. We use the same technology that we use in Changing, except we allow a personality to grow in the vatbody."

"Why didn't anybody meet us when we landed?" Molly asked. "If one of you had flown all the way out to Cereville we'd have turned out the whole place to welcome you."

Robin cocked her head, listening to a dozen voices, then stilled them all by saying, "We don't like surprises. Suppose—suppose you are somebody who's lived a hundred and fifty years, and you know that, by jumping from body to body—by Changing—you can live as long as you want. You do one of two things: either you go out and do every-thing, experience as much life as you can, or you shut down the part of you that wants to do new things, because there's too much of a chance that you'll either run out of new things to do, or one of those things might kill you. And, sure enough, over a century and a half, most of the people who want to try new things run out of luck, leaving the rest of us."

As she sometimes did, Robin tried to pin down her vague memories of sports, pre-Change. Skiing? Maybe. Surfing? Her thoughts shied away from the image of roaring surf. She had tried camping, and a sudden flash came of sleeping under canvas, of wrestling a trout from a stream. She hadn't enjoyed it; someone had talked her into it. She hadn't been that outdoorsy, that daring. Maybe that was why she was still alive. The memory slid away, as if it belonged to someone else. Which, when she thought about it, it had.

Molly shifted uneasily on her cushion, and studied the menu. "I'm getting a chocolate milk." She offered the device to John, but he shook his head.

"Over the years," Robin continued, "we get into ruts. None of us look around at our neighbors, much less up at the sky. About the only change that's acceptable is *the* Change, because that's what keeps us alive."

"What happened to your body?" Molly interjected. "Your other body, I mean."

"Oh that?" Robin waved her hand. "It was just meat." A strangled noise came through her link, and she winced. "That was insensitive of me," she added quickly, leaning forward and making eye contact with Molly. "We don't have much respect for flesh, I suppose, considering we put it on and take it off so readily. I was in that male body for two years, and was a female before that. But we really don't have the resources to bury or waste good flesh like that, even when it is a little on the old and stringy side."

Molly's drink had arrived, and she made a production of sniffing it and setting it aside before turning a half-frightened, half-determined glare on Robin. "You all are very different here on Earth, but it all comes down to this." She patted her belly. "Do you have respect for this baby of ours? Can we bring it into the world, and love it like we ought to?"

Robin chose her words carefully, aware she was trying to span the vast void between their worlds. "We understand your attraction to your... offspring. While we have no intention or desire to interfere with familial attraction—"

"What?"

Robin sighed. "We know you love your baby, but you have to understand. Population Control, NullPop, is not a flexible agency. We—they—have rules for immigration; they'll just delay two personality implants for you. But there is no option open for natural babies. It's not just illegal, it's unheard of. Everyone on Earth is made allergic to embryos. You'll have to give it up."

John was standing, folding his fingers into the palms of his hands in a way that made Robin vaguely uneasy. From behind him, Molly said, "Give up our baby? I don't want to give him up for adoption."

"Adoption?" Then the meaning of the word came to Robin, courtesy of her ear-machine, and she laughed in shocked delight. "Oh, no, it'll have to go in the hopper, of course. It's a rare delica—"

The movement was sudden, caught only in Robin's peripheral vision, then the man's folded hand caught her on the side of her head and neck, knocking the much smaller woman into the menu console, off which she bounced to crumple to the floor.

That's something else we've gotten rid of in the last century, said a voice in her ear she barely heard before chasing darkness down to nothing.

◆ ◆ ◆

"They call it a 'fist'." The doctor was hesitant, obviously as rusty at his skill as she was at teaching. "He appears to have used it to break a vertebra in your neck. I don't believe you will be able to move anything from there down."

Robin stared at the ceiling. "Where are they?"

"The Farmers? Oh, they were Changed. Some kind of law having to do with violent offenders, whatever those are." The doctor shone a light in one of Robin's eyes, then flicked it away. "Of course, they're much happier now. Are you ready to Change?" The question was a formality; already the mandala was forming in the air above Robin's eyes.

"I suppose," she said. "I suppose I'm ready now. Would you make me a male, please? A large male? With big hands." As the doctor refocused the mandala, Robin's last thoughts moved back to her teenage years, when she had been suicidal, sure that her wish to be the opposite sex had been perverse. She remembered, keenly, imagining the magic coming down and changing her: sprouting hair on her face, flattening her chest, narrowing her hips, sprouting her clitoris into a penis, and so on. The thoughts, newly minted, were yet ones she remembered from all the female bodies she'd had. It was comforting.

"What happened to the Farmer's baby?"

The man wheeled a portable terminal to the bedside and ran a sure hand over its diagnostic lightbuttons. "I'm not sure. I suppose I could check."

"No," said Robin. "Don't bother." She knew what had happened to it. Then the snapping, the tearing, and soon Robin came to himself.

Edd Vick, the son of a pirate, is a recovering Texan now living in Seattle. He is a bookseller whose library is a stuffed three-car garage. His stories have appeared in *Analog, Asimov's, Year's Best SF,* and about thirty other magazines and anthologies. He lives with novelist Amy Thomson, their daughter Katie, a dog, a cat, and five chickens.

"'Choice Cuts' was one of my earliest stories, and arose from my gender dysphoria as a teen, which though lessening has persisted to this day. It was first published in the Seattle street paper *Glyph*. I rewrote it as a furry story, which worked surprisingly well. That version was published in *Rowrbrazzle,* and was recently chosen for inclusion in *An Anthropomorphic Century.* As an author of SF and fantasy, I've written plenty of stories set in dystopian futures, but despite its darker elements the world of 'Choice Cuts' is one where I'd likely be happy to live."

Robinson Faces the Music

Ryan Kelly

I must express my boundless gratitude to one Ms. Harriot Heimensour, tireless intern at the offices responsible for publishing the volume in your very hands. It was she who recognized that my reminiscences of how I met the alien Robinson, and how I first entered into service as his valet, were not, as in the words of one short-sighted editor, "the narcissistic ravings of a cannibal." If anything, as the astute Ms. Heimensour realized, my treatment of those events was too cursory by half; justice demands a fuller treatment, perhaps in several volumes. But since such a richly textured memoir will require a lengthy period of research and reflection, Ms. Heimensour has convinced me that audiences may be receptive in the interim to some brief tales regarding what occurred after I entered Robinson's service, when I was just beginning my career as the alien's valet. Thus, gentle reader, I pray you will forgive a lack of overture and join me *in medias res*.

It took the better part of a day to remove the vestiges of the farewell party Robinson had thrown for himself, and another two days of reorganizing the contents of various drawers and cabinets until I was satisfied with the order of the house. Measuring the time in days was problematic as the house was traveling through a dark expanse of space and Sol was no longer distinguishable from any of the other glowing balls of gas looming outdoors. I didn't spend a great deal of time gawking out the windows, but from what I could tell in passing, we seemed to be moving generally in the direction of the front door.

Robinson had been melancholy since we left Earth, a state which I'd made every attempt to prolong as it caused his needs to be very basic. He would sigh and mope in his room and asked that his meals be brought to him. I enjoyed my solitude and used my time to explore the premises. There was a stocked larder, pantry, and kitchen. There was a library (largely disused), a billiard room (evidently worn), and a sunroom that stared into the void of deep space. And lastly there was a furnace room where I found Donald half starved to death and terrified.

As is the case with so many of these old houses, the furnace was located in the cellar just beneath the kitchen. Most old houses don't also have interstellar capabilities but they share a propensity for gathering forgotten belongings in their basements. This was no exception; in addition to a large rumbling metal contraption I took to be the furnace, there were also stacks of boxes and crates, three deep in places, containing discarded mementos. I found a bag of keys, kitchen implements of dubious usefulness, and what I assume was sporting equipment for some variety of alien athletics. I was not, as some would claim, "rummaging" through Robinson's personal belongings. Rather, as the sole employee of the house, it behooved me to organize its contents such that they might be retrieved at the owner's convenience.

It was during this organizational process that I heard a noise like an animal scurrying about.

"Who's there?" I said, a touch shrill. I've always had a premonition that I would die below ground level and I wasn't sure if this counted.

Receiving no answer, I crept forward and peeked around a column of cardboard boxes stacked on top of an old steamer trunk. And there, huddled and shaking in front of the furnace, was Donald. Poor, idiot Donald. Gullible, flimsy little Donald. He looked up at me and said, "Ryan! Oh thank God, it's you!"

Now in a story such as this one, in which aliens and phenomenon and great fashion are as common as bedbugs on airplanes (very common), it is necessary to mention that Donald is human. Otherwise you might take it literally when I say that, even at the best of times, Donald's bulging eyes and pallid skin caused him to resemble a deep-sea fish with very low oxygen requirements. And now he appeared to have neither eaten nor bathed for three days.

"Donald, what on Earth are you doing here?" A poor choice of words, I admit, and Donald seized upon it with all his unimaginative might.

"What on Earth? What on *Earth?*" Donald was prone to hysteria and I could hear it creeping into his voice now. "Don't you see, Ryan? The Earth is gone... I don't know, destroyed or disappeared! This house, it's just... floating in space. I don't know what's happening anymore." The furnace chose that moment to begin its deep rumbling, and Donald shrieked and fell away from it.

"Donald," I said, helping him up, "that's preposterous. The Earth wasn't destroyed. Well, to the best of my knowledge anyway. And we're not floating in space. We're shooting through it. More or less in that direction." I pointed toward the front of the house.

"Shooting through... what?"

"What are you even doing here, Donald? How did you get here?"

"There was a party. I drank too much and fell asleep in a closet. When I woke up, everyone was gone, and—"

"A party?" I asked. "Robinson's going away party? You were there?"

"You invited me!"

"That doesn't sound like me. Anyway, the short version is Robinson is an alien and the house is a spaceship.

Or a spacehouse. The nomenclature is confusing."

"A spaceship? But how are we going to get home?"

"Home?" I laughed. "Oh Donald, we're not going home. Come on, I should show you to Robinson."

"Robinson the alien?"

"Yes, for God's sake, Donald. Now hurry up or I'll suggest we maroon you or jettison you or something. I don't even know all the things that might be done to you. Most would be an improvement."

It so happened to be midday, and lest hunger drive Robinson to quit brooding in his rooms I needed to deliver his meal. His preferred lunch was three slices of turkey on white bread, a meal so uninteresting that I assumed the request was the result of hidden alien physiology. It turns out he just had a boring palate. In any event, I included the last of our fresh lettuce, a small amount of pesto, pepperoncini, and turkey on toasted focaccia. Robinson disliked each of these ingredients save the turkey, but it made me smile inside to see him wince each time I revealed his next meal. He would put on his bravest face and eat as quickly as possible. I hoped to find the combination of ingredients that would send him over the edge to bitter complaint, but so far he seemed to have a supernatural reserve of good manners.

I brought Donald along with me to the second floor and made him hold the covered tray that contained Robinson's midday meal. I was about to knock on the door when Donald stopped me.

"Wait, what does he look like?" he said. "I don't want to scream. Does he have a huge gray head? Tentacles? Cranial ridges? Legs—or maybe he levitates? I don't like things that float, Ryan."

I knocked on the door without acknowledging Donald and entered just as Robinson was saying, "Come in, come in!"

Robinson was sitting at a small wooden table by the window. Outside the vastness of space pressed in. Robinson was wearing the slacks and linen shirt I'd laid out for him that morning, though the jacket was slung over the back of the chair. He did not have any of the obviously alien characteristics that Donald had suggested. Nor did he have purple eyes, grotesque appendages, or an electrified exoskeleton. He looked human; but then again, not quite. He was tall, had rather longish fingers, very straight teeth, and most people found him breezily charming. How I knew immediately that he was an alien is a matter for my aforementioned memoir, but suffice it to say that neither Robinson's slim musculature nor his pleasant, if vacant, face were able to quell my suspicious nature.

"Well, hello," Robinson said, rising from his seat, "Who's this, then?"

Donald had followed me sheepishly into Robinson's room, holding the silver lunch tray like a shield before him. I said, "This is Donald. He seems to have stowed away, sir." Robinson hated to be called sir; I did it at every opportunity.

"A stowaway!" Robinson's eyes lit up. "How exciting! Well, come here then, let me look at you."

Donald took two steps forward, his fears forgotten in the face of Robinson's ineffable bonhomie. "You're an alien?" he asked.

"Well, on Earth I was. Out here we all are, you know. Or maybe none of us are. I don't know, sometimes people argue about that, but it's boring."

"But you don't look like an alien. I mean, you look human."

Robinson bristled. "Well, I am very tall."

"You're not that tall," Donald said. "Not alien tall."

"He has exceptionally long fingers," I pointed out.

"That," Robinson said coolly, "is unkind." He sat down again. "Anyway, what are we going to do with you?"

"I want to go back to Earth," Donald said.

It wasn't so much that I didn't want Donald to go back to Earth. Rather, my entire purpose in joining Robinson's employ was to avoid a few accrued debts to some uncompromising clothiers. I was not keen to return and risk being on the business end of their measuring tape.

"Donald," I said, "It's no use. We've been traveling at the speed of light for three days, which means that hundreds of years have passed on Earth. Everyone you ever knew is dead."

Donald's eyes widened and his body shook violently. "What? No! That's... No!"

Robinson waved his hand dismissively. "Don't listen to him. We're just zipping around, none of that speed of light stuff. Gives me a headache. Everyone is fine back on Earth, you know, barring comets and whatnot."

My comment about the speed of light had been designed primarily to wound Donald, but I was a little saddened to learn it wasn't also true. A comet sounded promising though.

Robinson looked mournful. "Still, I'm afraid I can't return you to Earth just yet. I've been summoned by my aunt and any delay will result in a fate far worse than death."

"Familial obligations often seem exceptionally dire, sir." I said.

"There's no 'seems' in this one, Ryan. My aunt is a monster. Well, an 'inter-dimensional entity' is what you're supposed to say. She had an accident with a quasar or some such, and now a good portion of her occupies the fourth dimension. I can only assume she's as much a terror in that one as the same familiar three we're acquainted with. Anyway, we can but answer her summons with all due haste or she's liable to consume my energy force. She's always saying she's a moment away from doing it."

"So we're going to visit your aunt?" Donald asked.

"Well, 'visit' is a cordial a way of putting it. She sent me this letter. Here, you ought to just read it."

Robinson handed me a folded letter. I was as impressed with the idea of an interstellar postal service as I was with the superb penmanship. The letter read:

> My dearest excrescence of a nephew,
>   Your fiancé has returned from her travels. Return at once or I shall consume your energy force.
>   Your affectionate aunt,
>   Cecilia

This Aunt Cecilia seemed like a savvy character. I liked her method of correspondence. I handed the letter to Donald for him to read. "I was not aware you were affianced," I said.

"I, er, well, you know, sometimes these things just happen in spite of ourselves. Here's a photo of yours truly with the offending article. My fiancé, I mean."

Robinson handed me a small framed photograph that had been lying face down on the table in front of him. It showed Robinson sitting at a dinner table next to a young woman in a fashionable gown—a woman with a bright eye, eager smile, and an admirable décolletage.

"She seems charming, sir," I said.

Robinson glanced at the photograph in surprise. "No, no. That's my cousin Anna I'm sitting next to. My fiancé is the girl standing by the table. The one with two antennae."

"Two antennae?" Donald asked.

"Well, two that you can see. That's her," Robinson said, tapping on the photograph.

I had been wondering about the figure standing next

to the table, an overturned chair at her feet. Her eyes blazed and she stood with her feet shoulder width apart, staring square into the camera with arms akimbo. She wore some kind of clingy elastic jumpsuit that it seemed no one had dared mention was wholly inappropriate to the dining room. And, as Robinson had mentioned, there were the two short antennae that protruded from the top of her head.

"The young woman is Gloria Wilbershire, and she is a danger to man and beast. She's mad for exploration, goes on long treks through unknown reaches, that sort of thing. She writes these endless books and goes on and on about our duty to uplift, and the grim realities of life, and the horrible privations. Very downcast stuff. And now I'm to marry her! My aunt's meddling is at the root of the whole damn mess. Her father is the Supreme Potentate of something or somewhere called Dimension Vee, and my aunt wants in. She thinks marrying me off to the nuisance Gloria will seal the deal. As if four dimensions weren't already enough!"

"So to avoid this arrangement you lingered on Earth, hoping the problem would resolve itself?" I ventured.

"Very cogent, Ryan. And it almost worked! But there's nothing for it now, with my energy force at stake. I'm not certain what would happen were it to be consumed, but I imagine it's unpleasant."

The rest of our little interview was concerned with providing Donald some sort of useful purpose while he was a guest of the house. At first, he thought to assist me in my duties but I rapidly disabused him of the notion. I am particular in household matters, and if the size of my responsibility had grown with my newfound occupation so too had my particularities. In the end, Donald took a small guest room and passed the time with Robinson's collection of detective, western, and paranormal romance novels, of which there was a tremendous number. His favorite series was one that combined all three genres: the hardboiled adventures of Detective Longhorn Werewolf. Representative titles included: *Ghost Murder at Lovers' Gulch,* the scintillating *Who Shot the Vampire Sherriff?* and *The Missing Virginity of Cemetery Ranch.*

Donald's presence would not have been so bad except for the effect it had on Robinson; he dropped his former melancholy, even in the face of his uncertain fate, and resumed his normal effervescent good cheer. I suppose this was partly a result of having shared his troubles with sympathetic ears, but it was also obvious that he was the sort that thrived best in multitudinous company. Even the meager increase of Donald's society was enough that, as a result, Robinson would chatter on endlessly to either him or I; crossing Robinson in a hallway at an unguarded moment would lead to a long-winded discussion apropos of nothing but whatever synapses happened to be firing at random in his alien brain.

Robinson had an absolute fear of silence. And through his endless prattle, I learned of his many other fears, which included moths, video footage played backwards, germs, his aunt, large and small dogs, anything striped yellow and black, and, in particular, fish served with the head attached.

"It's the staring eyes," he told me with a trembling voice.

"I will bear that in mind, sir."

A few days later we arrived at our destination. Robinson brought Donald and I to the sitting room just off the main entrance of the house, and we saw through the single-paned windows our first glimpse of galactic civilization: a turtle. It was difficult to judge its size and distance, but from the towns and cities dotted along its shell it seemed to be the size of Earth's moon. The turtle moved its feet as though treading water, but they found no purchase in the vacuum of space.

Robinson was giddy with excitement; he loved to play the tour guide. "Welcome to the center of the galaxy!"

"There's a turtle in the center of the galaxy?" Donald asked.

"Well, not the literal center. The actual center has this awful black hole. A really bad one. No, this is the cultural center of the galaxy. It's just one man's opinion, sure, but Winnipeg has everything a man could ever need: dancing, little theaters, restaurants, clubs, music, light, food!"

"I'm sorry," I said, "But did you say 'Winnipeg'?"

"Yes, I know, it has the same name as the city in Canada. I was as surprised as you are now. It's a big galaxy so there's bound to be some overlap in the naming of places. Still, the Winnipeg on Earth was a tad disappointing by comparison. I thought the food was just ok."

"A very diplomatic verdict, sir. Also, does the house require no pilot?"

"Oh my God, we'll be killed!" Robinson cried in dismay. "Ha ha, you should see the look on your face, Donald. No, just so, Ryan, the house can bing along on its own just fine. It should be taking us to the capital now. There's a spot for us in my aunt's neighborhood. Not normally where I prefer to lodge, but I must appear available."

The house swept over the enormous ridges of the turtle's shell, and we were treated to the sight of villages and hamlets spread out beneath us. These gave way to moderate townships and then the outskirts of a great metropolis. A nearby star came into view as the turtle rotated gently in space: morning on Winnipeg. An hour later found us moving more slowly over the capital city itself. There was more traffic to contend with, floating houses like our own, though few so large and well-kept. A fair number had been a long while since their last coat of paint and bore a number of cracked windows and other signs of disrepair.

The automated force piloting our home seemed also to negotiate with our neighbors such that we never collided, though there was an awkward moment when we found ourselves flying an arm's length from an upper middle-class home and its habitants, apparently a family of four and a female servant. We all happened to be standing near the windows so we had to endure one another's company until the houses parted ways. Robinson thought it was great fun and waved his arms with enthusiasm while trying to shout messages through the impenetrable glass.

At last the house came to its mooring in a respectable neighborhood redolent of established wealth. The streets were cobbled (with what I would later find out was tortoise shell) and wet with fresh rain.

"My aunt can't possibly know I'm here yet and my odds of surviving our interview will be much enhanced were I to give her a box of her favorite pastries."

"Are we to the bakery then, sir?" I inquired.

"Well it's never that simple, is it? Her favorite pastries are just ever so slightly illegal. You see there's this creature, sort of like one of your baby seals... You know what? The less you know, the better you'll sleep. Let's just say it makes foie gras look like corn flakes. They say the cruelty of its preparation really brings out the flavor. Anywho, let's go get some for my horrible aunt!"

Robinson lent Donald a heavy coat, and we walked outside to find a cab, our breath fogging in the air like a midwinter morning on some of the colder parts of Earth. Seasons are difficult to determine on a space turtle, so much depending on its yaw and pitch in relation to the nearby star. The cab was a large wheeled box with small windows and an insectoid driver that sat atop it like a hackney coach.

On the inside of the cab were two well-upholstered benches facing one another.

"Well!" said Robinson, sitting on one of the benches, "Well, well, well! The pastries we're after are called 'verbots' and the only man I know that might have a connection is a member of my old club. So that's where we're off to. I can't wait to show you two around! I wonder what all has changed since I've been away?"

Robinson's club was a gentleman's club of the sort that one sees rarely these days on Earth. It was not a dance club, nor less a venue for the burlesque. It was more of a large bar and fine restaurant, with rooms for billiards and darts, a variety of taxidermied animals of (incredibly) various origin, an endless assortment of leather-upholstered sofas and chairs, a morose man who could arrange wagers for sporting events, and a small army of discreet cleaning staff who tidied up after the mostly stupid class of rich sons who spent their afternoons at The Loafers', as it was called. This inventory of its contents I received second hand and have never confirmed because I was not allowed through the door.

An elderly porter stopped us outside as we approached. He had a bushy mustache and a bright red nose, but the redness appeared to arise from the cold and his bottled remedy to that ailment, rather than alien biology.

"I never! Is that Mr. Robinson I see? Welcome back, sir, welcome back! How long has it been?"

"Too long, too long by half!" Robinson replied. "I hope nothing's changed. Or everything, maybe! Ha ha! These two are my guests, of course."

The old man amiably watched Robinson and Donald saunter past but then stopped me with a hand on my chest, which I slapped away immediately.

"Begging your pardon," the old porter said, "but I

can't let you in. This is a gentleman's club."

"Excuse me?" I asked.

"Gentle. Man. Man's club. I can't let you in."

"What's this then?" Robinson said, returning from inside. "Is there a problem?"

"I don't mean to make trouble, Mr. Robinson, but I can't allow your friend inside. It's a men's club for men only, you see, and so I can't admit your friend here."

"But I am a man!" I protested.

The old porter looked uncomfortable. "Well, as to that, I suppose so, but it's men only and no others, if you take my meaning."

"Oh, I was afraid of this." Robinson said. "Ryan, Ryan my dear friend, come over here." Robinson drew me a few paces down the street. "I didn't want to say anything because it's none of my business, but you may find your gender situation a bit different in Winnipeg than you did on Earth."

"What do you mean? I'm male—a man."

"Well, yes, on Earth that may be true. But you only have the two genders on Earth. It's refreshing really; it's so simple! But on Winnipeg we've discovered two additional genders! Four genders total, you see. And you present as three of them simultaneously. Now I'm a progressive sort, it doesn't bother me in the slightest. I don't even consider it! In fact, that's why I hired you. But most people aren't so open-minded as I am, unfortunately. But don't worry. I'll be sure to tell them in the club what perfect asses they're being, keeping you out. Really give them a piece of my mind."

Robinson was making his way back to the club and was halfway through the door before I thought to call out, "Wait, what are the other genders? What is it I do?" But it was too late; the coward had fled.

I waited for them in a café across the street, determined to take my ease. But I was not at ease. I have been a stranger in a strange land, but this was my first experience being foreign of gender. I had not one gender, but three! I was hopelessly transgendered and every other patron in the café seemed to be ogling me with curiosity. Though to be fair, a few of them had non-standard faces with extra-sensory apparatus, so it was difficult to tell. For all I know, they were ogling me in wavelengths beyond my comprehension.

Robinson and Donald emerged from the club emptyhanded and downcast, their mission a failure.

"Our mission was a failure," Robinson said. "My erstwhile friend disavowed all knowledge of verbot pastries, lied right through his bifurcated fangs. When I pressed the point, he offered to fight me! He only backed down when I told him he'd have to fight Donald instead. A real man's man, our Donald! Anyway, we've dawdled enough, I need to meet my doom at a timely hour."

I am not now, nor have I ever been, a "man's man," and it's not a state toward which I'd ever aspired. But in light of my recent exclusion, this comment gave me the odd sensation of pricking my masculinity, a thing which I had not realized was so vulnerable to such minor slings and arrows. What a ludicrous notion! Donald was unsubtle, poorly read, and a hopeless dresser; why should I feel jealous of him? Him and his readily identifiable gender. Unfortunately, I was only readying my injury for the arrival of insult.

We took another cab to Aunt Cecilia's house which was suitably intimidating. It was three stories of aged brick ringed by a black iron fence accented with spikes that did not seem ornamental in design. The discreetly uniformed man at the gate admitted us without a word.

"Hello!" Robinson piped to him, but earned no response.

The inside of the house was an immaculate array of

polished floors, dark wood, and lavishly framed oil paintings. I was alive with envy. It was the sort of house where it seemed necessary to whisper, which Robinson did shortly before we arrived at a large set of doors.

"Listen, Ryan," he hissed, "I think you should stay out here. My aunt... well, in spite of her finer qualities, which I'm sure there's at least two, she's not very open minded about, well, you. We'll just have Donald here pretend to be my valet."

"Donald?" I said, forgetting to whisper. "Donald's not even wearing a tie!"

"It will be alright, old boy. It's just a ruse, and just for a minute. There's no telling what she would do if she saw you. She's very conservative about her notions of gender. I'll leave the door open a smidge and you pull out our corpses if we're psionically exsanguinated."

"Our corpses?" Donald said. "Hold on, maybe I'll wait out here with Ryan."

"Sorry, Donald, no helping it. Here we go!"

I was doubly furious from before, but there was nothing I could do. Robinson knocked at the door. A voice on the opposite side was required to repeat twice its allowance of entry before Robinson mustered the courage to open it. He slid in quickly, ushering Donald in front of him like a human shield.

I skulked by the door, hoping to hear their horrible fates. To have Donald, of all people, impersonating me! It was simply too much. I still wasn't clear about what other genders I was presenting as, nor to what extent, but it was infuriating to have something so inherent to my person labeled a liability. I vowed to have my revenge for Robinson's blithe positive attitude.

I strained to hear what was happening in the adjacent room but all I could make out was a sort of groveling murmur that I took to be Robinson and a sort of electric hum that bounced between octaves, sometimes low and insidious, other times shrill and threatening. I assumed this to be the voice of Aunt Cecelia, transformed by the ravages of interstellar phenomena, but it might also have been someone walking near a theremin.

"Hey, you there!" A voice to my side startled me from my reverie. It came from a person who seemed to me perfectly androgynous, neither male nor female. I thought this person may have been aligned to one of the other two accepted genders of which I had heretofore been unaware. He (if you'll excuse the pronoun) was wearing a black--on-black suit, the servant's livery of the house, and I found him immensely attractive.

"What are you doing there, eavesdropping like that?" he challenged, drawing near. He smelled faintly of rosemary.

"I am Mr. Robinson's valet. He thought it best I not attend him at present."

"Did he, then? That's nice of him; it's about fifty-fifty he walks out of there. Come along and give me a hand; it's going to be awhile one way or another. My name is Cassandra."

I followed this servant of the house down a flight of stairs to a different set of corridors, these apparently more suited to the traffic of persons in Aunt Cecelia's employ. Being sublevel and not intended for the eyes of guests (or even the owner), these hallways lacked the polished solitude of the rooms above. Indeed, they were a bit worn and positively crawling with the various staff required to keep the floors above as imposing and flawless as possible. There were green-skinned repairmen, cybernetic footmen, maids of various shapes, sizes, and species, and what appeared to be a bipedal crocodile in the same livery as my new companion.

I asked about the crocodile and Cassandra said, "That's my boss, the house steward."

"He looks awfully imposing."

"No, he's great, just gave me a raise. His wife is a giant bird who cleans his teeth, sometimes they do board game nights. They both have drinking problems. Here we are."

We entered the kitchens, which were more chaotic even than the bustling halls we'd just been through. The chefs were more or less human in appearance, though they all wore lab coats and dark goggles. In fact, in addition to the requisite ovens, burners, and cutlery, there was a small array of scientific equipment I could not identify and a number of whiteboards covered in either baking recipes or mathematical formulae.

"The dowager's menu has grown somewhat more complex since the… incident with the quasar," Cassandra told me. I was watching his lips move more than listening to his words.

"Cassy, who is this? You can't bring your strays in here," one of the chefs said.

I was about to issue a withering reply, but Cassandra spoke first. "This is the valet to the dowager's nephew. I'm keeping him out of sight for now."

"Probably a good idea," the chef said, placing a large box on the table in front of him. "The lady would not appreciate you. We could care less in the corridors, of course, but the lady is a bit of a bigot."

"Hush now with that talk," Cassandra said. "Lady C will want her pastries. Are they done yet?"

"Nearly. There's a batch ready to be processed in the chamber. Pull them out, and I'll put a fresh batch in."

Cassandra took me to the edge of the room where there was a large black contraption, long and rectangular, with small doors on either side. The chef took a huddle of small, yellow chicks from his box and pushed them chirping into one door of the device. Cassandra opened the door at the other end and we were assaulted with flashing lights, fog, and aggressive dance music issuing from within. A gaggle of yellow chicks, much like the ones being fed into the machine nearby, came tumbling out into our hands.

Cassandra explained, "You may have heard, but the dowager's favorite pastries rely on an immense cruelty to produce. Since certain members of government have made it unfashionable and illegal to produce them, we've had to make due with some lesser delicacies. The lady prefers her food to have been frightened and disoriented at the time of death, so we marinate them in this tiny disco."

The crocodilian head steward entered into the kitchen and called our attention. "The nephew has survived his interview. He's on the street corner now but he says he left his valet inside. Is that him?"

Cassandra led me through the tunnels to a servant's entrance on the street nearby where Robinson and Donald were waiting, both as frightened and disoriented as the small birds that Aunt Cecelia was probably now devouring. Cassandra shut the door behind me without a sound. I had hoped for some final parting word from him and was staring at the door with mixed emotions when Donald spotted me.

"Ryan! Ryan! Oh, there you are! We've been looking all over for you. Ryan, it was horrible. Unimaginable. I thought we were goners for sure."

"The skin of our teeth!" Robinson said with what positivity he could muster. "Just got by with the skin of our teeth. The bad news is that we have to host my prospective father-in-law for an early supper tomorrow. Six o'clock! Who can stand eating that early? Anyway, Ryan old boy, I hope I can trust the preparations to you. I have to find a bottle to crawl inside for the meanwhile. Ryan?"

"Sorry, sir. Yes, you can leave the preparations to me." I had just found Cassandra's card in my coat pocket. He must have slipped it in when I wasn't looking.

The Honorable Lord Wilbershire, father to Gloria Wilbershire, had wanted a rugged stern son, a man of exceptional derring-do and strength of character. That he had a daughter with all of these attributes had apparently not been balm to the wound of never having produced a male heir. In any event, it had been represented to Aunt Cecelia that though the grand prize of a dashing and heroic son had been denied him, Lord Wilbershire would accept the conciliatory gift of a son-in-law, provided he exhibited the aforementioned qualities.

Robinson had none of these qualities.

Longing for the keys to interdimensional transcendence that Lord Wilbershire kept hidden, Aunt Cecelia assured him that her nephew possessed all the requisite masculinity and adventuresome spirit. But Lord Wilbershire's suspicions were not quieted, and it's no wonder why. Robinson was seldom accused of an abundance of machismo and still less of an adventuresome spirit. He was a man of dalliances and carbonated alcohols, and it wasn't long until Lord Wilbershire heard rumors that his prospective son-in-law was something of a fop. Thus it was more in the nature of a demand than a request that Robinson host Lord Wilbershire for a rather early supper.

Managing the details of the supper was not so difficult as one might imagine; even though it was my first day in an alien civilization, there seemed to be a universal language employed when haggling with caterers, butchers, and wine merchants. And where my relative inexperience was a barrier, Robinson's fortune managed to pry open any door.

Robinson spent the entire day in the house, walking

out of one room and into another and then back again, repeating various phrases or grunts in an attempt to locate a more masculine mode of address. It was an abysmal failure. His attempts at athletic metaphors were particularly misguided. If Lord Wilbershire desired a rugged and daring son-in-law, he was due for a disappointment.

In the morning, I'd had some difficulty in convincing Robinson to dress like an adult. He had wanted to wear a paisley necktie, of all things. It took some painstaking minutes of explanation to convince him that paisley is the most despicable of all patterns, and I'm not entirely sure that my instruction took root. In any case, I destroyed the tie when he was occupied elsewhere.

You may by this time wish to accuse me of a certain antipathy of feeling toward Robinson, to which I can only admit my full and enthusiastic guilt. My recent vow of vengeance notwithstanding, it has never been easy to explain, even to myself, my motives in destroying Robinson. I envied his wealth, as I envy all wealth, but were Robinson poor and I rich, I would still wish to see him brought low. Was it his boundless optimism, his easy charm, his generous nature? I cannot say; I only know that from the moment I first met Robinson, I understood my role was to sabotage him at the most basic level I could conceive.

There came a knock at the front door five minutes past six o'clock. Robinson stood in the hallway wringing his hands.

"Sir, perhaps it would be better if you waited in the dining room, so as not to appear overbearing," I suggested.

"Swift thinking, Ryan!" And off he fled.

I opened the door and said, "Welcome, Lord Wilbershire. Mr. Robinson awaits you in the dining room. May I take your coat?"

The man who entered looked like any number of rich, paunchy old men. He had white hair thinned with age and was preceded into the room by preposterously large eyebrows that retained the echo of his youth's dark color. He had none of the extra-dimensional characteristics of Robinson's aunt; apart from the daunting specimens affixed above either eyeball, the most I could say of him was that his wardrobe was four decades too late. He handed me his coat.

"In the dining room? Couldn't wait for his guest, could he? Lead on, man. Let's get this over with," he said.

I led the way and announced Lord Wilbershire to the dining room where Robinson was attempting the disaffected nonchalance of a character he had seen in a cigarette ad. "Cool Flavor," I believe the tagline had been; for Robinson it was somewhere closer to "Dubious Aftertaste." He leaned against the table and put one hand on his hip, and in the other held a mostly empty glass of umber liquor. Donald, who was still nominally a guest of the house, had been invited to supper and stood very still on the opposite side of the table. He had been infected with Robinson's fear, and like a prairie animal, his instinct was to remain motionless until danger passed. This tactic somehow worked; Lord Wilbershire ignored him entirely.

Lord Wilbershire spoke. "I must apologize, Mr. Robinson, I lack my normal punctuality. I trust my tardiness has not discommoded you."

"What? Not at all, still quite commoded, thank you. Offer you a drink?"

"I never drink before dinner."

"What? Oh yes, of course. I mean, tea or something of that nature. Coffee if you're feeling wild, right? Ha ha!" It was hard to believe that the glass in his hand was anything other than alcoholic, but both parties made do somehow.

"Water will be fine," Lord Wilbershire said. "My doctor recommends I drink more water."

There was a pitcher of water at the table where

both men (and Donald) presently sat. I filled a glass for each and made to leave, but Robinson stopped me. "This is Ryan —works for me, you know. Prepared something special for us to eat, though he won't let me in the kitchen to see, big surprise, right? Ha ha!"

Lord Wilbershire had no immediate use for this information, but he did look at me with curiosity. "Yes, there's something... peculiar about you. Forgive me if that's too frank."

"Yes, sir. Will that be all?" I asked.

Robinson's eyes pleaded for me to stay. "Er, yes. I suppose so, I mean."

I left them. I would have preferred to stay within earshot and bear witness to what I am sure was a slow series of mortifying interactions that left Robinson feeling smaller and smaller. During quiet nights, I like to imagine what might have been said over that table.

"You lack even the barest odor of certitude required to begin to consider marrying my daughter," Lord Wilbershire might say, waggling his eyebrows. "You're like a sad experiment in bovine gullibility, gone awry; you're a petri dish for stupidity and no aspect of science could benefit from making you the object of its study."

"I know, I know. It's absolutely true," Robinson would respond. He would then look sadly down at his lap and no amount of time or charity would ever make him whole again.

Thus run my musings on occasion, although I've never bothered to learn the actual direction the conversation took, for fear that it would conflict with the version outlined above, upon which I've come to rely for a quick smile.

Lord Wilbershire's staff had communicated to me that the gentleman held peculiar notions about the proper way to serve dinner and eschewed anything other than a single, main course as an effeminate ostentation. The caterers I'd hired had supplied me with a competent chef, but I wanted to triple check that my instructions on the single, main course were being followed to the letter. After exchanging insults with said chef, I left the kitchen with three covered dishes on a wheeled cart. I lingered outside the dining room, waiting for the right moment to enter. From this position I was able to overhear their conversation.

Lord Wilbershire was speaking: "My boy, it is not 'Dimension Vee.' It is 'Dimension Five,' as in 'The Fifth Dimension,' and by convention, it is written using the numeral 'V.'"

"Oh, ha ha! That makes much more sense! I must have only seen it written. Gosh, and nobody ever corrected me. I wonder if a lot of people aren't calling it 'Dimension Vee' right now because of me? Whoever decided to write it that way anyway?"

"I did," Lord Wilbershire said, which I took as my cue to enter, wheeling the cart and covered dishes before me.

Robinson was visibly grateful for the distraction as I placed the covered dishes, one in front of each man (and Donald). Having but two arms I chose to lift the silvered lids from the plates sitting before Lord Wilbershire and my employer.

The accumulated steam wafted gratefully into the air, revealing to each a dish of some leafy greens, a bed of mixed grains and rice, and, topping this, a black and yellow striped fish, served with the head still attached. As an attentive reader, you no doubt realize that it handily combined two of the phobias Robinson had shared with me, unprompted, on our journey to the city. Even better was that its eyes were on short stalks and I had ensured these protuberances were aimed squarely at Robinson.

"Ah, fish—" was all that Lord Wilbershire had time

to say before Robinson overturned his chair backward and began shrieking like a tea kettle. Even I had not anticipated the extremity of his discomfort. Donald, again sensing danger, froze in place.

"Ryan, Ryan, cover it up for God's sake!" I'm sorry to say that at this inopportune moment the silver lids slipped from my hand, adding a metallic clamor to the noise of Robinson's caterwauling terror.

"Oops," I said.

"Have you lost your mind?" Lord Wilbershire demanded.

"It's the staring fish!" Robinson screeched. "It has stripes like a bee!"

Lord Wilbershire needed no further discouragement from allowing a union between his daughter and the sort of suitor who could be unmanned by a mackerel. He stomped out of the room, and I followed quickly in order to fetch his coat. Robinson had ceased his shrieking but remained gorgon-struck with fear.

At the front door, Lord Wilbershire whirled about to face me, his mighty eyebrows drawn down in consternation. "And don't think I'm not on to you!" he told me.

"Sir?" I asked.

"I knew there was something peculiar about you. As if his fits aren't enough, he has a gender bending valet! Totally unacceptable!"

"Very well. Good day, sir," I said to the door that had already slammed behind the old man.

I returned to the dining room and found that Robinson had fled. Donald, however, was still transfixed with fright.

"Donald, you ass, they're all gone now," I said.

"Oh thank God," he said, slumping forward in exhaustion. His capacity for fear was far beyond that of other lifeforms.

The taste of my victory was not as sweet as I'd imagined it would be. As I cleared the dishes, I thought again of Robinson's complicity in the discrimination I'd faced as a result of traversing the boundaries of alien gender concepts I didn't understand. It had been so easy to manufacture my revenge, and now his Aunt would drain him of his essential life force. Surely that's what I wanted? As if summoned by these cheerful thoughts, the doorbell rang twice.

It was a courier with a letter from Aunt Cecelia, addressed to Robinson. Why she wouldn't deign to use the telephone was a peculiarity I attributed to great wealth; communications were more dignified if they required several occupied persons to transmit them. I brought the envelope to Robinson's door and knocked.

"Go away!"

I entered anyway. "Forgive me, sir, but a message has just arrived from your aunt via courier."

"How could she have known so quickly? This is terrible! Ryan, how could you have forgotten my phobias?"

"There are a great many of them, sir."

"Oh, I know. Listen, it's not your fault—you mustn't blame yourself. You couldn't have been expected to know that I'd have such a powerful aversion to that... fish monster. God, it really was terrifying though. You must promise me to dispose of it well away from the house. I won't sleep otherwise. Ah, what am I saying?" He had torn open the envelope and was reading the contents. "Subject is moot; my sleep shall be eternal. My aunt commands an audience at once. Damn quick of her; you'd think she has the place bugged up with cameras. Ryan, be a pal and lay out a good suit to die in. I want to look the part."

To the last with his affable charm and wretched positivity. I laid out a black suit of excellent quality, fit for a funeral.

I am not one for crises of conscience. When I set my mind on a particular course, that is the course I stay. But since I had ruined Robinson's matrimonial prospects and doomed him to a horrific end, there was a foul niggling uncertainty rolling about my thoughts; certainly I had no affection for Robinson, so the source of my confusion eluded me.

We gathered up Donald against his wishes and hailed a cab for Aunt Cecelia's lair. Donald was much averse to going, still being terrified from his previous visit, but he became more agreeable once we told him that Robinson would be engaging with his aunt alone. The only time on the journey that Robinson broke the silence was when he glanced out the window and saw a restaurant he knew.

"They have a wonderful menu. Waitlist a year long but the chef is an old friend of mine. I would have liked to take you two there before I died. Alas, I suppose."

My newfound reticence toward Robinson's destruction bloomed further with this tidbit. There is nothing I love so much as jumping a queue.

We arrived at Aunt Cecelia's and the doorman led us to an immaculately furnished sitting room. Either Aunt Cecelia's previous engagement had gone longer than expected or she merely wished Robinson to agonize in the anticipation of his forthcoming ordeal. He wouldn't give her the satisfaction, in any event: he lounged comfortably on a sofa, kicking his heels up onto the small table in front of him. I admired the perfect shine of his shoes—my own handiwork from earlier that morning. I could see my reflection and that of Donald sitting stupidly beside me.

"Robin, can't you just hide out somewhere for a while until this blows over?" Donald asked. Donald isn't generally a valuable addition to anything, but this mirrored closely my own thinking.

"Oh, it wouldn't do any good," Robinson said. "I

had a cousin, Gary, he tried the old disappearing act when his number came up. My aunt found him in a bunker on a disused moon, hiding under a knitted afghan. She lives for the hunt and it's just better to not get her blood hot. Poor Gary. And anyway, we Robinsons always face the music. It's a family trait. Robinsons of yore would run to wherever music might be playing and stoutly face it."

At last the crocodilian head steward came to collect Robinson and bring him to his appointed end. Donald and I sat in miserable silence for a few minutes before an idea struck me and I excused myself to the hallway.

"Where are you going?" Donald asked. He was terrified to be alone in that house. Truly, I'd never met a more fearful creature.

"Just stay here, Donald. I'll be right back."

I checked three rooms before I found a maid cleaning in a billiard parlor. "Excuse me," I said. "Would you see if Cassandra has a free moment to speak with me?" I offered her the card Cassandra had slipped into my pocket at our last visit. The maid regarded me carefully, judging where in the hierarchy of servitude I stood in relation to her, but agreed at last to find Cassandra.

I was idly rolling billiard balls across the green felt of the table when Cassandra entered. He was wearing the same black-on-black livery as our first meeting, and he retained the perfect androgyny which renders inadequate my stock of personal pronouns. There seemed to be something lewd about the billiard table standing between us, like an unmade bed. He raised a perfect eyebrow, waiting for me to speak.

"I recall the mistress of the house has a fondness for a certain pastry…" I began.

"Indeed she does. Verbot pastries. Completely illegal and prepared with a staggering amount of cruelty." Cassandra walked along one side of the table and something compelled me to walk in the opposite direction, keeping the barrier between us.

"I think a gift of these pastries might save the life of my employer."

"I didn't peg you for the sentimental type," Cassandra said, still circling the billiard table. He was both menacing and extraordinarily attractive.

"It's strictly business," I said. "A suitable employer is so difficult to arrange. Do you have the ability to make verbot pastries in your kitchens?"

"We have the facilities but the not the ingredients. Verbots are impossible to come by. They're nearly extinct. They have no survival instincts to speak of. A verbot's greatest defense mechanism is the ability to hold very still when predators are nearby, and their extreme fear when in this state is what imparts the desired flavor. Their incredible capacity for fear is what makes them so delectable."

I stopped moving away, allowing Cassandra to draw closer. "I may have an adequate substitute," I said. "But we must hurry."

"Must we?" he asked.

♦ ♦ ♦

I had a cab waiting when Robinson emerged from the house and took his first few stumbling steps back among the living. He was pale and disheveled, and I noted with disapproval that he had managed to scuff his shoes.

He shambled to where I was holding open the door of our cab. "Ryan!" he said. "Ryan, I'm alive! It was the luckiest thing. I was to be killed, my essential life force consumed, and just then someone came in with a tray of fresh verbot pastries. Well, the whole mood changed at once, as you can imagine. I excused myself as quickly as I could but I don't think my aunt even noticed. What amazing luck!"

"Very fortuitous, sir. Shall we?" I said.

"Wait a moment," Robinson said, as I closed the door of the cab and we lurched into motion. "Where's Donald? We can't leave him behind! He'll never make it out again."

"Donald's gone back to Earth, sir."

"Earth? How did he manage that?"

"We also had some good luck. Donald happened to catch a ride with a gentleman traveling in that direction. I believe he intends to return to his uncle's farm."

"A farm? His uncle?"

"Yes, sir. He'll be very happy there, able to run around and play with the animals."

Robinson sat back in the cab, relaxing for the first time in hours. "Well, that's for the best then. I'll miss him though, he was good company. Send him a card from me, would you? Lord, I am famished. How about that restaurant I mentioned?"

"That sounds very pleasant, sir."

"Oh, but I have something to tide us over, Ryan. I was a bit sly on my way out, and I slipped one of those verbot pastries into my pocket! It's illegal to eat one and horribly immoral if you think about it, but I had to try one." He pulled a flaky pastry, wrapped in a cloth napkin, from his jacket pocket. "Would you like half?" he asked.

"Thank you, sir. Though I'm sure it will leave me wanting more."

Ryan Kelly is a cis male writer in Los Angeles, California. He writes short fiction, novels, and comics with the intent of irritating fascists. His upcoming novel of race and oppression in the 18th century will be finished early 2017.

THE THREE WAYS OF THE SWORD MAN
JAAP BOEKESTEIN

"An early Galactic sword, twenty-two hundred years old, complete with the avatar-imprints of the previous twenty-eight owners. You say it is called Windsinger?" The space trader looked at Lady Jes Okasthade. "We are interested in a trade. What do you want?"

Forgive me, dear forefathers. Giving up Windsinger was giving up the soul of the family. But she had no choice. With her twin brother Lord Jessam dead—prolonged melancholy ending in suicide a few days ago—she was the only one left. And she needed to trade the ancestral sword to continue the family. Which was not a lie, but it wasn't exactly the main reason for the trade. Not at all, actually.

Now or never. The idea was born from grief and desperation, and she still didn't believe she was actually doing this.

"Two things," Lady Jes said. "First, an exact replica of the sword, including the avatar-imprints. They must not know they are a copy."

"Acceptable," the space trader replied. Making an exact replica would be a matter of seconds with the technology on board his ship. Technology that was forbidden on Shurigyn since the days of the first colonists. For the trader, the replica had no value. In the Humanity, one could literally replicate anything, except time. An original, millennia old sword with a history attached to it, now that was priceless.

"Second, you transform me into a Lord, a *man*."

Technology that was not only forbidden on the planet but was also considered obscene in the extreme.

The trader was quiet for a few seconds, no doubt he was checking the legality of her request. Finally he replied: "This is not allowed on Shurigyn. I can offer you free passage to one of the planets of the Humanity where you can ask for asylum, if you desire to leave the rigid culture of your planet."

"Why would I do that?" Lady Jes asked hotly. "This is my home! I don't want to leave. But I want you to make me a Lord. And before you refuse me, consider this: you are not allowed to do business with a Lady here on Shurigyn. You need a Lord to hand over that sword legally. As long as I am a Lady, you have no deal."

Another moment of silence. "But who will you be? We need to purchase this sword legally."

"My brother died last week. Nobody knows. I am dressed in his clothes. The space station's cameras have registered a Lord looking like him. When I leave, I *will* be him. Or you can forget about this priceless antique that will bring you fame and fortune back in the Humanity."

The man from the stars made a sound that probably meant he was amused.

An hour later, a Lord who looked like Lord Jessam Okasthade left the ship. He carried a sword that looked exactly like his ancestral sword.

Lord Jessam burned the body of what was supposed to be his twin sister with the most elaborate rituals. The few guests—neighbors, some business contacts, a handful of acquaintances—looked on. They paid their respects and left shortly after, back to their own estates.

That night Lord Jessam got very, very drunk. He was free. He was what he always longed to be.

His joy mixed with the grief of the loss of his

brother—No, sister! He had to be his sister, even to himself. *Oh, why did you do it? You had it all! And you wasted it all. I will do better. I swear!*

The promises of the drink...

The next day, Lord Jessam woke up with the biggest hangover of his life. In a masochistic mood, he decided not to take one of the available cures but just sit it out, as a penance for the unspeakable—liberating!—thing he had done.

After two hours, he decided he was being foolish. He took a few pills, cleaned himself, and dressed. He had dressed hundreds of times in those Lord clothes. Ha, he even had chosen most of them! Now they were really his.

As a new Lord, he went to town.

As a man!

♦ ♦ ♦

Fleshpots.

What do young Lords do? They test their manhood; they test their steel. They make enemies and forge bonds for life.

Lord Jessam, a very minor poet and philosopher— basically an unknown—exploded in the nightlife of Refunse, the old Imperial capital before the Emperor moved to Neuvhalle about three centuries ago.

He partied, he fucked women, he fucked men. Over a month, he fought three duels and won them all. Not bad for someone who had trained mostly with his sister and was bested by her most of the time.

Windsinger's copied avatars cheered. So far Lord Jessam's avatar had been small and unimpressive due to insufficient input. From boyhood he had hardly carried the sword, always ill at ease with the digital ghost of father, grandfather, and the long row of demanding forebears. Now the Jessam-avatar grew stronger every day. The old ghosts were very happy, reliving their lives by the deeds of their living progeny.

Lord Jessam loved every moment. If he would die now, he would die as a happy Lord. He was what he always wanted to be.

◆ ◆ ◆

"You should court my sister, Lady Sakhai," Lord Tyram said. The seven drinking buddies, comrades in arms and blood friends forever, were sitting on the wooden benches in a sauna, recuperating from five days of partying.

The young Lord slapped Lord Jessam on his shoulder, indicating he meant him.

"Huh? Really? Marriage? How revolting!" Lord Jessam waved the idea away. "Marriage is for old Lords who want to be chained to a nagging wife and a bunch of crying daughters."

His friend persisted. "No, really. There is talk of a coming war with the Brown Hat coalition, who are firmly behind Lord Ramsul's preposterous claims for the post of prime minister. Before we know it, we are knee deep in blood and entrails! A Lord must think of the future of his family in such times. My sister is of the marrying age and a very... practical Lady. You will hit it off great together!"

"You sound like you are selling an unwanted horse," one of the other young Lords said. "Know what you are in for, Jessam!"

Minor insults were jokes between blood brothers. Lord Tyram ignored the jab. "Don't you have a sister, Jessam? We could make it a double marriage, cementing the bonds for our two houses forever."

"My only sister died last year," Lord Jessam replied. He was amazed how easily those words rolled over his lips. *Because they are true.* "But if you really insist, I will meet the Lady. But no promises! I will just be doing you a favor."

"Good enough!" Lord Tyram grinned. "Lady Sakhai will be delighted!"

"She hasn't seen Jessam yet!" another of the friends joked. "Maybe she will faint from sheer terror!"

"Or flee screaming!"

"Or start bossing him around."

Lord Jessam laughed with the others, but his heart was not in it. *What would Jes have thought of these jokes?*

◆ ◆ ◆

Well, no fainting, of fleeing, or bossing around. They sat in the tea pavilion, with a view on a misty lake while crane birds waded serenely near the banks, seeking fish. Lord Tyram's sister was a tall woman with delicate features and refined manners. She carefully hid that she wasn't very pleased with the whole forced visit. No Lord would be able to detect her subtle mood, except Lord Jessam. How many times had he hid his own thoughts and feelings growing up?

Lady Sakhai poured the tea and offered it to Lord Jessam.

"Your brother didn't do justice to you, my Lady," Lord Jessam said. He felt he was reciting lines from a play. How had he ended up in this situation? "You are far more beautiful than he had ever told me. I guess a brother is not a good judge in such matters, neh?"

"I trust the taste of my brother, Lord Jessam," she replied.

No, you do not! You think he is a fool. Where did that come from?

"I was impressed by the mood of your poems, Lord Jessam." A compliment for a compliment, that was the ritual.

Poems? Lord Jessam remembered his bro... the poems he had written years ago. Before... He didn't do poetry now.

"I used to write, but that was a long time ago. That was a different me, a softer me. Now I drink and fight and make my friend's sister uncomfortable."

She looked up. Surprised. "Lord Jessam, I am so sor..."

"Don't be, Lady Sakhai. I should apologize for being so boorish." He rose. "I am honored you like the poems, but I am not that Lord anymore. I... changed after my twin sister's death. It was either that or follow her into the grave."

The Lady looked up. "I thought I sensed a sadness. I am glad you chose to live, Lord Jessam."

"So am I." He bowed. "If you'll excuse me, my Lady. I hope your brother won't send too many foolish men to court you. But you know, we men... Sometimes..."

To his surprise, Lady Sakhai giggled.

He left confused.

◆ ◆ ◆

He even was more confused when he received a handwritten note the next day. Lady Sakhai thanked him for the lovely company and invited him for dinner.

"You soon will be wed, brother!" Lord Tyram joked. "Now give me a bunch of nephews and nieces, and we can take care of those Brown Hat rascals!"

"You want those before or after the wedding?" Lord Jessam replied deadpan.

"Ha ha! I don't care! But I am sure my sister wants to get wed first."

Don't be so sure of that, sweet Tyram. There is a whole world you know nothing about. Liaisons weren't uncommon, but nobody ever talked about them. Lords didn't only fuck droid-servants or other Lords. And neither did Ladies.

Hush, hush.

"But if we go to war, should you not also be married soon, Tyram?" The thought was logic, but the feeling was strange. Sharing Tyram with a Lady, with his wife? Jealousy was unnecessary, but still, Lord Jessam felt a hot sting.

Idiot! You are not a moon sick girl anymore... You are a Lord!

Lord Tyram shook his head. "Not I! I have two younger brothers. The lineage is secured! I can die a glorious death if need be. You need sons, Jessam. I don't."

That was true.

In a month's time, Lord Jessam wed his best friend's and best lover's sister, Lady Sakhai. It was a grand party; Lord Jessam's comrades toasted him.

Will there be children? Lord Jessam asked himself after the wedding night. He hoped so.

The autodoc on board of the spaceship had assured him he had fully become a man. No primitive butchery like in ancient times. No! Speed printed organs, internal and external changes, different body chemistry, a different bone structure, a thousand and one little things.

When the seven comrades left for war, Lord Jessam's wife was pregnant. A son.

I am going to be a father. My family lives on, whatever happens.

His forefathers in his sword Windsinger nodded happily.

◆ ◆ ◆

The battle with the Brown Hat coalition took place in the woods of Cathena. Under the dimly lit canopy of the ancient giant trees the two armies faced each other.

"This will be glorious!" Lord Tyram said after taking a sip from his coffee.

Lord Jessam just nodded and also took a sip, although he felt the need to piss. He was nervous, as they all were. Fighting duels was one thing, but this was war. Of course, both sides would abide by the ancient rules of armed conflict, anything else was unthinkable, but the duels fought on the battlefield were generally to the death instead of the usual first blood with civilian fights.

"The Brown Hat coalition is large. They brought many Lords. I reckon we are outnumbered," one of the seven blood brothers said, peering through his binoculars.

"So we fight better and kill more of them," Lord Tyram said. "We fight for honor and glory!"

"For honor and glory!" six voices replied.

I would not want to be somewhere else, to be someone else, Lord Jessam thought. This was what he was born for, this was the life he wanted to live.

A signal was given, and from both sides challengers stepped forward. They called out their names and lineage, and challenged the other party to come and taste their steel.

Lord Jessam and Lord Tyram were both in the first wave of challengers: by ancient tradition the young were first, to have a chance to win glory. The veterans would fight later.

The face of his opponent was hidden behind an elaborate helmet, but Lord Jessam could sense the man's nervousness. *Just like me.*

They fought; Lord Jessam won. In the end, he stood with a bloody sword over the corpse of the other, panting, sweat stinging in his eyes. He had won; it was an honorable fight.

He had fought to the death and he had survived.

Now he was a real man.

He returned to his comrades and found three of them dead. Among them was Lord Tyram.

"Who killed him?" Lord Jessam demanded, his heart cold as ice.

A name that didn't mean anything. Somebody from the Brown Hat coalition. The name was burned into Lord Jessam's soul.

He went out to the battlefield, shouting the name of

the man who killed his friend and lover.

The man replied and accepted the challenge.

They fought.

Lord Jessam lived.

But he was dead inside. He wanted to die. What was life worth without Tyram?

That day, in the battle of Cathena, Lord Jessam fought seven duels. He fought as a Lord possessed and perhaps he was. He made his name that day. His forebears cheered; his sword sang.

In the end, he fell down, his last opponent dead at his feet. He could not rise again, for the blood loss was too severe. But he lived and the seventh man was dead, just like the six before him.

◆ ◆ ◆

A few hours later, Lord Jessam came to in the field hospital, his wounds healed but not his soul.

Grief, deep as a sword cut, tore through him. Tyram was dead. Tyram!

He cried for his fallen comrade, his lover, his brother in arms.

So this is what it feels like to be Lord.

◆ ◆ ◆

Lady Sakhai was sad, but she had always known she would lose her brother to the sword; that was the fate of most Lords. She mourned the customary six days and asked her husband to join her in the tea pavilion where they had first met.

She sat there, pregnant, regal, sad.

Lord Jessam sat with her, defeated, empty. His grief consumed him. He hated who he was, what he was. Fate was so cruel! He wished he had never met Lord Tyram. He wished he had never been his comrade in arms. How could Lords live like this, knowing they would lose their friend to the sword one day, or otherwise—even worse!—grow old lonely, either with honor or not, but bereft of all their loved ones?

"You were a lonely child?" Lady Sakhai asked.

What? What is her question? Lord Jessam looked at his pregnant wife. *I am mourning my love, and you are asking about my childhood?* It was a very strange question.

"No, I had a twin sister. After father's death, mother raised us." *I don't feel answering her silly questions!*

Lady Sakhai shook her head. "That is not what I mean, dear husband. Were you *lonely*, growing up? You didn't have brothers; did you have many friends?"

Was I lonely?

Yes, I was.

Was Jessam lonely?

I...

"I guess I was lonely, yes. We were just a minor family and we didn't have many allies or friends. We very seldom had visitors. I grew up with my sister, but she... she was a headstrong girl who lived in her own world. Yes, I guess I was lonely. But why do you ask?"

Before she answered, Lady Sakhai poured some tea and offered Lord Jessam a cup. After he had sipped, she said: "Because your deep love for Tyram. I think you have been looking for a kindred soul all your life, and when you finally found him, you poured all your love into him. Even while you know it is a Lord's fate to die by the sword, and a Lady's fate to grow old and grieve for lost fathers, brothers, husbands and sons. Jessam, you are consumed by grief, perhaps ready to kill yourself. I don't want to lose you just yet. I want to spend many years together before you die with honor."

He was silent for a long time, pondering her words. *So open, so vulnerable.* She was showing her bare self, just to lure him out of his despair. *How outrageous, how courageous.*

I would never dare to be like her.
But I must.
She is my Lady.
I am her Lord.
I must trust her.
I can *trust her.*

Joy, grief, trust. These were all things that meant to be Lord.

"I..." started Lord Jessam hesitatingly, "I... I will tell you about my youth. And I will tell you about my sister. I think our spirits were switched when we were born, because in many respects, I became the man she was as a girl..."

Lord Jessam told Lady Sakhai everything about his sister and her brother.

Jaap Boekestein (1968) is an award winning Dutch writer of science fiction, fantasy, horror, thrillers, and whatever takes his fancy. Five novels and over three hundred of his stories have been published. He has made his living as a bouncer, working for a detective agency, and as an editor. He currently works for the Dutch Ministry of Security and Justice. Visit his website at jaapboekestein.com.

"Science Fiction has always been in one way or another a mirror of our own society, reflecting our own hopes, fears, dreams and frustrations. I believe one day we will be able to swap bodies as easily as a set of clothes, so writing a science fiction story where such a thing is hard was an interesting challenge. For my story, 'The Three Ways of the Sword Man,' I was inspired by one of my all time favorite authors:

Jack Vance. He was a master of writing about strange societies which put the protagonist under pressure. A lot of Jack Vance's stories ended with the hero destroying the society, but I certainly did not want to do that. My protagonist feels quite comfortable in his society, only he is born into the wrong body. For this story some dear gender fluid friends shared their tales and experiences, and I want to thank them all. They are beautiful people, and I hope this little mirror shows that."

LGB(T)
MAVERICK SMITH

The expectant news vultures glanced past me when I emerged from the building. I wasn't surprised. After all, someone had phoned in an anonymous tip to the planetary police that the Amazing Ashley and Bashful Betty had captured the notorious Marvin the Menace. The vultures of the media were waiting for the appearance of the two female superheroes clad in form fitting outfits complete with capes. The appearance of an anonymous young man wearing a hoodie was not even enough to make their cameras turn in my direction. The news media had dismissed me as a citizen straggling from the building.

Anonymity. It should have felt good. It didn't. Instead, the knowledge that Bashful Betty would be exiting the building in a few moments to manage the media felt like white hot silvers of agony driven into my heart. Or maybe that feeling was caused by the bullet wound. It was, after all, a mere thirteen centimeters above my heart. Close enough for me to confuse the origin of the pain.

I had had time to guesstimate the distance as I secured Marvin the Menace to a pillar in the parking garage and made two calls on my voice-only phone with numb fingers. The first call had been to Bashful Betty, who had been delighted at the chance to claim some credit for the capture of a notorious evil-doer. A probationary member of the League of Glorious and Bold, Betty had been assigned to this planet only a few short cycles ago. It was her ability to successfully complete tasks assigned to her by more senior LGB members like me that would help secure a permanent planetary posting. She was one of many probationary members and deserved a chance to shine a bit in the eyes of the public.

But sharing the credit galled me. It was infuriating enough to fill my vision with angry red spots. I blinked. The spots turned black. No, I revised my assessment. Those weren't caused by emotion. The spots were a side-effect of the bullet wound. A symptom of blood loss to go along with my increasingly numb right arm. A symptom I knew from experience was usually followed by me fainting.

I certainly felt like doing so right now.

Fortunately, I had made it around the corner of the building. I could collapse out of sight of the news vultures. But if I did that, I was not getting up anytime soon. Where in the galaxies was the recipient of my second phone call?

Nicole pulled up. The squealing tires of her electric car sounded faint even to my enhanced hearing. I could read the concern on her face despite the black spots that were rapidly merging to obscure my vision. She was ushering me toward the car when everything went black.

I woke up to the smell of lavender and the sound of heartbeats. Two things that under ordinary circumstances wouldn't be overwhelming. But the damned gunshot wound was making my hyper-senses go haywire. The effect was even more disconcerting given how my chest felt. Or rather, did not feel.

I could not feel my chest. But then, that was to be expected. At least the pain from gunshot wound in my shoulder had subsided. Even my hyper-senses only registered it as a dull ache. It was a welcome improvement over agony. Inclining my head downward, I saw that the gunshot wound was covered in pink-tinted bandages. The feminine color contrasted markedly against the sweat-stained surgical wrappings which covered the rest of my chest.

I looked over to see Nicole seated on the ancient ottoman she had pulled up beside our threadbare couch. The billet in this, my ninth planetary posting, had come with worn furniture Nicole was intent on replacing with neo-leather replicas from the central plants. It was good that we hadn't done that yet; bloodstains would prove problematic to get out of neo-leather.

Tight lines of worry bracketed Nicole's mouth. I managed to smile at her as I took a few deep breaths to get my hyper-senses under control. The result was much more manageable. I could appreciate this refuge from hectoring news hounds much more when I wasn't overwhelmed with scents and sounds.

Nicole broke the silence first.

"You cannot keep doing this. I cannot keep doing this. I was in a meeting today, an important meeting I had to leave when you called. My boss is getting tired of my excuses of sick relatives or family emergencies." She took a deep breath, meeting my gaze squarely. "You need to be able to ask the League of the Glorious and Bold for help. You need to come out, at least to Spider."

Spider, the superhero in charge of operations for the LGB, had gotten her name because of how she controlled and coordinated information for the League from the company office on one of the core planets. Spider even kept a database of the LGB superheroes civilian identities. My decision to transition medically was something I should have told Spider about ages ago. But I had been putting it off for a multitude of reasons. I tried some of them out on Nicole.

"The core planets have a strong stance against transgender people—"

"Trans people make up a significant portion of the population on any planet," Nicole replied calmly. "It is not inconceivable that the LGB would include a transgender superhero."

"The LGB is full of cissexist superheroes steeped in cisnormativity. If I disclose, they could conveniently 'forget' to be available for backup on missions."

"You have worked with and relied on the other LGB members for years. Do you really think if you announce a shift in your gender identity that all that shared history will count for nothing?"

"Spider, herself, could be cissexist, prejudiced against transgender people."

Nicole did not even dignify that fear with words. Instead, she simply arched her elegant red eyebrows at me.

"You're right," I acknowledged. "That is not likely."

"You could educate the rest of the LGB," Nicole argued. "Show them that trans people can be superheroes."

It was with this optimistic statement in mind that the two of us decided to make the long journey from the periphery to the core so I could tell Spider the news in person. Hopefully she would react more favorably than if I just sent her a holo-video. Bashful Betty was overjoyed to be left in charge temporarily, thanking me profusely enough that I wondered if I had ever been that grateful to merely be given a chance.

Thanks to Nicole's contacts we caught the next freighter off-world. Having a partner who was a lawyer and who was on a first name basis with many pilots at the space-port was useful. It meant that we switched to a courier ship, then a passenger vessel before paying an astonishingly low price for tickets on a transport ship for the last leg of our journey.

"I thought this would take longer," I commented to Nicole as we made our descent. "Are you sure you cannot convince the captain to hover in orbit for a bit longer—say, six cycles or so?"

"Sweetheart." Nicole adjusted my bow tie. "Six cycles or six centuries wouldn't change the outcome of this meeting. You're prepared. We've rehearsed your key points. I even booked a few extra days at the hotel in case Spider needs to contact corporate before agreeing to let you transition on the job."

Nicole always had been an optimist. Still, her confidence helped bolster my spirits as our ship descended. My partner was right. Spider would see the logic of letting me transition on the job. There was no other foreseeable outcome.

◆ ◆ ◆

"You have to die." Spider's multi-faceted eyes reflected my dark, drawn face back at me. Only the agitated tapping of her mutated, eight-fingered hand betrayed any emotion. "There is no other way."

"No." My mouth was dry. "There has to be an alternative." I couldn't set aside my cape, couldn't return to being just another pitiful person with mutated genes. "There has to be."

"Well, there isn't," Spider said bluntly. She turned to the vid-screen, putting her back to me. Small stone spiders had been woven into her dreadlocks. Combined with her eyes, the effect was eerie. I thanked the galactic gods that the peculiar people my polluted planet produced had been gifted with a different mutation.

Spider clicked her spider icon on a folder marked "cadets." Once. Twice. Then the pixelated spider vanished. The vid-screen now displayed a scrolling list of numerals. Spider clicked on the first string of numbers. A candidate profile appeared on the screen. A treasury of information, the databank included the obligatory picture. Even with the candidate's face deliberately blurred out, I could tell from the height, weight, and ethnic homeworld data that the kid looked nothing like me.

"You see?" Spider swiveled her chair to face me once again. Her pointing thumb indicated the profile on the screen behind her. "Nowhere near a height, weight, or ethnicity match."

"But—" I began.

"I know what you are going to say," Spider interrupted. "In addition to this aspiring superhero, I've got one hundred ninety-four other candidates that don't look like you." She stressed the last few words.

"That does not have to be a barrier," I argued. "Caleb the Chameleon changed ethnicities like other people change socks. By my last count, his superhero persona has been white, black, Asian, Latina and, once asteroid mining took off, a being of alien origin unearthed from an ancient asteroid."

"And the public noticed," Spider pointed out. "They noticed and our backers noticed. The result negatively impacted funding and made Chameleon a joke throughout the galaxy."

"I didn't know that." I thought furiously. "Well, can't we substitute—"

"No." Spider held up one eight-fingered hand, stopping my sentence in its tracks. "I am not going to tell one of the probationary members to give up their dreams of a unique moniker to take up your mantle."

"We did that when Deadly Daria got pregnant and went on maternity leave."

"Yes," Spider conceded. "But everyone at the League of Glorious and Bold knew that was a temporary substitution. Your situation is not temporary."

"That's true," I said after a moment. "But dying? Can't I gracefully retire? Like Sylvester Super-being did?"

"Sylvester Super-being served this company for forty-seven years." Spider's multi-faceted eyes were impossible to read. "His decision to 'gracefully retire,' as you put it, was understood and even welcomed by the civilian public. The man was suffering from dementia and had begun to mistake seagulls for enemy drones." She paused. "Unless you are neglecting something, we have no palatable reason to give the public as to why you, a young aspiring superhero, would suddenly decide to leave the LGB."

"No reason that would not scare off our generous, image-conscious corporate funders," I muttered.

"What's that?" Spider's tone cut through my self--pity like an iceberg through the seas of Old Terra.

"I asked if I at least get to choose my manner of death," I said, louder.

"But, of course." That finally elicited a smile from the director of operations. "Amazing Ashley is a superhero. She deserves to die as she lived." Spider leaned backward in her chair, a colder smile settling on her mutated features. "Within certain mission parameters as outlined by our backers, of course."

◆ ◆ ◆

"The entire meeting was like that?" Nicole parked our rented gasoline-fueled car. Unlike our planet on the periphery of the galaxy, this core world was still reliant on fossil fuels, a wasteful use of fuel most of the outlying planets had long since discarded.

"Yes." I ran a hand through my new, shorter haircut. I had had it cut during our voyage in an attempt to look more professional A wasted effort, like this entire trip. "It was exasperating." I fumbled with the clasp of my bag with furious fingers. "And then, when I was leaving she handed me—"

"Why don't you show me once we get inside?" Nicole laid a calming hand over the shaking sheets of legalities. It was a question, but her steady tone made it a statement.

"Yes. Fine," I agreed, cramming the documents back

into my over-sized man-purse. It was good that Nicole was sensible about these things. The two of us were not technically married anymore, so our conversations were not protected by spousal privilege. And Spider had handed me a non-disclosure agreement at some point in our morning meeting. The divorce was not my idea, but it was my fault. One of the mandatory requirements of transitioning was being single. This included getting divorced if you were already married. To her credit, Nicole had not complained about this ridiculous bureaucracy requirement.

I did not bring out the papers again until after dinner. This time I showed them to Nicole in her capacity as a lawyer and not as my romantic partner. She read through them carefully, the furrows on her forehead growing deeper each time she finished a page.

"The LGB makes no promises about rehiring you and state if they decide to do so your current seniority salary will not be recognized in this new position," Nicole quoted from one page.

"The means my salary will be reduced by half," I realized.

"It also says if you are rehired the monetary issues of marketing, moniker and costume will be paid for out of your personal salary for the first seventeen months."

"We are going to be so so broke." I groaned.

"And if you are rehired you will need to relocate."

"What?" I sat straight up on the couch. "That's ridiculous."

"It's also mandatory." Nicole said sourly.

"Doesn't the blasted document at least stipulate I get to die a heroic death?" I began to flip through the pages, looking for the right clause.

"Yes." Nicole took the pages back from me and flipped to the right page. "It says you get to decide between three options for your heroic death. Option A is you die rescuing a busload of orphans. Option B is you perish tragically rescuing a busload of kittens. Option C is that you perish heroically while rescuing a busload of orphans and their kittens."

"I think I am sensing a theme," I commented wryly.

"Yes." Nicole set the mound of sheets aside. "I think these methods of heroic death are intended to tilt public opinion against fossil fuels. But that's immaterial. The question is, what do you want to do?"

I edged closer to her on the couch and took her hands in mine. "I think the better question is what do *we* want to do?"

♦ ♦ ♦

Five Days Later

"Ow." I winced as the explosives expert tightened one of the straps on my protective armour. "Is it supposed to pinch this much?"

"Look, lady," the assistant retorted. "Would you rather experience a bit of discomfort now or legitimately explode into flames later?"

"Point taken," I muttered, squelching the urge to correct his mis-gendering. Surviving the next few hours was more important than striking a blow for transgender rights.

The busload of orphans rolled into the parking lot. On each child's lap perched a day-old kitten. I could hear the orphans chattering and the kittens mewing from the outside of the bus. The bus, the orphans, and the kittens had all been sourced by the LGB from gods know where. I had not asked, and Spider had not volunteered any information beyond the essentials.

The aforementioned director of operations spoke through my earpiece. "You know what to do?" I confirmed I did, and she had me repeat the plan back to her twice before she was satisfied. Static echoed in my ear.

"Is everything okay on your end?" I queried.

"Yes." Spider's voice was like the sound of shifting gravel. "I just wanted to say good luck. With this and with... what comes after." She still could not say the words "retirement" or "transition," I realized. "It has been... educational working with you, Amazing Ashley."

My heroic rescue made headlines across a large swath of the planet. There were several obligatory interviews with the rescued orphans and their soot-stained kittens. The kittens mewed piteously, their innate cuteness translating across numerous language barriers while the orphans were teary-eyed at the thought that the superhero had perished saving them.

And Nicole had been right; there was also a detailed engineering analysis explaining that the bus explosion had been caused by unstable fossil fuels and clearly a switch to alternatives was long overdue. My superhero name was added to the memorial outside the company's head office and a few politicians made short speeches about the bravery of caped crusaders. As we prepared to leave the planet, Nicole insisted on saving much of the media on a digit drive.

"For posterity," she said, when I complained about it. She touched her stomach when I continued to complain. The core worlds had less risky in-vitro procedures than the periphery planets and by mutual agreement we had visited a clinic a few days after Amazing Ashely's death. "For our children. Those ridiculous non-disclosure agreements we signed don't extend to your offspring. I should know. I read the legalese."

"I suppose that means we will have to get married again?" I sighed theatrically.

"Yes." Nicole said definitively. "And this time I want a fancy wedding. No 'I'm a poor fledgling superhero' excuses."

"I heard that the Cloud Nebula hosts the fanciest weddings in the core." I put my arms around her waist. "And in the time it takes to get there, I can fill out all the name and gender paperwork and get it processed."

"I know a lawyer who might be able to help with that." Nicole kissed me, quick and fleeting but she was grinning when she pulled away. "And by the time we get back from our second honeymoon, I wager Spider will have a new contract for you, complete with another ridiculous name."

"And a new posting." My smile slipped for a moment. "You won't mind? Starting again? With me?"

"Sweetheart." Nicole put a hand on my cheek. "I'm a lawyer with enough seniority to find work anywhere in the galaxy." Her eyes were soft, and her grin was cheeky. "You'll just have to reconcile your masculine pride with me being the breadwinner."

"Of course, dear." I returned her smile. "Good thing I'm a feminist."

Maverick Smith has always been interested in social justice and equity. A D/deaf, queer, trans, non-binary settler-Canadian, they engage with social justice and equity themes both directly and indirectly in their work. Maverick is extremely honoured to have a story in this anthology and has previously been published in *QDA: A Queer Disability Anthology*. More recently, Maverick was a featured author at *Naked Heart: An LGBTQ Festival of Words* which was presented by Glad Day Bookshop.

FLIPSIDE

NICOLE JINKS-FREDRICK

Rule Number Three: I don't seek people.

If I did, then I wouldn't be reporting to the station master's office at the top of a glass elevator which possessed stunning views of a neon marketplace below. The elevator shaft, supports, and frame were made of carbon fiber and titanium.

The entire star station was made of the stuff—a form of carbon modified to be as strong as spider silk, flexible enough to absorb the shock of most explosives on the military market. Bad news for povs like me, good news for the corps who had sleek new ships equipped with dispersive-energy blasters, DEB for short.

According to the stylized C engraved into the elevator door, Caipolu Corps presently owned this station. Last I knew it had been owned by Pokele and built by Delite Creations.

An electric, too-sweet voice seduced me over the speaker.

"Thank you for your visit and welcome to the Station Master Suite. May your conference be swift and productive."

With my eyes closed against the heights, I only knew the elevator had stopped because my stomach lurched and I heard the hiss of the vacuum sealing to the car. Pressure ran these things, pressure and luck, and I was glad mine hadn't run out.

Yet.

The hallway stank of titanium white paint and

butane. Beneath the smooth layer of fresh matte enamel, darker splotches showed through the pigment in a pattern which suggested Pokele's interior designer had gone for the always classy crime-scene couture.

The old corp's station master must have been fond of the intimidation the look provided, for there was a lot of splatter-pattern mingled with a few dashes of arterial spray. I stood there and thought that in the future I would avoid both Pokele and Caipolu stations.

Voices came through an open doorway, one a boyish tone with rounded vowels and a deliberate rhythm, the sort politicians use to enchant their constituencies. The other was the growl of a man who had put up way too long with fixing other people's errors.

"When I arrived, it was with the understanding that there was a private room available. You cannot expect me to take accommodations in the men's bunkhouse."

"Didn't know then that the Guarda would come, did I?" The Caipolu station master stuck a sunflower seed into his mouth and shelled it with his tongue, then spat it out onto the smooth black desk beside his shiny new ankle boots. From his lounging position, he waved me into the office as if he was done talking to the Privileged One.

"Are you a captain?" the priv asked upon seeing me. Pov and priv. That was us. Impoverished versus privileged, the war we all fought in this life. Half that war was won at birth. "Any chance that you have room? I would be most grateful for even a robotics closet, if you have an empty one."

He was a priv according to his tone, but his clothes told a different story. Navy trousers and a pale button down, both a size too large and as rumpled as a one-night stand with a dirty, rotten, no-good, bio-hacking pirate.

"Bunkhouse at least got a bed," said the station master, as if the priv had his priorities all wrong and he just didn't know it yet.

The priv stepped around the guest stool. "Please, I will pay. I would not have remained except for the privacy I was promised, and the Bullet Bus has left now."

The elevator door hissed open and we all heard the snap-snap-snap of military boots marching down the hall. Two sets came to an abrupt halt and about-faced outside the office door. The Guarda captain entered with black visor lowered and one hand on his stun baton, one hand on a security-film.

"Caipolu Station Master, I am Captain 24601 of the Interstellar Guarda Service: Nightmare Unit, reporting for confirmation of open docks of the following description: I84 through I86, J22 and J23, and single unit L50. There is a blockage in I84 and if it is not removed immediately in accordance with Interstellar law, we will tow the obstruction and charge this station for the fees incurred."

The station master, his feet now on the floor, stood and started an explanation of my presence, then went silent as Captain 24601 made to approach the desk. The station master stared at me, then back to the Guarda with the expression of a Terrellian hound belly-crawling to appease his angered owner.

I objected, "You can't evict me, I've ship problems. Faulty starboard thruster, might damage your station if it's not mended. And I'm a licensed seeker."

Seekers got preferential treatment in star stations, and scornful treatment elsewhere. The station master gazed at me with arms outstretched as if to apologize, and I realized that I could be the Caipolu's dearest daughter and still be spaced like so much toxic waste into a wormhole. "Can't I have a refund?"

Captain 24601 faced me now, his razor-edged jaw set in an analytical scowl. A red light blinked on his visor. He was scanning my facial features, matching the physical body in front of him with my virtual identity in cyberspace.

"Dorianne Freelancer, captain of the Fogcutter-class *Wulfbane*, Three-Star Seeker." A lip curl of disgust. "Outstanding service record marred by a sentient exception. If you won't break that limitation for Olivia J. Yates, you are part of the problem and I want you gone faster than I can order my Blade to haul your limping rustbucket out of port."

"Fine, I'll go, but I need compensation—"

Captain 24601 reached for the call icon on his wristring.

Urgently, the priv tugged on my elbow. "I'll pay your next docking fees, please," he whispered into my ear and it occurred to me that he was a cunning git used to weaseling his way around.

I stared at him, him with his bulging eyes. I knew what my answer should be. Any and all passengers and cargo are the responsibility of the Captain to ensure all regulations and legalities are fulfilled and complied with; any breach of the Law is to be accounted for by the Captain... I frowned at the priv with his pointed chin, disheveled hair, and those baby blues pleading for me to rescue him. I was a sucker for people in need, and I knew it. This time, and this time only, I would go against my better judgment.

I nodded at him.

To Captain 24601, I bowed stiffly and rudely, then left the station master's office wondering what could have compelled me to take in a leech off the star station floor. True, I couldn't afford food and shelter at the next station without first obtaining cold hard credits or something tolerable like Correllian gems, but I could afford even less to accidentally house a man with a past to hide from.

"I can pay in Lyrium credits," my elevator-mate said.

I stood in silent contemplation, making the priv

even more uncomfortable. He was clearly hiding something. But what?

Lyrium was standard currency and the main element used in the reactors of most space craft. Asteroids pumped full of it were free game for mining. Control over the asteroid belts traded hands often, frequently violently, and it was wise to stay away from these hotspots. Some planets are lucky enough to have their own mines, encouraging a prosperous civilization. The wealthiest planets are part of the Interstellar Council. They made the Law; the Guarda enforced it.

"That could have resolved far worse," added the priv.

Was this sorry sod as harmless as he appeared or was there deviousness behind that distressed facade? Was he ducking a gold-digging dame or a corporate investigation? As my stomach lurched in the elevator and the neon world sped closer, I pondered my predicament.

"Thank you, Dorianne. I can—"

"The name's Dorian. Only place it says Dorianne is on my homeworld birth certificate." And the Interstellar Watchlist, but the priv didn't need to know that. Nobody wanted to hire a seeker named Dorianne. But Dorian was popular enough.

"Dorian, then. I can pay for your starboard thruster, too."

I raised a brow at him, said nothing. Too many cameras here, too many mics and who knew what Terms of Service I'd signed by stepping aboard the station. For all I knew, I'd agreed that they could claim my soul in bright red letters across *Wulfbane*'s hull—but it was likely standard business arrangements and data sharing. Not that it mattered. It wasn't as if I could have made it to the next station before I'd fixed a few things.

My new-found walking wallet seemed to understand, as he remained silent through the gilded marketplace hustling with street-pharma, gambling, scantily clad exotic beauties and all other entertainment banned on family-centric stations. Once on the metal walkway in the docking bay, I tried to shake the leech by cutting through mobs of vice-tourists pouring out of buses. The priv held on, clinging to my shadow like a giggly chit to a Lyrium baron's coat-tails —or his tentacles, for that matter.

"This yours?" he asked, though the answer was obvious.

Not only was she parked in I84, but she was also a rose gold color thanks to the light armor electrospray all Fogcutters received. While the Blade-class ships humming with idling thrusters were bulky with more armor than space dragons, *Wulfbane* was as slender as a dragonfly and every bit as maneuverable.

Inside *Wulfbane*, I flicked on three switches. Engines fluttered to life before the priv even found his seat beneath my potted clementine that reminded me of love as withered as white petals on a cold night. The Guarda wasn't scornful towards Fogcutters because they were old or pink or designed for research and reconnaissance. It was because of all the ships in the nine systems, Fogcutters were nearly impossible to sink a laser or DEB into. They were too fast, too agile, too unpredictable.

Same as their captains.

Papa Detti's voice crackled through the cabin's old radio. "...avoid Hobbart region. Cameras have auto-detected Olivia Yates in the crowd on Endo's Central Hub, but all traces of her have been—" I snapped the dial off. "Yes, Papa, I know all about it. Stupid Guarda."

"I get the impression you are not upset with the Guarda alone."

"It's not right. She's not kidnapped; she's a runaway and you don't fix problems by running away from them.

Man up and buck up. Stop this excuse for Guarda harassment."

The priv was silent, and I was glad. One less irritation.

Mindful of the busted starboard thruster I was supposed to have, I navigated *Wulfbane* out of the bay and watched with contempt as the Blade craft took the dock I should have had twenty-one full hours on.

Once we were free of the station and had entered open space, the priv spoke.

"You have my eternal gratitude."

"I'd rather have your name and the reason you're so set on privacy."

"My name is Janus," he said, "and my reason is personal."

"Janus what?"

"Janus Freelancer-Wulfbane."

That name was reserved for my crew. If I had any. The cheek of him, to align himself with me as if I were a corp to join simply by walking aboard with a wad of cash. But still ... "Got enough to fix the environ stability system?"

"I thought the thruster was out."

"No, but if it was, it would have been in the station master's interest to let me stay or risk wrecking his station. But the environmentals? That's *our* concern. He doesn't care if we're breathing oxygen or dioxide."

"Oh." Janus thought about it a moment. "Yes, I have sufficient funding."

"Good," I said and kept my eye on the screens for any sign of trouble.

Because Rule Number Fifteen: Seekers always find trouble. They do seek it out, after all.

"It is twelve hours to the nearest environs service at Glamour Station," Janus said.

"It's eight to Tapira."

"Tapira's environs service shut down last week.

Glamour's services are speedy, however."

"How do you know?" I asked, and then realized he was doing more than just thinking when he went quiet. He was surfing cyberspace. "You're a bio-hacker! That's why you want your own room; you're afraid someone will turn you in. What companies did you hit? Tell me I'm not entangled in corporate espionage."

I gripped the arm rest of my chair, felt the blood drain from my face. The color rose on his cheeks and spread mercilessly down his neck. We stared at each other, both struck silent.

"It—it's not that situation." His eyes squeezed shut. "At all."

A bleep cut through the cabin. Someone was calling, but I wouldn't get distracted now. One tap on my wristring muted the noise.

"Then what situation is it?"

"I have not done anything wrong."

"That's a good start. Now, the rest of it."

Whoever was calling decided to leave a voicemail in a surly huff. His voice vibrated on the speaker between my wrist and the overly fancy bracelet. "Dorianne, payment is due to the Casablanca Club. This is your courtesy call."

Click.

Now it was me who felt a blush.

Janus opened his mouth. I knew what he was going to offer.

"No, no." I crossed my arms. "This is not about payment, this is about your biotech."

He shrugged. "It's all legal. I don't spy for corporations. Bioaugmentation is common when your family is like mine."

A priv. That's right. How ever could I have forgotten? Sour with the memory of gin and nanotech soothing a heartache, I said, "My partner was a bio-hacker.

That collection agent? It's the end of the story."

"I am sorry. I promise I am not wanted for wrong-doing. You can leave me at Glamour if you wish."

"I'll set a course for it. Your room is at the opposite end of the hall from here."

He opened his mouth, then shut it again. I could see he wanted to argue but did not. He walked to his room, the cockpit air thick with the fight we did not have.

◆ ◆ ◆

We had dinner at Glamour. It was a rough station. Orphans from Orm's Hydro Wars begged piteously, and you never knew if they kept the creds or if it went straight into their boss's fist. Our pub was in the upper storey, out of the bio-waste korati left from their orbital jumpers to cowboy's haulers.

The Whistle-Blower was a slice of civilization amongst rowdy shooting ranges and festivities in the lower decks, but it still had a rustic flare. Real, raw timber beams were displayed on the ceiling, the brass bartop so polished it showed every last dried droplet. A violinist played his notes over shiny leather booths. Janus had gone all-out with the spread tonight.

"Here's yah grub, sweet thing," the waitress said, chewing a wad of gangy root around her words. She left without asking if we would like anything else, and presently the barman left off his cleaning and there came a shrill giggle from behind the walnut counter.

We ate yuppa fish roe on thin wafers, slender slices of roasted korati and cheeses fresh from Terrellia, bread from the bakery on the third deck, and a regional ale called raka which tasted of smoked wheat and raisins. Janus had placed this order, as well as the one for *Wulfbane*'s inventory stock. He'd done better than I would have after a high--rolling job.

There were oranges in the fruit tray. Janus peeled

one, and commented, "It is unusual to have a clementine. They are hard to obtain, even for the right price."

My stomach lurched; a familiar face filled my mind's eye, suave and swashbuckling, a smile bright in the face of danger.

"A friend gave it to me." He'd also given me toys for the wristring and a coil of nanotrackers. But I didn't want to think of it. I returned to debating Janus's odd financial behavior. When I'd first met him, he'd clearly been skimping on maintaining his physical appearance and going cheap on the bus fares, yet now he was binge-spending his credits as if they were a final meal on death row.

"Were you on a case seeking oranges?" Janus leaned towards me, cheeks as wondering as a child begging his grandfather for exciting tales. He reminded me of an innocent me.

"No, I wasn't seeking a clementine."

He hesitated, catching onto my tone, but his curiousity was too great. He lowered his voice. "I heard you can only get them from pirates."

That was right. Pirates. Freelancers of the purest order. They played cyberspace and real space as if it was an endless sea with no consequences. They were the ultimate rovers. No homeworld, no citizenship papers. Born on star cruisers, die in battle. Space was their home, and they would answer to no one and nothing. They cared for themselves, their property, and their ship. They wanted a good time. That was all.

"I got it from a friend," I insisted.

"Tell me about this friend, the one who gave you the clementine."

Resigned, I said, "It's the rankest story in the book. Innocent do-gooder from a small star station meets dashing rogue who could make the world magical. The story is hard, fast, and unrequited."

Softly, Janus added, "And, it would seem, costly."

I grimaced. "Very."

We sat nursing our drinks a few minutes. He got me yammering on about my sidearms. I had a pair, unmatching. Lady MacBeth was a standard slightly-modded antipersonnel weapon. She had two settings: stun and kill. Tintin was my many-times-great grandfather's trusted sidekick, given to me by my father's father when I joined Jarrel Star Station security against my parents' wishes. She still bore a stamp from a little Earth town called San Francisco.

Tintin had one setting: bang.

There were no hassles with Lady MacBeth. She was as icy and deadly as her namesake, but without the madness. Guns didn't have feelings, and that was good. The artificial intelligence programmers working on Guarda weapons seemed to agree with my novice assessment.

There were a few hassles with Tintin. She was antiquated. She required special orders for ammunition manufacture. But she had two things going for her that Lady MacBeth did not. For one, Tintin was sentimental. And two, she had never been confiscated because no one, not even pirates, took a museum piece seriously.

Janus asked to see her. I wondered, briefly, if I had found on the station floor a friend whose mind rotated the same way mine did.

"Where do you go from here?" I asked.

"The gentlemen from Gilman Ranch are hauling an envoy of cattle and rare minerals to Fenala. The slave trade is weak, so I should be safe to trust them."

I nodded and squelched sadness to know he was leaving. "Might want to watch your tech."

"Naturally."

Janus sat upright; something had caught his attention in the main entrance that I couldn't see without swiveling in my booth.

A commotion reached my ears, the bouncers squaring off with someone whose voice was rough and raspy.

"What is it?" I asked. "Someone have one raka too many?"

Even as I spoke, I saw the ropey arm of a Guarda swing over a ducking security personnel.

"Are they resisting the Guarda?" I had never, ever in my life seen or heard of this happening. Since private security firms frequently paired with Guarda forces for stings and other thrilling times, the two rarely took opposing sides.

I remembered who had been throwing credits left and right.

"You paid them off." I stared, wide-eyed at Janus's frumpled clothes and ill-gotten haircut. "How? After all you spent on the ship?"

He drank his raka, cherishing the sip as if it were the best vintage wine he had ever found in a cellar. Janus said, unconcerned, "There was still plenty after I talked to the Casablanca Club on your behalf."

Now *that* was flabbergasting. "Who *are* you?"

Sad eyes lifted to mine, and suddenly, he seemed softer, feminine. When he spoke, his voice raised two octaves very quickly and very naturally. "My birth name is Olivia Janus Yates."

The daughter of Lyrium moguls Scott and Laurie Yates, the heiress whose worth was equal to the Persion asteroid belt, Kisn's moon, and Orin combined. The same girl whose parents had the Interstellar Council Guarda turning over every stick and stone searching for her. The one Papa Detti irritated me with news about every time he broadcasted.

"Well, joys of Avalon," I said dryly. "What do we do now?"

"Liberty for Glamour!" a skinny youth shouted shortly before hurling himself into the mass of struggling bodies. The youth's gang of a half dozen ragtags jumped onto the Guarda's black armor, wielding raka mugs and pigherding sticks. It did nothing to the Guarda, except for the one who fell and was beset by sharp-toothed shreels seeking shinies. The Guarda was delayed, at least for a minute or two.

I returned to find my companion watching me. I downed the last swig of raka and asked the obvious. "But why? How?"

"There is no time to explain. Soon, the Guarda will break through the resistance and they will have a unit in every hallway. Within ten minutes, I will be on their main ship heading for my parents. Once they have me, I will be diagnosed with a mental disorder of some sort, and they will treat me by removing the Noxeum gland I had put in last week. Do you know of the surgery?"

His news hit me so fast my brain struggled to process the information. So he was cross-dressing to avoid his family? It was a convincing disguise. I shook my head in answer. "Noxeum are from Drax. They're the sentient morphers, aren't they?"

They were equal parts legend and reality. I'd never met one, and Janus's extra gland was likely the closest I would ever get. But why go through all of this to get an organ from a rare species? It smacked of priv elitism, yet I could not see Janus doing this just for show.

"They can change their color and physical attributes at will." Janus was definitely female now. Slightly fuller cheeks, slimmer muscles, thinner fingers. Gazing at him (her?) was as if I were looking at his sibling. "They cannot, for instance, take on the appearance of a human but they can alter the shape of their nose or their scale color, or their height or anything else within their genetics. Their thyroidius gland controls this, and the wealthy or desperate can purchase one. For a price. In humans, the compatibility of Noxeum thyroidius varies widely. However, I haven't the experience to control it. It is why I needed the private room, do you understand? I couldn't be a woman one hour and a man the next, not with a roommate, and not without giving away my real identity."

It all made sense. The way he'd kicked up a fuss in the station about his private room, why he'd taken bus routes instead of cruising in style. Even the creds spent made sense. He'd have known that once he touched his money, the Guarda would coalesce upon his location. Well, almost everything made sense. I must concede there were a few vital points missing.

"Why?"

"Why what?"

"Why run away from the Yateses? Why hide? Why didn't they give you the surgery? Why even go through all of this?" I waved my arms to encompass the room, the brawl, the station. All of it.

Janus's voice wobbled between octaves. "Because to them, I'm their little girl. To them, I'm dresses and fashion and shoes and facial pigmentation. To them, I'm long hair and stylists and holoshoots. But that's not who I am. Have you ever had a bad hair cut and felt wrong? It feels like that, but to all of me. And it does not stop there. Everyone who sees me treats me as someone I am not, there are things I physically cannot do because of my body. You don't understand. Even now, you're treating me differently. But you have to know that I have been happier this last week than I have been in my entire life."

Hunted by every seeker in the nine systems, hounded by vigilant station security, and knowing that every credit spent was a breadcrumb to his location. That was the happiest week of his life. What was a person to say to a confession like that?

As fate would have it, I didn't have to say a word, because at that very moment the Guarda were beside our table.

"Olivia J. Yates?" Captain 24601 asked.

"That is me," Janus said.

The Guarda addressed me now. "The Yates family thanks you for your cooperation and commends you, Dorian Freelancer, for breaking your sentient limitation to ease their sorrow. They send their blessings, and pray for the safe return of Kate."

Of course, they would mention Kate. Kate was the reason for Rule Number Three.

A film-wrapped block of credits dropped onto the table. Enough to buy *Wulfbane* and stock her three times over, and Fogcutters were far from cheap. I looked up at Janus—Olivia?—and he smiled. He'd done more than just douse me in credits until the Guarda came. He'd called them in my name.

"It's a king's ransom," he said. "That's how much they value me."

"It is a pity," I said, "that they don't love you more."

Confusion, then pain flashed across his feminine face. I couldn't touch the credits.

One of the Guarda dropped a hand onto Janus's shoulder, and I saw him slip away behind a mask of docility and feigned sweetness. I lost it.

Twisting my ring around, I shook Janus's hand. "I'll see you again."

"No, I'm afraid not." He was afraid. He stank of the stench.

"Your parents are waiting, Olivia."

I waited on him too as the Guarda encircled Janus and took him away.

Their boots clacked into the hall. I sat quietly

accessing my wristring on its forearm display. Planning my next move. An Orm urchin slinked next to my booth, darted out a hand quick as a viper.

I struck.

His arm pinned to the table, the boy let out an awful howl.

"You after this?" I showed him a Lyrium stack.

Eyes wild and wide latched onto the creds. Yes, he wanted them.

"Go to Roundpen 35. When the lights start flashing, you open the gate and scare the daylights out of the korati. When they stampede, you come see me."

His eyes narrowed. "How do I know you pay?"

"What you get if I don't?"

"I get in trouble."

"You get in trouble for sneezing."

The boy lingered. "Three stacks."

"Argue with me again, and you'll be out the whole deal. You've got five minutes for job completion. Take it or leave it."

The urchin would do it. I let him go.

Credits packed up, I walked leisurely for the next-to-nearest banking box where I exchanged these stacked credits for a full cargo of Armorovian whiskey which could fetch double in the right system. That took three minutes. As I waited, I tapped my wristring into the station's wireless and ran a script called AdminAnywhere, then examined the NanoWatcher App.

The nanotrackers I'd shaken onto Janus's palm showed his location.

They were going to the L-Hall, stopped at the docking console to fill out paperwork and enter their flight plan. That done, the Nightmare Unit would enter the L-Hall to reach L50.

I waited until the L-Hall blastdoor opened and the

auxiliary Guarda entered the elevator to go to their own ships. Elevator doors shut. Pressure locked.

Showtime.

Through my wristring, I ran a visualization party demonstration on the station's system.

Never before had Glamour seen such a light show. Not even on New Year's with cowboys detonating modified lightning mines and the cowgirls showing them up. I smiled. The reviewers were right. ShockTartsDazzlingDisplay_33 truly was the best environs demo on the market.

Cattle bellowed through the station.

Time's up.

I ran through the halls. All security would be routed to the livestock hazard, elevators would lockdown, and nobody would bother me.

By the time I reached L-deck, the Guarda had discovered the L50 access port closed. I opened their blast-door. They startled, then realized I'd hacked the system.

Fire rang out.

I ran for the nearest shelter, held out my wristring, and let the hologenerator play a recording of me ducking around a corner. Six Guarda ran after.

"Search the rooms!" when they lost sight of the hologram.

Using the cyberjack, I locked the hall door behind them. That was the problem with these stations. Doors everywhere. Great for lockdown, terrible if the wrong person controlled it.

Captain 24601 stamped in front of me, gun leveled. "Hands off the wristring, down the weapon."

Janus shook his head, eyes round as saucers. I obeyed.

"Display the museum piece and prepare for arrest."

I displayed Tintin to the captain. Then I shot one round right onto his heart.

The captain fell over cold, no preamble, just flat to floor.

Janus gasped. "You killed him!"

I scoffed at the notion. "How can Tintin even pierce the breastplate? I shocked his heart, that's all. Come, before he wakes up."

Janus took one more glance at the captain's still form, then ran after me on our way to *Wulfbane*. "Why?" he asked. "Why did you do that for me?"

I let the question meander around my possible answers. "I had the opportunity to be who I wanted to be. Why should that be taken from you?"

"Oh," Janus said and his brow furrowed. "What about facing your troubles instead of running?"

"I said to face your troubles, not ride a pod into the Guarda fleet."

"You were to take the credits and go. Not rescue me waving around antiques."

He was so flustered. I decided to add to it. "Hardly the craziest thing I've done for a friend."

His steps faltered then sped up as *Wulfbane*'s ramp opened. "I'm your friend? Even knowing I'm... me?"

I threw a bunch of creds to the urchins standing outside my Fogcutter. "Sure as shreels have spines."

We gunned it out of Glamour, and I didn't spare a glance at the clementine forgotten on the floor.

Nicole Jinks-Fredrick was born and raised on a fish farm in Idaho. She began storytelling at an early age by terrifying her cousins with tales of stranded travelers entering haunted houses during terrible thunderstorms. She is cis female. Instead of taking up the family farm, Nicole now writes fantasy novels in the UK under the name Nicolette Jinks.

"'Flipside' is the lovechild of dreaming and heartache, and is my first plunge into a story based in space. I loved using emerging technologies coupled with a reluctant-to-change social order, which resulted in a natural gender role tension. Though Dorian is female she exhibits many traditionally male behaviors while also embracing a male-dominated archtype; Janus questions pre-conceived notions of masculinity by being soft-spoken, thoughtful and refined when other males in the story are rough, tough authority figures. 'Flipside' is influenced by my childhood culture, which mandated feminine females and masculine males with little tolerance for anything else."

THE NEXT GREAT RACE
JES RAUSCH

On the third beep Colin rolled over, groaning, and dragged himself out of his thermal sleeping bag into the cold. By the fifth he was out of his tent and shuffling to the sled. He smacked the panel, and the beeping was replaced with Hector's voice, accompanied by live feed of him sucking down a steaming coffee. A real coffee. The fucker had real coffee.

"Morning," said Hector, far too upbeat for day eight. Colin tried to shrug the tension out of his shoulders and neck and only succeeded in giving himself a cramp.

"Shit."

"Bad night's sleep?"

"No," said Colin. Hector's grin told him his lie was obvious. "I'm going to feed the dogs."

The remaining ten dogs were hungry and went at breakfast eagerly. Colin lingered a few minutes to watch them, allowing himself a rare smile. Huskies, all of them, old but with fire still left in them. Most teams took the full sixteen dogs allowed; he and Hector had only thirteen to start. The other three dogs had been left behind at checkpoints over the past few days, pulled out for their own safety.

"Today's strategy?" asked Colin when he returned to the screen on the sled. He put together his instant breakfast and instant coffee and used the sled's outdated heating unit to warm them.

Hector set aside his real coffee and pulled over a pad. He was a black first-generation Plutonian. He had grown up with the New Iditarod, unlike Colin, and it showed in the excitement in his eyes, the angle from which he viewed the race. Colin understood how it all worked, the rules and guidelines, the basic tactics and ways to run a team, but Hector *knew* it.

"You're not going to like this," said Hector, then covered a yawn with the back of a hand. "Gina made up almost all your lead last night. I expected something like this now that we're getting down to the final stretch. Dustin must've told her to run the team longer to—"

"How close?" asked Colin. He was being short with Hector, but it was day eight, Colin was tired and sore, and his shitty instant coffee was worse than cold—it was luke-warm.

"I figure she'll pass you today if she keeps pushing like that. Might lose a few dogs off the team at the next checkpoint, but they're only down one anyway and they started with the full sixteen."

Colin downed his coffee in one go and swore.

"And *our* strategy?"

"I'm working on it," said Hector. "I had a few ideas, but it depends on what you think the dogs can handle."

"They can handle anything," said Colin, mouth full of lukewarm instant eggs.

"Distractions? People?"

Colin paused to glare into the screen. Hector put up his hands.

"I know, tourist attraction dogs. I'm only confirming. I'll need to check weather forecasts and pester a few people for construction schedules..."

Colin listened to Hector babble to himself and take notes, oddly calmed by it. Colin liked the routine and the normalcy, liked feeling that there was a way through any problem a person worked hard enough on. He completely trusted Hector to get them to the finish line, even after taking home the red lantern two years ago. That had been Colin's fault anyway.

"You know I like listening to you mutter," said Colin once he had finished the best breakfast dwindling funds could buy, "but some of us have places to be. Any suggestions before I prep the team and get on my way?"

Hector was frowning at something on his pad. He had probably let his coffee go cold.

"Stay ahead," he said. "Stay the original course. I want to check a few things and see what Gina and Dustin are up to before we make a move." Hector yawned again, scratched the back of his head. "I'm going to take a shower and work on this. I'll be in touch by the time you get bored."

"Thanks," said Colin and ended the transmission before Hector could catch the expression on his face. Damn, could Colin use a shower about now.

◆ ◆ ◆

By the time Colin packed up the tent and readied the sled, the dogs were eager to be on the way again. He mushed them off into the snow and through the perpetual twilight of Pluto, less irritated now that he was on his way again. Hector probably deserved that shower anyway. He got up hours before Colin and stayed up hours after him, keeping up with the other teams. Some started earlier than Colin did, while others, like Gina and Dustin, ran their teams late. Hector, like any good second member who remained behind, kept on top of every little development, and two years ago had confessed to Colin that he barely slept three hours a night, even though he could get a solid five when the race was going.

"It's Dani Dormer," he had said then. "I was six when it happened, and I'll never forget it. They completely rewrote the New Iditarod after that, Col. Smart sleds were not just allowed but mandatory, and the second teammate was added."

Colin had nodded. Anyone doing the simplest search on the New Iditarod was buried under an avalanche of Dani Dormer hits. Before she and her entire team perished, the rules had been archaic, virtually no tech allowed. There had been protests in every major city on Pluto and many others on both Earth and Venus, although Colin suspected many people turned out more for the dogs than the woman. Regulations changed; now every team was required to have a sled that could scan injuries and linkup. Second team members were permitted, either to ride with or stay behind and monitor, but no one chose to drag a second person over the terrain.

His and Hector's smart sled, easily meeting regs two years ago, barely passed the requirements this time around. Colin considered worrying about what they would do next year. A waste of time at the moment, although Hector occasionally fretted. Hector repaired the sleds for Kuiper Krossing resort and had barely scraped together the funds to buy one of their old models when they had upgraded. If he had not been a genius at patching up the tech it never would have worked, but Hector was fucking brilliant.

Colin guided his team onto one of the bridges between water ice sheets. Pluto was a messy patchwork of human-made gravity and atmospheric pockets over natural water glaciers, strung together by bridges and hope. It was only recently that work had been done making the surface nitrogen ice inhabitable, but despite the harsh atmosphere, the dwarf planet bustled with tourism and research.

The dogs kicked up ice crystals as they exited the bridge and Colin passed through a shimmering wall, heart racing. He had come here three years ago, a new man with his illegal documents and the hope that people would not look into the background of a white Terran too hard. They never did.

First he'd gotten a job hauling shit off space freighters, work no one would ever have bothered to hire him for had they seen the gender on his legal papers. With top surgery and T, he was man enough for anyone at a glance. But the government would not change a person's legal gender without specific kinds of surgery, and with no more money Colin was stuck.

He was hired on by Kuiper Krossing not long after that to tend to their dogs and run the sled attraction. The work was more fulfilling, even if the company was shit. He tended to the dogs that got too old for Kuiper Krossing, but they never took them for rehoming if he took them out on a team once a week. They were more than willing to sign the old dogs over to him, too, shift some of the costs off themselves. Colin had lost his apartment two months ago, unable to keep up with the price of rent when he had dog food, vet bills, T, and prepping for the race to pay for.

It was all worth it. Kuiper Krossing had not fired him yet for staying in the kennel overnight, and this year he and Hector were going to win. The prize was enough money that, even with splitting it in half, Colin would be set to buy his own little one-bedroom house in full, if he wanted it. And this time would be different. No red lantern this year.

Colin tapped the screen halfway through the first beep.

"I'm back," said Hector. "Let's talk rest times for old dogs."

◆ ◆ ◆

Gina passed him on lunch break. Colin was resting the dogs and having another lukewarm meal with shitty coffee when she skidded past, a blur shouting triumph. He and Hector had been solidly in the lead yesterday.

"Fuck," said Hector, glaring at his pad. "I heard her and watched her go past you. You couldn't stick out a leg?"

"And get us disqualified?" asked Colin, choking down his coffee.

"Nevermind. How much can you push the dogs?"

"They're old dogs. I'm not going to run them down to the last six."

"Gina and Dustin—"

"Hector, I'm not running my dogs into the ice. I'm not going to win like that."

Hector looked up and their eyes met through the screen.

"Right, sorry, Col."

"Your amazing plan would be great right about now," said Colin. "Day eight's almost over and last year Gina and Dustin won in ten."

"Don't let me down, then," said Hector, turning the pad so that Colin could see the map that was on it. "See that little green dot? That's you."

"Red must be Gina," said Colin as he watched it move beyond him.

"Staying the traditional course. But you know us, we're not traditional." Hector gave him a nasty grin and Colin figured he was referring to the time when they had both come out to each other, Hector as ace, Colin as trans, just before their first race together. Just before they had earned the red lantern for last place.

Colin swallowed his gelatinous reconstituted beans and waited for Hector to continue.

"See ahead rather than left where she's going? It's quicker that way."

"Off limits?"

"No," said Hector. "But most people don't use the shortcut because they can't make it faster. The bridges are smaller and there's a pesky town that tends to distract the dogs. Everyone comes out for a sled. But if you say yours can handle people…"

"Absolutely," said Colin, pulling the cloth scarf back over his face.

"And loud construction won't bother them? The town is expanding. Can you handle detours if there are any?"

"My dogs have had their tails pulled by toddlers and been screamed at by angry adults. They can handle a little mayhem."

Hector grinned.

"Good. I'm hoping that Dustin will watch us do this and think we're making a desperate move to not lose again. When he finally realizes we can handle the shortcut it'll be too late. Even running her team late and early Gina can't make up the distance. We'll have it this year."

"As long as this works," said Colin.

Hector glared at him. "As long as you do what I tell you to," he said.

Colin switched the image on the screen to a map, biting back a retort. He did not care to look at Hector when he knew he was right. Last time they'd raced, Colin had ignored a few of Hector's directions and it had led to last place. Even though Colin had admitted in the end he was wrong, Hector brought it up now and again, mostly to keep him in his place.

"Don't worry about it," said Colin.

♦ ♦ ♦

"What a fucking joke," muttered Colin as he exited the town. Hector had been right about the eager people crowding the streets to catch a glimpse of him and attempt to pet his dogs, but he had not stopped for them. At a few places, he had to slow and some of the children had put hands on the dogs, but more or less they backed down when he refused to stop.

The dogs had handled the noise and detours of the construction well, too. Colin figured he could have gotten through the place faster, but he did fairly well regardless. Once they were well through the town and over a truly small bridge he stopped for the night, fed the dogs, pitched the tent, and waited for Hector's update.

"They're confused," said Hector when he appeared on screen, beaming. Colin made himself another serving of shitty coffee.

"Gina and Dustin?"

"Yeah. Looks like she took a late lunch break and just kept sitting there. Probably to watch us fail. We're both safely enough in the lead that she can waste the time. And rest her dogs."

"They don't stand a chance at all then," said Colin, feeling smug. He and Hector were really going to win this year. He was now standing on the edge of what had seemed impossible, and it felt damned good.

"See what happens when you listen to the genius?"

Colin ignored him. "Instant bowl of chicken taco goo or instant portabella pasta?"

"Come on, Colin, you can't be that stupid. Go with the pasta," said Hector. Colin refused to look over and see what Hector was eating; it would be real food. "How was the town?"

"Fucking ridiculous," said Colin, watching his pasta reconstitute and heat to lukewarm. "Who blocks the road for a sled team? Or lets their kid grab at someone else's dog?"

"You made good time. You must have surprised them. No one goes through there anymore."

"We did get most of the way through before it got really bad," said Colin. "How much bad luck do we get for talking about the prize money before we have it?"

Hector laughed. "Everybody does it anyway," he said. He was in a good mood. "You first."

Colin shoved adequate pasta into his mouth to avoid

answering immediately. The first thing to mind, of course, was enough of the appropriate surgeries to become legally male, but then, he knew even that was an unattainable dream here on Pluto. The cost here for anything like it was astronomical; he would have to go back to Earth. And while Hector knew he was trans, Colin had never mentioned he was using falsified documents. It would have meant having to enter the race with a different name, and he was not about to win as anyone other than himself.

"House," he said. He liked the idea of that too. "Nothing too fancy. Pay it all off and never get kicked out again."

"You get evicted again?" asked Hector. Colin shrugged. "Col, you have to pay your rent. What do you even spend your money on?"

"The dogs."

"Let Kuiper Krossing rehome some of them."

"And leave us with no team for New Iditarod?"

"Hell, come live with me then," said Hector. "Have you been living out of the kennels again?"

"Your turn," said Colin, mouth full of instant mush. "Your half of the money?"

Hector shook his head but dropped it. "Start a business. The traditional Plutonian dream, right?" He chuckled. "Not sure what kind yet. Have to narrow down the options."

Colin gave him shit for not going with the obvious recreational tech or imported bot store, then Hector gave him the updates on how everyone else was doing at the race. All other teams were at least a half a day behind Colin and Gina, and Gina herself seemed to be staying put where she was, at least for the night.

"I might even turn in early," said Hector, sounding shocked.

"Like hell you will."

Hector laughed. "Get some rest, Col. Winning's hard. Night."

◆ ◆ ◆

Someone was in his tent.

Colin woke. A shadow hovered in front of him in the dim light filtering through the fabric of the tent walls. He did the first thing that came to mind: he rolled. He struck the person solidly in the legs and himself solidly in the side and he heard a muffled shout. By the time he had extracted himself from the sleeping bag, the shadow was standing again.

"Stay where you are," said a familiar voice, and Colin's still-sleepy mind struggled to place it.

"What do you want?" he asked.

"Other than you staying there? Nothing I don't already have."

Colin took a step forward. He had determined he was talking to Gina, and he wanted to see what she would do. She held her ground.

"Don't be like that," she said. "There's no point."

"Why is that?" asked Colin, and took another step. She ducked out into the cold. He was not dressed for it, but he did not want to let her get away, so he stepped into his boots and left them untied, shrugged into his coat and left it unzipped. She was standing by his sled when he stepped out, hands in her pockets, scarf down to reveal a smug smile on her white face.

"You know I'm going to win," said Gina. Colin stopped where he was and stared at her. The obscenely cold temperature, even in a controlled gravity and atmospheric pocket, immediately snagged hold of him from every angle.

"If you're here, it still looks like an even chance to me," said Colin, thinking Hector would be pissed he had to come up with a new plan now. She must have gone through the town in the night to avoid the crowds. Gina laughed.

"And you should make it look like it. But Dustin and I are winning."

Colin eyed her. She was too confident not to have some scheme.

"What were you doing in my tent?"

"Securing what I needed to win," said Gina. "I now have images of your *real* documents. Racing under a false ID? I'd have to brush up on the rules, but I'm *pretty* sure that's grounds to disqualify."

The cold vanished as Colin's entire body flooded with the heat of fear and rage. He had kept his original birth certificate and other forms of identification with him since he had been kicked out of his apartment, not trusting to leave them in the Kuiper Krossing kennels where he had assumed they would be discovered. He had thought they were safe here, next to him on his sled by day, in his tent by night.

"I don't want to take everything away from you," said Gina. "It's been an interesting race."

Colin took a step forward, but her smile vanished and she glared.

"Here's what's going to happen," she said. "You're going to come in second—it's not a bad place, enjoy it. I'm going to cross the line first, fifth year in a row. And your harmless little rulebreaking never comes to light."

Colin wanted to go over there and tear whatever data device she had recorded the information on out of her hands. But any kind of violence against another team was also against the rules, and he did not doubt for a moment that Gina would report him for so much as grabbing her arm.

"Congrats on second place," she said, turning back to where she had left her sled, dogs in their harnesses. "Not bad for someone who won the red lantern last time they raced."

Colin watched as she got on her sled and waved at him. He only realized he was staring at her sled trail when the anger had started to fade and the cold began seeping back in.

◆ ◆ ◆

"Shit." He smacked the panel again. "Work, you fucking technological wonde—"

Hector's face appeared, and he looked concerned, but Colin breathed out in relief. He had dressed, stuffing his documents in his pockets though it no longer mattered, and speed-collapsed his camp, expecting at any moment for Hector to beep him awake but never hearing the noise. The dogs were all harnessed already, and Colin was sucking down his second serving of the worst coffee in the solar system.

"Gina is a piece of—" began Colin before realizing that Hector's mouth was opening and closing, but he could hear nothing. "Hold on."

Colin worked on the sound settings, even turned the sled's linkup off and then on, although he was only supposed to disconnect in emergencies. Nothing. Hector was speaking, but it was not going through. Colin tried the text function next, but that did not appear to be working, either.

"She broke it." He stared at Hector's agitation on the other end. Gina had sabotaged his sled, and Colin knew shit about fixing it. Fuck. Maybe he could go back to that town...

Hector was holding his pad up to the screen. Colin peered at it, read what Hector had typed.

They must have had two GPS trackers. I swear the one where she was yesterday was still active 20 minutes ago. Then it's off and the one by you is on. They'll probably claim tech glitch.

Colin did not care what the hell they claimed. His

lead was gone, his personal information was in the hands of someone who had no problems using it against him, and he was sick of shitty coffee. He gestured at Hector, hoping he understood Colin wanted directions, not explanations. They could argue about what happened later. For now, all Colin wanted was to regain his lead.

Even if he chose to give it up tomorrow. He wanted the option.

Hector pulled the pad back and began typing again. Colin wished he had something he could communicate with, but he had no pad because he was traveling light as he could. The camera on the old sled model was not adjustable, either, so unless he could figure out how to write into thin air, scraping words into the ice was not an option. He was at the mercy of how well Hector understood him.

I'm tracking her new course. There's still a way to get ahead, if you push the dogs and take some bridges too narrow for Gina. The old sled's small enough that you should have a good half inch room on either side through them.

Colin motioned the pad aside with a hand and then shot a thumbs up. Done. He could navigate through that. Would be a challenge, but he needed something to focus on to override the anger. He could not believe how fucking awful his luck was. Maybe he should consider getting off this dwarf planet when this was all over. Maybe he would have to, if Gina did not keep her word.

You're going to have to check in every 15 minutes since I can't beep you. And before and after bridges. Got it?

Colin flipped him off.

Good. Your map still work? Head for the western bridge.

Colin turned off the screen and mushed the dogs in the direction of the western bridge, leaving Hector to do his mental calculations and try to figure out what was going on. He was bright, but Colin doubted even Hector could guess Gina's threat. And it was not as though Colin could actually tell him what was going on. He gritted his teeth. He hoped Hector was putting in one hell of a complaint with the race managers.

◆ ◆ ◆

Made it? asked Hector, then, when Colin gave a thumbs up, *You're going to go through an old science post next. Up ahead there are two bridges, take the smaller one on the right.*

Rage had melted away to confusion and that familiar feeling of being trapped, plastered in somewhere he did not want to be. The first narrow bridge had been a challenge, the second, a little less. He had just come out of his fourth, and he no longer got the jolt of exhilaration from navigating such a tight space. His mind was free to focus on the problems he wanted to forget.

He rushed to the next bridge without having decided what he would do in a few short hours and took it faster than he should have, angrier when he came out on the other side perfectly fine. If he got stuck in a tiny tunnel then it was all out of his hands. He and Hector could console themselves that they lost only because Gina and Dustin cheated.

Colin smacked the screen at the other end of the bridge but only glanced at the new directions, too pissed off to look at Hector. Had it really been last night when they could taste the victory? He was disgusted with himself for ever thinking he had a shot at anything like a home of his own.

He noticed the noise first. Clanking, thudding, carried through the chill air with smoke so warm Colin could actually smell it in this cold. He gagged on it, the scent biting with the tang of something industrial and foul. He turned to look back over his shoulder.

Pop-up buildings were strewn about the ice, like shipping crates in appearance, gusting out pillars of smoke. He recognized these as cheap mining shacks companies would get brief permits for, to strip resources for a small, set period of time. Colin stared, trying to work out what could possibly be profitable here. Some deposit in the ice, obviously. As he watched, a person suited up in biohazard gear exited one of the structures and went to the next.

Colin swallowed and turned back around. He did not think he wanted to be here.

Hector was waving frantically on his screen, worry in his eyes. With the angle of the sled camera, he probably caught sight of what was going on behind Colin.

GET THE FUCK OUT OF THERE

Colin urged the dogs on faster. If he had any doubts Hector's freaking out confirmed this was a bad place to be. The operation he was hoping to put rapidly behind him was probably not at all legal, and even he had heard stories about people disappearing in remote or dangerous areas. Usually they were activists of some sort, but he wanted to be in no way caught up with this. He urged the dogs to the nearest bridge and in, half expecting to get stuck now when he least wanted to, but they made it through.

Hector's image disappeared from the screen. Colin resisted the urge to stop the dogs at that and kept on, blank panel blossoming with a recorded message a moment later. There must have been sound but all he could get on his sabotaged sled were the bold, red letters on grey.

YOU HAVE ENTERED THE PRIVATE OPERA-TIONS OF SYSOLCO PRODUCTIONS. YOU HAVE BEEN SCANNED, IDENTIFIED, AND RECORDED. ANY AND ALL MENTION OF WHAT YOU HAVE WITNESSED HERE WILL RESULT IN IMMEDIATE LEGAL RESPONSE FROM SYSOLCO. THANK YOU FOR YOUR COOPERATION.

Colin's screen went blank again, and after a moment Hector's panicky face appeared. The relief Colin felt at seeing Hector was reflected back at him.

What happened? asked Hector, then took the pad back. *You okay?*

Colin gave him a thumbs up and nodded. No, he was not okay.

◆ ◆ ◆

They pushed on for a few hours after they should have stopped, Colin wanting to put more distance between himself and SysolCo's illegal mining, Hector unable to really argue him into stopping with their mostly one-way style of communication. Colin made camp eventually, fed the dogs, and reconstituted his shitty meal.

Gina and Dustin know what we're doing. Hector had not brought up SysolCo again, but Colin knew he was unsettled by it as well. Colin had been lucky. Probably the corporation had run everything they could on him and discovered what Gina had. They had too much on him to bother getting rid of him, and the GPS tracked body of a New Iditarod racer would be a harder thing to disappear than an activist. As common as activists were now, people pissed over how Earth had been trashed and resisting a repeat on other planets, they still regularly "got lost" in the harsh expanse of someplace like Pluto. Sometimes their bodies were found, always someplace in the middle of nowhere as though they actually had been lost.

Colin had received a warning. He took it seriously.

She's been pushing her team hard today, Col. She shortened all her breaks and hasn't made camp yet. Cross a few more bridges tomorrow morning and you'll pop out in front of her by a little over half a mile, and that's only if she camps late and gets up two hours before you.

And if he decided not to delay to give her the lead. Colin still had not made up his mind about it. With SysolCo and the fact that he had to make the decision for both himself and Hector without discussing it, he had been avoiding thinking about it.

We have it. Hector grinned silently on the screen. *We have it!*

Colin forced a smile.

I'll be at the finish line waiting for you tomorrow. We'll get you a shower and then we'll celebrate.

Not even a shower could make Colin feel better now. He nodded and gave the screen a thumbs up. Hector made excuses about having to get to the finish line and really monitor Gina now that they were in the last stretch before telling Colin to get a good night's rest. But it was impossible to sleep. Colin lay in his tent, low dim light all around him, awake with a distant buzz in his brain.

He was from Earth originally, grew up in Alaska and had heard of the Iditarod races of old all his life. It always seemed preposterous that Earth had ever been anything other than the chaos it was, that Alaska had once had a winter worth racing in, but Colin had seen the old footage and images, as well as the preserved wildlife in museums. Five years ago, he would have never suspected he would be on course to win a New Iditarod race, stuck with several weighty choices and a friendship he was certain he would lose regardless of what he did. If he let Gina win, he doubted Hector would be happy. And if he won, they would be disqualified.

Then there was SysolCo. Hector had absolutely seen them, too, and more than that, they had the footage from his sled. Colin was not even sure they would be safe after the race. And if he won, and Gina went through with her threat, SysolCo would no longer have anything over him that could possibly serve as reason they should not silence him.

Colin knew what he should do, knew what the

smart thing was, knew Hector could probably find less to blame him for with the easy decision. But Colin also knew he hated anyone trying to manipulate or exploit him. His entire being had always resisted it.

He could tell himself to do the smart thing all he wanted. He doubted he would listen.

♦ ♦ ♦

The dogs ran well. Colin passed over his last few bridges and popped out in the lead about a half a mile ahead of Gina, just as Hector had predicted. If his sled screen still worked, he would be listening to the sound of Hector cheering among the crowd at the finish line. As it was, he could see Hector's shaky image jumping up and down.

Time was running out. If he was going to spill out of his sled and let Gina pass him, he had to do it now. Colin had talked himself into throwing the race last night, letting Gina and Dustin win their fifth year in a row, and asking Hector to forgive him. Prepare harder for next year. Understand that Colin did it to protect them from disqualification and from SysolCo going out of their way to keep their silence.

But Colin did nothing. He had not expected himself to listen to reason anyway. He would deal with the consequences later; he always did. For now there was winning, and there was refusing to let anyone else dictate his fate. So he and Hector would be disqualified. They would make news on all the inhabited planets, and maybe the ID laws would change. Colin could always hope.

Crossing the finish line was so exhilarating his senses went numb and time slowed. He pulled the dogs up and when he finally got off the sled, Hector was there in his coat and hat, shouting. He flung his arms around Colin.

"We're about to be disqualified," said Colin.

Hector pulled back and held him at arms length.

"What the hell?"

Colin explained quickly. One glance back over his shoulder let him know that Gina would be crossing in about a minute, and reporters were circling, just waiting for him and Hector to pull back enough to descend.

"Wish I could've discussed it with you," said Colin.

Hector's cheer had completely vanished. "You fucking should have. Before the race. Damn." Hector ran a hand over his face as cheering filled the air for Gina. Colin waved off the more aggressive reporters, trying to think.

"Say it was me," said Colin. "You didn't know. They'll probably still disqualify us, but I'll be the only one banned. You can find a new musher and—"

Hector was shaking his head. Gina was talking to the crowd and the reporters now; casually Hector put his arm around Colin's shoulder and led him off like nothing was unusual.

"No. You know I got image of the SysolCo shit, even though the rest of the sled was down, right? I made copies and checked every possible thing along the route. That's illegal mining going on there. That plus our Gina problem, and we're in a lot of shit."

"We have to get off the planet," said Colin, Hector's nod telling him he should have realized this sooner.

"I was hoping for the money," said Hector, shrugging. "But we'll have to do without it."

They were nearly at the lineup of parked shuttles now. Eager reporters still trailed them, curious, but none had taken a chance at accosting them yet.

"You planned for this?" asked Colin. He should have realized Hector would do something after stumbling across SysolCo.

"I'll tell you as we go, but you'll have to leave the dogs. Kuiper Krossing will take care of them. You have your ID and anything important on you?"

"A little late to ask, but yes," said Colin. He resisted patting his coat.

"Good. My cousin Annette works at the spaceport and already has a couple spaces for us on a freighter. My aunt is a professor and activist on Venus. We get out, we get the images to her, and we keep our asses low for a while."

"You really are a genius," said Colin. He tried not to be annoyed that he had not considered the need to leave Pluto. They were at the shuttles now, and Hector led them down to the end of the lineup. "Why aren't you pissed at me?"

"I am pissed at you," said Hector as they got in. "But anyone can see it's unfair to disqualify us for something like this."

"I thought you were going to..." said Colin as they got in and Hector set the controls for the spaceport. He should have felt more tension from the constraints of the race, but time felt more rushed now than even the last stretch to the finish line.

"Don't make me save your ass again," said Hector.

The shuttled pulled out. Colin's mind was on overload. He had just won the New Iditarod, but the next great race was just beginning.

Jes Rausch is a bigender transmale/nonbinary writer living in Wisconsin, with too many pets and too much beer for company. Nir fiction has appeared or is forthcoming at *Crossed Genres*, *Apex Magazine*, and Lethe Press. Find nem not updating nir Twitter @jesrausch.

COYOTE DOG BITTEN
DAVE RISER

Walker's shoulder throbs, pain radiating in waves down his arm. He holds it close to his chest as he stumbles along half-familiar paths. The electricity in the air buzzes and makes his vision hazy. His heart is still beating too fast. He can't breathe right.

He half slides, half falls into his den. He has to cut his way out of his outer jacket, tears in his eyes from the pain of it. If he'd been shot by a homemade phaser like the one he wore on his own belt, he'd still be laughing it off. Or if it had been regulation—but fucking blackcoats always have to be meaner, have to bite harder than everyone else. The wound even looks like a bite, like something's snapping jaws took a chunk out of his arm. He could nearly swear he sees the teeth marks.

Safe in the darkness, he lets himself breathe, counting backwards from ten over and over, until he's settled enough to get his medkit. His hands shake as he preps the antibiotic shot, but he's pretty sure he manages to get most of it in. If he were smarter, he'd do the searing shot too, but he can't bear the pain. *Tomorrow,* he tells himself.

He does not think about Ghost-Girl, haunting her wreck, and the unread pings on his receiver. He does not think about the way her face will fall when she realizes he can't help her anymore, that both of them are stuck here forever, to wither away under the desert sun. He does not wonder what she'll say when she realizes he's pissed away her chances. He pours a jar of water onto an old rag and grits his teeth. He barely manages not to puke, pawing and scrubbing the worst of the dirt away. All he can smell is burnt flesh.

There's blood after he scrubs himself down. Walker covers the bite with an old shirt. He stares around his den and manages not to see anything. He closes his eyes, takes deep breaths. It must be almost dawn in the world above.

He's not sure how to get his binding off without ruining it, so in the end, he leaves it on. His chest hurts but his chest always hurts, so he tells himself he'll be fine. If something comes for him in the day, he wants to be ready. He wants to go down with a little bit of dignity, so when the crows come to search his corpse, they'll know what and who he was.

With that comforting thought, Walker curls up in his blankets. He has fifteen unread pings from Ghost-Girl, but he can't bring himself to check them.

Ghost-Girl—*It's Vanessa*, she keeps telling him— lives in the crash site. The half-collapsed shell of a once magnificent ship that still flickers and sparks, even now. Walker remembers the crash, the awful sound it had made, all the bodies. All the shiny things that hadn't burned.

Ghost-Girl had scared the shit out of him at first. She sounded strange, flickered occasionally, and she didn't smell like anything. It was different from the way most ghosts sounded strange, flickered, or didn't smell. She'd asked him to bury the bodies, and he had, thinking she would disappear after. She hadn't. Walker was used to ghosts, liked them even, but he'd never had one hang around as long as Ghost-Girl. He'd never had one laugh at his stupidest jokes or send pings to his receiver at all hours of the day.

He sleeps. Then he wakes, passes out, wakes, and sleeps again. He dreams of the crash, all the screaming, and smoke wrecking his throat. The smell of burning flesh. His stomach had growled at the scent, days gone without protein, and when he'd cried it had been half in shame.

He wakes again, can't get comfortable; his arm, his fucking arm, feels like it's on fire. He dreams he's digging up jar after jar of water, then wakes up and does it for real. He gets half of the first jar down before he starts worrying about puking it back up and choking. He passes out again.

He has twenty-one unread pings from Ghost-Girl.

Walker wakes silently, mind clear, muscles already tense, aware of something leaning over him. He launches himself up and hits the intruder in the stomach, then the chest, knocking it across the room and away from him. The thing makes a sound—pain, surprise, fear. When it goes down it stays down.

Walker watches and waits. His arm screams with pain, and tears bead at the corners of his eyes. His mouth feels like it's full of sand, and he's aware that he's shaking. He thinks, *This would be such a shitty way to spend the last seconds of my life.*

After a pause, so full of tension it could bend time to last a millennium, the intruder cautiously pushes itself up. It goes slow, only far enough to get its legs under it and stare over at Walker.

A boy in the ragged clothes of a desert scavenger. Younger than himself, probably, with big dark eyes, dark hair, and darker skin than Walker. He's thin, the kind of thin that's only a few steps above starving. Small, too, with a soft face that makes Walker think, maybe—

His expression though. His eyes, the set of his jaw—

Jackal, Walker's mind supplies. Smelled rot on the wind and tracked it down to his den, just looking for a meal. Walker tries not to think about the way it feels to stick his hands into the pockets of dead strangers.

"I'm not going to hurt you unless you hurt me," Walker says, hoarse even to his own ears.

The jackal stares at him, half crouched on the floor. His hair hangs in his face, but his eyes burn bright and even. *Intelligent*, Walker thinks. Not lost to the desert yet. Walker is still glad he's not between him and the door. He cocks his head and considers the jackal on his hearth. The jackal shifts his weight, as through preparing to flee, and panic makes Walker's pulse surge. He could *use* this tiny, frail, angry thing.

"You hungry?" he tries. Magic words.

The jackal shifts back, eyes darting from Walker to the den's exit. He hesitates, then nods.

"I'd like to formally invite you to dinner, stranger. I'll need some help digging it up, but that's all. No strings attached," Walker says.

The jackal has no reason to believe him, and he stares at Walker long and hard to make sure he knows the jackal knows, before nodding again.

"Up we go then," Walker says, and gestures to the entrance.

It's night again, in the land above his den, and warm wind blows his short hair back. The jackal is waiting, just out of reach. He has his arms crossed like he's trying to keep himself together by sheer will. Walker knows how that goes.

It's a little ways to the cache. Not Walker's best, but the closest. Despite the adrenaline still buzzing in his system, his legs feel like they've been tied to sandbags. The jackal doesn't follow, and he doesn't lead, maintaining his uneasy proximity despite the brush and the occasional withered cactus.

"Here," Walker says. He uses his good arm to drag the sagebrush back and points down. "Give me a hand, yeah?"

He kneels first, and after a moment, the jackal approaches and takes a knee across the dirt. Walker holds the sagebrush. Hesitantly, the jackal digs. Walker watches his nimble fingers pull up clumps of dirt and rocks and unidentified, nameless bugs. He does it all without a whisper. Walker wonders if silence is the jackal's protection, or his curse.

Before long, the jackal's fingertips collide with the wooden cover, and he wipes most of the dirt away. He pauses, looks at Walker, then down at the cover. He slides one of the knobs to the left, then one up, then one to the right. All the correct moves, swift and precise. He's faster than Walker would've been, and Walker bites down on a grin.

The cover opens.

"Avast," says Walker. "You've done it." The jackal raises an eyebrow.

Walker gets up and the jackal stumbles back, wiping his hands on his stained and tattered shirt. When Walker kicks the cover aside, the jackal's eyes get even larger. Walker pretends not to notice, but part of him warms. It wasn't long ago that he would've done the same.

Walker grabs a package of protein bars and slides the cover back. He kicks most of the dirt over it himself, because now the jackal is waiting for the other shoe to drop and won't come near him.

"Here," Walker says, because the distrust annoys him. He rips the package open with his teeth, breaks a bar in half, and holds it out.

He thinks for a moment that the jackal won't take it. His mouth is curved in a frown, and he squints like he's trying to see through Walker right down to his bones, but eventually he edges closer and snatches it. The jackal tears into the protein so violently Walker is lucky he doesn't lose a finger handing it over.

"I'm going to call you Jack," Walker says. "It's not original, but it's a name. Blink once for sure, blink twice for hell no."

Jack glares at him and doesn't blink at all.

"Alright, fair," Walker says. Then— "Are you a boy?" He knows better than to assume, and he's been wrong about these things before.

Jack glances from Walker's face, to his binding, then back up. Walker doesn't cross his arms over his chest but he thinks about it. He shifts his weight instead, opens himself up, to show that he knows what he is, to show he's not ashamed. Jack nods. Something in the harsh set of his shoulders eases.

"Cool, me too. If you want more, you'd better come back down. Anything could be out here," Walker says, wincing internally at his own words. *It only sounds like a trap because it is,* he mentally soothes Jack. *Just not the kind you're afraid of.*

Walker has to go in first, and he half expects to be felled by a blow to the head halfway down. He's isn't. Jack creeps in and sits next to the entrance, legs folded in just the right position to make sudden flight easiest. Walker parks himself a few feet away and sits cross-legged, busily breaking the protein into equal sized pieces. *See?* He tries to say with his tangled limbs. *Harmless.*

Jack looks around Walker's living space like he's wandered onto a spaceship. Walker is familiar with the feeling, although, besides the wreck, he hasn't been on a ship since he was small. There's the pile of blankets, of course, and the open medkit on the floor where he left it. The remains of his last meal. Dirt and grime and dried blood; signs of active life, signs of thriving. Walker's surprised that alone didn't scare off the jackal.

There're also the books, stacked along the walls. He'd taken some of them with him after leaving his parent's den, some of them he'd found, and some he'd stolen. Most are about him—Coyote being stupid, Coyote being cruel, Coyote surviving. Some of them are about jackals, or dogs. Walker find the fictional ones easier to get along with. Some of them are about humans, people, but he suspects they're a metaphor for himself: Coyote hiding in the skin of a man. (Some of the books are about that, outright, and Walker likes them the best.)

"Can you read?" Walker says.

Jack flicks his gaze from Walker, to the books, to the food, and back. He nods once more. Walker grins; the unlikeliness of it all charms him.

"You can pick one up," he says. "Whenever. It's alright."

Jack's stomach growls so loud it nearly echoes.

"Or later," says Walker, hoping it's dark enough that Jack can't see his face flushing. He slides about half the protein over, careful to keep his fingers out of the way. This time, though, Jack eats slowly, and only glances over at Walker once every two bites.

Walker regards his own portion with distaste. His eyes feel heavy, and his head feels hollow. The pile of blankets calls to him, but as good as he feels about Jack, he knows passing out in front of him would be like dangling a mouse in front of a cat. (Or a handful of scraps in front of a jackal.) Walker wonders where or what Jack's running from, how long he's been in the desert. Walker's eyes aren't good enough to see if his cuticles are cracked, if there's sand under his nails.

Jack catches him watching and slows, going tense. Walker waits a beat, to see if he's going to attack, and when Jack doesn't, he smiles.

"You look like an intelligent, enterprising young man," he says. "Want to meet a friend of mine?"

◆ ◆ ◆

Walker's sweating by the time they get to the crash site. He hopes it's just strain and not infection. Probably it's too early for him to be moving around like this but: extenuating circumstances. Jack walks next to him, shooting looks at Walker like he's waiting for him to change his mind and bare his teeth. Walker remembers when he used to look at everyone like that; in fairness, some of them eventually tried to eat him.

The ship looks worse than it had after the crash; not even Walker can fight erosion. There's some graffiti too, because nothing on this planet is untouched by it, advertising that *Cameron sucks cock* and *the dog in this junkyard is unfriendly; beware*, and *Stephen and Olli 4ever* and *No one is ever coming back for us.*

Walker bangs on the metal frame of where a door used to be and steps into the shadowy hallway of the ship.

"Ghost-Girl," he calls. Jack looks at him like he's grown two heads; in any other circumstance, Walker would be offended. "Vanessa," he says, instead, voice pitched to carry. "I brought you a puppy."

"You what?" says Ghost-Girl, appearing suddenly in the way she usually does.

Jack jumps nearly three feet in the air, clapping a hand over his mouth and makes a sound between a squeak and a hiss. Ghost-Girl doesn't look impressed, but Walker almost is. He'd been a little worried about Jack being able to see her; coyotes and jackals are similar, he knows, but he wasn't sure if similar would be enough.

"This is Jack," Walker says. "Jack, this is Ghost-Girl, as you probably guessed."

"Hello," she says. Then: "Are you crazy too?" Jack's eyes are as wide as they can probably go. He shakes his head.

"Well, that's good for you, I guess. I've been stuck here for so long I'm out of my mind, and Walker is desert-

batshit," she says, then turns to Walker. He'd thrown a jacket over one shoulder, but hadn't been able to move his injured arm into the sleeve. When she catches sight of his burn, her entire body goes stiff, and she flickers out once.

"It's not as bad as it looks," Walker says, knowing that it's probably worse.

"Walker."

"Blackcoats, you know how they get." He knows she doesn't. Even when she was alive, she wasn't pulling the kind of stunts he is. Part of him thinks it's unfair, that he's alive and she isn't.

When she yells at him, he ducks his head and allows it, trying to fight against the way his vision sways.

"—and for the sake of all the stars and engine oil, go take a fucking nap," she finishes. "What are you doing, all the way out here?"

"I brought you a present," Walker says, and then looks up to find his present has vanished. His face falls and he can't help the way he draws up tighter, as though compensating for the way his stomach has dropped.

"Don't look like that," she says, waving a hand at the rusted wall behind her. "He's still in the ship."

"Oh," and just like that, Walker feels like he's swallowed the sun. He allows, graciously honest with himself, that the injury might be making the rest of him a bit unstable.

He thinks, if ghosts could spit, then Ghost-Girl would spit at him.

"You've always been unstable," she says. Walker hadn't realized he'd spoken out loud. "Desert-crazy."

Walker could argue that he'd been space-crazy before he was desert-crazy, just like her, but his tongue feels tired, so he just rolls his eyes at her.

"Go take a nap," she says, and then turns away from him. Walker follows her into the forgiving dimness of the ship, ears straining for Jack's footsteps. He doesn't intend to take a nap any time soon.

It's a short walk from the entrance to the shuttle. The path there is littered with sand and scuff marks and dropped scraps of steel. The ship feels smaller on the inside than it appears on the outside, even after all the stripping Walker's done. After the desert, it should be claustrophobic, but Walker sort of likes the way he can see everything around him without straining his neck. Sneaking isn't easily done in a dead spaceship. Limited entry, and barely any whirring to cover footsteps.

Jack is waiting for them at the shuttle's door. He has his arms crossed across his chest, but there's dirt on his nose. The way he hunches forward has Walker searching his clothes for telltale signs, but then he catches himself and stops.

"Can't figure it out?" Walker asks. Jack just stares at him, a practiced, empty gaze. Walker can almost feel Ghost-Girl's reluctant approval. Maybe he can—the rules for ghosts are strange.

Jack kicks the door, the suddenness of the movement startling, and it opens with a hiss. Walker laughs. Jack looks at him and he's not smiling, but Walker can read the way his skin crinkles next to his eyes and knows he's pleased.

Then Jack catches sight of the shuttle itself with a loud, abrupt intake of breath. Walker's grin widens; he thinks, *the trap snaps shut.* It's a rusty, pasted-together thing, but it's definitely a ship. Small, functional, and more than he'd ever allowed himself to dream. Walker's never been one for mechanics, but he's strong and good at doing what Ghost-Girl tells him to do. His arms are covered with old burn scars but, in return, he has hope.

"Always pleased to show off," says Ghost-Girl. "When this is my project. You're just the arms."

"Not anymore," says Walker. Jack's already inside, methodically inspecting the panels and wires and everything else that makes up a shuttle. Walker tries not to feel smugly *right*, fights off the urge to point at Jack and shout *I knew it, I knew this was inside you.*

Ghost-Girl turns to him, something curious in the shape of her mouth.

"You brought me a replacement."

Walker shrugs. "I've got a good feeling," he says. It comes out softer than he intended, more honest.

"Stars."

"He can't stay with me. Can he stay here?"

"If he chooses to," says Ghost-Girl. "This isn't a place for the living."

Walker finds a place in the docking room to sit, and watches Ghost-Girl order Jack around. He takes to it pretty well; his hands are quick, and he almost seems familiar with the tech. Ghost-Girl snaps at him less and less as they go on, less even than she snaps at Walker. Every so often, he shoots a bewildered look at Walker. Still trying to decipher the end-game.

Walker's arm is on fire and he knows it's bad, knows it's only going to get worse, but he doesn't have the where-withal to get another antibiotic shot. He ignores it to grin at Jack. Jack makes a hand gesture Walker's never seen before, but with the accompanying expression, he's sure he knows what it means.

He laughs. Jack turns away instead of glaring at him.

He doesn't mean to, but after a time that could be a year or just five minutes, Walker closes his eyes. *It's the light*, he tells himself. *It hurts.*

◆ ◆ ◆

He wakes up sometime during the day. His mouth tastes like dust and his skin feels like it might fall off at any moment. Ghost-Girl is wherever she goes when he isn't around. After a few minutes of investigation, Walker finds Jack curled up in an empty room a few doors down. He's in the corner, head pillowed on his bag, one tattered shirt thrown over his shoulders as a blanket. His shoulders rise and fall in time with his breath. There's an empty water jar next to his feet. Walker picks it up before he leaves, carefully silent.

The trek back home is worse than it had been to the crash site. He has to rest in the shade and drink another jar of water before he can muster the will to pull his shirt off. The shirt wrapped over his wound stinks like pus and death. Walker holds his breath, pulls it off, and then crawls out of his den just in time to puke.

"Things aren't going well for our favorite four-legged friend," he intones to himself, wiping his mouth.

Once, after his parents had died, he'd found a strange animal. It looked like a picture of a deer viewed through a kaleidoscope. Too many parts all coming out the wrong way, disjointed. It was dead, and vultures had been picking away at its flesh, but there was still some meat on the ribs. Walker had been hungry all the time then, at a low point in his scavenging, and he'd brought some home.

He'd roasted the meat over an open fire, but it had still smelled bad, even when it was bubbling. Walker had only been able to eat a mouthful or two. He'd hated himself for it at the time, he'd felt wasteful. He'd also spent the next week shaking and puking. He'd stayed alive by pure luck; he'd stumbled on someone else's cache not long after, before he got too weak to stand. He'd done better, had made the best of his second chance.

Walker thinks he might be out of second chances.

It makes sense to him this way—he's used up his luck but Ghost-Girl still has hers. He's found her a way out, he's found some desert kid who can still use most of his brain. He's made them a beginning, to make up for the all the ends he's caused, and now he's done.

He kicks dirt over the vomit and crawls back down.

It takes almost an hour to take off his binding, and when he does, his chest still feels like he's been kicked by a mule. He coughs, trying to compensate for all the short breaths over the past however-many days. Only then does he allow himself to curl up in his blankets. He doesn't sleep so much as passes out.

◆ ◆ ◆

Later, when he can stand again, he prepares a bag to bring to the crash site. He packs the last of the protein bars, water, about half his blanket pile, and some books he thinks Jack will like or that he'll at least be interested in. He also brings his favorites, tucked at the very bottom of the bag, packed first.

Walking away from his den, his stomach twists, but Walker won't allow himself to be sentimental. He leaves the door propped open and covers his tracks on the way to the crash site. He definitely reeks now, his covered arm radiating sickness. It could be the darkness, shielding him from the sun, or the knowledge that this is the last trip he has to make, but it feels easier than it had before. He only has to stop and rest twice.

"Good morning," he says to Jack, when he finds him in the shuttle room. Jack looks up at him from his place on the floor, bleary eyed. He looks surprised and Walker tries not to wonder how long it's been. "Where's Ghost-Girl?"

Jack shrugs, stretches. Walker averts his eyes. With his jacket off, Jack's arms are exposed, a collection of scars. More than Walker, more than anyone could ever get by accident.

"I brought you some things," Walker says, and sets the bag down. The loss of its weight almost sets him on his ass. He kneels to cover his loss of balance, busying himself in emptying it.

Jack's footsteps are even, measured. He sits down next to Walker—not within grabbing distance, but close.

"Here." Walker tosses him a protein bar. Jack catches it, looking surprised for a half second, and then it disappears into some hidden pocket in his shirt.

Jack picks up a book. He deliberately meets Walker's eyes, then rips the cover off.

Without hesitation, Walker's on his feet, grappling the book away from him and curling around it. Jack's up against the wall, covering his face with his hands, but Walker doesn't move toward him. Rage, red and snarling, blossoms in his chest but he swallows it down. Counts backward from ten. His ribs and his arm scream a duet of pain.

"There," he says, and watches Jack slowly lower his arms. "Boundaries tested. Good?"

Jack stares down at his criminally-shabby boots. Walker takes it as a yes.

He sets the book down, and steps back. Jack waits until he's sitting before approaching the book. He picks it up again, and this time, he flips through it. Walker picks up a protein bar and tries not to watch him. He picks at it while Jack picks at the book, frowning. There's a crease between his eyebrows that Walker wants to reach out and smooth over.

The ship whirs, faintly, so Walker isn't surprised when Ghost-Girl flickers into the room.

"You look tired," he says.

"I do not," she says. "I don't look like anything. My face literally never changes."

"You've got bags under your eyes."

"Walker." When she tosses her hair, it clips through the doorway, just a little.

It's an old argument, worn enough to have holes. Walker looks down at his fingers, stained from the protein bar and the desert dirt. He hopes she won't be too mad when he's gone.

He flicks a crumb at Jack, to see what he'll do. Jack flinches, then scowls. He sets his book down, carefully picks the crumb up between thumb and forefinger, and flicks it right back.

"Leave Jack be," says Ghost-Girl.

Jack fails to hide his grin, just a little quirk of his lips, and Walker's breath stutters.

"I'm being friendly," he says, trying to cover it.

"You're horrifying. You smell terrible."

"You can't smell," he says. Then catches Jack discreetly tapping his nose.

"Yeah." Ghost-Girl flickers out, appears behind Jack, who doesn't even react.

"Snitch," says Walker. "Like you're any better." Jack makes a sound in his throat that could be outrage or just a cough. Walker flicks another crumb at Ghost-Girl. Of course, it goes right through her.

"Are you done?" says Ghost-Girl, hands on her hips.

Walker flicks yet another crumb.

"I found the next piece," she says, and he stops.

Jack glances at Walker, waiting for an explanation.

"Of the engine," Walker tells him. "Ghost-Girl can check the local networks, and if someone marks it in their inventory, she can tell." It's more complicated than that—technically, she shouldn't be able to access the records. Not remotely. Walker had asked her once but zoned out while she was explaining, and he knew if he asked again, the same thing would happen. Jack though. He's sure Jack would pay attention, would understand, might be able to help her even.

"Denim Drag, in town, has something that'll work," she says. "I sent you a picture and all the info I could dig from the files."

Walker fishes out his receiver and squints down at the hazy pixels. Jack goes stiff; Walker is suddenly struck with a brilliant idea. He wishes he hadn't already sold off the receivers he'd found in the crash.

"We're on it," he says, and extends the receiver to Jack. "You can man communications."

Jack snatches the receiver in much the same way he'd taken the first protein bar. He immediately hunches over it and starts tapping. Ghost-Girl blinks, then laughs, her eyes momentarily unfocused, reading pings. Walker is jealous for only a second. This was the plan, for them to get along without him.

Jack types the whole trek into town. Walker talks a little bit, nothing in particular, keeping himself focused and upright. Occasionally, Jack makes a sound like a sneeze, and it takes several repetitions for Walker to figure out he's laughing. His insides squirm. He stops talking for a while until the lump in his throat dissipates.

Since it's dark, the town is alive with movement. Bright lights casting longer shadows, people yelling and laughing and drinking. Some nights, Walker can't get enough, the spell of it drawing him in. It feels like a marvel: a doomed town on an abandoned planet, but people still sing and fight and hold hands. It's almost enough to make him forget that none of it's for him.

Tonight, it just feels like a pleasant distraction. Jack's with him, head up now, eyes wary. No one looks twice, too busy with their own affairs. Walker leans over, trying for casual, pleased when Jack doesn't move away. He starts pointing out local landmarks—the place where Walker had broken his arm when he was still a kid, where he sells his scavenges, where he used to sell his scavenges before things with the owner went sour, the best place to get a drink.

Jack nods. He doesn't laugh, but Walker reads amusement on his face, once or twice. It's close enough for

Walker.

Then Jack hesitates on Main, staring at the message wall. Walker follows his gaze.

"Is that you?" he asks. Jack doesn't even glance behind them before he rips the message down. It's not unlike a missing poster, but Walker doesn't think Jack is lost so much as escaped.

"They don't even have your name on it," he says, because he can't say *Stars above, you're worth a pretty penny.* Or *Engines fail, that's where you're from? I can't even imagine*—He doesn't want Jack to think he's having stupid ideas.

Jack rips the paper in half, and then again, and again, until it's just shreds and he's breathing hard. Walker keeps a watchful eye on their surroundings, but even this isn't so unusual. Anyone can leave anything on the message wall. Anyone can take anything down.

"It's this way," says Walker. He wants to put his hand on Jack's shoulder, but he doesn't think it would go over well.

They walk, easy and unconcerned, until they can duck behind the burnt-out ruins of a bar to huddle outside the Drag. Part dive bar, part racing venue, the Drag is a haven for anyone with a love of engines and things that roar. It smells distinctly of piss and gasoline. Walker usually keeps his distance, but he has knowledge of the place. Two buildings—one storage, one public. The public building is brightly lit and always full to bursting. Laughter and hard, loud voices pour out the half-open door.

Storage is dark, used only when the owner wants to show off or someone brings something to trade. There's a door that's no doubt locked, but two of the windows they can see are obviously missing glass.

Jack keeps looking at him, not only with suspicion. Walker's got an old shirt tied around his arm in a vain attempt to keep it clean, but he knows it doesn't smell good and probably looks worse. He concentrates on not passing out, or at least not looking like he's about to pass out.

"Quietly," he whispers to Jack. Jack gives him a look that could evaporate water. Walker winks, enjoying the disbelief he reads in the shape of Jack's mouth. Then he pulls his hood up and tries to think shadowy thoughts. He slips into that other self, the quiet one, the one that's kept him alive so far.

Jack follows, just as silent, and no one shouts as Walker boosts himself through the window. He hits the concrete ground hard, there's a second when his heart stops, but nothing happens. No one comes running. He has to haul Jack up the last few inches, Walker's good hand and both of Jack's clasped together. His skin is drier than Walker expected, and freezing despite the heat in the air.

Then Jack is sliding down next to him, flinching away, always flinching. He wipes his hands on his shirt, looks everywhere but at Walker. Walker takes a deep breath and works on not taking it personally.

He picks his way through boxes and shelves, touching as few as possible. Jack breathes behind him, further away, as they both search. It's dim, but the moons are shining; Walker is used to the dark. If circumstances were different he'd like to live in a den like this, full to the brim with shelves and pretty, useful objects. Maybe he'll get to haunt it when he passes.

When he stumbles over a box of spare receivers, he slips one into his pocket. He feels a little silly—for not thinking about it before and for the giddy feeling that settles into his stomach. He digs around for a few more moments —stooping to look in worn boxes covered in dust, standing on tiptoe to look on top of stacks upon stacks of oil cans. His arm hurts, rhythmic waves of pain washing down and over his chest, but it almost feels as though it's happening to someone else.

Jack makes a sound in his throat, soft enough for Walker to almost miss it, and he turns. Jack's holding a box in careful hands. He nods. Walker is glad for the bite on his arm, as his face breaks into a smile all on its own. If he'd stayed healthy, Jack would never have found him, and Ghost-Girl would be stuck with the rest of them for all of eternity.

Walker has to boost Jack up again, and when he does, he feels something pop in his bad arm. He ignores it, easy enough now, and crawls out after. They walk, don't run, away from the Drag, away from town. They could be anyone—just desert kids going home after running errands.

Grem, the slip of a man who always gives Walker the best prices, nods to them as they slip away. Walker waves.

Then it's just the sky and the desert paths, just the two of them and their ticket to freedom tucked in Jack's arms.

The giddiness is worse the longer they walk. Even Jack seems to be feeling it. Walker wants to wrap an arm around his shoulders and swing him around, to knock into him and to hear him laugh. *You amazing creature,* he wants to call him, and take his magic hands and hold them up to the sky. Instead, Walker's head is spinning like a dancer, so he does a few lazy spins himself to match. He's not really surprised when his legs give out. He sprawls in the dirt. Dark spots flicker in his vision, a few at first and then more, crowding his vision smaller and smaller.

The last thing he sees is Jack's face, backlit by the twin moons, all of them staring down at him.

◆ ◆ ◆

He thinks Jack must have had to drag him the rest of the way, but he doesn't remember it. He does remember the cold of the ship on his back, Ghost-Girl shouting and then speaking softly. There are lights and, he thinks, rain.

Someone hits him in the face—Jack, it must be—and Walker blinks up at the ghostly specter trying to hold him.

"What happened?" he tries to ask, but his tongue is too heavy in his mouth. It comes out as just sounds.

Ghost-Girl puts her hands over Walker's arm, and even though he can't feel her, he still winces.

"How hot are you running?" she asks him, her voice distorted but still kind.

Walker has to lick his cracked lips before he can reply. The world swims unpleasantly.

"Grease fire hot, baby, all the time." He tries for a smile. Ghost-Girl strokes her hand over his hair. It doesn't feel like anything. Walker closes his eyes and pretends.

"Jack," says Ghost-Girl, soft.

Walker tries not to pay attention, sure he won't like what comes next.

He's right.

Jack has to pin him because Walker can't stop himself from shaking. He knows he's crying, and he wants to tell Jack it's alright, not his fault, just his body's natural reaction to pain. He would, really, would promise Jack he was doing everything right, except Walker can't remember how to do anything but wail as Jack cuts through his favorite jacket, as Jack preps the antibiotic shot and as Jack gets out the rags.

It hurts, the roughness of the rag and the burn of whatever's cleaning him from the inside out, it feels like Walker's being carved open. He tries to push Jack off, shaking his head wildly, but Jack holds him down. His knees dig into Walker's arms like more needles. He's making sounds, little *shh shh* noises, as though trying to hide the sound of him preparing the second syringe. The searing shot. Walker sobs. His chest shakes with the force of it. He hopes distantly that Jack won't shame him for it.

The searing shot feels just like its name, but it, or the pain of it, puts Walker out, and then he feels nothing at all.

◆ ◆ ◆

Walker blinks up at the stars. The shock of waking, of the unexpected, makes thinking feel like swimming through mud. It takes him more than a few moments to piece his surroundings together.

Ghost-Girl's sitting next to him, illuminating the shuttle dock with her sky maps. She spins them incrementally so Walker can imagine he's watching time pass as stars and comets and planets move through the room. She speaks softly, telling him again of a place she found. He finds it in the map, the place they can go that's green and fresh and breathing. Except for Ghost-Girl's crash, the last ship to ever enter orbit had been a small load of families and their supplies, twenty-odd years back. Walker remembers it, and his parents, so excited for their new life before they realized it was made of nothing but dust and dead ends.

"Vanessa," Walker rasps. She cuts off and shudders, not quite losing her shape but coming close.

"Hey," she says, carefully keeping her voice steady. "We almost lost you there."

That was the plan, he doesn't tell her. He thinks she must already know.

"I was there," he says, instead. Then—"Water?"

"I'll get Jack," she says. She leans over, as though she was going to whisper, her eyes going unfocused while she sends the ping. "You're in so much trouble," she tells him.

"You can't yell at me if I can't stand." He raises his good arm, and she twines her fingers with his, careful not to phase through them.

"I can do what I please. You're lucky I like you."

"Always," he says. Jack arrives with a jar. He holds it

while Walker drinks. He looks tired, but his hands are steady. Walker is glad for that water, glad he can't apologize, can't ask *Did you weigh my heart while I was out, jackal?*

When the jar is nearly drained, Jack pulls away and drops Walker's receiver into his lap. He's got several messages from someone unknown.

You are the biggest fucking moron on this whole desolate planet, reads the first.

Walker grins; Jack is looking down at his own receiver, tapping away.

I should've left your ass in the desert to rot away and *You kicked me in the junk you bastard you owe me forever.*

"I really do," Walker tells him. "Also, foul mouth, damn, wash that out with soap."

Suck a thousand asses, Jack types back. *You smell terrible, probably because your brain is literally made of bat shit.*

"You two are disgusting," says Ghost-Girl.

"This is a private conversation," Walker says.

There is no such thing as a private conversation, she types to them both. Walker catches Jack's gaze and rolls his eyes. Ghost-Girl swipes her hand through his good shoulder.

They pass the hours like that, the three of them in the shuttle room. Walker can't tell if it's light out or not, and everything feels timeless, like he'd left his internal clock behind when he'd fallen. His arm still hurts, but in a different way. It feels like something his body can handle.

They don't talk about Walker's collapse or the work they've done while he was out. He looks around the shuttle dock and sees it with new eyes. He knows it hadn't looked so disorganized—so worked in—before he'd brought Jack there. The shuttle looks almost whole—Jack's doing.

Walker watches Jack watch him; there's something he doesn't recognize in Jack's eyes now, and sometimes Jack will touch him. Just little touches, his hand on Walker's good arm, tapping his knee when he wants Walker's attention, but still. He's amazed every time.

Eventually, everything ends. Walker read that somewhere.

He's outside squatting behind a bush to piss when he hears them, familiar barks and jeers. He finishes as quietly as he can, shimmying his pants back over his hips, while he hears the blackcoats from the bar hunt him.

"— gone to ground."

"Grem saw him. I know it was Walker; he's just playing dead." There's Ripper, the leader, her voice high and unmistakable. Walker's pulse flutters like a moth against a lantern.

"His bunker looked deserted to me," says Spots, her second-in-command. Walker has only once heard them agree. He would've been charmed if it hadn't been the decision to jointly kick his ass.

"He's been living out here his whole life," says Ripper, which isn't true, but is what Walker had told her. "He knows the desert. He'll try to hide in it, blend in."

"If that's true, then he's too smart to hide in the wreck," says Spots. There's a murmur of discontent from the others, arguing among themselves. Walker doesn't have nicknames for most of them; the ones he does have he can't remember.

"Walker only thinks he's smart," says one. Walker peers through the brush and sees him hold up a receiver, twin to the one he stole for Jack.

Of course, he should've thought—the Drag has a tech kid too. They'd know to put trackers on their devices. He would've remembered if his blood hadn't been on fire. They say more, but Walker doesn't think it matters. He's quiet as he sneaks backward, until he can't anymore, then he's running on shaking legs, desperation lending him strength.

When they catch his scent there's shouting, the baying of dogs on the chase. He's got his receiver in his hands as he runs.

Run, he sends. *Blackcoats r coming.*

He takes an alternate route through the wrong side of the ship, winding through the skeleton, glad of the hours he spent learning the paths. He hears them behind him, further and further but not gone.

Then Jack is there. Walker almost punches him, heart hammering. Jack doesn't even bother with flinching; he grabs Walker by the arm and pulls him sideways. Together, they make their way to the shuttle dock. Ghost-Girl is waiting there already, but Walker can tell she's also somewhere else.

"I'm sorry," he tells her, knees wobbling. He barely gets the words out; they keep sticking to the lump in his throat. *I'm sorry I keep fucking things up.*

"I know," she says.

"I didn't—"

"It's okay," she repeats, sounding far away. "We just have to work fast."

Jack's already in the shuttle, moving things around, trying to secure the bay doors.

They work fast; it's not enough.

Ripper screams at them, says she can smell them through the metal. Walker tries not to focus on the actual words; he just keeps looping the wires like Jack showed him, over and over.

Ripper shouts, "Did you really think you could hide that thing?" and Walker doesn't know if she's talking about the shuttle or Jack.

"Fuck you," he says, not loud enough to carry. One of them starts shooting, then all of them, their blasters making the walls shake.

In the same moment, the shuttle dock opens from the top, showing off the vast expanse of dark space. Walker hopes so hard it might kill him.

Jack drags him into the shuttle. Ghost-Girl is already there, hovering around a bundle of wires and boxes. There's a huge window and something that might be flight controls. Walker slips into the control chair, lays his shaking hands over them, and waits for instructions.

"Pull hard," Ghost-Girl is saying to Jack, both of them crouched by what must be the engine. "If it doesn't spark, we'll have to start everything over again."

"No pressure," says Walker. "But we don't have time for restarts."

Around them, in the dock, the walls are starting to melt, from the blackcoats and their ridiculously overpowered phasers. Something shorts; there's the smell of smoke, a flash of light. The whole wreck goes dark, shuttle included. Ghost-Girl vanishes. The last expression on her face is fear.

Walker doesn't even have time to swear. There's the dread that comes before the *oh shit,* and then he grabs Jack's arm and tries to pull him away, to make one last run for it. But Jack turns on him and—

His teeth are filed into neat, narrow points. There's blood from where he must have bitten his tongue, a half-formed lumpy thing. Walker can't help his recoil. Jack—truly a jackal, Walker knows now he was right—doesn't even bother with hurt. He boosts himself up, leans over the engine, and does something with his hands.

A heartbeat where time feels suspended, where the blackcoats crash through the door and Walker reads his end in Ripper's trigger finger—the shuttle whirs to life. Light burns Walker's eyes. Ghost-Girl flickers and steadies, staggering as though she can actually feel the ground beneath them shudder.

They lift.

Ripper shoots upward, but they're rising too fast. She misses. The ground falls away. Walker grins so wide his lip splits, and he doesn't care. Jackal grins back at him, teeth and all, and Walker howls.

"I can't fucking believe this—" says Ghost-Girl. "I've got control, I've got nav—we're gold. We're fucking gold." She sounds like she can't believe it. Walker wonders if she'd be crying, if she could.

Jack makes a noise, a guttural, choking echo of Walker's howl. Walker opens his arms. Jack flies into him, grip hard, and rough, and perfect. Walker swings him around the engine room, knocking him through Ghost-Girl, who spins and laughs as the ship lifts off toward the faraway stars.

Dave Riser is a trans guy who lives in an attic somewhere in the Pacific Northwest. He spends his time writing about monsters and learning from his mistakes. Find him on twitter under @davevriser.

THE TREE PLANTERS

EVERETT MAROON

He grabs a spruce seedling out of his thick canvas bag where it is lined up with the others like arrows. In one quick motion, he drops it into the hollow metal pole. As the baby slides down the tube, it makes a quiet noise reaching higher timber, a change of a couple octaves by the time it reaches the bottom. It reminds him a little of a didgeridoo, or at least, what he's heard didgeridoos sound like—*schuuk*. The tree sits ready for planting only a moment before Hax hits the trigger and injects it into its place in the brand new soil, the very youngest in a staggered row of conifers.

The first sun isn't quite over the ridge yet, but Hax is ready for it, tired of squinting in the pre-dawn light. He and his coworker Marnie will have three solid meta-ticks of planting time before the second sunrise, and then they'll need to take cover because radiation from two stars is harsh on human skin. Like, third-tier burn harsh. So many people have died trying to make Valus habitable that Hax has lost faith in the expertise of the Health Service.

Schuuk. Marnie tamps down the moist dirt with her boot, just enough for the seedling to stay put but not enough to force her to break stride. She and Hax have an ongoing bet about who can get more trees in the ground in a solar rotation, a six-set rotation, and a mountaintop. So far for the six-set she's ahead by 327. It's too close a margin for him. Hax's contraband beer is on the line, after all. Way better than the piss they serve at the company-owned tavern, even on tournament nights.

On the next peak ahead the earth-maker machine rumbles, like a gigantic bulldozer working in reverse. It's as close to Earth soil compositions as the brightest Valus engineers can create. It stinks like rotten broccoli and after a rotation of seeding the mountain, they get back to base reeking of it. The smell is so bad they're both grateful for their face masks.

They need the trees to make enough oxygen to support the intended population, even with the polar ice cap factories churning out all of the surplus oxygen that the interior of the planet can give. Barren ridges on either side of theirs stand as testament that there are plenty more mountainsides to enforest. They've only been at it for fifteen months and already it feels like forever.

"I didn't see you at Woulf's last night," says Marnie, her voice muffled by the mask but repeated in the speaker at his ear. Everything they say is doubled and a quarter-second out of unison.

"Yeah, I didn't go. I just wanted a quiet evening."

Schuuuk. 187. 188.

"Okay. So what did you wind up doing?" she asks.

She's in one of her chatty moods, he thinks, pulling another seedling from his bag. All of their Forest Service equipment is painted some shade of green or yellow, and all of it is beat to hell.

"Just played video games." *Close enough to the truth.* With a couple pints of homebrew at his side, but he doesn't want to tell her that the latest batch is ready or she'll come over and drink everything in his quarters. Hax steps up his pace a little, thinking about their competition.

Marnie snorts. Hax knows everyone thinks he's some kind of loner. He's happy to cultivate that perception.

"Well, you know we'd love to see you. Jance is not a great tournament partner. He nearly took Ragienld's head out with a bad miss at the board."

"Ragineld has a big head. And Jance couldn't hit the side of the depot if he were standing in the depot."

Condensation from his breath has started collecting in his mask, making his beard scruff damp. He tries to hide his irritation by walking in silence.

Schuuk. 235.

"Well, I did okay without you at tournament," she says, taking a peek behind them. She glimpses their progress every so often. Hax never turns around. He never wonders about his planting; he has other shit to worry about. Probably they gossip about him at tournament, but he won't let himself speculate about that. He heard that Jance thinks he's having some über secret affair. Ragineld, the tournament host, once told Marnie he thought Hax was in some kind of witness relocation project, and according to Marnie, she didn't correct him. "People get some wild ideas when they're all stuck building a new planet," she'd said.

Up ahead, the newborn soil stretches out, curving away in a stinky swath of dark brown on a gentle slope. Maybe someday Valus will be beautiful like Earth was. He doesn't know because he left Earth when he was just a few years old. But somewhere in his bones, he can feel vibrations or echoes... something that tells him Valus is all wrong, too artificially reproduced. He hopes someday it will feel all right to him.

"So who lost?" asks Hax.

"Kenlee lost," says Marnie. "It's too bad. I like Kenlee."

"Damn, I thought Kenlee would get to the finals." Between both of them, five more tiny trees stick out of the ground.

"I know, right? Meanwhile that slime ball is still in the running."

"Slime ball, slime ball, there are so many to choose from, so who could you mean? Do you mean Deeble?" he asks.

"Yes, that's his name. I always forget." *Schuuuk.* "I repress it. I swear he cheats, but I can't figure out how."

"A lot of them cheat. Why wouldn't they, since the stakes are so high?"

"It ruins the competition."

"Well, the tournament means a lot to people."

Marnie pauses for a moment. Hax takes the opportunity to install three more seedlings, all in a row. Marnie curses at him.

"I get what you're saying," she says, double loading and plunging trees into the soil in a few seconds. They aren't supposed to do this. Forestry Service has calculated growing efficiency, and the seedlings have to be a certain distance apart.

"So you admit that competing is more than just within the tournament. We're all in a grand contest, really."

"No, actually we're not," says Marnie. "We're here for the common good. The tournament is about getting us all to step up and be our best selves."

"Come on, if the tournament were about making a better planet, the reward wouldn't be a one-way ticket to Balta, the luxury planet."

Marnie is silent. Hax figures she's turning over his comment in her mind.

He laughs, making his oxygen mask get unbearably greasy inside.

"Damn it," says Hax, taking a big gulp and ripping the mask off.

"What are you doing?" asks Marnie, her eyes as big as the second sun. "You can't breathe the air!"

Hax rubs his uniform shirt tail inside the mask in two, three strokes, and slams the mask back over his nose and mouth. They have completely stopped planting seedlings for the moment, despite the risk. Those happy green tubes will summon General Management Service if they're idle for too long and it's not an authorized break time. Hax's tube flashes a warning signal. He grabs a tree and loads it.

"I just couldn't stand it anymore," he says, and they get back to their usual pace. *Schuuk, schuuuk.* Marnie grumbles to him that he's made her lose her place, but the pole meter will tell her how many she planted at the end of their shift.

Across the meandering valley, the sky looks almost blue, like in the pictures they've seen at the Library and History Service Building. This is usually when Marnie says it's all worth it. Not today.

Finally, it's only about fifteen ticks until lunchtime and the second sunrise, when they'll meet up with the shuttle and head into their bunker. Hax will miss being outside, despite its insufficiency.

"I shouldn't have picked testosterone," he says, almost to himself.

"What?"

"I should have picked the other."

"Estrogens? Why? I thought you wanted to go masc."

"I did, I guess. I mean, I don't know. What if I feel kind of in between? Testosterone makes everything so greasy and gross."

"Well, estrogen isn't all cheesy breezy, either. You went to the Health Service presentations, you filled out the questionnaires. They said we had to pick one or the other to become more like we used to be."

Now I'm stuck talking about this, he thinks. *Fine. Let's talk about it. It will feel good to get this crap off my chest.*

"I don't buy it. I think we should just be us as we are. Maybe no sex is okay. Or being in between. I don't know.

What do we need synthemones for?"

"I wonder if you're depressed."

"I'm not depressed, Marnie."

"Then talk to Health Service. Maybe they can switch you?"

"I can't do that!"

"Why not?"

"Are you stupid? Jerrent did that last year, and do you know what happened to him?"

"I'm not stupid, Hax."

"Okay, but do you know what happened?"

"I'm not talking to you anymore until you admit I'm not stupid." She walks away from him, casting new trees into the ground. *Schuuk.*

"You're not stupid, you're not stupid, Marnie, come on." Hax trots off after her. *Damn it now I need to finish this fucking conversation.*

She stops, turns around, still planting in a new line back to her original trajectory.

"You think pelvis expansion is a cakewalk?"

"No. No, I don't. I just—"

"They're just hormones. It's for the common good, remember?"

He sighs. They are in this together. Maybe he should go to the tournament one of these weeks, see if he can qualify for a larger home unit. Or win one of the annual prizes to Balta. Nobody needs an oxygen mask on Balta.

"It's just different and I don't like change," he says, lying. *Different is not my problem.*

Schuuuk.

"Look," says Marnie in a whisper. Rumors pop up from time to time that their Forestry Service gear has listening devices embedded in the paint. "It's hard for everyone. At least we're not in the coolers down below waiting for the planet to be ready, too frozen to even hope that we survive the thaw. Would you prefer that?"

Hax takes a moment but then shakes his head. But he thinks: *Maybe.*

"So keep planting trees, and stop complaining, and shut up about Jerrent. Jerrent had a lot of issues."

Yeah, thinks Hax. *Like Jerrent didn't want to be so masc. And I don't, either, maybe. And now I know I can't talk to anyone about this, not even my best friend. I can't believe I had the chance right in front of me and I blew it and now I hate myself and I'm on this shit-smelling construction planet.*

Schuuuuk. The row of seedlings stands behind them, ready for the second sunrise, eager to soak up as much radiation as light beams can carry.

Maybe tonight, Hax thinks, *I can figure out how to finally get off of Valus. Soon. It has to happen soon.*

She can't stand this body or this place any longer and nobody here understands that.

Everett Maroon is a pop culture commentator, fiction writer, and the bestselling author of *The Unintentional Time Traveler.* He has written for *Bitch Magazine,* GayYA.org, RH RealityCheck, The Daily Dot, and Global Comment. He lives in Walla Walla, Washington, with his partner and their two children. He blogs at transplantportation.com.

If You Can

Bo Balder

I am Peony. Mummy and Daddy made me. They took flesh from their thighs and kneaded it into the shape of a human baby. Doughyson helped them. He knew how to shape flesh and give it a spark.

Two hundred years later, I sat with my feet in cool swamp water, my back against a spongy fern tree, and considered how to avoid taking root.

"Peony, hey!" a human voice cried behind me. Aidizig, my wife.

I wanted to get up, but one of my feet had sprouted a radicle and anchored itself in the mud. I absolutely didn't want to plant myself yet, and now my body was preempting me? I tore the rootlet loose from the grasping orange mud and turned to face Aidizig. I blinked my human-like eyes against the bright light. It was a hot, humid day, as always, and Aidizig's brown skin and pale grass skirt barely stood out against the predominantly sacred green vegetation.

Aidizig stared at my foot.

I broke off the shoot and kept it against my thigh until it was reabsorbed.

"You're not going to take root here, are you?" she asked. "Too close to Doughyson. He wouldn't approve."

I craned my neck to view the great white mountain that was Doughyson, a thousand feet away in the swamp, surrounded by pale gray profane plants. Doughyson was a Mound, the mature stage of us Wan, immobile and rooted deep in the earth, with only the taste of water and wind to amuse himself. Exactly what I didn't want to be.

"You *look* like you want to plant yourself," said Aidizig. She looked up at me. She was by no means a small woman, but I still stood a head above her. I'd become very large and heavy lately. I kept my shape symmetrical and human-like, as I'd always done. I looked like a fat middle-aged man, although chalky-white.

"If I stay this heavy, I'll have to. But I won't."

We started to walk back to the village past the fields of sacred foods. Away from the Doughyson-saturated water, the sacred growth was denser, and we walked over a lovely path, cool and moist to the feet, shaded by green and blue ferns.

"What *do* you want?" she said.

I shrugged. "I don't know." I lied to her. I feared her derision if I spoke my true desire out loud. "My parents were people once. They raised me as a human child."

Again I swallowed what came after: *I want to be a man*. Although I was clearly a Wan.

Aidizig sniffed. "Without a human body, you can't be a man. If you're born a man and become a Wan, you can stay human for a long time. But even they change into something else after a while."

She always knew where my sore spots were and didn't hesitate to press them. I wanted her not to be right, but it had gone exactly like that with my parents. Daddy was thirty years old when he'd been bitten by a whitefish, one of our smallest stages, and his flesh changed into Wan flesh. After a hundred years or so, Daddy was the first to leave our little family. Mummy dutifully stayed on for years, but at some point, she couldn't cope anymore. With me.

The baby that never became quite human enough.

I believed Daddy had planted himself, only I never found out where. What happened to Mummy, I had no idea.

"I'm pregnant," Aidizig said suddenly. "And Doughyson says a message from your mother has arrived. He wants you to visit him."

I fell down, I think. Next thing I knew, I was looking up at the fern bushes. Aidizig's black curly hair hovered into view. "Peony. Are you all right?"

I sat up. "I don't know. Did you just say you were pregnant?"

"Yes. And then you fainted."

"That's impossible," I said. "I don't have circulation."

She stuck out her hand. As if she could heave up my three hundred pounds. But she meant well, I guess. And she was pregnant. Not from me, obviously, and I hadn't noticed. She'd smelled odd for weeks now. A real human would have connected the dots, but not me.

"You fainted. Maybe you have more humanity inside you than you think." Why were we talking about my humanity or lack of it? And not about her pregnancy?

My wife was pregnant. Not by me. What did that mean? Should I feel betrayed or happy? What would my human friends do? Feel anger. Check. Feel loss. Check. Confide in loved ones. For the first time in a century, I felt the desire to see my mother again.

Would an angry man hit his wife? A blow from me would kill Aidizig. I didn't want her to die; her life would be short enough anyway. And then I knew. A human man would *leave* his wife.

I scrambled up. "I feel pain. I feel anger. I miss my mother. And my father. Is that human?"

She looked at me funny. "I should think so."

I sent those unwelcome human feelings to my hand and broke it off. I didn't want them. I began to toss the hand away, although it went against the grain of a Wan's mass-p-reserving ways, but Aidizig stopped me.

"What are you doing?" she said.

"Dumping mass," I said. Even without a human body, I knew very well what she meant. She thought I should keep the feelings. Because human beings had no choice, they were forced to deal with theirs.

"Bullshit," she said. "Eat that hand. It will tell you what to do."

I looked at the hand. It was a well-formed, perfectly human hand, except for the color. Thick sausage fingers, shiny nails, even fake hairs on the back. I turned it around. No fingerprints or lines in the palm. Those I can't manufacture, I don't know why.

I stuffed the fingers in my mouth and swallowed them without chewing. The pain and longing flowed back little by little as I reabsorbed the hand.

Aidizig had been right. I even experienced a kind of relief, because now I saw what I needed to do. I was going to find my mother and in doing so, leave my wife. Two birds with one stone, as the humans say.

I paddled towards Doughyson in a borrowed boat. The closer I rowed to the white hemisphere, five times or more my height, the sharper the smell became. *Come here*, the scent said. *Come near, let me take you in.* That temptation was intended for his walkers, but this close I found it hard to resist. It was risky, getting so close to Doughyson, but I thought it was worthwhile. I needed to talk to him about my father and mother.

Doughyson was very old. His parent had been the cleverest of all the Mounds, I think. I say parent, not mother, because we Wan have no sexes like humans. Mother Doughy had figured out that humans weren't just pesky creatures that built on your surface and tried to grow their green crops everywhere, obliterating the pale Wan vegetation. Perhaps Doughyson's parent became so smart by eating a lot of human beings who'd been transformed into Wan.

Doughyson was a piece of his parent, with part of its memory and cleverness. We store our memories in our flesh, so as we grow, we become wiser. But at some point we grow too big to move. We feel the urge to root ourselves and become sessile Mounds. Afterwards we create puppet Wans called walkers, to bring us food and news, which to us is the same thing. Otherwise, life is boring. Sitting in a swamp waiting until you're big enough to explode into a trillion pieces, which all then try to get big enough to become smart once more, that is the life of a Mound.

Doughyson must already have smelled me. He'd formed a big head near the cove where I tied up my boat.

"Greetings, Peony!" he boomed. "What joy that you come visiting."

He hadn't completely discarded human manners.

"As you asked," I said. "You have a message from my mother?"

The head bobbed slowly up and down. I was flattered that he took the trouble to move. "Give me some of yourself. I want to record your unique perspective."

I tore a large piece of flesh from around my belly button. I'd been planning to dump mass anyway. I put in a dash of loneliness and aimlessness, two emotions that I was sick and tired of.

I put the lump on his extended lower jaw and pulled my hand away just in time to escape his bite. His little joke. I kind of liked Doughyson, and had great respect for his wiliness, but I trusted him not at all.

"I want to get something about my parents in return," I said. I just couldn't resist saying it out loud, even though Doughyson would have heard that question loud and clear in my flesh.

The face didn't respond, but there was no point

expecting human reactions from a Mound. Moments later, the mouth opened again and offered me a piece of his own substance.

He'd known my parents well. He'd taught them how to shape me. No doubt my mother had fed him knowledge, and he'd fed her information in return. That was the way we talked. You could never be sure, though, that such a piece of meat knowledge would not multiply within you and take you over. Each exchange was a risk. If Doughyson knew about the void within me where I longed for my mother, he might try to slip something dangerous by me.

I put it on my tongue to let it melt. Doughyson was famous for his meat poems, and for a moment I thought I'd gotten one. But then I realized it was just a memory—not Doughyson's but someone else's. One of his walkers, maybe. I saw an island in a green sea. Strange spiny trees grew on it. The sky was blue instead of white.

Then another memory, this time with sharper details, more smells, and tactile sensations. This sea was leaden gray, more like the sea that lapped against my island. But it wasn't my island. It was larger and flatter, and many humans lived on it. I heard metal clattering on metal, as though there were more than one forge, and big wooden structures towered over the trees. The beach was littered with behemoth skeletons. A village couldn't eat that much meat in a hundred years. The person who'd made the memory swam closer to the shore and focused on one of the people. It was my Mummy. She looked sharply at the memory carrier with her narrow white eyes and then made a shooing gesture in my direction.

I awoke from my dream and looked long and thoughtfully at Doughyson.

"Why are you spying on my mother?"

Doughyson whistled air out of his mouth hole. "I want you to find out about the first memory. I very much want to know."

"Why?" I asked. I needed to hear my mother's message but he seemed to be evading the issue.

"Once before, long ago, I've seen such a memory. I don't remember who I gave it to. But the memories surrounding it make me think that I should find out. And finally, I have a message from your mother I promised her I'd give you at the right time."

My mother's message had been sent out years ago, passing from ship to ship and from island to island, and I would have to follow the trail back. A miracle that it arrived at all. The message consisted of a piece of her flesh, carefully wrapped in palm leaves, kept moist for years by conscientious skippers.

I ate the message. It was on the verge of being dry, but the inside was still fresh. It came from Frog, one of the two personalities that made up my mother. She'd looked in a mirror and spoken her message. "Dear daughter," she said —she didn't know that I preferred to take a male shape now —"I have made excellent progress with my life's work. Come to me and help me. You won't regret it."

That was all, besides directions. It must have taken years to reach my destination. A huge chunk of meat containing only this message, repeated thousands of times. I guess she'd wanted to be sure it arrived.

"Why did you give me this message now? How long did you keep it for?" I asked Doughyson. The wily old creature never did anything without ulterior motive.

He didn't answer and withdrew the head into his Mound body. I would get no more from him.

♦ ♦ ♦

I said goodbye to Aidizig. She cried, holding her still-flat belly. Not because she lost a husband, but because she was losing a friend. For good, probably. I took my leave of the other villagers. I dumped their names and faces when I needed to lose weight, but I kept that one image of their faces at my farewell. As if I wanted to remind myself that they'd been my friends.

Maybe Aidizig would disapprove of me throwing away so many memories, but she no longer counseled me. I'd chosen to sail by my own currents.

I got on the rickety wooden boat that would bring me across the sea to the next island. I didn't think I would ever come back.

◆ ◆ ◆

After that long and difficult journey, nobody was waiting for me when I stepped on the wharf of the far island just after sunrise. Nobody remarked on my being a stranger. I soon understood why: the island was so crowded with people that no one could know everybody.

I didn't have to ask the way. It was clear that everyone was on their way to the same place, and I soon became surrounded by a crowd of people. Although I'd discarded half my weight after a careful selection, and therefore half my memory, I'd kept my height. I was a tall thin man instead of a big fat one.

About half of the crowd consisted of chalk white Wan, while the other half was brown humans. They spoke like ordinary people, with a strange accent, and yet I understood only half of what they said, they used so many unfamiliar words. They were building a ship that was going to make a long trip to a faraway island. They often mentioned Ing's name. A memory from my childhood rose up. My mother drawing circles in the sand, telling me about suns and stars and planets. I never quite understood what she meant, but the passion in her voice had thrilled me.

The crowd shuffled around the corner and came to a large open area. The people and the Wan disappeared into the buildings that stood around the square. I saw ironworks, carpentry workshops and weavers. People stirred huge vats from which giant greasy clouds were rising. It smelled like rendered behemoth.

In the middle of the square stood a large wooden scaffolding containing a cylinder with a pointy tip. People called it the ship, but it didn't look like one in the least. It carried no sails and no deck. No windows and only one door at the top. Like a watchtower with no place for the watchers to enter.

"Peony?" my mother's voice said near my ear.

"Mummy!" I said. And then, when I saw her face, "Ing."

Because it was Ing, the tightly-wound, intellectual aspect of my mother, not Frog, my warmer, more loving mother. Ing was taller than Frog, her hair was straight, and her face leaner, tighter, with narrow eyes and a small mouth. A handsome face, certainly, but without a trace of kindness.

Her mouth twitched. "You speak my name like it's a dirty word."

"What have you done with Frog?" I asked. "Did you throw her out?"

Ing's eyes filled with tears, and briefly seemed bigger and softer. "No, dear child. I'm both. But without Ing I can't build this ship."

I glanced at the cylinder, but it still didn't resemble a ship. "I think that without Ing you wouldn't *want* to build it. Ing is the one who wants to go home. And Frog has to tag along, I suppose?"

My mother shook her head. "Without your father, Frog didn't feel at home in White City."

"Where is Daddy?" I asked.

"I can't find him."

"Has he planted himself somewhere?" I said.

"I think not. He always remained very human; he wouldn't have wanted to. But whether he's still alive..."

She meant if he was still whole. Wan can be eaten or lose coherence.

"Come, I'll show you the ship. We're almost ready to leave. Actually, I've only been waiting for you."

I walked behind her. The crowd parted, full of respect for her. She was probably loving it, especially if Ing had dominance.

"How can this ship sail?" I asked. "I don't believe any of it." I was eager to contradict her, angry as well, but felt inhibited by the crowd. It made my stomach ache. Was I more human than I thought? Psychosomatic pain, my mother would have said. Actually, even then she'd already sounded more like Ing than like Frog, who'd grown up in a swamp and had never learned to read.

Ing looked back at me. "Wait and see. It's a space-ship. Hadn't you guessed?"

I didn't want to admit that I didn't know what a spaceship was.

We left the heat and the sweaty odors of the half-human crowd and entered the space inside the palisade. The wall of the vessel was covered with heavy fabric, which shone and reeked of behemoth oil.

"Does that oil waterproof it?" I asked. I'd wanted to seem clever, but Ing burst out laughing.

"Water? Peony darling, don't be silly. This ship will fly through the air, and then through space. Didn't I just say that?"

I chewed on the inside of my cheek, but found no inspiration. "I don't know what space is, Mummy."

Ing's eyes narrowed. "Did you throw that knowl-edge away?"

I wanted to snarl at her. *You'd never throw away knowledge, only feelings! Do you even love me?*

But I said nothing of the kind. "I don't remember."

Ing shrugged. "Fixed easily enough. Here."

She broke off a few fingers of her right hand and gave them to me. I took an involuntary step backwards, but forced myself to accept the flesh. I was no longer a child, but next to Ing I still felt small.

The knowledge shot in like an arrow and unfolded like a flower. We were on a planet, which revolved around the sun. The sun was a star, a kind of island. The sea of space contained a lot of islands. The Wan came from this planet, people from another. Ing had been trying to return to her home planet for a long time. She had needed that time to build up the scientific and industrial complex to get there. Among these snippets were hidden a lot of facts about speeds, orbits, gravity, friction, and acceleration. Ing wasn't poetically inclined like Doughyson, but the orderliness and logic of her knowledge had its own kind of beauty.

That explained everything. I looked with new eyes at the rocket. I also saw many flaws. "It's very cold in space and there's no oxygen. It will take you take years to travel that distance. I see no facilities for people."

Ing smiled approvingly. "Exactly. But we would only need them if human beings went along. We're the only ones going."

"Mummy, are you crazy? I'm not going. Why should I? I was born here, made here. Why should I go to your island?"

"Planet," she said, then bit her lip. She just couldn't resist correcting me. "Listen. You wouldn't have come if you'd had to leave something behind on the atoll. I know you. You want to be a human being, but you'll never be one. You make friends, they grow up, have children, grow old and die. You've now gone through that a few times, and you've had enough. Am I right or not?"

I ground my teeth to keep from shouting. Then I grew a new set, which I also gritted. She was right, of course, and that gave her the power to wound me.

I counted to one hundred. Ing stood there, very patient and motherly. And calculating.

"Suppose you're right," I said as calmly as I could. "Does that mean leaving this world is the solution? Maybe I should just gather mass and plant myself, if I am not a man as you claim."

"That's your choice. But if you wanted to, you would have done that already. So. Your Wan physiology will give you the advantage you need to survive in space. The trip will take years. Human beings don't get that old."

I shook my head. "Leave me out of it. Why are you going?"

She looked away from me. Her chalk-white profile was sharply outlined against the brown fabric of the rocket. "I want to see if humanity has survived. When we fled, we thought the war would kill everyone, maybe even destroy the planet."

"And then? What will you do if there are still people, and what when there aren't?"

She stared up into the clouds. "If there are still people, I want to find my family, or their descendants at least. Say my goodbyes. Become human again." There was a false note in these words. As if someone else spoke in her mind and influenced her. "And if there are no more people, then I will fall apart and no longer exist." That last bit I could well believe. Ing's passion and focus hid a deep despair.

"What does Frog think?" I said, sharper than I intended.

She shot me a quick glance, then looked away again. She was planning something.

"Come on, Mummy, I know you're holding some-thing back," I said, speaking in the tone of voice I'd heard my Daddy use when Ing had been up to her usual shenanigans.

She came very close and looked around to make

sure no one else could hear us. "Don't you feel it? The urge to go to another world and propagate? I have to do this."

I felt cold and my face drew tight. I hoped that little of Frog remained in the Ing-Frog combination, because Ing had never been good at reading body language. "I understand what you mean," I said, nodding. "But I didn't think we could?"

She broke off a knuckle. "A gift I got from Doughyson, before I left. The reason I left."

Doughyson. A white finger in every pie. Had he managed to influence my mother into this gigantic, insane undertaking because he wanted his genes dispersed throughout the universe? I no longer wondered about the purpose of my life. I needed to restrain my mother and protect mankind. Even if I wasn't a real human being and never could be, I loved the humans and wanted to save them from the Wan.

I consumed the finger tip. It was a short image that flashed briefly and disappeared again. A giant white sphere floated within a solar system, with a small, unbearably bright white star and a cloudy gray planet. I looked up at our own impenetrable clouds. It had to be this planet.

I began to whisper as well. "You mean the Wan are not native to this planet? That Mound floated in space without any protection."

Ing nodded. "That's why we only need to get into orbit around the planet and then find a navigational window to take us to the humans' sun. One of us will take in enough mass to initiate spore dispersal. That will give us the initial acceleration we need to leave the solar system. From there, we'll use solar sails to get to Earth."

"You know where to go? Okay. How do we get the mass to be large enough to sporulate?"

Ing looked guilty and cunning at the same time. I looked around at the busy Wan. They were destined to be eaten to turn one of us into a Mound. A fine woman, my mother.

"How did you manage to convince them?" I asked. "Or do they also feel that compulsion to seed themselves?"

"No, no," said Ing. "Wan or Mound walkers are totally useless for academic work. These are all humans who have elected to be changed so they could live longer and finish their work."

And those were the dedicated people that my dear mother was planning to sacrifice.

"When are you going?" I asked. "It'll take dozens of years before the Mounds around the world grow big enough to explode. You sound like you want to leave tomorrow..."

"I think if we are in space and have sufficient mass, sporulation will happen automatically."

A lot needed to be done before we could leave. Test rockets had to be fired off, and so on and so forth. More and more people and Wan arrived on the island. Fish became scarce, there wasn't a behemoth left, and we'd emptied their grain stores.

The humans—mainly men—wanted to be transformed into Wan so they could participate. The native Wan, strange-smelling, asymmetric emissaries from distant Mounds, wanted their chance to hurl their cells into space.

I worked side by side with my mother, sometimes infected by her enthusiasm, more often paralysed with doubt. I wanted to stay close to her, and yet I sensed that her motives didn't pass muster.

We were ready to go, strapped to springy wooden beds. It looked nothing like the few memories that Ing had shared with me about her departure from Earth. The noise of the takeoff would have deafened a human. The world lurched and a great weight pressed down on me. The rocket rattled and shook. I reabsorbed my teeth to stop the clacking. Then came weightlessness. Ing had taught me that this meant we were in orbit.

"Gather round," Ing said. "Hold hands." All the Wan did, facing inwards. Only Ing faced outwards into space. The vessel rolled, the dotted stars twirling past disconcertingly.

I obeyed, as always, but couldn't help questioning. "What are we doing? Praying?"

Ing rolled her eyes. "Computation. Close your eyes. Give your flesh in my command and do as I ask."

We melded our fingers and let Ing's commands flow through us. I didn't understand them at all, but my flesh did and responded. The commands made the ship fire thruster rockets.

A shockwave traveled through me. I fell over and inadvertently opened my eyes. The stars no longer rolled.

"What are you doing?" I repeated.

"Navigating," Ing said with a thin show of patience.

Like on an actual ship. Of course. Skippers used sticks and shadow and sightlines to move from island to island. This must be the same.

Several times Ing used us this way to thrust us into the right path.

"We're waiting for a window to slingshot us around the sun," she said.

After that, Ing decreed that that breathing was superfluous. Talking was a human affectation; we Wan could communicate by sharing our flesh.

Waiting for the tide and wind to drive us through a tricky channel. I got that, but still couldn't grasp the instructions she sent through our flesh. As long as Ing was here to steer us, that didn't matter, but how would I cope if something happened to her?

The gray cloudy ball below dwindled as we accelerated away from it. The thread that connected me to everyone I ever knew broke. Snap. My father, whom I'd never really said goodbye to. Aidizig, the child, the friends from my village. How long had it been since I'd seen Aidizig? Without people being born, getting old and dying it was hard to keep track of time. Would she still be alive, and had the child survived? They would die in any case during my long journey to Earth. Only my mother left now. The thoughts hurt, and I kept all of them.

The vessel grew hot, then cold again. Ing said we had slingshotted around the sun and were now on our way out of the solar system to Earth. Nobody apart from Ing quite understood what this meant, so there was no feeling of celebration. Ing declared a period of rest.

Ing and I waited until everyone had settled back in their bunks, then grabbed the nearest Wan. We tore him to pieces and stuffed him inside us. He was a sour old carpenter who had become Wan late in life. He left a bad aftertaste in my mouth.

It didn't take long before the others realized what we were doing—we couldn't hide the extra mass. Ing and I grew into enormous spheres. A few of the other Wan copied what we were doing. We didn't need to act. There was no room to move, so we took the remaining Wan in simply by pressing up against them as we grew bigger from our eating. The ship broke apart.

So we floated in space, two large and three small globular creatures. It was difficult to maintain functioning eyes. The delicate tissue froze and broke off. But I didn't want to risk missing the supreme moment. For if we two were the only Mounds left, which one was going to explode, Ing or me? Mother or son? But I knew who had to be the designated explosee. Family ties don't mean a thing to Mounds. Our race has no families.

I attracted one of the globes. After a brief struggle,

he or she gave in. The more mass you have, the more charisma. The mass with my personality won over theirs.

When I last made eyes, I saw that there was only one smaller ball left. And two Mounds, me and Ing.

I had thought about it in advance. Whoever had the most mass could affect the other. And the heaviest was the one most likely to sporulate. I'd viewed some sporulation memories of Doughyson (who had seen it from the inside, up to a point) and my parents (who had been watching as long as they could), and I knew it took time to explode. Our scent would change—the chemical signature of our flesh— and pink stripes formed around the middle.

So it would be worthwhile to keep making eyes. I needed to see what Ing did. My expectation of the future looked like this: Ing's intention was for me to explode. The extra push from the explosion, plus the solar sails she'd taught us how to deploy, would get her to Earth eventually.

I constantly watched the remaining Wan and Ing circling around each other. Before us, it was dark; behind us the light from the sun battered us. That damaged my eyes as much as the cold, but I became very adept at creating fresh ones.

What was Ing going to do? She had always been relentless and a bit disturbed. I thought she'd push the remaining ball towards me so I'd have to start the sporulation cycle.

The last ball floated almost imperceptibly toward Ing. I had no muscles to tighten, never had, but I imagined tensing up to prepare myself. I was sure she had a plan to turn this around somehow.

The final Wan drifted against Ing. It flattened, and clung to Ing in that pancake state, adding its momentum to hers.

Ing took the mass into herself, by choice.

Ing, my mother, was sacrificing herself for me. She

was going to explode into a million tiny spores. All sense of time dissolved. Pink striae appeared on Ing's equatorial band. Black zigzag chasms opened on her white surface, just south of her equator. The fissures widened and deepened. She exploded from the inside out, funneling the power of the explosion through the hole she'd made, directing it towards me as long as she could. A cloud of tiny particles from the inside spewed out, followed by bigger chunks. The pellets and spores sped towards me in absolute silence.

I didn't really understand why she was acting like this. The Ing part of my mother had always baffled me. I'd distrusted her and figured that Frog was the one who really loved me. But now Ing was maneuvering herself into dying so that I'd survive.

The first chunk hit me like a bomb. It felt as if I, too, would disintegrate into fragments. Too late, I realized I could have ejected mass and evaded her gift.

The bits and pieces of Ing bombarded me. I took in the extra mass and momentum. I accelerated away from home.

Her personality dissolved in the destructive sporulation. I needed to absorb the Ing-stamped material and the stuff from the smaller Mounds she hadn't completely assimilated yet. My defense system labored to turn these bits and pieces into my flesh, instead of the other way around.

I isolated a single large piece of Ing inside myself, by creating a neutral shield of flesh around it. Maybe someday I would take the time to savor it properly. To read the poem of Ing and weep.

I couldn't cry in this shape because I lacked eyes or tears. I cried inside, where I was the most protected from the cold and radiation of space. Maybe I should start to consider that core my heart. I never had one. Or hormones. I could never feel the same way as a human whose mother just died, and yet I knew that I did.

Because it hurt.

I had endless time to think through the potential consequences of our actions. Maybe I should have killed myself, blown myself up while still in my own solar system. I could have changed course to another star.

In the end I decided to follow my mother's plan and travel to Earth. I'm not sure why. Maybe her cells or Doughyson's were making me do it. Maybe I was kidding myself if I thought I'd been the dominant partner in the merge. Whatever the reason, I felt a burning curiosity to see where humans came from. Where my mother was born when she was still human, where her strange ideas came from. Something like that.

So, centuries later, I floated into a new solar system, my body shaped into a solar sail as thin as a bed sheet. The third planet from the sun, that was Earth. During the journey, I'd changed my mind about Ing's sacrifice many times, and back again. Had she intended to send me from the start? What would happen if I reached the Earth? During my journey I never had enough mass to start sporulation, but what would happen if I experienced gravity again, when I crashed on the planet of the humans?

I'd disintegrate into small particles, and those particles were going to follow the primal urge of the Wan. To clump together in ever larger masses, and once they grew big enough to become whitefish, to bite and infect humans. To continue growing until they were large enough to form a Mound that would eventually burst open and send out its trillions of spores.

I could very well be the end of humanity.

The pressure of my race, the pressure to survive and multiply battled with my human part, or, if you will, my heart. Deep inside, I felt like a man. And I refused to condemn the human race to extinction.

I steered myself to the third planet. I'd assimilated Ing's knowledge of the shape of space and how to find my way in it. Not as much like sailing a boat as I'd first imagined.

The blue planet grabbed me with its gravity and pulled me towards it. I went into orbit. I'd never thought I'd get this far. But now my task was to destroy myself, so I wouldn't pollute this planet with my avid Wan flesh.

I created many eyes, each in its turn freezing as I gazed longingly at the green and blue and white of Earth. A planet without a permanent cloud cover like the one I knew. Just like the picture that Doughyson had given me. Would the sky be blue as well? I so wanted to stand on the surface and look up to it, if only for a moment.

But that couldn't happen. I was like an oversized pathogen that might infect the human race with a deadly disease.

The planet pulled me closer, a few meters per revolution. On the dayside, I drank in the blue and green, on the night side, the light of the large satellite glittering on the sea. Did I see lights down there, to signal human life? A fire or an oil lamp wouldn't be visible from space. But I needed to stay on the safe side and burn myself up in the atmosphere. I made myself as large as I could, like the solar sail. That would slow my descent, while assuring not a single particle of me would survive.

The familiar urge prodded me. It told me I was a Wan, not a human being, and that I should stop whining and just be who I was. I remembered the Doughyson meat I'd eaten. I'd never wanted to procreate before. Had it been Doughyson engineering this all along? Had my suspicions of Ing been unfounded?

But after all, I was a Wan.

A deeply hidden memory provided the round-tipped arrow shape I should to take to minimize reentry damage. I held on to my present shape with everything that I had. I wouldn't do what Doughyson wanted. I'd vowed to protect humanity against the Wan.

My edges caught fire and charred. The flames crept inwards. If I kept my vast diaphanous shape much longer, I'd burn. All my memories would be gone forever. What if I did what my flesh urged me to, what if I seeded the Earth? Would that be so bad? Wasn't it pointless to want to protect an alien species like humanity?

Doughyson might get his way yet.

The moment of no return loomed closer.

I will decide in a moment.

I *will* decide.

Soon.

Bo Balder lives and works near Amsterdam. She's the first Dutch author to have published in *F&SF* and *Clarkesworld*. Her short fiction has also appeared in *Nature Futures, Futuristica Vol. I* and other places. Her SF novel *The Wan* was published in January 2016 by Pink Narcissus Press. Visit her website: boukjebalder.nl.

"I wrote this story because I couldn't stop thinking about my novel *The Wan* and how I'd left my protagonists. So I wrote a kind of mini sequel on how their daughter fared in the world they'd left her."

TRANS MARE COGNITUM
MICHAEL TAKEDA

1. Simon

I made a mistake coming here, Simon thought as he
tightly clutched at the pack that contained all his earthly
belongings, and pushed through the jitney cabbies that
crowded the port exit. Or rather—he amended to himself—
there was nothing *earthly* about his belongings anymore.
He'd left the Earth behind to come to Quadrant 46 for
nothing more than a promise.

A promise that he'd finally have a place where he
could *belong.*

First, though, like all travelers to the Moon, Simon
had the misfortune of passing through the satellite's only
space port, a horrible place called The Hub.

From above, The Hub was deceptively inviting:
sleek and modern as a mechanical otter. The windows of its
tall buildings shimmered like silver sheets of clean water at
the sun's zenith, transforming into a warm honey glow as
the sun slipped beneath the horizon.

Up close, The Hub displayed a different face. The
streets were filmed with the ubiquitous moon dust that
swept in from the western crater, and the gutters were
heavily littered. Crime was rampant; the port's knife-narrow
alleys housed hordes of delinquents ready to prey on unsus-
pecting travelers. Lower-level business owners daily
mumbled quiet curses as they scrubbed the blood stains
from their stoops.

Even once he was somehow ensconced in the relative safety of the bullet train, the view through the dusty windows did nothing to change his initial impression. Beyond the sharply delineated boundaries of The Hub, the landscape unfurled in never-ending shades of gray. Gray sand, gray rock, without a scrap of the greenery he'd become so accustomed to while living in rural Carolina. Barren, alien, and cold.

Silently, Simon fretted over his decision. At least until the announcement, in muted robotic tones, of their imminent arrival at Quadrant 46. The edge of the colony at the far side of the *Mare Cognitum* gradually appeared in view. Surging up from the basalt, the settlement was a riot of colors so vibrant that, after so many hours of washed-out dimness, it almost hurt to look at it.

Wide-eyed, Simon gazed in child-like wonder at his new home, marveling at how his future kin had made something of such exquisite beauty in such an ugly place. In fact, Simon was certain that he'd never laid eyes on anything so beautiful that it had literally taken his breath away.

At least until he met an infamous man once known as Mama Hydro.

◆ ◆ ◆

At the train station, Simon was greeted by a smiling couple, neither much older than his own child, the one he had left behind. They stowed his meager belongings in the trunk of one of the Community's few electric vehicles, all the while filling the silence with cheerful chatter about life in the colony. He knew they meant well, but their enthusiasm made him feel tired and far older than his forty-five years. Seated in the tiny passenger seat, he smiled and nodded as the driver, a tall, angular woman, continued to talk about what he could expect during his transition—here, both his greeters smiled—to moon life.

This was merely a formality. Simon was old enough,

unlike his welcome committee, to have seen the original footage of the first attempts of the Phase Project. He remembered the drama of the solar mirrors in the Shackleton Crater that began the process of melting the lunar ice, and then the worldwide celebration when advances in the newly-emergent field of hydropunctalation created the lunar atmosphere far sooner than its initial prediction. What should have taken five generations was complete in a decade.

Once the moon was habitable, the Earth governments had selected the prime locations for their own purposes—nefarious, profitable, or both. Then the private citizens of the overpopulated planet had been given the opportunity to group together to form their own settlements based on commonalities.

The commonality of the inhabitants of Quadrant 46 was that they were all transgender.

After a short ride to a suburb called Leisure World, Simon was given the keys to his living quarters, directions to the clinic where he would meet with Doctor Euclid in the morning for a physical exam, and an explanation of his new job. The clinic appointment was also a formality, as Simon had already supplied results the requisite documentation that proved that his brain, if not his biological sex, was male.

As for the new job, every adult resident was assigned a task that benefited the Community in some way in return for food, lodging, and a small stipend. As there wasn't much need for an ex-museum conservator in the colony, Simon's task would be to assist the doctor at his clinic.

It turned out that life in Leisure World wasn't perfect. Simon missed his collection of art objects, his books, his friends, and, most of all, his child. But he was grateful to have food and shelter, work that was meaningful, and the opportunity to live freely as himself, without

fear of ridicule or violence.
     It was enough.
     They were safe.
     Or so he thought.

◆ ◆ ◆

     The day after Simon arrived, a young man mysteriously and quietly disappeared.

◆ ◆ ◆

     Simon had been in Quadrant 46 for three weeks before he saw a child.
     The day was bright with thin wisps of clouds drifting overhead in the man-made atmosphere. Restless within the tiny confines of the housing unit he'd been given, he'd decided to stroll through the park. Though far from his neighborhood, the park was one of his favorite places in the city, and featured a splendid variety of perennials around a clever fountain that played music. It was in this fountain he saw the child—about eight years old, thin and brown as a stick, dark hair slicked wetly to his oblong head—laughing as he dashed among the pulsating jets of water that spewed from the pursed lips of metallic fish.
     Children were rare in the Community. At the unexpected sight of the innocent and joyous exuberance, Simon felt a pang deep inside him, in his ghost womb. Lingering, he sank down upon the nearest bench, so caught up in the feeling that he was scarcely aware of the man seated at the other edge. At least until the boy ran up to them, slapping wet hands down on the other man's knees.
     "Mom! You promised we'd go out for ice cream! Can we go now?"
     The man made a small huff of exasperation, his voice low. "Hem," he muttered. "What have I told you about calling me that in public?"
     The boy blinked. His expression turned sheepish, voice small. "Sorry. Dad."

How familiar that was. Simon chortled softly. As the man's eyes snapped to him, the laughter died along with the catch of breath in Simon's throat.

Eyes dark as teak, glinting like a dragonfly's wing, and warm as sun-soaked amber. When the man looked at him, Simon felt a strange familiarity, as though they were connected by an invisible thread—one that had been drawing him here all his life, to this moment, to this man.

Drawing him home.

♦ ♦ ♦

Alek Kurtz was one of the hydropunctalators of the original Phase Project that terraformed the lunar landscape. Although much of his work had been performed in a government laboratory of Earth, he held the distinction of being one of the first non-astronauts to set foot on the moon.

The first thing he'd done, he'd told Simon during one of their early dates, was to crouch down in the settling cloud of moon dust, and filter the soil through his fingers. To commune with the *tierra*.

Having seen Alek perform this particular gesture while working in the Greenhouse, Simon could picture Alek as a young man sifting the dust in his still-pristine spacesuit. Even though Alek hadn't transitioned back then, Simon couldn't picture him as anything other than male.

Alek's role in the Phase Project had not only guaranteed him a one-line mention in the history books, but had made him into a sort of folk hero among the Moonlanders. There was even an infamous gang that circulated through The Hub, tagging corporate walls with obscenities, tossing bricks through windows, and hijacking water from the trucks transporting the precious liquid from the Points. They called themselves the Hydropunks.

Alek also shared details of the long journey that had brought him back to the moon, this time with his children, in search of a quieter life as his authentic self.

Soon there would be little that Simon did not know about his beloved. He would learn about Alek's love of nature, his deep-seated need for solitude, the fierce, protective love he bore for his offspring, the sounds he made when he came, and his not-so-secret weakness for milkshakes.

On their very first date, they'd gone to Tea Time, the Community's only tea shop. As Simon listened to him talking about how *water is life* from across the mismatched, floral-patterned crockery, it was already too late. He was already in love. Madly and inexplicably.

◆ ◆ ◆

Two days after their first date, another young man vanished without a trace.

◆ ◆ ◆

2. Alek

The first time Alek paid Simon a visit, he circled Simon's home like a cagey panther, scrutinizing all of Simon's possessions with the purposeful intensity of an archaeologist at a dig.

Because he was single, Simon had been given a unit with only three rooms: a kitchen and living room area on the ground floor, with a bedroom upstairs. Alek was acutely aware that Simon was watching him as he studied the framed photographs on the walls of the living room. Each one, Simon had told him, was an object he and his team of conservators had restored during his work at the museum.

Alek was surprised to recognize the image in the first photograph. His right eyebrow twitched as he flashed a curious glance at his host. "This is a Monet."

"Yes."

"You worked on this painting," Alek said, tone somewhat dubious.

A hint of a smile played on Simon's lips. "My

specialty was restoring paintings. Yes." Stroking the dark blond hairs on his chin, he added, "It had been left in storage for a long time. No one knew about the leak in the museum's storeroom. So every time it rained... well, there was some extensive water damage to a number of the canvases. Including this one."

"I see," Alek said. He then let his gaze roam over the other photographs in the room. Other than the framed pictures, Simon had not personalized his quarters. Everything was minimalist—so clean and tidy that Alek suspected some hardcore OCD. "Well. I guess you could say Monet left quite an *impression.*"

Simon groaned.

Chuckling to himself, Alek moved onto the next photograph. "Tell me about this one."

"A bowl with chrysanthemum blossoms. Japanese, early eighteenth century."

Alek continued around the room, listening as Simon described each object, spinning silky-webbed tales artfully, almost magically, out of thin air. He noted how the quiet man's blue eyes would light up as he described each precious object that he and his team had once repaired. Alek found that endearing.

This man... he's unlike any man I've ever met. Do I dare disturb the universe?

At the end of the tour, decision made, Alek climbed the stairs. He didn't glance behind him to see if Simon would follow.

The bedroom contained a bed and a dresser. Upon the dresser a few articles for grooming sat, neatly arranged.

Definitely OCD... but absolutely amazing.

Simon, leaning in the doorway, coughed awkwardly into his fist as Alek turned to him. "As you can see... there isn't much of interest up here."

A playful smile curled up into Alek's dark mustache.

"On the contrary, there is one thing in this room that interests me a lot," he said. Stepping forward, he slid his hands up over Simon's shoulders, his eyes glinting with open hunger. "You."

On the day they'd met in the park, they'd struck up a tentative friendship. But Alek had made it clear that he wasn't interested in anything more. A series of bad relationships had left him sour. He had his children, and his work in the Greenhouse, and that was enough for him now. He wasn't interested in romance. It had been a long time since Alek had let anyone see all his scars.

Tenderly, Simon kissed all of them. Every single one.

In that moment, it was too late for Alek. He was already in love. Madly and inexplicably.

♦ ♦ ♦

What love felt like:

It felt too good to be real. Fragile and as easily crushed as the membrane of an eggshell formed in a low-oxygen climate.

It felt like a blessing from all the gods that mankind ever dreamed of, a reward for all his suffering and pain.

It felt like the most wonderful and beautiful gift, wrapped in a smile starlight-bright, and warm arms to hold him, and the promise of never having to be alone again for the rest of his life, and knowing deep down in his heart that he'd found the one thing he'd never had, but had secretly longed for always.

True love.

♦ ♦ ♦

Three days after Alek spent the first night with Simon, another transman mysteriously disappeared.

♦ ♦ ♦

"They don't even realize how lucky they are. How easy it is now. They have no idea what people like us had to go through."

It was an unusually warm day for winter, all bright sun and cloud-wisp sky. Alek and Simon weren't the only ones who had decided to take advantage of the weather. Sitting on the bench with two steaming synth coffees, they were half-observing as Rue, Alek's seventeen year old, played touch football with a group of young guys on the grassy knoll of the park, while his youngest, Hemlock, cheered from the sidelines, and Basil, the middle child, sat with his nose buried in a book.

To the others in the Community, Alek's being with Simon seemed fitting somehow. Although there were many women their age and older, most of the guys were in their early twenties. That there were two single, middle-aged men who also happened to be gay... well, *match made in heaven.*

"If by 'people like us,' you mean smart, funny and wickedly handsome, then you could be right, *mi amor,*" Alek said, then laughed.

Simon chuckled in appreciation. "You know what I meant, sunshine."

Alek did know. Like Simon, he had decided to transition many years ago back on Earth, before advances in gene therapy had made changing one's biological sex much safer and easier. Nowadays, painful weekly injections of testosterone were a thing of the past, and surgeries were practically perfected.

"What I don't get," Simon continued, indicating some of the shirtless players, "is why some of those guys actually *ask* for scars. And wear them proudly, like some badge of honor."

"Maybe they just want to honor our trans history," Alek suggested.

"They could honor our history by waving a flag, and go with a nice, smooth, manly chest."

"I'm not ashamed of my scars," Alek said quietly, after a moment. "They're part of me. Of the shit I went through. The shit that made me strong."

Pensive, Simon ran a finger along the cold metal edge of the bench. In response, he merely grunted.

Alek glanced at the field. Once he ascertained that his children were still alive and not bleeding, he shifted, leaning forward to peer into his beloved's face. "Simon. Is something wrong?"

Simon turned the coffee cup in his hands. Drew a breath. "You haven't heard, then."

"Heard? Heard what?"

"You know Jenna? Who works at the bakery?" When Alek nodded, Simon said, "She's gone missing."

"Oh," Alek said, as he felt his heart sink. Of course he knew Jenna. He and Hemlock had loved to watch her work, nimble hands piping icing onto cakes, or twisting bread dough into knots. "Fuck. And nobody knows what happened?"

Simon shook his head. "Doctor Euclid said they're going to discuss it at the next meeting. He told me that the disappearances started a few months before I got here. But they don't know anything. No witnesses."

Mouth grim, Alek's gaze snapped instinctively towards his boys to reassure himself that they were safe. He didn't want to consider what horrible things might have happened to his friends. He'd seen enough of that on Earth. Enough of that had happened to *him*. Mind spinning with ugly memories, he felt his heart lurching dangerously in his chest. Air suddenly refused to inflate his lungs. He couldn't breathe. He couldn't—

"Alek."

Simon's voice echoed in his ear. He felt Simon's hands on his shoulder. Simon's blue eyes—*kind, patient, loving*—were fixated on him. Drawing him back.

Before Alek could speak, a voice boomed across the distance. "Lisa!"

Alek stiffened.

♦ ♦ ♦

He'd been a girl once. An innocent little girl with blood on her dress.

♦ ♦ ♦

Simon's pale face filled the screen as he leaned closer. Still, Alek caught the movement as Simon's hand traced along the edges of his tiny and naturally uncluttered desk. "Alek? Who was that man in the park?"

Ripple of pulse. There were certain things he hadn't told Simon yet—not because he would ever dream of hiding things from the man he loved, but because some things were difficult to dredge up from the past, and present them, still writhing and gasping like a cuttlefish, at another person's feet.

Whenever he had to confront that past, Alek would recite TS Eliot under his breath, like a magical chant.

Let me be no nearer in death's dream kingdom...

"Alek?"

Simon's eyes. Blue as Aegean sea water. Patient. *Kind.* All he had ever wanted. He drew in a breath. "My ex," he said softly. Then, to clarify, "Ex-husband."

"You never told me you were married."

For a second, Alek bristled. Then he realized that it was no judgment, merely a statement of fact. He responded lightly, with a hint of sass. "Did you think I made all those children by myself?"

Simon smiled. "Well, no, but... not all babes are born in wedlock," he said teasingly. Then his smile vanished. "He's the reason you left Earth, isn't he?"

Let me also wear such deliberate disguises...

"Yeah," Alek admitted. "And he wasn't too happy about that."

Simon's expression became grim. Alek could almost sense his mind working, even through the screen, as though no distance could sever the mystical connection between them. An invisible braid of love, respect, and trust.

"Given what he said..." Simon paused, his frown incising deeper lines around his mouth. "He doesn't seem too happy about you being a man, either."

Rat's coat, crowskin, crossed staves...

"Alek?"

"He wasn't," Alek said. "But that was *my* choice. He didn't accept it. He didn't accept *me* for who I really am. He didn't want me to transition. He wanted me to stay a woman."

Simon hummed thoughtfully. "But you never really *were* a woman," Simon pointed out. "Not really."

"I didn't know what I was," Alek said. "I only knew that I was unhappy. But now..."

"But now?"

At the hour when we are trembling with tenderness...

Alek paused to consider. But, really, there was nothing *to* consider. It was cold truth, the kind one felt way down deep in one's soul, hard and brittle as ancient bones. And truth, however harsh, always demanded to be heard.

"Now, for the first time in my life, I'm comfortable in my skin," he said, voice thrumming with the steel buzz of conviction, like a premonition. "I'm finally who I was *meant* to be. And I would rather kill myself than ever go back to living as a woman."

◆ ◆ ◆

Brushing the dirt from his hands, Alek thought for a moment before composing the following message:

Simon,

When I see you, when I think of you, when I smell you, when I feel you, when I make love to you, everything about you to me is masculine. I hope you know that. Men have always been my weakness, and you bring me to my knees. I love you, mi amor.

Your sunshine.

Kicking at the lava rocks he'd unearthed, he chewed on his lip as he stared at the screen, waiting for Simon's response. When his handheld's screen lit up, he nearly squealed.

Two words.

Marry me.

◆ ◆ ◆

It couldn't have been predicted. The last time Alek had seen Simon, there had been no signs that it would be the last.

Simon had been grousing again—almost compulsively, one of his hobbies—about the younger generation of transmen in the community, and how they took all the modern technology for granted.

Lying side by side in Simon's bed, curled up slippery and soft like snails, Alek was watching as Simon thumbed over the screen of his handheld, flicking though photos of results of the newest surgical techniques.

"These young guys," Simon mused as his finger hovered over one revealing image. "They have it so easy. You remember what a phallo used to look like? Like a Frankencock. Jesus. Nowadays you can't even tell the difference."

Alek sat up, brushing back a dark lock of his untamable hair. "Your anatomy isn't what defines you as a man," he said. Then, as an afterthought, "Simon. I thought you didn't want bottom surgery."

"I don't." An automatic response.

Alek hummed. "I'd do it. If I had the money." Saucy, he grinned down at his beloved. "It would be worth it just to be inside you."

Attention caught, Simon let the device slip from his hand, rolling over to give Alek a look, one eyebrow cocked. "And what makes you think I'd like that?"

Alek blinked. Then smiled as he noticed the curve of Simon's teasing grin, the nerves of his skin igniting as Simon's light fingers sketched a poem down the hard, hairy length of his thigh. It was like that with Simon—just the touch of his hand and Alek was ready to go again.

Testosterone really is magical.

With a growl, Alek launched himself, pinning the blond below, and they rumpled the sheets until the small hours of the night.

◆ ◆ ◆

In the ordeal that followed his kidnapping, Alek remembered that night with frequency. The memory kept him sane.

Until it didn't.

◆ ◆ ◆

From the muffled sounds that seeped in, Alek recognized that he was in the Hub. The sounds of the Hub tasted like the copper of blood, burning metal, and acetylene.

They'd locked him in a dank and suffocating room, no larger than a prison cell. Which is what it was. He spent his time in captivity pacing the walls and plotting his escape. When the door finally opened, he lashed out like a rabid ape, all fists and fury.

Alek wasn't a large man. But what he lacked in size, he made up for with ferocity. He managed to draw blood and crush nasal bones before he found himself pinned face-down against the vaguely moldy carpet. It had taken four men to take him down.

Lisa. Don't fight it. We're just trying to help you.

Alek gritted his teeth. He wouldn't be afraid of *that bastard* anymore. He wouldn't shed another tear. He wouldn't beg. The scratchy carpet dug into his jaw as he hissed into it. *My name is Alek.*

There was a lengthy pause in which he only heard the soft rub of denim as his ex shifted, barely audible over the surge of blood in his own ears. *You're sick, Lisa,* the bastard finally said. *We're going to fix you.*

He didn't know what that meant. There was no time for fear. Mind consumed by rage, Alek cursed as they dragged him away.

There was the needle's prick, and the sweet, sickly scent of ether thick in his nostrils that stole away his thoughts. Then darkness, cold and deep, creeping over him like a shroud of mist.

Later, there was pain, diluted by the heavy haze of sedatives.

And bandages.

◆ ◆ ◆

3. Simon

Without Alek, joy vanished from Simon's life. As if the very sun had been stolen from Simon's sky.

At first, he felt numb. Euclid diagnosed it as denial. Gradually, it began to feel as though his thoughts were wrapped in a heavy, wet wool blanket, his senses deadened. As if all color had been leeched out of his eyes. Ordinary sounds were now strident and shrill. And the very air tasted constantly of moon dust and despair.

When the realization struck, it was if a hole where Alek used to be was ripped into Simon's soul, and the universe poured in all of its pain and suffering.

It hurt.

Jesus fucking Christ, it hurt.

Simon tried to put on a brave face for Alek's children. Someone had to look after them, and Simon had not hesitated to assume responsibility. But living in Alek's quarters meant that he was confronted by Alek's absence at every turn. Curled up in the familiar bed, he breathed in the ghost scent of his beloved.

He was wallowing in this sorry state when the children knocked on the bedroom door, their expressions set as if in stone, a series of antique Roman busts all in a row.

It was Basil who spoke.

"We need Dad," he said. "What are you going to do about it?"

◆ ◆ ◆

The darkest, most unsavory section of the Hub was unaffectionately referred to by the locals as "the Rat Hole."

They should have called it the "Spider's Web," Simon thought as he hastened along the narrow, interconnected walkways towards his destination: the Hydropunks' hideout in the center of the Hole.

He'd paid dearly for this information. His slim savings account drained, he'd sold his only possessions of value: the collection of museum photographs of the precious objects he'd restored. So much time had passed since Alek's disappearance. But the den of thieves was his only hope.

The greeting he received was only slightly warmer than he'd expected.

"You! What the fuck you want, asshole?"

This from a kid—no, barely a kid, practically a *baby* in Simon's eyes—in a patched-up flak jacket, combat boots, tattooed skull, who was perched up in the scaffolding that served as the look-out.

Simon wasn't particularly courageous, but he'd spent years carefully studying men's posturing. Shoulders back, chest out, he jerked out his chin. "Word on the street is that you know everything that goes on in the Hub. I need information. And I'm willing to pay for it."

Simon's words had their intended effect. Suddenly he was the the center of attention, surrounded by a half-dozen or so young men and women, dressed in a similar manner as the young look-out. A tall, beefy male that Simon assumed was the leader warily eyed him. The cambot set into the man's left socket click-whirred as it briefly flashed red. "What kind of info, mate?"

Simon told them about the disappearances from the community. About Alek. About Alek's ex, who Simon believed may have been involved because—

Bot-eye lunged. Suddenly a large hand choked off the words from Simon's throat. Angry spittle spattered across Simon's face. "What makes you think we give a fuck about a tranny faggot?"

There was once a time, when he was a younger man, that such words would have filled Simon with rage. Currently, the lack of oxygen was a more pressing dilemma. Clawing at the hand, Simon managed to suck in enough air to hiss out, "'Cause he used to be Lisa Kurtz."

The grip loosened. Red flash of mechanical pupil. Then a sneer. "Bullshit."

A soft voice. Commanding. "Back off, Bruiser."

Simon rubbed at his neck as his attacker and the others slunk away, some regarding him curiously over their shoulders. Ignoring them, he focused on the woman in front of him. With a fire-engine-red fauxhawk, ears modded into elfin points, and lips tattooed in candy-cane stripes, she was about thirty.

And—Simon realized—the actual leader of the Hydropunks.

She regarded him curiously for a moment with cat-like green eyes. "Your boyfriend—he's really Mama Hydro?"

It felt wrong to agree to that, but Simon nodded.

He could almost hear the calculations abacus-clacking in her head. "We'll get the info you need. Come back in one week. But it will cost you. Twenty liters of water. We have a deal?"

Twenty liters of water. A princely sum. The community had promised to help Simon but, even so, he wasn't sure he could manage to pay this price.

For you, Alek... anything.

There was no other choice.

He put out his hand. "Deal."

◆ ◆ ◆

4. Alek

They kept him sedated. His head a jumble of cotton weeds as time trickled away, his new body healing into its deformed shape. When he tore out the tubing in a fit of rebellion, they strapped his limbs to the bed, fluids drip-drip-dripping from the IV, adhering him to life.

He knew little about the radical zealots who had kidnapped him. He only knew that he wasn't their first victim, and that somehow the bastard had found them. Shackled, there was no escape. He was prisoner here, and prisoner to the pain. Something had gone awry with the surgery—the hack of a doctor had removed some of his axillary lymph nodes, causing his right arm to swell with life-threatening infection. Lost in fever dreams, he called out for his children. For Simon.

Veiled like nuns, the women eventually came. Supported his shaking legs. He refused to look as they peeled back the surgical tape and unwound the blood-stained bandages, revealing the shadows of sutures dissolving into his newly-softened flesh. With fingers like iron, they gripped him by the hair and forced him to regard their handiwork in the mirror.

A strange, but familiar woman stared back at him.

For a long time, he didn't even realize that the high-pitched keening was the desperate sounds torn from his own throat.

Broken and in his weakened state, he was taken by

the bastard and the sisters to an unfamiliar place.

They called it home.

Time passed. The sisters dragged Alek through the days until it became routine before they quietly withdrew. He let his body move. He nodded at dinner when the bastard spoke of bringing the boys with them back to Earth, to start again. *Man and wife. Happy family. The way it always should have been.*

"Lisa? Where are you going?"

Alek realized that he had stood up from the table. Staring down at the grease-streaked plate in his hand, he forced himself to speak. "I'm going to take a bath."

With a dismissive wave, the bastard turned back to his handheld.

Alek left the dish in the sink, took an object silently from the drawer, then headed up the stairs. Everything in the apartment was white—a transitory space, lacking the warmth of a real home. He missed the vibrant hues of the fruits and flowers of the Greenhouse. He even missed the gray sands outside the colony—if one looked closely, they could see in the grains a glorious spectrum of colors, from rose quartz to obsidian and all shades in-between. As he climbed the stairs towards the bathroom, he trailed his fingers along the wall, picturing Simon's photographs of all the precious, broken things that he had restored.

Toothbrush dish. A Delacroix. Bowls with chrysanthemum blossoms. Monet water lilies. 120 sapphires in filaments of gold.

Once in the bathroom, he shut the door. Tapping the faucet, he let the water pour out, until the tub was filled, and the mirrors filmed with steam.

In his more pessimistic moments, Alek had wondered if Simon had viewed him as just another beautiful, broken thing he could fix. Now that Alek was broken, his beloved wasn't here to fix him. And Alek could not, would not exist solely as someone's broken doll.

Never again.

Lalique orchid comb. Japanese iron crabs. Silver bound books. Syrian rings of electrum. A pocketwatch in the shape of a skull.

Still dressed, Alek stepped into the tub. The water was hot, but not unbearably so. He let himself sink down until he was mostly submerged in the water. He ignored the prickling at the corners of his eyes, reaching to dig out the object he had taken from the kitchen drawer before coming upstairs from a pocket in his pants.

In the filmy light, the thin blade glimmered like a promise of relief.

Against the flickering pulse of his radial, he poised the point of the knife, then pressed deep once, twice.

Porcelain inkstands. Ivory skeleton with pearls for eyes. Urn clock.

Memento mori.

◆ ◆ ◆

Into the water, the hydropunctalator's blood began to jet, billowing out from his wrists like scarlet ribbons unfurling in a lunar wind.

◆ ◆ ◆

A strange thing happened as Alek lay bleeding out in a bathtub in the Hub.

There was a ruckus. Incomprehensible shouting. The sounds of smashing doors and shattered glass. The thunder of footsteps hammered like a heartbeat up the stairs.

The door crashed open.

Crimson butterfly wing. Illuminated manuscripts in scarlet ink. Ruby-encrusted crown fit for a king.

And in the very moment he was ready to let go, he was saved.

Michael Takeda is a transman who sometimes writes things. To read more of his writing, please visit his website at elvesfromiceland.weebly.com.

FIRE FILLS THE BELLY
NOA JOSEF SPERBER

There aren't any coroners on Coroner Street anymore. In other places, other communities, the main street is called Main Street, or First, or Grocer, or Market, but when this community was established, the coroner set up shop in the middle, for her convenience. Then the community's average lifetime expectancy went up and the coroner moved to Forth Street, where she became a part time florist.

Raphael, who lives on Coroner, does what all men like him do. He sells his dignity as he sells his words, as he sells his time, as he sells his skills. When he needs to get something from the market he has to pay with coins instead of barter goods, because his wages are so small he is pitied. "Buy yourself something you really need," people would tell him, instead of trading him little things. The coins jangle in his pocket all week until he can swap them in for potatoes and beets and dairy products. Water he can buy straight from the building manager.

Where and when Raphael was born, the adjustments hadn't been so widespread. He can remember driving with his parents and sisters to school, when everyone still had cars. He remembers posing for an ID photo in a dingy hall. It was like a passport picture, which he'd had taken when he was very little, but it wasn't. Not really. It wasn't made of the same material, and he found that with a match he could warp it, bubble it to hide certain information.

Raphael's apartment has almost nothing in it and it is not a homey place. There's no knick-knacks on the shelves like there were in his childhood. There aren't even shelves. He has a stuffed mat for his bed and his clothes hang from the low ceiling beams, where he's hung up sheets of molding plastic to divide the room. He's got an icebox in the corner that holds nothing but ice and bricks of coffee; there's a wood tub beneath the pipe where he washes his clothes and his body. He's lined the room with waterlogged books, the old sort, where characters fill their days with aimless activities, or fantasies where heroes fight dragons.

It hadn't been completely easy to fit into this new life when he had first fallen into it, but it was better than he thought it would be. He wakes up with the sun and busies himself. He lives well, performing on the street every morning before working every night. He knows this body, and what he can do, all the limits he can press against and all the points he can reach. He knows the things people like about it, and him, and he is okay.

One day he wakes up, splashes water on his face, chews a mixture of baking soda and mint, and spits off the balcony on his way to the outside stairs. His neighbor leans out their window and laughs, and they are nothing but flyaway hair. Skin just darker than his, and a long loose shirt. They look so gentle, so good.

His face heats. "Good morning," he mumbles, and his neighbor smiles.

◆ ◆ ◆

There is nothing shameful about how Raphael lives. He tells himself this over and over. There's nothing shameful about him. He is only a man, or something akin to a man, and he's only making his art, or something akin to art, with his life. Art like his tattered books and art like his sister used to buy on expensive paper. It's just—art with his limbs, the strong edges of his body.

There is no shame in me, he thinks. He cannot believe it. Maybe there is some shame in what happens inbetween, the not-so-soft street he chooses to walk down every night. He can hold his own, but he always lowers his gaze and ignores what he hears, the dogs that trail behind him.

It's foolish to call his stunts art, however. A woman, a true artist, taught his craft to him, and what she taught him was the act of imitation. Imitating fire, beast, natural world, imitating man.

Stripping off his shirt in the middle of the road doesn't fail to draw someone's eye, despite the undershirt he leaves in place. The curve of his body is something beautiful, the firm V of his hips and the soft way his ribs turn into the swell of his chest. More alluring is the way he tilts his head up, baring the long curve of his neck, before snapping forward and spitting a live fleck of coal into his palm.

This is what Raphael is, a professional danger. Officially he is a street sweeper, but this is what he does. He can coax the flames dancing across his shoulders, hold his whole body in the air by the pads of his fingers, stand statue still while people prod his skin with soft hands.

A woman stares in drifty-eyed amazement at the flame he holds in his hand. She rests a toddler close to her side, its little feet drumming against her rounded belly. Another on the way. She fumbles in her pocket for the single coin she can find and offers it to him, but Raphael shakes his head. He shifts the fire to his upper arm and holds it at bay there, pulling a handful of change from his own pocket, and hands it to her. The baby she holds takes the largest bit and bites it before she gently pulls it away.

"Be well, mother. Blessings to you," he mumbles. "To you too," he adds, a slip of a smile curling back his lip, and reaches out his fingers. The baby smiles back, toothless and lovely, grabbing Raphael's thumb.

No shame, he thinks, but a flicker of something curls in his gut. He's glad for her, but something burns just inside his own stomach, a place of possibilities. What could have been, if he had done different: creation. The burning spreads over his shoulders and he smiles at the next person that comes near him. He bows low. Honor before duty, he figures.

◆ ◆ ◆

The market sells bread if anyone can bake it that day and Raphael will buy it, eat it in thick slices smothered in butter or stacked with vegetables. It's a luxury that he allows himself and he only has it for dinner, sitting on the rusty steps in the outside air. The butter is thick and salty, spread on his tongue, spread on in excess or left to go rancid in the heat.

Raphael leans his head on the railing and licks the crumbs from his fingers. He never learned how to cook, but he learned how to be happy in some ways, sometimes. The feeling sits in him. Above him, the monorail clangs as it rushes over the tracks, *hushusha-hushusha*, and he can hear the faint fluttering of the bats, disgruntled, that flap their way off into the lavender dusk.

His neighbor unbolts their door and steps out, bare feet light, toes slipping between the grates.

"Hey," Raphael says.

"Evening."

He doesn't know their name, but he would like to. They're beautiful, more so than everyone else, and they look at him sometimes, through the window. Not strangely, just clear-eyed and hopeful. It's the way he looks at the people who are happy, the way his sisters used to look at his parents.

Raphael's love for people is something he can't exactly explain, but they are extraordinary, all of them—a pristine and alive thing that he's still longing for. He's past the point of feeling untouched, like he's not damaged by what he's done to himself. Maybe all people feel like this, but he's never been very good at knowing.

"You look like you wanna ask a question," his neighbor says suddenly.

All he can do is shake his head.

"Oh," they say. "Your face is just pensive. If you can think one I'd like to answer it."

He looks at them and parts his lips, but the sound that comes out is soft, and it floats away on the heated breeze.

His sisters looked like him, hair curled in a halo of fuzz and eyes a dark, syrupy brown, but that's all he'll think about. They probably look different now that he's begged and borrowed and gone to the government for what hardened his jaw and made him have to shave whenever he can get the lather. When he last saw them, he was young, but for the life of him, he can't recall the specifics. It wasn't planned, so there were no tearful goodbyes. One moment they were all there, braiding green, fragile weeds into a crown, and another moment, he was standing in a hallway, back pressed against the wall while his picture was taken. He hadn't been told the specifics of why he needed identification, but there were people being deported left and right, and anyone with eyes could see that, so he carries it always, inside a matchbox in his coat pocket. The same matches he burned off an F that was printed in smudging ink.

His sisters had to be somewhere; he'd just never know. After receiving that little plastic card he wandered around for days, begging people to bring him to his family until someone called for the police. He slept for a week in a jail cell while the women there murmured about him but stroked his hair anyway.

He and his neighbor stand considering each other. They're leaning on the building wall, hair wet and twisted up on top of their head.

"You're the fire eater?" they ask.

Raphael shrugs. "In a way. More the opposite. Fire regurgitator, if you will."

They smile. "The fire regurgitator. I'm sure that looks great on your government forms."

He shrugs again. "I think technically it says 'mercy fed', as tossing around fire rarely counts as a real skill." He waves a hand. "I'm sure your form has something very dignified. Doctor, maybe."

"Engineer," they admit. "Have you thought of a question yet?"

"No," he says. "Afraid not." A moment passed before he adds, "I have something I want to know, but I'm not going to waste my question on it."

"Oh?"

"I'd like to know your name."

His neighbor nods and Raphael's breath catches in his throat.

"Adison," they say. "Save that question for something good. I don't give my answers to just anyone."

"No? Just to charming fire swallowers?" he asks. "There can't be too many of us."

"I have yet to meet one," Adison smirks.

"Oh, come on," Raphael moans. "That's not fair."

◆ ◆ ◆

The woman Raphael studied under is clearer in his mind than his own life. He was with her for years, since he was sixteen and his limbs were long and coltish. He was thinner, hands unsteady, and his book collection was confined to what fit in his waistband against his hip.

Her name was Rachel, in a cruel twist of fate that sent bile up into Raphael's throat: the name of his youngest sister. It was meant to be.

Rachel was so beautiful that he had wanted to paint

her, not that he would have known how. Her skin was dark, almost the same as Raphael's own, her hair tied back and covered with a scarf.

The first day they met they sat on barstools while Raphael struggled to decide if he should have the whiskey in front of him. It was almost pretty, the way the sunlight reflected off the sparkling amber liquid. He'd never had a real drink before, just a sip or two of wine when his parents could get some.

"You should drink that," Rachel advised. "There's nothing that good anywhere else." The bar was empty, sunlight twinkling through the broken stained glass windows. There was a deep gash in the wood, and he traced it with his pinky.

Raphael squared his shoulders and downed it in one go. He could barely swallow the resulting cough, the whiskey burned going down and his head felt sideways for a moment.

Laughing, Rachel pounded him on the back. "There you go," she said proudly. "That's it." Rachel took him home with her, washed his hair, fed him often. Lit him on fire when he begged to be taught, pushed him down when he shouldn't have gotten up.

He wonders what happened to her.

Bathing is done standing up in the tub, pouring sun-warmed water over himself. There's not enough room to sit down in, but he uses what's left at the bottom to wash his clothes. The rationing is getting worse these days, less food to go around and water still difficult to make.

"Would you have fought if you were born twenty years earlier?" he asks Adison. He's on his knees carving coffee off the block on the icebox, collecting the scraps on a piece of paper.

Adison makes an I-don't-know noise and a ruffle

that might be a shrug. He can't see them. "Not sure. Is this your question?"

Raphael grunts, almost jabbing his palm with the knife. "Nope, just *a* question."

"You're got to ask it sometime, Raphael, and that's not a fair question anyway," they admonish. "What's done is done."

"Cool worldview, for someone living on Coroner Street in a recovering war zone."

"What, you don't think we're thriving in the 'communities of the future?'"

"Nah, I'm living off welfare and petty cash. The world was supposed to be solar and kind, not rattling," he laughs, shoving the coffee packet under Adison's nose for inspection. "This is enough for a cake, right?"

"Sure," they say, confusion written across their face.

"Children's homes down by the park," he explains. "The big building under the monorail endline. Kid almost died a few weeks ago, so I figured I'd send this over? I do it a couple times a year, in every place I've lived." He brought the coffee from his time with Rachel as a self-gifted going away present. The hassle of lugging it across districts and arguing with border guards aside, it was the smartest thing he could have done.

The world, he had learned, was big, and certain things lagged behind while other things rushed ahead, and some areas had been desolated by the war while some were only affected by the lack of trade with the others. Some places had fresh water from the generators, and the coastal cities were even renewing the oceans. Some places had electronics everywhere and no one hungry. His childhood had been easy, but there were thousands of children like him who had died young and starving.

"You're odd," Adison says out of the blue. "I don't understand how one job can get you enough money and how the mercy feeding system works and where did you get that much coffee?"

"Community where I used to live, it had a port. We had some pretty good stuff."

"Okay, but that doesn't—"

"The mercy feeding system is there for people who are excess to a society," he explains, not looking them in the eye. "If you can prove that you're useless and stuff, they can give you a menial job with no chance of transfer or benefits except through the system. Like, with your fancy job, I bet you don't have to go into a government office if you want a day off, or if you want to work somewhere else, or if you want to do anything. It's not a big deal or anything," he mumbles. "I sweep the streets; you know that. It's like working for the government but without the old prestige. That propaganda, you know, about everyone being equal."

Adison says nothing.

◆ ◆ ◆

The children have filled up the yard by the time he gets there, walking though the monorail is free to all citizens. Filled is the accurate word: the yard is small, the children many. They're all just a little small, a little dirty, a little wild, but all of them good. A few of them go running up and down the street to meet him; three have shoes, two have their feet wrapped with cloth, and three more are barefoot, but they are all laughing. The smallest one smashes their face against his leg, a mess made of syrupy eyes and fuzzy halo. Again.

He asks his entourage at large, "Who was sick? Can you show me?"

Children, he reflects, as they all pull him somewhere, little ones climbing onto this back, *make sounds that are remarkably like* chirping.

◆ ◆ ◆

One of the children follows him all the way home,

not saying anything to him at all. Raphael keeps looking at her out of the corner of his eye. She's about ten years old, knees scraped, her hands working nervously over her skirt.

When they get to the middle of the community, a place that must be unfamiliar to her, considering how she looks around, she stands in his way so he can't climb the stairs to his balcony. "Fire man," she calls him. Her voice is so thin. "Teach me?"

He imagines her, standing in the street with flames licking her skin, and he can see the fire in her eyes.

"Not tonight," he finally says. "Come tomorrow. Early."

"You promise?"

He nods.

The girl is named Rochelle, and he laughs loud when she tells him. Of course it is. Her eyes narrow but he reassures her it's a good name. "A strong name," he tells her. "Names like that don't burn down."

"I picked it out myself," she says, like a challenge, and he smiles.

He has her hold a burning match until it burns down to her fingertips. He has her stand with her hands outstretched for an hour. He has her read one of his books out loud as she stands on one foot with a match ablaze in her hand. She is so steady she's like a rock, and he sends her home with strict orders not to try swallowing the stuff yet, for god's sake. Adison watches the two of them sometimes.

More and more children tag along now. He doesn't give any of them matches, because they haven't asked yet, but they're all trying very hard. They sit on the fire escape, warily considering the flame, flip through Raphael's books with interest, or encourage Rochelle when she tries to master something new. He teaches them in his home, on the stairs, in the street. Rochelle beams when strangers gather around to watch her.

"Who taught you?" Rochelle asks one night, as he's trying to send all the children home before it gets dark.

"A good woman," he tells her. "You're like her. You both clenched your teeth like that—" She looks startled and relaxes her jaw. He laughs. "—when you've got something important on your mind. You're like my sisters, too. You're all stubborn."

"That's right, I am," Rochelle mutters.

"I thought of my question," he says to Adison, rubbing his hand over the back of his neck.

"You have?"

"Uh-huh," he says. "I just—"

Raphael looks at them, really looks at them, at their curious eyes and all the rest of their face. Adison is a human, he thinks, and humans are so imperfect, but humans are so perfect, every one of them.

"—just, why did things turn to this?"

That's not what he intended to ask, but it slips out anyway. Adison says nothing.

"And how do you make your life, your body, feel like home?"

Adison doesn't look at him.

"And why—and why—and why—" He takes a deep breath. "I'm sorry. I wanna know why I don't feel right, and I know you don't know the answer."

"No, I do," they say suddenly. "Raphael, no one feels right. What on earth is right supposed to feel like?"

"I don't think I see things like normal people do," he says defensively. "I don't think I'm not right in the way that other people are."

"Yes, you are," Adison says. "I promise you are. There's nothing wrong with you. Just live your life."

He stands in the street and closes his eyes. There are

people everywhere, passing him, watching him, ignoring him, and he tries to love them. The heat of the flames spread out across his skin. He doesn't know how he doesn't burn to a crisp, but that's okay. When he raises his arms the fire jumps and his heart soars. For a moment it looks like great wings stick out of his back, and then it looks more like ocean waves, and then he looks like a man, something small and fragile and insignificant, standing on his feet.

"It's okay," he says, keeping his eyes clenched shut. "I'm not worth your time."

There is no shame in the world.

Noa Sperber is a sixteen year old agender trans boy, born and raised in California. They have a soft spot for sci-fi and a passion for trans characters in art.

EDGE OF EVERYTHING

M. RAOULEE

"I stayed longer than I meant to," said Idris. He set his teacup aside. The last splash at the bottom glinted until the china settled.

Brahne gave him a sidelong look from behind the counter. "That's all right. I like the stories you tell. They're heavy, but they make me feel like I'm in the right universe, you know?"

She had to be needling him. He'd hardly said a word the whole time he'd spent in her shop that morning. As he collected his coat, he held back a laugh, managing to tell her in the end, "I guess that's just me."

"And you're always welcome here."

"I appreciate that." Idris lifted his hand in farewell and stepped outside. After the stained glass windows of Brahne's cafe, the streets washed out pale. He held his hand over his eyes as he headed to the market, but he could have found his way there blind just by the rustle and bang, the off-kilter music of people in their factory uniforms moving between stalls.

None of Idris's clothes matched. His coat, once white, had been dyed gray to cover the stains it had taken over the years, and his stall umbrella showed the color of every festival and paint accident it had lived through, though he still hadn't been able to justify the price of a replacement to himself.

When he popped it open, there came a break in the flow of passersby, someone stopping short and getting jostled as the crowd moved on. A small figure in a cloak staggered backwards through the other footfalls until they came to the pylon Idris used as a counter.

Their face had the untouched smoothness of a service worker. That made enough sense. Most of Idris's customers surfaced out of overbooked rideshares down to the corporate district. Still, there was something like a skipped beat in this person's smile, small but out of place. "Ferry?" they said.

"Ferry anywhere in the universe," replied Idris.

"You make it sound tiny."

"It kind of is."

They then leaned closer, though they never did drop into a whisper. "I need you to take me to the Edge."

Idris sighed, crossing his arms. "Sure, as long as that's not a bad pick-up line."

"It's not." They spoke on without glancing away. "I left something there. I want it back."

"Sure. It might even have fixed itself if it was broken. Of course, it could also have up and atomized. It might not be a *thing* anymore."

The customer's eyes grew wide, as if they'd never heard of *things* coming undone before, despite how many half-drunk yarns in the Valley depended on the phenomenon.

Idris looked them straight in the face and asked, "You okay with that?"

"I think..." They shook their head, not disagreeing, but coaxing a thought loose. "...yes."

"Then, I guess I'm taking you to the Edge."

"Good! And thank you."

"Meet me here two hours into first shift tomorrow."

"Oh. So, we're no—"

"I'll need time to change my rigging. It's fifty round trip, by the way."

The customer folded their arms up inside of their

cloak, making themselves the very picture of explaining why they couldn't pay. A moment more though and they held out a first full of credit counters that looked like they'd been walked over a few times.

Idris took them. The first read as real on his pocket scanner.

"I'm Ansil," the customer said meanwhile. "Male pronouns."

"Idris. Likewise. Don't be late, okay?"

Ansil's shadow bobbed in a nod. Before another detail passed between them, he had hurried off, one more person out in the crowd without a uniform, and then gone.

Idris shrugged it off. He still had until second shift started to catch a small fare or two.

In the crags past the marketplace, the grounded old starships that had seeded the whole world creaked. A skyboat took flight from the *Merrimack*, vapor stretching out behind as it reached upwards, then turned sharply and headed for the *Allura*, which had hung over the Valley so long that her underside had gone blue with lichen.

Part of Idris still said, *I should be asleep. There's a function tonight, a whole list of people I'm supposed to dance with and nobody even trying to call me by the right name.* There was always a function or five on the *Allura*. Her people lived for pretending respect at one another over liquor.

Without anything to drink by himself, he brought a succession of sick workers out to one of the agriplants and, once he'd disinfected his seats, some children to their music lessons. After, he would have gone back to market for one more fare, or perhaps, as a matter of old habits, stepped out to somewhere serving harder drinks than Brahne's. Instead, he brought his skyboat around to the far side of the *Graceland* and rented a spot at a garage.

Most of the other occupants were only halfway out

of their green mechanics' jumpsuits, their toolboxes over-flowing with ratchets and old coils covered in black crystals. Once they'd gotten over Idris darkening their bay doors without an announcement, they proved just as loud as any after hours crowd in a bar. Their music spun on, wistful about one ex-lover and then angry about another.

Idris buffed the scratches out of his windscreen. Someone nearly cold-cocked him with one of their oar fins as he was setting his own. It happened. No one took a scratch.

They worked until the the only lights they had were lanterns jittering with gelflies. The owner had to order some of them out. Idris left without complaint. He drove. The *Allura* floated above the valley no matter where he stopped. Beyond her, figments of other islands held their paths in the impossibly far away space stretching on in all directions.

Except one, Idris thought almost wistfully. Not long after, he put his seat back and he slept well enough for someone camped out in a skyboat.

At the bell for first shift, he stretched himself awake and headed back to his flat to change his clothes. Most of the grocers had opened by then, and he took his pick of what he wanted for his cooler before excusing himself to Brahne and his landlord.

Ansil was waiting for him at the market. He wore the same cloak as the day before, not a wrinkle to it. The two of them walked off to the docks without much in the way of hello. Ansil bounded into the passenger seat of the skyboat as Idris jiggered the oar wings in that ceremonial way most ferrymen took to, as if to prove they knew everything about their craft.

That done, he climbed in himself. "Our ETA is two hours into second shift. Help yourself to whatever's in the cooler. Oh, and the goggles are highly recommended." He offered up a spare set from the glove box.

Ansil yanked them out of his hand, then turned to put them on, ducking his head close to the side port and scruffing around with his hair. When he popped back up, he had them fitted more or less right. Rapping his thumb on the center of the lens, he said, "These are what made that dent in your nose, huh?"

"It was that or calluses on my hands." Idris did have a small one of those, a wrench mark in his palm, and he felt it as he pulled the ignition levers into place. The engines lit, and with a sigh in the body of their vessel, it lifted from the moorings. A cargo runner passed them, then a rideshare. Idris pulled out after, and they began to climb.

Ansil's peculiar smile widened as their speed picked up.

"What ship are you from that you want to go build dust castles at the end of the world anyway?" asked Idris.

"I'm not sure."

"Seriously?" He expected an answer, not because he was owed one, but because an answer struck him as the only thing that would fit into the conversation from the point where it hung suspended in the seconds after. A silence held in the passenger's seat nonetheless. Idris came to the place where fragment after fragment of his own attention fell off into wondering. Was Ansil adopted? Disowned? Had he lost something besides whatever he'd dropped at the Edge? He took his eyes off of the skyway to glance his way.

Ansil looked back after a moment. "How about you?" he finally said, a good minute and a half out of sync.

"Me?" Idris gave half a shrug and made a conscious effort to take the next turn as smoothly as possible. "The *Allura*."

"Really? Her engines still almost work, right? And they had that thing a few years back with the children protesting because..." Ansil trailed off, mouthing on a few more words, though none of them made any sound.

"Yeah. I know all about that. How'd you think I got down here?"

"I wouldn't have guessed that was your ship, so I didn't think anything about it. But, now that you mention..."

Idris pulled them towards the inside track of the skyway. "You can mess with me once we clear traffic, Okay?"

Ansil nodded, which was to say agreed to mess with Idris.

Idris didn't know if he even realized. Besides that, and as the agriplants wound further and further apart, he considered just how he would tell Brahne this particular story. She was going to ask to hear it, and he was going to slide her at least a few lines, even if halfway unintentionally. Ansil seemed set to come off sounding a little strange regardless of what he wanted back from the Edge.

Did Idris actually think of the other man as strange? Just because of one fallen off conversation and a smile that didn't quite make sense? Wondering turned, little by little, to memories of the time he'd spent looking down from the *Allura*. At the borders of the Valley, that train of thought at least made sense.

The last skyway marker read "Travel Safely." Past that, ferrymen flew by sight rather than traffic signals if they meant to travel to the Edge—west, to the place where the wind always headed. Without the skyway to force a path, the skyboat felt as if it had lost its bottom in the sudden vibration change. Ansil pressed his lips together as it happened, then blurted out that he wanted the some music.

"Right, right. I did say you could mess with me once we were clear," Idris mentioned as the first song hit its bridge.

Ansil turned out to be something of a shoulder-swayer for some of the brighter tunes. His right dipped further than the left. This might have been because of the angle of his frame in the seat and anyway, it didn't seem to be bothering him the few times Idris caught it in the rearview screen.

The Valley could be crossed in an hour or so. The rest of the island humanity had settled, that went on in a greenish blue eternity. Wells of clouds thinned and crashed and sometimes gave up blooms of lightning even in calm hours. Here and there a hermit's house would pass the low side of the windscreen. Idris, at sight of one familiar settle-ment, noted a crack in the greenhouse roof. Perhaps no one lived there anymore.

Meanwhile, Ansil leaned against the window, his gloves creaking on the polymer. He held out to the end of the current song before he reached into the back seat to spring the latch on the cooler. "That's a lot of tea."

"Brahne's my friend," replied Idris. "Did I get the kind you like?"

The cold packs knocked into each other and Ansil sat back with a bottle of triple-filtered water clasped to his chest. "I don't drink tea," he said. It took him a moment to unscrew the lid, but he did manage, sniffing at the throat of the bottle before he drank. "This's nice."

"Good." Idris especially didn't mind if that tea was all for him.

A finger from the far side of the cabin nipped into his shoulder, just to disappear back into Ansil's cloak as his passenger began to sway once more.

Half a dozen more questions flitted underneath his tongue where he couldn't quite make them words to someone who wouldn't tell him where they were from. "Okay. That's me being poked. Exciting?" he ventured.

"Very." That left the next move for Ansil.

In the otherwise silence that feathered in again, Idris drifted into the westward glide of traveling, of just how much sky there was, even without the *Allura* to lift him higher.

He brought the skyboat upwards without much thought to it, steady on their speed otherwise. Its wings hissed gently between songs and the first shards of black crystals started to form on his goggles. The next time Ansil took a sip of water, he swished it around in his mouth, plucking a dark fragment off his tongue after. Idris turned the rearview camera onto one side of the engines, then the other. They looked rougher than they should have.

He was stretching to get a look over his shoulder when he spotted movement in the distance. "Hey, you ever seen a lauscha up close?"

"No. I haven't, actually." Ansil went to the window, water bottle pressed between him and the polymer as he wriggled, searching the horizon that tilted as Idris brought them around.

The lauscha finned against the wind, meaning all he had to do to meet them was choose a current to ride in on. The skyboat jittered, fragments of crystal from the windscreen seams skittering free as it streaked forward. Its windows fogged at the edges with the sudden rise, but the neon twinge riding the sky showed clear in the center.

Between their wings, the lauscha carried dark exoskeletons. Only their pod feed and their faces, all slow-blinking eyes and snouts, showed any softness. One pair at the front of the flock moved in symmetry, their bodies weaving in echoes of one another. A younger member circled past, pausing to look straight into Idris's skyboat. With a whinny it dove far off to starboard and into a clot of low clouds.

"Did we scare it?" said Ansil.

"Or it's playing. Or being a lauscha. I don't..." The

skyboat banked hard to port. "Damn it! Hang on." Idris jerked the wheel in the opposite direction. The wings rattled. A blow of crystal shards hit the cabin.

The lauscha flock plunged by after their smallest member. In the skyboat, Ansil clutched at the door. Idris hauled upwards on the wheel. By the time he'd corrected their bearings, they'd lost most of their altitude. They landed with a thud. The music stopped as the engines cut, leaving them in the thick of the plucking, whistling cries the lauscha made as they gathered and circled not too far off, before diving over the side of the island and elsewhere into the sky.

"That was beautiful," said Ansil. "But, ah, what happened here?"

"Can't be all majestic and not cause downdrafts." Idris sighed. "Bad choice on my part. Anyway, while we're down, why don't you stretch your legs? I'm going to check on some stuff."

"My legs are as good as they'll get." Ansil nonetheless climbed out, and went on to finish his water while leaning against the side of the skyboat. He moved off only when Idris's inspection brought the two of them close to bumping into each other, and then he made his way towards the jagged margin of the island that the lauscha had passed.

Idris found less crystal than he'd expected from flying so long. However, feeling around the underside of the right wing stirred up a place where his hand grated to a stop instead of sliding on the membrane. "Hey, I need to do a quick clean here."

"That's fine."

The starboard side of things did turn out fine after a few brushes. The port, which had been facing the clumsy mechanic in the garage the night before, turned up a loose shard of metal in one of the clips. It wasn't the usual sooty gleam that it had grown underneath, but a feather maze of stress marks.

Idris kicked the side of the skyboat. "Make that a long clean and a beating."

"I said that's fine." Ansil shrugged. He lifted his water bottle to the precipice. He drank as if toasting someone at a party.

Idris worked in silence outside of his own sounds. He ended up hanging onto the wing from the underside, twisting out the screws by hand so he didn't ruin anything that could still be saved. Nonetheless, the clip broke into about twelve pieces when it came loose. Some of them got in his hair as they fell. They stuck. There were soot crystals everywhere.

He spent a minute swearing and scruffing at himself before he got back to his repairs. This job wasn't hot, or the dirtiest he'd ever done, but he started to sweat just the same. At some point between banging on the hull and wondering why parts that involved screws were called clips, he threw his shirt out of the way. The new clip didn't want to seat, even after the third time he took everything apart and scrubbed.

Idris finally felt it click into place. He thought of how much time he must have wasted. The sky answered next time he lifted the screwdriver, washing out in a violet hush. The wind stopped a moment after. As he lay beneath the wing, staring at the shadow where the last screw was supposed to go, he heard the lauscha singing each other to sleep.

He dropped his tools back into their box. He brought half of them right back out to wipe down or stuff absently into his pockets. When he did approach his passenger, he found him back at the edge of the island. Ansil seemed content waiting, though the only music he had was his own intermittent humming.

Idris cleared his throat. "So, we're stuck. I'm not flying in the dark."

"I figured," said Ansil. He squinted through the dim grayness. "You can't do anything about it, anyway."

The expression didn't quite fade when Idris lit the lantern between them. Insects' evening trill around them stuttered on the sudden brightness and just as they always did, the gelflies came, leaving shadows like spines between the two of them.

Ansil pursed his lips.

"Sure you're not scared?" said Idris.

"It's hardly my first time out at night." Ansil used the old word for third shift through a half a glance back to the edge, the last one he gave before he stood.

Their eyes met across the lantern glow.

"Anyway, don't worry about me."

Idris looked down at his chest and his ratty binder. Then, he stretched his empty hand behind his neck. "Because you're worried about me," he tried.

Ansil's attention deepened for one long, shimmering instant before he pulled himself back to a smile.

Thinking on that might have been part of why Idris kept speaking himself. "Allurians don't float just because our ship still does. We don't have wings. Some of our men have breasts and some of us like work even if we came from a wrecked luxury liner. It's not my first time out at night either."

"How could it be? You're a ferryman."

"And if it's all the same to you, I don't sleep with a shirt on."

Ansil blinked. "Why... why are you asking me?"

Idris handed him the lantern. Without his sweaty clothes, he reached down to touch his toes, then stretched back to stare at the ghosts of all the other islands stranded empty up above them. "There've been people in my life who cared."

"The only reason I'm not joining you is I'm cold."

"That right? The superstrate here stays pretty warm. You'll probably do better under the wings." Idris stepped out of his shoes and into the back seat. The cooler he set aside, then the binder, before he fell backwards. He'd been sitting for hours, lying on the ground for more than that. Getting to spread himself out on something soft felt so sweet on his skin.

Ansil rustled about for a while; how long Idris couldn't tell without a clock. When he did happen to peer out of the skyboat to check on him, all he saw was the cloak balled up beside the hull. It hardly looked like it held anyone. Idris hummed on the chance of an answer.

"I can still kind of hear the lauscha if I put my ear to the ground," Ansil murmured. "They were pretty and I'm glad I got to see them."

They had a few words off and on between that. Idris would doze and the next he remembered, they'd be talking about traffic or windy days or something small like that. He thought they came back to "Are you sure you're not cold?" but that lay distant from the peace in his muscles and all of the stirring quiet blinking around them.

In time and past where he was sure he'd nodded off at some point, he asked, "You're not asleep, are you?"

"Not really," said Ansil.

He opened his eyes to a flushed sky. They had no reason to wait after that. Idris rubbed some dry shampoo into his hair and put his binder back on with his spare shirt. He nibbled out of the cooler while Ansil waited for the first kicks of the wind.

In the moment, it grew light across the universe, Idris started the skyboat and Ansil turned the music back on. There were more words, still small, off and on between songs for the first hour. Silence followed for the second since the speakers turned to clanging even after the music had been shut off.

Crackles of light that left no sound reached along their flanks. The horizon darkened or grew blinding. By the time the Edge came into view, Idris and his passenger were both rapping on their goggles to keep them from faceting over.

They had to leave the skyboat and slog the last few miles on foot through the flickering dust. A field of silver silt lay at the threshold of the Edge. Not every ship had made it past intact. Pieces of those that hadn't loomed over from the hills, bits of them gone in gleaming bites or still claiming their own personal lighting. The wind ended there and a chill covered the air on those last few aching steps to the place where the universe *stopped*.

Idris really had come this way before. He'd already thought of eternity while looking at the remains of the hulls, watching his footsteps. "Here we are," he said when they came upon the Edge itself.

The rift took up no space, and yet it seemed to go on forever, somewhere past its shattered perspective.

"Thank you for bringing me." Ansil held out his hand. The rest of his payment rattled there. Once more, he smiled, and when his grasp was empty, he unfastened his cloak.

Ansil as Idris would have recognized him ended at the wrists and at the throat. Past that, his skin was gone. Only a silvery undercoat remained. Damage to the right of his chest and shoulder had been patched in mismatched yellowish metal. One of his calves was down to struts and joints and wires.

"You're a..." Indris faltered, though, bit back. Ansil knew what he was. There was no reason to hold it to him.

"A C4700 companion android." He almost made it sound wistful, being able to stand there and say it at all. "I've been here longer than the *Allura*. What I left in this place, that's everyone who knew. I was the only one who made it through."

"I... I'm sorry."

"No, you're not. My life took the place of a real person's." Ansil shook his head. "It doesn't matter now. I'm tired. I'm going home." As he turned, he gleamed like water in the light from the Edge. "Thank you for bringing me all this way." From there, he stepped off. His shadow flashed and grew and still looked so very human.

Idris's shock bled towards enchantment. Androids—autonomous, thinking androids—didn't exist in the Valley. Except, he stood there in witness, watching one as his heart bobbed in his throat and black sparks covered his goggles.

Memories washed in after. He'd thrilled on the first day of the protest on the *Allura*. He'd waited and he'd sung. He'd danced to songs he didn't know. He'd thought of jumping when the other children started to talk about that, but...

He was just a *boy*. He wanted to go home and hear someone call him Idris. Just once, and still, just always. The other children said nothing when he told them.

If Ansil hadn't been there to listen to him so long ago, if he had metal where most people had bones, none of that mattered, watching his silhouette shrink. Idris hardly felt himself move. He shot after him through the dust. "Hey! You're not going to let me drive back alone!"

"I'm sorry." Ansil walked on. "I promise I'm sorry."

"Then stop being sorry! This's really stupid!"

"I already paid you." That, he wailed. "I can't do this anymore. I want to go home." He broke into a run, or tried to.

Idris seized him around the waist, tight with his hands latched together. They reeled. The thump in his frame as he held him, that stunned both of them to stillness for an instant.

"Please let me go," came the whimper, soft against his ear.

Ansil was heavier than he looked. He threw himself one way, and he left bruises behind. On the other, he creaked and he growled, his chill fingers lighting on Idris's face.

Indris took a deep breath. He let go.

Ansil lost his balance, toppling into the dust. It wisped around him in the split second Idris looked back. Since—he did look back. He couldn't move forward without that.

The light of the Edge stung, but so did its cold, and the slicks of black that rose and spread and thinned out to nothing across its surface. The rift towered above him and slipped past the mist below.

He'd been there before, but never as close as he came in that moment. Stars peered out of the sheaf of space that rose before him, thousands of them so white they were almost violet, streaked across the arms of the galaxy that had made them.

Their cold bit through his gloves and the crystals on his goggles grew thick. He'd lost all sense of his fingers even before he squeezed onto his ratchet and he held it out into the glittering darkness.

He breathed. The other universe tasted blissfully of nothing through the pain of waiting, though Idris did wait. He waited until turning away made his pounding heart ache. The galaxy faded away and his arm burned.

Something in him remembered that emptiness, even if he'd been born a thousand years after the *Allura* came so close to crashing.

Frost and crystals rose and shattered on his sleeve as he made his way back.

Ansil's stripped leg sparked. Dust had gotten into the joint. Ansil himself, he kept saying *why, why,* and *why* again.

Idris knelt beside him and held out the ratchet.

A few points there, stained with particles from the far side of Edge, caught alight. They glowed like embers as they rose. The ratchet, then the outer layer of his glove likewise lifted upwards and shone so deeply and were gone, undone *things* all.

By the time they had gone out, Idris's hand was shot over with crystals.

Ansil blew on them and they vanished.

It had been almost a week since Brahne had seen Idris. She considered worrying about him, but storytellers, ferrymen, men with hearts at all, they had their own journeys and those didn't have to involve teashops, let alone hers. She still missed the sound of him not speaking.

She was on her way over to his chair to chase away a gelfly nymph that had settled onto the arm when the door chimed.

Idris had his right arm in a sling. His coat was missing. He hadn't come alone.

"Brahne, this is Ansil. He's got a story. I think you might like it."

M. Raoulee is a lesbian author and artist living in Virginia with several cats, more plotbunnies, and a hoard of vintage beads. This is her first published story.

The author would like to thank her family for all of the 80s science fiction comics they left lying around, and her housemates for allowing her to continue the tradition during her midnight writing jags.

ACKNOWLEDGMENTS

Editing an anthology is not a solitary activity. The editor would like to thank the following people.

Thanks to Geoffrey Godwin, who initially helped shape the project and encouraged me in this endeavor.

For their feedback on some of the stories that were submitted to this book, I would like to thank Deven Balsam, Jordan Tao Mambert, and especially Bill Racicot, who also gave me the seeds of the idea for my own story.

For aid in editing, thanks to Josie Brown for the expert editorial suggestions, and to my copy editor Trisha Wooldridge, who made sure that the version you now hold in your hands is in top shape.

Most of all, I would like to thank all the transmen and transwomen who have shared their experiences with me and helped me through my own transition. Remember never to apologize for who you are. Regardless of where you are in your transition, you are all valid and you are beautiful.

ABOUT THE EDITOR

Michael Takeda is the founder and Editor-in-Chief of Pink Narcissus Press. He started his editing career with student papers at the University of Oregon over two decades ago. Since then, he has also worked as a translator and teacher of English and Italian, had a brief stint as a music reviewer for local newspaper *PDXS*, completed two degrees in Italian literature, and is a published author of various fictions. He currently lives in Worcester, Massachusetts.

ABOUT THE ARTIST

Dante Saunders is a New England based graphic novel artist. He has created official promotional artwork for NBC's *Hannibal,* cover art for *The Kelpie,* and *Ben Fox: Zombie Squirrel Specialist,* and is the co-creator of the webcomic *The Vampire Aurelio,* as well as having contributed to several anthologies and completed several solo original projects. Dante has a strong interest in promoting art and characters featuring marginalized topics, especially regarding transgender subjects, as he relates to them on a personal level being a transman himself. He blogs about comics, art, environmental issues, dinosaurs, and new projects on his tumblr account, the-kingsman-dante. You can also find his art tumblr-blog at the-artist-dantesaunders.

ALSO AVAILABLE FROM
PINK NARCISSUS PRESS

DAUGHTERS OF ICARUS

New Feminist Sci-Fi and Fantasy
"Throughout, the authors explore themes of gender, identity, and autonomy, with characters as diverse as miniature clones, stripper vampires, aggressive mermaids, and mystical crones. Many of the stories focus on gender roles and the pull of relationships, whether parental, familial, or romantic, among all kinds of people." —*Library Journal*

ISBN: 978-1-939056-00-9

NARCISSUS IS DREAMING

A science fiction novel by Rose Mambert
"*Narcissus is Dreaming* reminds me of some of the work of the late Theodore Sturgeon, who also dealt with concepts of otherness, loneliness, and the endless varieties of love." —*Analog*

ISBN: 978-1-939056-05-4

THE WAN

A science fiction novel by Bo Balder
"Inventive and energetic, with a truly unique SF premise. A promising debut from one of my favorite publishers."

—Jeff VanderMeer, author of
The Southern Reach trilogy
ISBN: 978-1-939056-10-8